Flagged Victor

Flagged Victor

A Novel

Keith Hollihan

HarperCollins*Publishers*Ltd

Published by HarperCollins Publishers Ltd

First edition

HarperCollins books may be purchased for educational, business,
or sales promotional use through our Special Markets Department.

HarperCollins Publishers Ltd
2 Bloor Street East, 20th Floor
Toronto, Ontario, Canada
M4W 1A8

www.harpercollins.ca

Library and Archives Canada Cataloguing in Publication
information is available upon request

ISBN 978-1-44340-997-1

Printed and bound in the United States of America
RRD 9 8 7 6 5 4 3 2 1

To friendship, in all its states and stages

Then call it fiction instead. Append a note: "I made this up."
Then you will be guilty of betraying no one . . .

—Philip Roth, *Operation Shylock*

Flagged Victor

1

Milan Kundera got me laid at a particularly trying time in my life, but it was the way he told a story that left a mark. His novel *The Unbearable Lightness of Being* is about love and freedom (among other predicaments) but it begins by exploring a premise. Building on Nietzsche's myth of eternal return, Kundera talks about the dialectic between lightness and heaviness. If we only experience this life once, then the many things we do along the way actually have an existential lightness to them because their impact is so cosmically trivial. If, on the other hand, we're forced to experience every moment of this life eternally, then even the most trivial actions become heavy with consequence. In such a case, the desire to buy, say, a mere cup of coffee is fraught with weight because we will be buying that same cup of coffee over and over again, forever.

In other words, that cup of coffee had better be worth it.

A life of lightness, however, in which nothing is experienced twice, means consequences aren't worth worrying about. You can buy that cup of coffee, sleep with your best friend's girlfriend, or, for the sake of argument, rob a few banks, and, if you're so inclined, let your existential worries drift away weightless as a puff of smoke. After all, time will pass, the cells in your body will eventually be replaced, memories both exciting and horrible will lose their sharpness, and life, as they say, will go on. Ultimately, you sever yourself from the thing you did, the moment in time that marked you, and even the person you were. You're someone else now.

A life of lightness gives you permission to do whatever the fuck you want.

It's not often my heart starts thumping when I read something, but I remember thinking, Now that's the way to start a novel. Begin not with a scene or an establishing shot of your hero but with a rush of ideas that serve as a petri dish for the events and emotions that get cultivated over the next several hundred pages.

Actually, I read Kundera's novel after I saw the film. And while the film was impressive, the impact it had on me was enhanced, as I mentioned earlier, by the fact that it got me laid. I caught the movie on a whim while on a first date with a young woman who was my lab partner in Introductory Biology, a science requirement I was taking two years late. A foreign student at Dalhousie University in Halifax, she was far too exotic looking to be with me, and we didn't have much in common—she was earnest in her desire to be a medical doctor and save the world; I had less pure motives, rounded out by an interest in books and travel, along with a smidgen of charm. But I took a reckless chance at the end of the term and asked her out. By coincidence, *The Unbearable*

Lightness of Being happened to be playing at the revival house near campus around Christmas of 1989. She was eager to see it—I was willing to see anything as long as she was part of the evening. Afterwards, it seemed imperative to both of us, her as much as me, that we go back to her apartment for a vigorous session of sweat-soaked, furniture-rattling, consciousness-obliterating sex.

I've been an especially keen fan of art films ever since.

I finally read the book a few months later in a hut on a beach in Thailand. I had left school, fled Halifax, and was trying to write, and Kundera's novel impressed me at a different level than the movie. The way his motif of lightness and heaviness had been folded into the argument of the story hit my nerve endings with voltage, a stimulation that flowered what felt like brilliant new thoughts and realizations. I'm not discounting the pleasure I associated with my memory of the film and its aftermath. Indeed, if all philosophical lectures could be sensorily enhanced with sucking and fucking, classes would be full and professors would party like rock stars.

But, stimulated as I was by the horny remnants and the great writing, I mainlined the Nietzsche bits and could not help but see the things that had happened to me and Chris in an alternative way, a way that was starting to become manageable, like grief. I didn't understand everything yet. But I knew I had a story to tell. That had always been part of the deal. My desire was not to explain, exactly, but to turn confusing memories into something narratively coherent and hopefully guilt freeing. I tried to write that then, and it didn't work. So I wrote about something else instead, concocting out of some heat-stroked speculation and plenty of Mekhong whiskey the tale of a couple who backpacks through Asia robbing other backpackers to keep travelling. I threw into it everything I understood at that point in my life about morality and consequence and the lightness of being and the relief of a reckless fuck. I was circumventing the original impulse or question in a very roundabout way, which is one path in the process of making fiction.

Chris, to me, was lightness. He made decisions easily. He was oriented toward action and, for all his power and force of will, he had a quick and graceful way of doing things. He was utterly confident in his capabilities. Even when he made mistakes, he dismissed all failure, shrugged off consequence, laughed lightly at himself, and strode happily to the next adventure. I was his dialectic opposite. When it comes to consequence, I am like Prometheus chained to a rock, an eagle eating my liver each day, the poor liver regenerating each night. Or like Loki—to do homage to the topless Scandinavian women on the Thai beach near my eternal hut where I remain, in some parallel universe, still typing—bound to another rock by entrails, a constant drip of acidic snake venom falling on my forehead. Each consequence, the same as the last, the same as the next. It doesn't matter if it's a cup of coffee, a reckless fuck, or a mad dash through a mall parking lot with a bag full of money. It doesn't matter if I've already committed the crime or am only contemplating the doing. Drip. Drip. Rip. Chew.

Loki. Prometheus. Liver. Venom. Eternal return. Topless sunbathers. That's the postcard I would have mailed.

Actually, the film I saw on that date wasn't *The Unbearable Lightness of Being*, it was *Betty Blue*. In fact, I don't recall exactly when I finally saw *Being*, though I do remember being knocked flat by the book when I read it in Thailand. But *Betty Blue* was also foreign and had a great deal of fucking in it and was even about a writer, which was the clincher for my lab partner, so a certain mutability between the two movies occurred in my mind. Eventually, reality and the poetically plausible became indistinguishable, as often happens when you're making fiction. Needless to say, this kind of convenient truth-making is a hazard among memoirists, compulsive liars, and the criminally minded too.

If you treat life lightly, does life handle you lightly in turn? If you are heavy by nature, will you bear the weight of consequence everywhere you go? In the case of Chris and me, the evidence was so complicated I don't know how to parse the many pieces. The light one bore the burden. The heavier one lightly walked away. Except, naturally enough, for the heavy one, even lightness had terrible weight.

It was that shift in lightness and heaviness I remember most clearly on the last free moment of our lives, one pleasant August evening. We stood on the grass outside the house where I had a basement apartment. The job was done, and we knew we would never do anything like it again. That in itself was a relief from a terrible weight, at least to me. Perhaps to him it was the shedding of lightness and the grudging acceptance of weight. He was, after all, enrolled in police academy and scheduled to begin in a few weeks. (You should laugh here; you should blink once or twice in amazement.) We congratulated ourselves modestly, without any of the chest-thumping and fist-pumping that had characterized other occasions. We acted—if I dare connect the word to either of us—with maturity. We had no plans to party or to blow through dollars. We were calm and easy, even satisfied, a condition that felt connected to some deep sense of finality and fulfillment. I think we'd both spent so much energy over the years striving to become bigger and greater, to achieve some unspecified potential, that when we eased down and throttled back, the mood that overcame us contained within it a contented sense of accomplishment. I've had the same feeling when I've finished writing a book. For an hour or two, an abiding calm, a cessation of doubt.

I said goodbye. He said that he would see me later. We'd used my car for once but he got into his own. A black Fiero, no less, a sort of Trans Am in fibreglass. It was leased but seemed to be part of him, like his impressive mullet (this was Canada in the eighties, after all), or the loping and deceptively fast stride he had when he ran. The gym bag was on the front seat beside him. Inside the gym bag were some workout clothes, the bundles of cash, and two handguns with loaded clips. He drove away slowly, around the corner, up the hill, out of sight, and it was over. What was over, exactly? His life. It ended on the highway. And part of my life ended too.

Four months later, I asked my European lab partner out to a movie and experienced the lightness I mentioned before, but what I did not mention was that the lightness in that moment was a blessed relief, a visit by a nymph who, for one night, chased away the eagle tearing at my liver, held a bowl over my forehead to catch the dripping venom. She was a stranger who barely knew me. No one who really knew me wanted anything to do with me. Three weeks after that, I flew to Hong Kong, my belongings stuffed into a pack that I carried like the proverbial weight on my shoulders.

Southeast Asia in the early nineties was the kind of place where you could still pretty much disappear. You could forget your own past, lie to anyone you wanted, and more or less shed your identity except when you handed over your passport.

And I was told by a reliable source even that could be bought.

One of our favourite movies back then was *Butch Cassidy and the Sundance Kid*. We watched it on video in my basement, using a Betamax machine my father had pilfered from the bank where he worked. Since he was the district manager, that wasn't considered stealing.

We identified with the two romantic outlaws, who shared our grim sense of humour. Like Newman and Redford, we were both blond, virile, and irresistible to women. Although we had not yet robbed any trains, we figured we might someday, and that we would enjoy it as much as Butch and Sundance. And we knew, without declaring it, which parts we'd play when it happened: Chris the charismatic schemer with vision, me the reluctant but loyal sidekick. We even knew the differing emotions we'd experience. A persistent anxiety on my part, a love of adventure on his. A bitter-sounding but actually friendly repartee between the one with the plans and the one with the skeptical doubts. The way desperate, arm-flailing leaps into rivers always end with a joyful splash and escape.

Actually, the ending of the film was something we argued strongly about. It was blatantly clear to me that Butch and Sundance are completely fucked when they're holed up in the hacienda by Bolivian soldiers. Admittedly, there's never any hard evidence of this. When Butch and Sundance reload their pistols and rush out, the moving picture fixes suddenly into an unmoving frame, and the last we see of the two friends is a shot of them side by side, locked in a running crouch, guns blazing eternally.

It was all very impressive.

What a cool fucking way to die, I said to Chris.

I meant it. I would be proud to die like that, heroically meeting my fate side by side with a best friend, rather than huddling like a coward hoping to evade the inevitable.

But Chris had a different take.

What do you mean die? he asked. Who says they're dead?

I scoffed at his lame humour, but then I saw he wasn't joking at all. Naturally, I rose to the bait.

Of course they're dead, you moron. They're surrounded by thousands of pissed-off, gun-toting badasses.

Chris disagreed. In fact, he utterly denied what he called my interpretation. To settle matters, we reversed and played the ending over and over, the Betamax whirring and clunking with each repeat performance.

Calmly, Chris asked: Did you see anyone die?

Frustrated, I answered: No. But they're dead.

Reasonably, Chris suggested: Prove it.

Increasingly emotional, I declared it obvious: There's no way they can make it. They might have survived tight spots before but this time they're dead.

Socratically, he continued my education: How do you know?

Desperately, I went literary: That's why the camera freezes, you asshole. To show the end of their journey together, to stop the constant movement, to prove to anyone with half a fucking brain that they're finally totally dead.

I'm not sure I believed my own argument, as convincingly as I tried to lay it on. It was the kind of premise a master debater (and God knows I did my share of that) throws out with utter conviction in order to baffle an opponent and score a cheap point. At the same time, I suddenly wondered what *had* been the reason behind the mysterious freeze-frame shot? There was a deeper mystery in that aesthetic choice, and I was not sure I understood it.

Not to be out-scholared, Chris turned my film-school argument upside down.

You've got it wrong, fuck nuts. They only froze the camera so they can duck down, drop out of the frame, and sneak off.

This was so provocatively ridiculous I lost my shit.

Chris, they're fucking dead.

I bet they're back in the US before the credits even finish rolling. Robbing another train. Getting ready for the sequel.

They're hanging by their ankles from some tree limb with their throats cut.

Enjoying a whiskey. Watching the sunset somewhere. Shooting cans off a fence.

Executed.

Escaped.

This went on for several more rounds until I screamed: Dead dead fucking dead!

I could have wept in frustration. It did not help that I knew he did this sort of thing to me all the time.

Of course, I recognized what was happening. The intensity of our argument had begun to echo the kind of childish fights Butch and Sundance had in the movie. This was no comfort to me, however, just as it clearly annoyed the shit out of Sundance when Butch insisted on something impossible. I also knew that Chris's ability to twist circumstances to serve his needs, the very persistence of his self-delusion, reflected an actual and potentially combustible difference between us. Chris refused to believe anything but victory was inevitable. I anticipated defeat around every corner.

Later, when I thought about that frozen frame in the light of Kundera's novel, in my beach hut, still typing, each key exploding like a gunshot, I understood the scene and my emotional response to Chris more clearly.

Butch and Sundance weren't just frozen for aesthetic purposes, they were nailed to the eternal cross of consequence. Drip drip rip.

The black Fiero. The warm August evening. The gym bag within reach on the passenger seat.

Chris was driving to see Susan. He never arrived. I felt self-servingly bitter whenever he spent time with her. It cut me both ways. He was my friend first, so there was some jealousy of her. And, of course, as is only to be expected with a friendship like ours, I had complicated feelings for Susan, too. The situation was impossible, and I'm sure I preferred it that way. I was made to be the jaded extra—the amusing, cynical, but secretly pining sidekick. These are the limiting but potent terms you see friendship in when you are young. If Chris knew any of this, he didn't acknowledge it. He was good about overlooking my complicated handicaps of conscience and soul, my many personal weaknesses. He had few jagged edges himself, and it seemed rare and noble for someone of such ease to be so large-hearted and accommodating about the limitations of others.

He took the highway because that was the fastest way to get to Susan's house on a Saturday night. He was eager, even anxious, to spend time with her. He was coming down from the high of what we'd done, and he wanted comfort and compassion as much as sexual release. He was also feeling very tenderly toward her, and that was not always the case. He could be dismissive, cruel, and deceitful at times, and Susan put up with it, saw it, I think, as part of what made him compelling. His present emotional state might have been a passing mood, a letdown from the earlier excitement, or it might have been a tilt toward maturity. I view it as tragic, however, because I think it indicated the beginning of a new him and a different level in their relationship, the place you get to when you learn to actually care about others and their feelings.

He was driving too fast, so it was no logical surprise, though still a little heart-knocking, when the blue and red lights came on behind him. He hadn't seen the speed trap. Fuck me, he thought, and gave a laugh. Only Chris could have laughed in such a situation, with so much at stake. Only Chris wouldn't immediately assume the worst, because he did not experience the universe as oppressive, as out to get him, as lying in wait. He eased his speed down and pulled to the side of the highway carefully, put the gear in neutral, and pulled up the handbrake. He threw his track jacket over the gym bag. The highway was dark all of a sudden. The sun had gone down during a few unnoticed moments and dusk had settled in with the permanence of night. The side of the road did not have a wide shoulder, and he wondered if the cop would be pissed off at him for not pulling over farther. Fuck it, he thought. There was a ditch and then a dense pine forest. The evening was airless and calm. No traffic passed by. He rolled down his window and waited.

Do you know why I stopped you? the officer asked.

The question echoed a similar question Chris often asked, but he didn't think of that at the time. Talking to the man's belt buckle, Chris admitted that his speed might have been a tad too fast. He apologized like the pleasant and polite middle-class young man he appeared to be.

But something about the ongoing moment and the police officer's demeanour sharpened his attention, a nervousness, a touch of formality and strain. Chris knew many cops personally—his own father, his father's friends, the cops who frequented the Billy Club, the bar he bounced at on Tuesdays and Thursdays—but not this one. His mind worked, in delayed fashion, to interpret this condition of wrongness and understand what, if anything larger, was going on. At the same time, he prepared himself to hand over his documents. Driver's licence in the wallet in his hip pocket. Registration and insurance in the glove compartment. The police officer did not ask to see those things.

What's in the bag? came the question instead.

And that's when Chris understood exactly what was happening.

He thought about the bag and wondered what to do. The obvious answer was to jam the car into gear and gun it. Maybe he could put some distance between himself and the cop, then toss the bag away unseen. He hesitated, however, and those three or four seconds of indecision were sufficient, in the micro-battle between will and circumstance, to allow the moment of action (uncharacteristically) to slip by.

With a foreign sense of defeat weighing him down, he answered that the bag was filled with workout clothes and added optimistically that he had just come from the gym. The police officer, however, asked to see inside. So Chris dragged the bag toward him slowly, while fumbling as casually as possible to pull the gym clothes closer to the surface and hide the rest of the contents.

As he started to look back around to the police officer, he felt the muzzle of a handgun against the little hairs of his temple. This forced his gaze forward, his skin sparking under the electric touch of metal. He could not see the man's face, but the burst of blue and red lights behind him, the number of police cars such brilliance indicated, was a gauge of how heavy everything had become.

Heavy wins out over light, and there's nothing you can do about it. But for every someone who insists on living lightly, there's always another someone who tags along, living lightly too for a time, not out of natural inclination but because they have been momentarily convinced by the sheer certainty of a person who refuses to see the world any other way.

I suppose it's telling that when I think about me and Chris, I think about Butch and Sundance. And I also think about Tom Sawyer and Huck Finn, and Don Quixote and Sancho Panza.

You're probably starting to see a pattern.

Actually, it's not the force of certainty or the lure of adventure that convinces a Sundance to share the delusions of a Butch Cassidy, or a Sancho Panza to follow a Don Quixote.

It's love.

2

Like many memorable duos, our friendship started with a fight.

When I was twelve, I broke my arm. It happened my last year in elementary school, right before summer. I was new to the school, new to the neighbourhood. My family had moved from somewhere else. My parents wanted me to attend the new school, even though there was only a month left and I would be going to a different school in the fall, because they felt it would give me an opportunity to make some new friends. Nobody at the school thought that was a good idea—not the principal, not my teacher—but my parents forced the issue, knowing what was best. Then, a week in, I broke the arm, and it was a bad fracture, and it took another week for the swelling to go down, and by that time it seemed pointless and possibly hazardous to send me back for ten measly days. (I'd have to struggle with the cast and avoid falling or jostling my arm in the playground, impossible for a boy.) So they let me stay home instead. The weather was unseasonably hot that week. I suffered in my jean shorts and tank top, lying awkwardly on the couch in front of the TV, never comfortable. The cast was solid plaster and dry to the touch but so heavy it seemed soaked with bad luck and humiliation. It hooked around my right thumb like a belt loop and came to a crusted and crumbly end at my shoulder. I felt like a fallen gladiator permanently braced with a shield.

I was happy to skip school. It was a source of great relief. But I was also bored to be at home with nothing to do and no one to play with. My father didn't like my lying around. Whenever he walked past, his stern eyes were averted and he moved faster than usual, as though making up for my self-indulgent immobilization with his own vigour. But, at some level, he must have felt guilty about my plight because he bought a few comic books to keep me company. Batman, Superman, Justice League. They were ordinary classics, brilliantly coloured with fantastic storylines, but they lacked the intensity and intrigue of the weirder stuff I preferred. Nevertheless, since comic books had been forbidden in our house until then, the gesture conceded the seriousness of my condition, a nearly lethal combination of injury, loneliness, and boredom.

Sometimes, when I was sick of being inside, I went out into the backyard and lay on the newly sodded lawn and read. Midday with everyone at work or at school, the neighbourhood was so quiet and still that once a little blue bird hopped up close to my propped-up comic, as though curious about the world behind the cover. I was in awe of its lightness, the way it flicked with each hop and flutter. For a brief second, that bird was my closest friend, and I was filled with hope for a new beginning, one in which the universe and I would be finally in sync. Then the bird got bored and flew off, as birds do.

I got used to the cast by the time the school year ended, and I started running into some other kids from the neighbourhood on the street. Since I was new and had a broken arm, I was the object of some curiosity. They asked me where I was from and what had happened to the arm. It turned out one of the boys had been in my class and knew some of the details. He filled everyone in.

He and Lewis had a fight lined up—

Lewis Garner?

And practically the whole school followed them out to the field under the overpass—

I heard about that.

And they started fighting, and it was more or less even until all of a sudden Dusty jumped in and booted him right in the face. Twice.

Booted him?

In the fucking face. Boom. Splat. He flopped over like a sack of shit.

At first, I didn't quite know what had happened, not just because I didn't see the kick but because I didn't understand where that kind of anger could come from. Lewis and I were only going at it half-assed. He wasn't nearly as strong or mean as I'd feared and I became comfortable, or at least complacent, realizing I could hold my own. The entire fight seemed staged, a storyline we were forced to follow to satisfy the audience's whooped-up depravity. Maybe Dusty sensed something bogus. Maybe he just hated me too much to hold back when I appeared to be winning. All his rage came out when he kicked me. And afterwards, I lay passively on my back with my hands on my face, incapable of doing anything else, not because of the pain, which was surprisingly mild, but because of the shame. The kick to the face was so humiliating and unjust, so morally wrong, that it gave me the excuse I needed—an excuse I didn't know until then had been available to me—to do the unthinkable and just give up. All the weight I felt, the reign of terror I'd been experiencing as the new kid, the anxiety of being battle ready while also staying open to any gesture of kindness, all of that heaviness vanished when Dusty gave me the boot. The worst thing had happened. And so the dread lifted.

I didn't know, however, that Dusty wasn't through. He pulled my hand back from my face. Part of me thought it was a gesture of regret, that he was trying to apologize for his impulse, for the rage that had come over him, that he wanted to examine my face to see if I was all right. Then, while I was still puzzling through his motives and as passive as a patient with a doctor, I felt him straighten my arm, hold it still, and stomp down.

He stomped on it?

Like he was breaking a stick. Like it was kindling.

I heard it snap.

I almost puked.

And then Mr. Henderson showed up and we all ran like hell.

Except for me, on my knees, with my arm cradled, gulping air. I don't know if it was shock, fear, misery, or an act of defiance in the face of immense cosmic injustice, but when Mr. Henderson, one of the teachers, asked if I was all right, I said yes. I stood up, managed to wipe my flushed and tear-streaked face, and carried my broken arm in my good arm all the way home.

Dusty's psycho.

No kidding.

He can fight though. Remember that time he caved the guy's face in?

Fucking brutal. They had to pull the guy's nose back out with surgery.

That's because Dusty boxes. He knows how to punch.

Yeah, it's the boxing and the insane killer part that makes him scary.

Is he going to Westphal next year?

Fucking hope not.

Should be going to jail.

He'll get there.

He's already been in juvie.

You can't go to juvie when you're barely twelve.

Sure you can. Where the fuck do you think you go—to your room?

I didn't verify or dispute the story or interject with any information of my own. I just listened to their analysis and took some solace from the indirect way they were commiserating with me. For some reason, perhaps because I lived in their neighbourhood and school was over for the year and local ties were stronger in the summer than during the winter, I was now suddenly one of them. And it made me feel a little better that in their shared awe over Dusty's cruelty, I got the message that there was little any of them would have done differently in my position. Dusty was the car wreck you didn't see coming. If you were lucky, he hit the guy next to you and spared your pitiful life. If you weren't lucky, you stood around and listened while others talked about your broken arm or your surgically recon-structed nose.

Then one of the boys said: Someone ought to break that fucker's arm back.

And that was the first time I knew Chris.

He was a year older, already attending middle school, and one of the tallest and certainly the strongest in the group. A fringe of curly blond hair framed his high forehead and he had a hooked and slightly crooked nose, so that he looked a bit like a youthful Roman centurion who'd just taken off his helmet. He had wide shoulders and noticeable biceps. He was rumoured to be a tae kwon do brown belt, and his knuckles were raw and chapped as though he spent his off-hours breaking bricks in half. He was quick to laugh but rarely the first to speak. He held himself back a little and was unusually watchful. What impressed me about him at that moment was his tone. The quiet, offhand way he spoke about breaking Dusty's arm was a signal that he wasn't bullshitting or throwing out some wildly implaus-ible suggestion. And that made him seem capable of doing it. Moreover, this unexpected reaction reawakened in me, in delayed post-traumatic stress fashion, a sense of moral outrage. I'd been wronged. I'd been dealt a serious injustice. The surge of gratitude I felt got mixed together with instant hero-worship and marked the beginnings of a true and lasting love.

The conversation moved on to other subjects, but with the strength that Chris's sympathy had given me, I was able to slough off my self-pity and join these new friends in a game of street hockey. Although the cast limited my ability to shoot or pass, it served as an excellent blocker and I gamely offered myself up as goalie. Once, when a wicked wrist shot hit the plaster, a hollow *thud* sounded. Everyone thought that was so cool, we spent a half hour trying to make it happen again.

A few weeks later, I saw something else from Chris—his unusual determination and follow-through. Many of us made bold statements but few were capable of heroic deeds. All alone one Saturday morning, as if setting off to take care of a neglected errand, he made the journey over Somerset Hill and down into the neighbourhood near the elementary school. Fate put Dusty out front of his duplex, chucking rocks at parked cars. Words were exchanged, and the fight started with a detached and almost professional manner in the empty driveway. The melee lasted several minutes before Chris's strength and reach overcame Dusty's speed and viciousness, and Dusty lay on the ground wincing through a bad eye and puffed lip. Chris's nose was bleeding and his shirt was stretched, but he was the one still standing. Then, casually and deliberately, because this had been the point all along, he grasped Dusty's arm, stretched it out, and stomped down.

I never asked him why. It seemed self-evidently about doing what was right.

There's an alchemy to close friendships. The ingredients are compiled haphazardly, with desperate abandon. A mixture of laughter, anger, fun, resentment, safety, betrayal, redemption, outrage, and time go into them. Unique external forces create unpredictable dynamics. Pressure or weight counts. Lightness often results. The effects cannot be reliably reproduced.

Like a magician's illusion, a close friendship creates its own reality. There's a cloistered quality. You disconnect from the outside world. You lose perspective, meaning you fail to be able to understand or justify your own behaviour from any angle but the one supplied by internal logic.

I'm trying to explain how we became capable of walking into the pastel-tiled lobbies of neighbourhood banks, wearing masks and carrying high-powered weapons.

Halifax was the far edge of the world. After Halifax there was nothing but ocean. The heavy flotsam of memories, the cold whitecaps of futility. Even the sunshine and the seagulls seemed to know this. There were enough good weather days, plenty of blue air and warmth to fool you that it was a reasonable place to live, but the sky was often dark, filled with roiling, embittered clouds cut by sharp shards of light. You got a migraine just being outside, blinded by the brilliant wet blink all around.

What we called Halifax was really three distinct cities surrounding a lagoon-like harbour. There was Halifax on one side, Dartmouth on the other, and cupping the far end a nondescript municipality called Bedford. When my family moved there, in 1981, we lived on the Dartmouth side. For years, I thought Dartmouth was south of Halifax, because south felt subservient or lesser. But when I looked at a map, much later as an adult, I saw to my astonishment that Dartmouth was actually north of Halifax, sitting on top, the ceiling to the open cave. I still have to think that through just to reorient myself mentally.

I did not know then that Halifax would become not a home for me but a place of exile. I've lived in a lot of cities since, and I occasionally feel as though the geography of my brain has collapsed. Streets in one neighbourhood remind me of streets in another. I turn a corner, glance at an old clapboard house, a vine-covered wall, a cobbled lane, or a shaded sidewalk and think I remember it well, only to realize my memories wormhole back to Halifax. It's as if that's the original Jungian forest, where heroes and dragons still live.

Dartmouth was insignificant compared to Halifax. A trivial abutment. We all felt so back then. Unless you had to admit it, you never said you were from Dartmouth. There was no excitement there, and nothing to do. Dartmouth was residential, filled with neighbourhoods and low-rise buildings, lakes and forests. When you looked across the harbour, you saw Halifax, the downtown clustered with skyscrapers, a string of lights on each of the two bridges spanning the water, and you knew that's where stuff happened.

After I moved to New York City, I often got the same feeling whenever I saw Manhattan across the East River. Naturally, I was living in Brooklyn, the Dartmouth of the five boroughs.

Though I never told anyone, there was a specific reason Dusty hated me so much he felt compelled to boot me in the face and break my arm.

Being new to a place is not easy, and when you are a boy, there are extra difficulties. I was seated in the classroom alone that first Monday morning when the other students arrived. In their shorts and T-shirts, they looked feral, and so impatient for summer that they resented everything between them and it, even the walls and desks. My presence was an affront. Was I a spy? Had I been forced on them as some kind of a challenge? Everything about me seemed to spark up their hatred.

What are you doing here? I was asked at recess by a crowd.

I had my standard response. I just moved here. But it was an insufficient explanation.

A routine of cruelty began. I was ignored at recess when I was lucky, surrounded by tormentors when I was not. I got shoulder knocks during gym activities, took a basketball off the side of my head unexpectedly. I was the brunt of hard laughter whenever I got tripped in the hallway. Smirks appeared whether I hesitated over an obvious answer or answered an unexpectedly difficult question correctly.

Dusty was the cruellest boy of all. I knew—the way you know a dog isn't right or that the crazy person on the bus will direct their attention toward you—that he would mark me. He was shorter than me, but he came from a broken home and lived in a shitty duplex and had taken boxing lessons and could do forty-seven push-ups at a go and beat up anyone. He walked with a purposeful swagger wherever he went, a hair-bouncing, knee-flexing pimp roll I realized later had been copped from John Travolta in *Saturday Night Fever*. Being marked by Dusty meant that I was given regular promises of my imminent doom. Sometimes the promise came from Dusty himself, hissed into my face; sometimes, gloatingly, from the girls in my class or one of Dusty's several minions, like Lewis Garner, or even from the few kids who were sympathetic toward me but accepted Dusty's reign of terror as a fact of life and were just helplessly relaying the message.

What was the reason for Dusty's persistent and calculated fury? He'd found, on my desk at school, a page of writing. It was a short story, something I began when I had some free time because the others were finishing an assignment I had never started and wasn't required to do. I'd always wanted to be a writer. I figured Halifax, if it did nothing else, would give me a fresh start to get that writing life going. I vowed after I moved there to write every day—even as a twelve-year-old I felt that kind of weight. But I forgot to hide my page of writing before lunch, and Dusty found it on my desk when class resumed in the afternoon. I was writing a mystery about a college student who gets a letter from a professor who disappeared while exploring a cave in Mexico. I had in mind that the college student would form an expedition to follow the professor's trail, explore the cave, and discover a lost city inhabited by a humanoid species that were actually aliens, stranded on the planet for a thousand years. I thought the story had great potential but Dusty didn't share my enthusiasm. It wasn't the content or even the quality that seemed to piss Dusty off; it was the simple act of writing.

I didn't tell my parents how I broke my arm. I pretended nothing at all had happened until I banged it accidentally at the dinner table that evening and began to retch with the pain. When they asked me what was wrong, I said I'd fallen. I added that the fall had happened in the playground and that the other kids had been concerned, but I hadn't mentioned it to any teachers and never realized the injury was serious until that moment. I lied for complicated reasons. Mostly I was afraid of disappointing my father, the businessman who sat at the end of the table in judgment of everything I did. Given how it had happened, Dad wasn't sure a trip to the hospital was necessary, but Mom took me anyway. After many hours in the waiting room, the X-ray, we were told, showed a long fracture in the radius with a spiderweb of microfractures at the radius head. A strange split and twist, seen occasionally in episodes of child abuse. How had I done it? I just fell, I said, and elaborated to explain the odd manner of the fall. The doctor lost interest until I stopped talking, and then he brightened. I was lucky. The injury was about as close to needing surgery as a break could be, but he'd set it expertly. We went home, my arm encased in plaster and throbbing from being moved this way and that. For doubting me, and perhaps in apology for moving to Halifax at all, my father bought me those comic books.

I later told Chris that I wanted to write books, meaning stories, novels, and so on. Anyone else would have mocked me outright or used the confidential information against me later in front of others. But Chris thought it was cool and made nothing more of it, which was exactly the response I needed.

Actually, some of that isn't true. I did get picked on mercilessly by Dusty, and I did get pushed into a fight with Lewis, and I did get kicked in the face by Dusty during the middle of that fight, and Chris did suggest someone ought to break Dusty's arm for his blatant transgression of schoolyard code, but no one, including Chris, made the walk over Somerset Hill to take care of the deed and right the wrong. Still, when I think about everything that happened, I can come up with no better story to explain how my friendship with Chris began.

The neighbourhood was called Manor Park, a name that was strictly aspirational. It was a new subdivision and there were still houses going up when I first moved there. We played guns or hide-and-seek in the half-built structures, hanging from rafters, huddling in dank, gravel-floored basements, shuffling along the narrow ledges outside second-storey windows high above the ground, or crawling across tar-papered roofs and leaping into the piles of pink fibreglass insulation stacked below. Most of the neighbourhood kids were twelve to fourteen, with a few brutish fifteen- or sixteen-year-olds thrown in. When school was out, we all played together. There was Derek, who was a little manic and clumsy, but who knew how to throw a knife so that it stuck in a tree, and could tie impressive knots. There was Geoff, who had a slapshot you could barely see and who could spit between his teeth a squirt of saliva that was marvelled at for distance and accuracy. There was Hughey, who was so tall and big-haired that we called him Franky, for Frankenstein. There was Jay, Robin, Paul, Sheldon, and Tom.

We played games of street hockey or baseball in an undeveloped cul-de-sac called the Horseshoe. We went swimming in a lake called Oathill, which was long and narrow and surrounded by forest. Sometimes we cut through a different forest to Penhorn Mall and played games of Asteroids or Space Invaders in the arcade, bought an Orange Julius or a bag of bulk broken chocolate bars if we had extra scratch, or just wandered the wide corridors past all the stores without any good reason or objective. If it was only me and Chris, we often ended up in the bookstore. We spent a lot of time in the fantasy and science fiction aisle judging books by their covers. We particularly liked covers with half-naked women or muscular swordsmen. I also judged books by how closely they adhered to stories I had in mind. I tested some of those story ideas out on Chris, and, through his grunts and supportive laughs, I understood he believed every one to be worthy of the Nobel Prize in Literature.

I remained in a sling all summer. I broke the arm two more times, once falling from the rafters of a half-built house, once tripping violently during a game of hide-and-seek. I was still a new kid, but I now had special status as some kind of fallen soldier. My status had been lifted by Chris, who was respected and yet treated me like an equal. This, undoubtedly, puzzled many since it flew in the face of my obvious deficiencies. A true friend is someone who hangs with you no matter what everyone else thinks.

At first, I did not walk to the new school with Chris but with the neighbourhood boys who were my own age, like Franky and Derek. We collected at the base of Somerset Hill and moved forth together, a troop of weary soldiers, and gained a little levity as the distance got covered and the curse words became more inventive and amusing. We wore blazing white Stan Smith sneakers in the fall, and we clomped and scuffed in Kodiak workboots in the winter, the laces always untied. Downy vests of enormous bulk were popular, and preferable to full-sleeved winter coats. Nobody wore a hat or gloves unless their mother was in sight. To carry our books and lunches, we used vinyl brown Adidas bags that looked like dachshunds without legs. Inevitably, the bags got so full over the course of the year that the straps could no longer take the strain and snapped. When one strap broke, you tied the loose end to the other strap, and you could loop it over your shoulder and carry the bag like a backpack, the weighty contents bulging out the bottom. If both straps broke, you were fucked. When there was ice on the ground, we flung our Adidas bags along the road like curling rocks.

I was unsatisfied with the boys in my own grade. They didn't cut it and I hungered for a different kind of companionship. By the end of the year, through the dint of many demonstrations of cruelty, violence, and mayhem, I was permitted to occasionally walk with the older, tougher boys, including Chris. Once in a while, it was just me and Chris the whole way.

My parents were the detached rulers of my life, overseers who asserted authority without much sympathy or interest, having many more important things to do.

My father worked for the Royal Bank of Canada. There were five major banks in Canada then, and the Royal Bank was the largest. While my personal status was bolstered by the dominant power of this bank, I was secretly bothered by the vigour of its number three competitor, the Canadian Imperial Bank of Commerce, or CIBC, whose yellow and brown colours I quietly preferred. One day, I decided I wanted to open my own savings account. Chris, Derek, and Geoff thought that was a good idea, too, and it was one of the few times anyone followed my lead. Instantly, however, I was paralyzed with anxiety. It made sense, given my father's job, to open an account with the Royal Bank, but there was no branch at Penhorn Mall, the only place within walking distance. Penhorn was CIBC territory. I worried myself sick for days about this, even as my idea took on a horrible momentum with the other boys. They kept trying to get us all organized with a lump sum to bring over to the bank and open savings accounts. Finally, I worked up the courage to ask my father if I could open an account at CIBC instead of at his bank. He okayed the idea without much comment, but I could feel immense disappointment in his indifferent shrug.

My account passbook was small and vertical, brown and gold, and blazing with guilt. But I liked to put even small bits of money in to see the numbers go up, and I liked to get the passbook updated every month or so to see how much interest had accrued, each new series of numbers punched unevenly into the page, like a telegraph message from some distant and lawless country. Twenty-three cents might be added in, or $1.62. Once I got over seven dollars in interest in a single update. I couldn't believe it. Seven freaking dollars showing up out of nowhere. I wanted to tell Dad how good that felt but feared bringing up the bank betrayal thing again.

Derek's father owned a sports store, though Derek and his father hated sports. Paul's father was a dentist. We avoided him, and his overly clean hands, as though he were a leper and treated Paul, too, with such disdain that he gradually stopped hanging around. Franky's father was supposed to be a salesman

of some sort, but even Franky didn't think it worthwhile to figure out what his father plugged. Geoff's father worked at the
oil refinery, and he seemed so red-faced and angry, we pictured
him surrounded by boilers and pipes, clanking them madly with
a heavy wrench, screaming for the hissing to stop.

Most of the other fathers did nothing special for their jobs,
they just worked. Everyone's mother seemed to be a nurse.
Except for Sheldon's mother, who was uncomfortably attractive
and worked as a stewardess and part-time aerobics instructor
before settling on real estate.

Chris's father, on the other hand, was a police officer, a
distinction that set him apart. Better, he was RCMP, the Royal
Canadian Mounted Police. Mr. R worked in an office now but he
had done a lot of straight-up policing earlier in his career, some
of it in tough, remote communities up north, and to further
bolster his bona fides, he had a collection of weapons, ranging
from pistols to semi-automatic rifles, in preparation for the end
of the world. Briefly, he'd even owned a grenade launcher and a
genuine Nazi dagger. Sometimes he took Chris and me shooting
at the armoury gun range. He carefully taught us how to handle
guns, how to aim and fire, how to clean them and care for them.
I was a decent shot, but Chris was a sharpshooter, a long-range
assassin, and he also had a knack for the mechanical aspects
of loading, breaking down, and cleaning. Sunday afternoons,
Mr. R cleaned his guns on the kitchen table on a green felt cloth,
and we would watch and ask him what certain guns could do to
a person.

He told us: This one will pop a three-quarter-inch hole in
your chest and churn around inside, in the process causing

enough internal damage to bleed you out within thirty minutes. Approximately.

What about that one? Chris asked, pointing to the stainless steel .357 Magnum with the fitted rubber grip, which we both thought was the coolest handgun in the known universe.

No internal bleeding with that one, Mr. R said. Tends to blow the head clean off the shoulders.

And that became one of our favourite jokes. We laughed with pure pleasure every time it came up. Tends to blow the head clean off the shoulders. Ha ha ha.

Mr. R and Chris had the same laugh: a deep, rolling cackle that grew in cruelty and mirth until you thought of evil geniuses hatching plots while wringing their hands.

One day, Mr. R drove Chris and me to school in a squad car. As an officer, Mr. R needed to do a day in the squad car every six months or so, even though he worked at a desk. We loved sitting in the back, behind Plexiglas and cage wire, but it was even cooler when Mr. R sounded the siren. Some guy in a beat-up Mercury Monarch had rolled through a stop sign and Mr. R thought it would be fun to pull him over and show us what it was like to give a ticket.

He stepped out of his car and walked to the front driver's side window, then he returned with the offending driver's licence in hand. We were out of our minds with excitement.

Mr. R called the licence number into dispatch and waited. He listened as the dispatch announcer gave him a long explanation. It was unintelligible to us. But Mr. R didn't explain what she said. He stepped out of the car, handed the licence back to the driver, and the big car pulled away.

When Mr. R sat back in the driver's seat, Chris asked him what was wrong.

He was flagged victor, Mr. R said.

Before we got to school, we learned what that meant. The V was for violence. The driver had been flagged as a violent offender. And so, Mr. R let him go rather than continue his stunt with two children in his car.

We felt like we'd had a close call. Like we'd accidentally bumped into Jesse James.

Flagged victor became one of our secret code-word expressions ever after. Doing something wrong, getting away with it, grinning an evildoer's grin. That was very FV.

Mr. R had a *Playboy* collection in the basement, and it was okay for us to go down there and look through them. The issues were all from the early to mid-seventies. The women stood differently then, often on tiptoes, their calves straining, like awkward ballerinas reaching for something on the top of some imaginary shelf. Their breasts were different then, too, starting higher on their chests, sinking lower and hanging rounder, and their shoulders and hips were wider and fuller. Beyond their bikini tan lines, their pubic hair was far, far bushier, a wide swath of mysterious wilderness.

One day, I was exploring the woods around Oathill Lake with Derek. Together, we found a stash of pornographic magazines. There were no *Playboy*s in the pile, only titles we'd never heard of before with pictures inside that were far more graphic than anything we'd ever seen. There were around thirty magazines total, so we each claimed approximately fifteen and worked on a plan to get them home without detection. We decided to risk hiding them in the forest until that night. Then Derek, who had a bedroom on the ground floor, would sneak out of his house, grab the loot, and deliver my share to me at my front door.

I woke myself up at two in the morning, the designated time, and crept downstairs. I stood looking out the glass of our front door for about ten minutes until I saw a dim figure in the haze, running down the middle of the street. I opened the front door when Derek arrived, breathing hard, with my stack of magazines in his arms. He handed them to me without a word, then took off again, running just as fast.

Oathill Lake was our main destination for recreation, winter and summer. In the winter, we skated and played hockey there. Early in the season, the water around the fringe of the lake was barely frozen, so we tossed our skates onto the more solid inner ice and hurled ourselves after them, hoping the surface would hold. If the ice was wet and your jeans got soaked, they'd freeze and you could stop a puck or take a whack with a stick against the shins and feel only the dull thud. In the summer, we swam from the pier on the wooded shore out to the floating dock in the middle of the lake and played there for hours, cannonballing into the water, rocking violently side to side to tip others off, or lying on our backs with our hair afloat like weeds, enthralled by the way the sky got turned into an inverted bowl of blue. I had a rubber dinghy, a heavy vulcanized beast that I carried on my own to the lake most days. To manage this, I lodged the rubber seat against my sweaty forehead, straining my jaw and neck to keep it in place, and got into a rhythmic bounce with the bottom end *thwock-thwock-thwock*ing against my heels, a sound like a rock ricocheting around the inside of a metal pipe. The dinghy summoned all light and heat down to it. Some days, we just lay within, frying in the sun. Once or twice at the beginning of each summer, I burned so horribly that only hours in a cold bath could stop my feverish shivering. Some afternoons, we used my boat to row across the lake and explore the other shores. We found the old lock that way, a stone sluice overgrown by marsh reeds and muck, as mysterious as the remains of a lost temple or city. The swamp around the lock stank so badly of raw unfiltered fart that it earned the status of a forbidden zone, an unmapped region where the only life was mutant and evil. We braved it whenever we could.

We liked to go snorkelling and look for sunken treasure. We liked to pick blueberries on the marshy sides of the lake, and we liked to kill frogs. At first, we killed frogs by throwing rocks at them, but this gave most of the advantage to the frogs, who disappeared with a splash at the first miss. Then we made the move to slingshots and we became better killers. Eventually, Chris and a few of the older boys graduated to BB guns, and a wholesale slaughter ensued. We could, with the high-powered pellets, even kill the large pollywogs that hovered like elongated eyeballs below the surface of the water. Chris lent me his rifle and told me to aim slightly below the pollywog's trajectory to account for any deflection caused by the water surface. I braced the butt against my shoulder, as I'd been taught, and took careful aim, until the pollywog and I were the only two sentient beings in the universe.

It's either you or him, Chris said, when I still had not fired.

So I squeezed the trigger, and when the cloudy water cleared, I saw my handiwork. Chris congratulated me with a pat on the shoulder.

Good kill. Very FV. Now you have to drink its blood to let the spirit of the frog into you.

Fuck that, I said, and lined up another amphibian to deaden my horror at what I'd done.

Chris seemed to feel no such pangs. Some days, I could tell whether he'd been down to the lake before me by the number of pollywog and frog corpses floating on the water, little grey holes in their heads. Eventually, we no longer heard the bellow of frogs in the evening. I honestly think we wiped the entire population out.

We built our forts in dense thickets of forest, out of old wooden shipping pallets and found boards and odd-shaped pieces of plywood and throwaway cuts of shag carpet, tar paper, and plastic. The best fort I ever helped build was constructed over a pit in the ground that had been created when a giant tree fell and ripped up the earth with its roots. This fort was at the edge of the swamp close to Penhorn Mall. Derek and Franky and I built it, without the knowledge of Chris, Geoff, Sheldon, and the other older boys. It had multiple rooms, and in one room you could lift up the floorboards and descend into the cave beneath.

I decided the cave was a good place to store my porn magazines, since I'd become too nervous to keep them in my bedroom any longer, and offered them magnanimously to the members of our fort.

Even more fun than building a fort of your own was destroying a fort belonging to someone else. The older boys heard about our fort but they didn't know where we'd built it, so we changed routes every time we visited. Despite these precautions, we must have been spotted or followed, because, one day, we arrived to find it utterly destroyed. The walls were toppled, the boards smashed, the cave below the fort reeked of piss. My porn magazines were ripped into ten thousand shreds, scattered puzzle pieces of unmatched breasts and hips.

The fort had lasted only three glorious weeks. Although disappointed, we weren't overly bitter. The building and destroying of forts was another example of natural law. It had been our duty to build it, just as it had been their duty to destroy it. Everyone accepted that.

While building the fort, Derek and I had gone searching the nearby forest for planks and plywood pieces. Just off a path that exited to a field surrounding Penhorn Mall, we found a nest of women's purses. We puzzled over what it could mean to find a dozen or so handbags in the weeds and brush. Eventually, we understood that someone must have stolen the bags from women shopping in the mall and dumped them in this spot. The industriousness of the activity—more than a dozen purse-snatchings—and the calculated route—each time the snatcher had left the purses in the exact same hiding place—spoke of something dark and obsessive about criminal activity.

We searched the purses idly and discovered that many of them still had spare change, a few forms of identification, and other odds and ends like brushes and compact cases. I believed the spare change to be fair game, but Derek considered it part of the evidence that needed to be turned over to the police. It would never have occurred to me to bring the purses in, and it shocked me that Derek was so insistent. I saw the crime as completely outside our realm of concern. The only thing that mattered was the treasure we had found and the good story. The purses had long ago been written off as lost. The purse-snatcher would not be caught just because we found the stash. The crime itself was a mystery, hidden in a thicket, beyond the reach of whatever light shone in the moral universe. It was something to laugh about, not to make better.

Derek hastily gathered all the purses and driver's licences and credit cards into his hands, while I just as hastily scooped up as many coins as I could get. We parted in mutual anger. Still indignant days later, I asked Chris, whose father, after all, was a policeman, if he would have brought the purses to the police too.

Fuck that, he said. And we laughed in FV fashion at what an idiot Derek had been.

Then we learned about Paul's new tree fort and plotted to bring it down.

The situation was tricky from a tactical standpoint and slightly dubious from a moral or legal one. Paul's house was on the street that bordered the lake. His tree fort was not exactly in his backyard but in the woods immediately behind his backyard. Wrecking it was a bit like wrecking his property. Still, we figured Paul hadn't built the fort himself and his father had probably done the work. This gave us enough scorn to go through with what needed to be done.

On the day we discovered the fort, we climbed the makeshift railing and clambered in. Astonishingly, there were three levels, each higher than the next offset like the sprawling wings of an elaborate house. There were ladders cut through floors, and there were railings and rope swings and toys lying about, some of them clearly belonging to Paul's younger sisters. We stood in the highest reaches and admired the view and the superb construction. Then we put the boots to it, kicking in plywood walls, wrenching up railing boards, tossing toys into the abyss. I found a rusty nail and stabbed a Stretch Armstrong doll, something I'd always wanted to do, and squeezed until fluorescent green goo oozed out of the tear in the chest.

The fort, however, was well built and resistant to our destructive activities. We'd made frustratingly little progress when Paul's mother stormed out of the house waving a broom and screaming at us. No one feared the broom or her threats but it was also fun to run away, so we jumped down to the forest floor and tore off through the woods, laughing like lunatics.

Being thwarted only inspired us to greater determination. We made the destruction of Paul's fort a burning objective. We thought about the ways it could be done and debated the options among an ever-amassing group of boys. Several smaller groups of close friends came together in one large super-group, bound by a common purpose and the righteousness of a holy cause. Should we wait until Paul's family went on vacation? Should we bring hatchets and crowbars to tear more quickly into the walls and do as much damage as possible before discovery? Should we gather branches and leaves and light a bonfire below it? Finally, one of us came up with the perfect idea, and we gathered on the appointed night.

We waited until pitch dark. There were perhaps nine or ten of us in total and no one had thought to bring a flashlight. We started off into the forest, excited and eager, far enough away from our destination that anyone who saw us entering the woods from the road could not possibly have guessed where we were going. We moved silently, except for the occasional grunt or curse whenever someone got jabbed by a branch, swallowed a bug, or walked through a spiderweb. We knew the paths well. This was our lake and our woods; Paul just lived here. We turned off the path at precisely the right point and crawled up the slope in the dark through thicker forest to Paul's backyard.

There were no lights on at his house. We hushed each other's laughter, though each hush seemed to coax more hysterical giggling. Finally, we stood below the tall tree where the fort was perched, cherishing the intensity, trembling with the anticipation. I heard a rucksack open, then a twig snap. Someone shushed us all again.

Then a chainsaw coughed twice and throttled into a glorious roar.

The noise obliterated every other sense. The chainsaw set to work, in whose hands I didn't know, biting and spitting its way through the trunk of the tree. We stood back from the splinters, as though from flying sparks, glee in our hearts. Lights came on in the house. A voice yelled a warning. We ignored it. There was work to be done. Then someone else yelled, Cops! We refused to believe it. It was impossible for the police to be summoned so quickly. And yet there was no denying it when we heard the wailing siren and saw the blue and red lights strobing through the trees.

Run!

I don't know who called out the command, but the word, as though it knocked a hornet's nest, sent us scattering. We couldn't see anything in the darkness, and when we ran, we ran straight into tree trunks and branches and brush and each other.

I found myself on the edge of the path closest to the swamp, alone and breathing hard. I knew the path ahead was doomed, and the path behind was trouble too. The police could cut us off at either end. They would scoop us up as we came out of the forest, and there was no way I could sneak by. I could hear bullhorns now too, muffled orders, and I saw blazing white lights arcing through the woods. That's when I heard a whispered voice.

Bang, you're dead.

I ducked in confusion and fear, and then experienced pure relief.

Over here.

The words lifted me up from my crouch.

Stay low.

I couldn't tell where the voice was coming from until I saw a head pop up above the high grass in the swamp and a hand wave my way. Whoever called me was hidden behind the stone lock, probably the only cover in the area.

The stench was overwhelming, layers of stink with foul nuances like swirls of flavour in a complicated tub of ice cream. I stepped carefully but my foot immediately sunk in spongy moss and got sucked into the muck. I pulled out, losing a sneaker, and winced at the sucking sound and the pucker of dank air that rose up. Then I heard the bullhorns and knew the cops were closing in. The voice hissed for me to hurry, so I ran, *suck suck suck*, feeling lashes of tall, wet reeds against my face and tasting splatters of muck in my mouth.

It was Chris, of course. He was perched on a lip of stone, like an expert rock climber, perfectly dry. I thought he'd mock me for showing up so covered in stink and wet, bleeding from scratches, one sneaker in my hand, but he only grinned. His good mood affirmed everything right about what we were doing, and affirmed me in the process. I wasn't mistake prone, clumsy, or stupid. I was in on a great adventure.

It took minutes for my heart to stop knocking and my breathing to settle. We waited and listened, our heads down. The cops ran down the path one way and then back again. The lights pointed beyond us and strafed through the trees, above and around.

During a quiet moment, I offered my assessment of the situation.

We're fucked.

It was obvious. But Chris was in no mood to concede defeat.

Why would you say that? he asked.

Because we're surrounded by cops.

So were Butch and Sundance. But they blasted their way out.

We'd seen the movie a hundred times, and still the argument continued.

Right, I said, and managed, even then, to snort in derision.

Actually, Chris said, we've got them right where we want them.

You think so?

In ten minutes or so they'll give up.

You figure?

I know cops.

I couldn't argue with that.

Then, he added, we can cut back up to the tree house and give it a shove. I bet it falls right over.

That's when I knew he was insane.

Maybe not, huh, Chris said, conceding he was joking.

Maybe not, I said.

Next time, we bring explosives. Stack them up under the tree. Light the fuse.

Boom, I said.

We giggled, and then stopped. A noise out there. We were so fucked.

How are we going to do this, Chris?

Blow the tree house up?

Get home without, you know, the whole getting caught thing.

Fuck if I know.

He said it casually as ever, but a wave of sympathy came over me because of the rare honesty. It seemed tragic to me, in that moment, that Chris should experience the reality I knew so well, that the universe conspired deliberately to thwart you, that cockblocking your goals and pissing on your dreams was part of the overall purpose of the cosmos. So, bravely, I resolved to work with him to figure a way out.

We considered the options. Even if the cops gave up on the woods, they could just park in the darkness of the street on our side of the lake and watch for boys walking out. The safest way home was to approach from a secondary street farther out on the orbital rings. If we had the rubber dinghy, we could row through the swamp into the forest and climb out the far end. But we'd never get there in the dark on foot. What to do?

I got it, Chris announced. We'll swim.

Swim where?

To the other end of the lake.

The idea was preposterous. Like climbing Mount Everest. We'd never once swam the entire length of the lake, even in daylight, even with the rubber dinghy trailing alongside.

If we can get to the other end, Chris continued, we can hook around and cut through backyards until we're at my house.

As if swimming the lake in the dark was a given.

I don't want to drown.

In this fucking lake? I bet it's been ten years since anyone drowned here.

Thanks. I feel much better. What about our clothes?

With Chris, it was always best to argue in terms of practicality. If you argued for better judgment or out of fear of the consequences, he only got more determined.

But Chris had thought about our clothes too.

We bundle them up and hold them over our heads.

So we took off our clothes, everything but underwear, and wrapped them tight around our shoes and stepped into the water. The temperature seemed warm and pleasant at first, but then began to cool. I tried to glide sideways, as Chris was doing, and hold my clothes above my head. We made our way like dark otters.

But the distance was farther than we realized, which was the predictable flaw in Chris's otherwise perfect plan. Soon my arms grew too tired to hold my clothes aloft, and it was either sputter and drown, or lower my arms and hug the clothes as best I could to my chest. By the time I got to the shore, I'd lost both sneakers and one sock, and my jeans and shirt were sodden with water. Even Chris's clothes were wet. Still, we were alive, gloriously alive, and we lay on our backs, breathing hard and staring at the benevolent stars above, filled with joy at our audacious escape.

Then we slogged home. My bare feet slapped the pavement, my clothes trailed water. When we got closer to our immediate neighbourhood, we cut up through a series of backyards to Chris's house. His parents were in bed. I waited in the basement while he went upstairs. A few minutes later, he came down with the clothes I would need to get home. We toasted the whole adventure with a couple of well-earned beers stolen from the fridge.

That was the most amazing thing we ever pulled off, before we robbed a bank.

3

In 2008, long after his reputation as one of the world's great novelists had been established, Milan Kundera faced an accusation. I had lived for a time in the Czech town Kundera grew up in (one more stop for me in a lifetime of serial getaways), so I took particular notice of the controversy. Although the Cold War was long over in the West, it lingered in living memory in the Czech Republic. There was a heaviness to the place, a sense that the geography was the dense region of the mind where nothing escapes or is forgotten. The Communists had been into consequences. They'd made a fetish of responsibility. They kept good track of every transgression and misdeed, criminalizing ordinary life, casting every act or utterance as suspicious, regardless of context or intent, in order to retain the threat of accusation for whenever it might be needed. And so the past kept resurfacing, especially as old files got exposed to the light, like clay vessels in which prophecies or heresies (depending on your point of view) had been buried.

In one particular file from 1950, the young Milan Kundera had been referred to as a police informant. According to the bureaucratic notes, Kundera had given information to the secret police about the identity of a citizen who'd become a spy for the West. As a result of Kundera's statement, the accused man served fourteen years of hard labour and narrowly escaped execution.

The news was a shock, which some refused to believe and others savoured. There were many Czechs who resented Kundera for being an intellectual and an emigrant, but in the public record, and certainly internationally, he had long been viewed as a noble opponent of totalitarianism. After all, he'd written novels critical of the insidious malignancy of the Communist government before and after abandoning his homeland in 1975.

Kundera himself had always denied he was a dissident or a communist or a leftist or a rightist. He was a novelist. His stories were not about right and wrong or good and evil but about love, laughter, forgetting, beauty, and lightness as well as weight and the other opposites. But given the new information that surfaced in his old file, it was possible to interpret Kundera's abandonment of Czechoslovakia as psychological rather than political, a personal expediency rather than a moral stance. After all, in the eighties, he'd even ceased writing in his native language. Perhaps the need to sever himself from the oppression of his country had not been the driving force. Perhaps he'd escaped from a more internalized oppression as well—the weight of old connections, of guilty memories, of a distasteful or even shameful past, you name it.

Accused sixty years later of being an informant, Kundera denied it utterly, and many great writers came instantly and indignantly to his defence. Even the imprisoned man's wife believed Kundera was innocent. The accusation seemed like a deliberately cruel and malicious stain on his reputation, a nasty, degrading, provincial kind of revenge. Yet, the amateur psychologist cannot help but wonder. There are aspects of Kundera's early novels that tangentially resemble the details of the long-buried report. Likewise, in several later works, there are passages that depict the pressures of interrogation and forced confession so keenly, the reader understands the complicit guilt of the good person who succumbs.

Did Kundera write those passages to manage his own convoluted shame and pre-emptively argue his innocence? Did he leave his country and abandon his native language because he wanted to escape an unbearable weight?

Mr. Kundera, please rise and defend your work.

It seems possible, even likely, that Kundera's insights came from his observations of people who did inform on others. With his personal understanding of the pressure of a repressive society, it would not be difficult for him to imagine and depict such inner turmoil. It also seems entirely plausible that Kundera was set up, that the files themselves were bogus, the information planted by some crafty plotter. In any event, regardless of speculation, there is also the sombre truth that he was only twenty-one at the time of the alleged incident. As Kundera himself argued in an essay many years later, how could it be fair to judge anyone for the moral choices they made in the fog of an opaque and youthful moment? A half century on, Kundera was more or less a different person. And, ultimately, his writing is so remarkable that it begs the question: Shouldn't any crimes (real, imagined, or speculated) that went into the making of it be forgiven? Shouldn't we even thank the youthful Kundera for making such real or imagined mistakes?

Nevertheless, if there's a shred of accuracy to the report, then it is at least biographically interesting—in the way that gossip or therapy is interesting—that his work served in part as an elaborate, obtuse, artfully woven confession, written in the guise of fiction. Kundera himself could hardly have come up with a better plot, a better elaboration of lightness and weight, a better illustration of the personal cost of institutional oppression and the social cost of secret, double lives, than by constructing such a meta-metanarrative.

I think every novel, at some level, is a confession. And every account contains its share of betrayals.

In the weeks that followed the tree fort incident, we all wondered how the cops had gotten there so fast. Chris figured he had the answer. Near Paul's house, in the Horseshoe, the cul-de-sac that had once been barren and served as our street hockey arena, there were now several new houses, and a number of young families, one of them a cop family. The cop's name was Drury, and though he was local police, not RCMP, he was a friend of Chris's father through some brotherhood of the badge thing. Chris suspected Drury had the cruiser home that night when the call came in to the dispatcher. Maybe Paul's parents called Officer Drury as soon as they heard noise outside. Or maybe they'd even consulted him in advance about the gang of kids who were trying to vandalize their property. Drury must have taken it personally. Three cruisers patrolled the streets of our neighbourhood that night looking for us, catching no one. We were proud of that escape, and I tried not to allow the extreme heroic lengths Chris and I went to in order to avoid capture be diminished by the fact that everyone got away no matter what route they took.

Here's the truth: I didn't run into Chris down by the lock. He clung to the edge by himself and stayed hidden and dry until he decided to swim across the lake on his own. I did not know he was there. In my panic, I fled by myself through the swamp. At one point, I lost my footing and fell hard, splitting my chin on a tree root or rock. I stumbled up, dizzy and teary-eyed, and tried to slow down, but I was afraid—I felt like something dark and evil was trying to stop me from getting away. Believing that I needed to get out of the woods immediately, I fought my way through tree branches to the street that cupped Oathill Lake.

I was covered in mud, I'd been flayed by branches, and I was holding my bleeding chin. The whole thing had been a game of hide-and-seek gone terribly wrong. Despite the seriousness of the trouble we'd summoned, in my mind, I was dismissing all consequence by simply giving up, the way you do when you decide you no longer want to play something. That's a decision fraught with weight when you're a child. When you play with other kids, there's a tacit assumption that rules are not to be trifled with, that they're sacred. When you give up—because the game has gotten too rough or you're not being treated fairly or you're insufficiently in command—you're doing violence to the shared fantasy world, destroying it in a way, and betraying everyone else who wants it to continue. But I didn't give a shit anymore. I was going home.

I didn't see the police car parked in the shadows until I was halfway up the street. It bleeped its siren and burst its blue and reds. I stood there, paralyzed, sick with the sudden understanding that some acts do indeed have consequences, that the real world will intrude on the world of delusion. I also realized in that moment that there was something wrong with me, some mental defect that had allowed my brain to ignore reality, to consider real life just another version that could be dismissed or embraced at my choosing. I raised my trembling hands into the air as you are supposed to, at least according to all the movies I'd ever seen, and a policeman in the front seat shined a flashlight on me. He saw the mess I was in and told me to get into the back. I think he was going to cuff me until he decided I needed a free hand to hold a pile of tissues.

That was Officer Drury. He spoke quietly into his radio and told whoever was listening that he had picked one up. Meaning one of us. Meaning me. A voice mumbled something back. Officer Drury didn't say much for a long time after that. We sat in the car, him in the driver's seat, me in the cage, and waited for another lost idiot to wander out of the woods. But no one did. I was the only one. I began to shake, as if very cold, and my nose ran and I sniffed and fought to keep my crying sounds quiet. I knew my life was over. Officer Drury knew it too, but he had clearly seen lives end before.

Then he broke the silence and spoke to me as directly and honestly as anyone had ever done. The conversation has never left my brain. Not the words, exactly. But the inquisition. The stark assessment of my worth. It's still in there, rattling around, working its way through many otherwise unrelated moments of conscience and shame.

What's your name?

I told him.

Where do you live?

I told him.

You realize how stupid it was to operate a chainsaw in the woods in the middle of the night?

I said yes. Because I did realize it now, acutely.

How many of you were there?

I told him.

What are the names of the other boys?

I told him.

You all live around here?

I said, No. Some of us do.

I'm going to take you home. Your parents need to drive you to the hospital to get that chin stitched up.

I begged him not to.

He told me that my father would understand. I knew that he wouldn't.

All grim and businesslike, my father thanked Officer Drury for bringing me home. My mother took me inside and looked at my chin under the bright kitchen light. Then, as I waited for my father to appear, I heard a strange sound. After a minute of strained listening, I realized to my horror that my father was sobbing in the hallway. That sound was the worst thing about the whole night, perhaps my whole life.

I was devastated, naturally. Until you've made your father cry, you do not know the disappointment a child can bring to a parent. But I was also angry. I was furious. I knew suddenly that I got caught because my father was the kind of father who would cry in the hallway when his son was brought home by the police. I also knew I was destined to be the kind of kid who didn't have the grace and moxie to escape trouble, who lacked ease or competence in a crisis, because my father cried. My father was devastated by my failure. And I was devastated by his.

None of the other boys, as far as I know, were picked up. My parents, in the stern quiet of morning, decided I would apologize to Paul's parents and to Paul. But they let it slide. I felt sick to my stomach all weekend waiting to be told to walk down the street and explain myself. But the order never came. As a result, I escaped further public shame, and I was able to play off the events lightly with my friends. I kept vague about my own path to freedom, dismissed the eight stitches on my chin as only a flesh wound, and laughed all the harder at Chris's ordeal. The swim had not been such a brilliant idea. His clothes got soaked and he lost a shoe. He hobbled home, half naked and freezing, hiding occasionally behind hedges and parked cars, too exhausted to think clearly. Chris carried his own buffoonery off effortlessly and made it seem cool. The others of us, who'd been relatively unscathed by the experience, felt gypped in comparison. At least that's the disappointment I projected. Inside, I was terrified of the consequences still to come. I waited for Officer Drury to visit each of my friends' houses in turn, to round them up based on my information. When that didn't happen, I began to doubt my own sanity. I came down with a fever because of the stress, unable to think about anything else. Had I been picked up at all? Had I sat in Drury's car and answered his questions? The only proof, even to me, was the scar on my chin and the shame of my father crying.

When I fled Halifax and travelled Southeast Asia, the other book that I carried with me was *Lord Jim* by Joseph Conrad. In retrospect, it's easy to understand why I was attracted to it. *Lord Jim* is also a meditation on lightness and weight, in this case, on the alluring lightness of youthful fantasy for a life of adventure, and on the naive but understandable desire to be tested by the worst this world can throw at you, followed by the sodden weight of shame you bear when you find yourself wanting. Lugging my backpack, contemplating the freedom and lightness of travellers in general, a participant-observer in the subculture of do whatever the fuck you want with or to whomever you want, I saw myself as another Jim. I was an exile in the same tropical ports. I had acquired a similar ease with my surroundings, the kind you get when you've travelled a long time and seen many strange things and have no particular plans or limits. Moreover, I was not readily knowable by the backpackers I met, and had a mysterious air. The reason was simple. In contrast to most others, I rarely talked about myself and the places I'd been and seemed, as a result, to possess dark secrets, maybe even a dark past. This was appealing to women as well as to men, and I'm sure it was not entirely surprising when, after any long and partially revelatory conversations over the course of an evening, or a reckless fuck one night, I would be gone the next day, without a message left behind. You were permitted to be rootless, taciturn, and cavalier about the feelings of others when you were a backpacker. Lightness was practically demanded of you, even, or especially, when you trafficked in weight.

I understood why Jim wanted to go to sea in the first place, how he could imagine that such a life would be one way—filled with adventure, dangerous tests, and honourable triumphs— and I could relate to his disappointment when that life turned out another way entirely—soaked in boredom, banal duty, and the pettiness of others, interrupted by brief moments of contentment and unexpected bursts of humiliation and fear. I had seen and done a fair bit myself by this point in my life, but the incident with the tree fort struck me in retrospect as having marked an unheeded warning of the many disappointments to come. Of course, I know my experience then was insignificant compared with the perils of some listing ship or violent storm, but I had been tested and found horribly wanting. I had been betrayed by my own weakness and I had betrayed others in turn. The fact that my shame was not made public, that I could disguise, cover up, and ignore the evidence of it, allowed me to rationalize such failure. I assumed at the time that the incident would not be characteristic of my entire life and personality but was only an aberration. Better yet, I told myself, it was a gift. It was a lesson that allowed me to prepare for a real test, when I would not be found wanting.

Jim thought so too. After a few early misadventures that rattled him badly yet lacked severe consequences, he pushed on in his career as a sailor, confident that his luck would be better next time. But in Conrad's world, the sea wins every toss of the coin. Jim's life-turning confrontation with fate occurred when he found himself the chief mate on a dubious freighter loaded with Muslim pilgrims making its way across the Red Sea from India to the Arabian peninsula. Life and work on board a freighter was a particularly grim comedown for Jim. Nevertheless, on the fateful evening, the sea was as smooth as glass, the sun set to the sound of the Islamic call to prayer—an eerie, exotic, yet deeply peaceful wail—and Jim felt briefly at truce, if not in harmony, with the vexing world. Then, in the night, the ship slid over a submerged object, perhaps (as speculated later in court) a waterlogged, half-sunken wreck. In the awful aftermath, it became obvious that the freighter would sink and there were not enough lifeboats for even a small portion of the passengers. Facing certain death, as they say, Jim made his terrible choice. He escaped with the ignoble captain and crew, abandoning their human cargo.

The horror we feel at our own weakness and failing—is it made worse when the consequences are also horrible or when they are banal? In a particularly cruel twist, the freighter did not sink but was found listing on placid seas and towed back to port, the human cargo bemused by the adventure, confident that God had preserved them. While Jim was relieved so many lives were spared, this fortunate ending only highlighted his cowardice and exposed his missed chance. He knew in hindsight that he should have stayed on board, the only remaining crew member, and that if he had done so, he would have been seen as a hero now, the personification of valour, as though his virtue alone had kept the ship afloat. Wishing he had done so, however, was a kind of torture, because he understood, at the raw pit of his soul, that bravery without consequence was mere vanity, a show of virtue rather than the real thing. He was nailed to the cross of his shame twice over. There was an eagle ripping at his liver and a snake dripping venom on his forehead both.

Of course, not everyone would feel such complicated self-loathing, and ultimately that is what makes Jim noble and makes his story worth telling. He earned the scars he'd always wanted, but he could not appreciate or accept the accomplishment they marked. The crew, on the other hand, was light about its guilt. The captain and the others sneaked away from the trial like thieves in the night while Jim remained behind to face the consequences of judgment alone. As a result, he came to bear a disproportionate weight of the blame and responsibility for what happened.

It is the willing acceptance of this weight that interested Conrad, or his narrative stand-in, the famous Marlow. That sense of burden, that weight, is revealed over the next several hundred pages in Jim's delicate, almost aesthetically refined sensibility. He told Marlow his story, exposing his shame, agonizing over every detail of his failing and every facet of his cowardice. He bore the punishment and the shunning of his fellow men. He tried to make a simple but honourable life for himself, incognito, in ports across the region, and so he lived as a wanderer, almost a monk, moving ever eastward into the obscure depths of the Orient whenever his true identity was discovered. He did this despite the fact that many were willing to forgive him. Indeed, some even admired him because his self-delusions had been so cruelly stripped and the remaining virtues were so exceedingly pure. But Jim could never accept this forgiveness or admiration. It was intolerable to him.

I wanted to believe that of myself as I travelled the same Far East, a region still replete with the exotic mysteries Conrad described. Like Jim, I watched sunsets off the sterns of ferries, and listened to the call to prayer on the glasslike sea. Like Jim, I experienced quick storms that seemed accusatory in their malevolence. Like Jim, I recovered from injuries in breezy hospital wards and spent endless hours in open-walled cafés, surrounded by expats but separate from them. I wanted to believe that I was in search of a new code. That I was learning the virtues of simplicity after a period of excess and delusion. That I had been tested by a cruel fate not entirely my own fault and that the harsh knowledge of my personal weaknesses had scarred me. That I was burdened by consequence and untethered by wreckage. That my character had been polished as a result. At the same time, proving that self-delusions are forever dangerous, I hoped that this mysterious past made me a more enticing encounter, a more desirable sex partner, a more cunning writer.

Unlike Jim, however, I hadn't faced my trial or borne any undue burden of justice, and I knew the truth of that even though I could tell a good story when I hinted at the particulars of my past in suitably disdainful but actually self-flattering ways. The vanity of unearned virtue was strong in me.

Not all of childhood is so heavy or dark. In fact, if you're lucky enough to escape abuse, hardly any of it is. As a result, you forget lessons easily. You don't know who you really are, so you go on trying illusions and fantasies of the self, and sometimes they are very comfortable, and the world is tolerant enough to let you wear them for a while. I'm not sure if that's the reprieve of youth or another manifestation of its cruelty.

We roll forward a few years, from the night of the tree fort, and its unknowable consequences, to the summer before I began college. We move from age fourteen to age eighteen. That's not so long to jump, though it seemed an eternity at the time. A similar span, say from thirty-nine to forty-three, would not feel nearly as significant. Though you round the hump of a fourth decade and enter middle age, you're likely to have the same job, the same family, the same monthly mortgage payments, the same car. Your progression through that phase in your life is incremental or gradual even though it can pass in an eye blink. In contrast, the years between fourteen and eighteen are filled with abrupt disruptions, noticeable changes in your physical body, your outlook, your understanding, and in the kind and intensity of your experiences, and yet in spite of all the excitement, the many events, nothing in particular seems to happen, and you crawl through the desert of time on your hands and fucking knees, delirious for some longed-for destination. Maybe mathematicians would chalk the difference up to the proportional amount of time experienced to that point. When you've lived only fourteen years, piling on another four means making it a third further and then some. In comparison, four years when you are forty is only a tenth of your lifespan and a relatively lesser portion. But I don't think the mathematicians have it quite right. There's something else going on, and I can only point to the episodic eternities of youth, the way conversations and homework and summers and awkward feelings constitute little forevers among themselves. Math is not quite up to the task of explaining time, just as it falters when trying to explain motive.

Fourteen to eighteen. In the movie, two actors would need to play me to make the transformation convincing. And yet, I don't want to sweep over four such years without suggesting some of the things we did and felt in between. After all, those were the four years that tightened our friendship. If, when I was fourteen, I was one friend among many walking through the dark woods to Paul's tree fort, by the time we were eighteen, the gang had fallen away, and only Chris and I remained. It would not be correct to suggest that we spent zero time with others, but he and I were always together and had achieved the semi-permanence of best friends. You can imagine the many different things we did as a duo—we played baseball and hockey, we stole alcohol and got drunk, we climbed trees, groped girls and once or twice got groped in turn, we punched brick walls just to see how it would feel, killed frogs, complained about parents and school, revisited old jokes and old experiences, made up new ones, laughed until our sides hurt, wandered shopping malls, and had many, many what-if conversations about things we might do, things we ought to do, things we wouldn't dare do, things we'd dare that no one else ever would. One of those persistent conversations involved a life of crime, but I did not take it seriously then, and I don't think Chris did either.

Even with so much time spent together, Chris remained a mystery to me. I knew where he lived and I knew his parents and I knew his grades and how remarkably far he could throw a baseball and that he did not like potato chips but did like ice cream. But I still worried about what he would think about the things I said and how he would react to the things I liked or did. I did not trust that we would always be friends. He was above me in too many ways. Bigger, stronger, more graceful, mistake free. He always said or did the right thing at the right moment. I may have been wittier, but my wit was of the reckless, floundering kind. I played the self-mocking fool, perhaps because I feared that's exactly how I came across. I was ambitious, but my ambition was loud. Even when I didn't talk about it, you could hear the banging and clanging in my brain, see the herky-jerky nerve spasms pass through my limbs. I wanted to be a writer, and Chris supported that, but I feared the writing profession was a shameful, unrealistic, and unworthy goal, a bit like choosing to be homosexual. Chris had plans too, but they were quieter, somehow better conceived, and more daring and awe-inspiring. Specifically, he wanted to be a police officer, perhaps after serving a stint in military special forces, and I had no doubt that he would be a trained expert called upon to handle dangerous missions and that he would live in a spare penthouse apartment overlooking the city, visiting it after bouts of extended international travel involving the occasional assassination.

It goes without saying that he got laid before me. Getting laid was our abiding obsession throughout most of our teens (and beyond) and for a time, Chris and I paced each other in failure. I took some comfort in that, some solace in the shameful number of times I jerked off daily, knowing that if even Chris remained a virgin, my own predicament must not be entirely my fault. But then, when he actually got laid the summer before his senior year in high school (by screwing the daughter of a family friend, who happened to be a prosecutor, in town for a visit), I never felt so alone in my life. Those who say virginity is no big deal are standing on the far side of the great divide. There is an enormous and devastating distance between zero and one, between yes and no, between have you or haven't you. To my eyes, Chris carried himself differently after that, he was even more self-assured, and I felt more desperate, ridiculous, and clownish. It did not help that he continued to get laid, on a persistently regular but randomly partnered basis over the next few years, while I continued to grope and flounder more or less pointlessly, except for the occasional encounter that went much but not all of the way, during which I would feel relieved as hell that someone else was masturbating me for a change, even though I probably could have done the job better myself.

In the last summer before we started robbing banks, the summer after high school for me, I was once again forced to confront the extent to which our lives had diverged. It started out as an innocent mid-July afternoon at the lake. I had a day off from the bank where I worked as a temporary replacement for tellers who were on vacation. Chris had decided to take a day off from his summer job, pulling rickshaw in the city. In our bathing suits, it was glaringly obvious how our different choices of summer employment had affected us. Actually, I'd had no choice in employment at all. I'd wanted to pull rickshaw with Chris but my parents wouldn't allow it. They seemed to think it was a sketchy job and wanted me to earn a steady and regular paycheque while gaining useful work experience. I didn't put up much of a fight because I knew I couldn't win. I didn't have any freedom. But I could see now what a terrible mistake I'd made. Chris was tanned from head to foot and had gained the physical tautness and brute strength of a gladiator. His calf muscles, when he dove into the water, had the sinewy carved quality of knotted tree roots. His shoulders and biceps were rounded and swollen. A swimming race to the floating dock left me heaving for breath, pale and flat chested, a half-dead flounder, him smiling easily, slick as a porpoise.

Still, we were having a good day until the girls showed up and further exposed my pitiful life. We spotted them on the far shore of the lake. We could tell they were girls because they wore bikinis and lay down on towels. We were the only four people at the lake that afternoon and it was impossible not to be aware of each other's presence. Chris and I sat Indian style and debated what they looked like, how much they wanted us, and what delights they could offer. Then, to my heart-pounding surprise, we realized they were waving at us.

It was the kind of mating dance teenagers do all the time, but this time it was happening to me. We waved back, Chris with amusement, me with a shipwrecked desperation. A few minutes went by and we resumed chatting, though I couldn't concentrate. Then a voice carried over the water and asked what we were doing.

Chris arched an eyebrow and grinned. I could think of nothing to say. So Chris yelled on our behalf.

Watching you!

A dialogue started up then, but it was the most absurd conversation ever. Each time they spoke, we had trouble making out their words and needed to yell for them to repeat. Whenever we called over, our words seemed to collide with theirs halfway across the water. After yet another miscommunication occurred, Chris gave up.

This is fucking stupid, he said.

He was right. But I could have cried and torn out my hair in frustration.

Come on over and get us.

I was sure that was what they yelled, but Chris disagreed.

What the hell do you think they said, then? I asked.

Chris shrugged. Maybe they said, We like burritos with lettuce.

He could be such a motherfucker sometimes.

Had they seen my rubber dinghy? It was the only possible answer.

Let's row over and get them, I said.

But Chris refused.

Come on.

No.

Come on!

Forget it.

Why not?

Are you kidding me?

I was not, in any sense, trying to kid him, and I wished he would stop kidding me.

It wasn't in my nature to be wilful or impulsive, but I felt half-crazed with desire. Stepping into the boat with ungainly haste, I picked up the ends of each oar and asked Chris, one

65

last time, whether he was going to join me. He laughed again. I suppose if I was a member of Ulysses's crew, I would have been among the first to head for the Sirens.

It took ten minutes to cross the lake. I felt more humiliated and yet more hopeful with each inch of progress. I didn't dare to check too frequently over my shoulder, even though I feared the girls would flee before I arrived. Rowing evenly and steadily to the other shore, I kept myself skilfully on course by locking my eyes to the floating dock, where Chris was suntanning.

When I reached land, I saw with relief that the girls were still waiting for me, and I couldn't quite believe my good fortune. They seemed amused and pleased by my gallant gesture of having crossed an ocean to meet them. And they were indescribably beautiful. Lithe and barely dressed in the smallest of bikinis, they were perfectly tanned—tanned on their feet, on their toes, on the tops of their ears—without any variation of colour, an essence poured into the glass vessel of girlhood, contained in there without any spilling, the caramel of youth and endless summer. Both were thin. One was taller, with red frizzy hair, and cartoonish brown freckles on her cheeks, and jaw-droppingly rounded breasts. She seemed, despite her size and robust sexuality, the more innocent, cheerful, and therefore stupid of the two. The other was shorter, flatter chested though prominently nippled, with dark brown, almost raven-black hair, large dark sunglasses, a thin gold necklace, and a sarcastic and mocking line to her mouth, the kind of knowing humour that has always indicated intelligence and the excitement of danger to me.

Nice boat, she said, and I knew she was making fun.

Can you drive all of us in that at once? the other asked.

I marvelled at the distinct but delicious differences between them. Although I naturally preferred the dark-haired disdainful one, I could imagine either of their breasts held in my hands and sucked by my mouth and knew I could finger-fuck each without prejudice, or both at the same time, and enjoy the variant qualities of slip and sticky, the change in pungency. I practically fainted with curiosity and need.

At the same time, I was also efficient and competent. I managed to get them both on board—the initial victory of any pervert—and huddled up on the far seat before heaving the boat away from shore. It was awkward and slow to row the three of us back. But I was astonished, with each pull, to look up and see two bikini-wearing girls across from me. They had their towels bunched on their laps, but their toes were near mine, and their hands dangled in the water, and they laughed like sparkling beads of light whenever I said something funny. Their names were Leah and Susan. Leah was the taller of the two, the older and possibly stupid one, the one blissfully at ease. She'd graduated in the spring from the other high school and had, it seemed, no plans to ever go back to school again. Susan was from my high school, though I did not recognize her without clothes on. Despite being a year or two younger than me, she had the composed and intimidating aura of a fully mature woman.

Chris perked up by the time we arrived, peeving me and making me feel proud at the same time. He helped hold the boat tight to the floating dock while the girls deboarded.

Now what? Leah said, with her hands on her hips, and a tilt to her head.

I could think of so many unmentionable ideas, but we went swimming instead. We dove or cannonballed into the water. We splashed each other. We raced out, turned around, treaded close to one another, dove under, grabbed a foot, kicked away. We laughed and tickled. (I feared rising from the water because I didn't know whether my erection was fully formed and steel-rod stiff, or just bobbing playfully.) We did handstands and back-flipped into the water. The girls, with their lean, proportionately exquisite bodies, could do them perfectly, and somehow I knew they would never be so beautiful again. Chris could also manage a handstand, rising like a great redwood, the muscles on his shoulders and back straining formidably before he tottered and crashed into the water. My own attempts were typically pathetic. I wobbled, collapsed, and landed on my neck on the floating dock, before tumbling in agony into the water. Chris laughed mercilessly. The girls laughed, though they were also suitably concerned. I showed enjoyment in my buffoonery, but I could already feel a stiffness setting into my neck and knew I'd barely be able to turn my head the next day.

When we got cold, we swam to the pier onshore and lay face down on the warm planks, smelling the sunshine soaked into the splintery wood. We watched through the cracks for min-nows swimming by. I noticed that Leah's foot was almost touch-ing Chris's leg and that he had raised himself on his elbows in such a way that his shoulders looked even more rounded, like a powerful animal's haunches before a sudden forward spring. Some sense of pheromones became obvious to us all, and Susan mentioned that she needed to pee. Then, to my amazement, she asked me to accompany her.

I jumped to my feet and glanced at Chris as I left. We laughed silently to each other, barely capable of disguising our delight. This was the summer experience we'd always longed for and imagined. The spontaneous double fuck.

I followed Susan's small steps along the mossy path.

I always wondered what was on this side of the lake, she said.

I asked her if she lived on the other side. She told me that she did now. The houses were more expensive over there, and she seemed like someone with money. I was trembling as though cold and I couldn't trust my own voice.

Wait here, she told me, and disappeared into the woods.

I knew that she was peeing. I knew that, somewhere, she was crouching and her bikini bottoms were around her knees and urine was leaving her vagina and puddling the earth between her tanned feet.

There was a boulder nearby, set partly in the water. It made a good spot to cast from because you could span out beyond the weeds. I clambered up and sat down. The surface was hotter than I expected, and I winced and forced myself to get used to it. I waited. I suppose I would have waited forever.

When she returned, I was calmer, almost resigned, as if our relationship had progressed further in the interim, become something more intimate and knowing. She climbed up beside me and sat close. My arm touched her arm. My feet dangled near her feet. I pushed the side of her foot with my toes, she kicked back playfully. A frog jumped. So we hadn't killed them all, I thought.

Leah's weird, she said.

What do you mean? I asked. I did not want to talk about Leah. I wanted to nuzzle Susan's neck and nibble the lobe of her ear.

I thought it was weird to call you over. Don't you think it was weird?

I shrugged. I guess, I said. Yes, it was weird, but I was glad.

I've seen you in school, she said.

Have you? I asked, heart thumping.

You're very noticeable.

I gulped. Is that so? I wanted to ask why, to gain some insight.

How come you don't have a girlfriend? she asked before I could pursue my line of thought.

I was taken aback, did not know whether this was criticism or invitation, and I tried to recover with something cool and confrontational.

How do you know I don't?

She looked at me strangely. You're sitting with me like this for one thing.

I had no answer for that. Even if I had a girlfriend, the situation seemed innocent or at least plausibly defensible (which was the same thing in my moral universe). Were my intentions so obvious?

How about you? I asked. Why no boyfriend?

She took a shard of rock and threw it into the water.

You don't ask a girl something like that.

And I thought, Jesus, which way am I supposed to turn here?

We sat silently. And then I did something I'd never done before while sober, and rarely since. I moved toward her. She did not move away. We leaned into each other. Our foreheads met and rested one against the other. Her mouth opened slightly. Her warm breath smelled like blueberries. I could see the lashes of her eyes. This is it, I thought, this is the one I will always be with. I had the sense that I knew her, that I always had, and though our spirits did not jostle easily, they were already entangled and always would be. We complicated each other. We were puzzles and accusations both. All of this in the time it takes to remember to breathe. My lips touched her lips and her tongue bumped quickly into mine, like a fish darting through water, and I felt a peculiar emotion, part anxiety and part ease, about the depths I knew I could never fully explore.

We've been gone a long time, she whispered, after mere minutes of this.

She made me feel, in that moment, as though we'd been cheating. My hand was on her chest, just above her breast, my thumb was edging her nipple, my fingers clinging to her collarbone. Her hand gripped my other wrist tightly, as if holding onto me for balance or keeping me from reaching down into her bikini bottoms.

I waited. I did not dare to speak.

She put a finger on my chin and pushed until I looked up.

You, she said, are strange and dark inside. I think you're trouble. And I think you're very smart.

I did not know what to say, or how to express my astonishment at this oracular pronouncement. What did it even mean? She's only sixteen, I reminded myself, as if to dilute the message. But I felt as though she knew me better than anyone had ever known me before.

Such soft skin, such a warm mouth. I felt tenderly toward her, like a killer does. I moved in again, this time with more hunger.

Take me back, you big brute, she said, and gave me the kind of smile you cannot argue against, so bright and sudden it made me realize all her smiles before had been guarded. Perhaps it was the only kind of smile that could break the spell and allow me to release her. So I raised myself from the rock and hopped to the ground with longing lodged painfully in my throat, and I gallantly offered to lift her down as though she were a figure skater in the air. I felt her full weight in my arms, and I placed her neatly before me. She laughed and gave me a quick and furtive hug around the waist.

Come on, you, she said.

We'd walked a fair ways, and she seemed to have more trouble with the pine needles and sharp sticks on the way back. As we neared the pier, I heard a strange squeak, and an odd laugh, and I feared we might be interrupting something. But Susan either didn't hear those noises at all or was too focused on her footing to understand what they meant. It was only when we came to the clearing that we saw what was happening.

They were stretched out along the length of the pier and half-wrapped in a towel, but it was impossible not to know what they were doing. I saw his legs and bare back, and her knees and arched feet locked around his hips, and the long, smooth skin of her extended throat and, I swear, the animal flaring of her nostrils. A rude growl came from her. It seemed to start in her belly and uncoil through her torso and tremble as it left her parted mouth. Her hands gripped his hair and held his head down, and a fluid speed possessed his whole body even as his toes searched for grip between the planks.

Can you get my towel please, Susan asked me.

I didn't understand, and I couldn't move. I was too distraught and amazed. I felt betrayed and in awe, horribly alone, tearful, viciously envious, and fiercely proud.

Can you please get my towel, she repeated.

Susan's head was hanging down, her hair like a half-curtain around her face. Her mouth was stern and angry, and I thought I could see tears of rage forming in her eyes. I did not know how to respond but to step gently onto the pier and approach them. Leah's eyes were closed tightly shut. Her feet were planted on the wood now, her knees still clenched on Chris's hips. I could sense Chris's irritation and read his glare through the back of his skull.

I just need to, I said. This, I added. And I pulled and tugged and removed the bundled towel from under her back. And then I turned and fled.

No boat this time. We walked. I accompanied Susan all the way around the lake to where I'd picked them up. We did not speak much. I shook my head a few times and tried to say now I understood what she'd meant about Leah being weird. Susan barely seemed to hear, except once she announced, Leah doesn't have a father, you know, as if this odd and somehow surprising psychological detail explained something about what had happened. When we made it to their side, she retrieved her sandals and a bottle of baby oil and left me with only a disinterested wave. No kiss. No hug. I hated her a little. I did not feel like walking all the way around the lake again. I walked into the water instead and angled my course for the distant swampy corner, away from where Chris and Leah and the dock and my rubber dinghy remained. I set off. It took a long time to get across, and there were a few moments when I wondered if I might drown, but I didn't really care. When I neared the marshes, the weeds started clinging to my limbs and the water around me got cloudy and tasted brackish in my mouth. I swam until it became too shallow and then I tried to stand and sank through the peat without finding any footing and mucked my way desperately to shore, falling repeatedly.

For the rest of the summer and into the fall, as my first year of college started, Leah became part of our lives while Susan was as absent as a shooting star. It was difficult to resent Leah, she was so light and good-natured, even as I was distracted by the memory of her bare legs stretching skyward, her pink nipples, her elongated throat, and the wish that I'd experienced something like that with Susan, on the mossy forest floor, under the cloak of the trees, dappled by the sun. Chris and I attended the same school again, for the third time. Chris was a biology major with a minor in sociology. He had in mind a master's degree in criminology, believing that such a path would move him up the pay scale faster when he became a police officer. I was an English major. We often met for lunch in the Student Union Building. He, thank God, was showing me the ropes. Where to eat. Where to drink. How to cut between buildings to avoid going outside as much as possible. One or two days a week, Leah joined us on our lunch break, dressed in business clothes from whatever receptionist job she was temping. I associated her menial work and the heavy earrings she wore with a lower-class upbringing. She looked older, more composed, less wonderfully at ease than in her bikini, but friendly. It seemed, amazingly enough, that we were her closest, or even only, friends. Although I resented her, I could find nothing specific to complain about, and enjoyed her company. She wasn't, it turned out, stupid at all. She did not seem to know much about university studies, but while she was not unduly impressed by our status as students, she was interested in our courses. She noticed one day a philosophy book I had in my stack and asked to see it, flipping the pages and reading the full foreword while Chris and I ate. Where do you get this kind of stuff? she asked. Somewhat patronizingly, I told her about the campus bookstore but said the prices were quite high. There were other cheaper second-hand stores around the neighbourhood. She nodded and the three of us talked about other things, and then it was time for me to go to my next class and time for Leah and Chris to go back to a friend's dorm room and fuck. Chris had expertly scheduled all of his classes to be over by noon, in time for a quick lunch and some midday sex. Mine were clumsily strung along all day. Another stark difference between us.

Leah herself was a female revelation, and a conundrum. She was as eager for sex as Chris, and they went at it with industrial frequency. I wanted to know details, but Chris was surprisingly coy and gentlemanly about it. All he said was, Oh, man, the things she will let me do to her, it boggles the mind. And, for once, he didn't provide any dirt on what was being boggled or how. They did not seem to have a serious relationship, in the boyfriend-girlfriend sense. They didn't hold hands or act affectionately in my presence. They were merely friendly and comfortable, and that was mysterious too. Any guy would sign up for a no-commitment relationship, but was it normal for a woman? Maybe because we didn't have the term for it back then, I couldn't grasp the concept of a fuck buddy.

Their collision and subsequent arrangement left me in a daze. One day, he told me, She can never wear underwear around me. It's our rule. If she comes to meet me for a date, or even for lunch, she can't have underwear on. If we run into each other unexpectedly on the street, no matter what else she's got going on, she has to excuse herself, go somewhere private, and take her panties off. Weird, huh?

I could never see Leah again, naturally, without thinking of her free of panties, and this was happening in the early fall when coeds in class wore little but shorts and tank tops. I'd never seen so many beautiful women, and the distraction was often so intense I felt afflicted by a kind of malarial insanity. Despite my pain, Chris even had the nerve to occasionally complain about his situation. He felt overly confined by their schedule and irritated by vague behind-the-scenes discussions and arguments. Leah, apparently, could be a pain in the ass once in a while. It seemed an awfully small price to pay. But the human capacity for dissatisfaction is boundless. No wonder we were kicked out of paradise.

It all culminated on Halloween. Some friends of Chris were holding a house party. College house parties equal wild orgiastic sex, Chris informed me casually. For a week or so in the lead-up, I was beside myself with anticipation. And then, on the Tuesday before the weekend, I ran into Susan on a downtown street. My life stopped. I remembered everything that should have happened but hadn't. I was ready for it to begin now.

Susan. Again. She was with a friend, an East Indian girl, and they were coming out of a cheap costume store that I was heading into, looking for vampire teeth and a tube of fake blood. With her clothes on, Susan seemed shorter than I remembered, and less physically striking. Still, in her scarf and sweater, she was fresh faced and cheerful. She surprised (and thrilled) me by hugging me like an old friend. She introduced me to Radha, whose eyes, I noticed in a moment that felt like a betrayal of Susan even before our relationship really began, were strikingly bewitching. She'd lined them with eyeliner and had a wicked and mischievous way of watching you and laughing. Susan asked me how I was doing, how college was treating me. I understood, then, how she saw me. For a high school girl, a college guy who stops, gives her a hug, and spends some time chatting was a kind of trophy. For the first time in my life, I actually had some cachet. I told her all was good, and I asked what they were going to be for Halloween.

Belly dancers, Susan answered. And I almost fainted.

Well, instead of going door to door begging for candy, why don't you come to our party? I asked.

Suddenly, it was our party. I did not even know the guys who were throwing it. But I was confident that two belly dancers would be welcomed.

After the words escaped my mouth, I worried that they might scoff at my idea. But they were thrilled, fucking titillated. I gave

77

them the address, said goodbye, and went into the store to get the kind of teeth I would need to tear a chunk out of the world.

Chris was not as thrilled as I would have expected. He groaned something about Leah. It turned out that, since the incident at the lake, Leah and Susan were no longer friends. Leah had tried to make amends, but Susan would not be persuaded. I was defiant, however, and for once, I did not get myself worked up about consequences. Let the cat fight begin.

My vampire costume was low-key but did what I needed it to do, exposing throats to me that I would never have had access to ordinarily. Naturally, I was completely outshone by Chris, who went as a Chippendales dancer with black suit pants, a black bow tie, and no shirt. His pectoral muscles were big enough to set a beer onto. Leah had painted her face white and made her lips red, and set her shock of frizzy hair vertical so that she looked like an electrocuted witch. She also wore a miniskirt and black boots that were thigh high and, presumably, no underwear. The house was full. It took effort moving between rooms. Every floor was wet with beer. The air was clogged with cigarette smoke. I was anxious for Susan and Radha to arrive, counting on my college mojo to give me a fighting chance, not taking into account how much that mojo was diluted by the presence of forty or fifty other college guys.

When they showed up, in long winter coats, I was surprised to notice how young they seemed. They were only high school students after all. But when they removed their coats, all was forgiven. The bikini at the lake had been a burka in comparison, and they were glittery with gold speckles. Every half hour or so, with plastic beer glasses raised above their heads, they began to gyrate in unison as if to the distant winds of Middle Eastern music, hips propelling their stuttered rotation, bellies fluxing wildly, and every male with a view cheered heartily in appreciation. I should have charged a fee.

Around eleven o'clock, Chris grabbed me and shouted in my ear that he needed to take Leah home. She was tired and feeling sick, though I got the impression she was also upset by some interaction with Susan. Chris was my ride, and I would be stranded without him. He wasn't apologizing, however, just informing me of the situation.

I'll probably get stuck banging her or something, he added.

I nodded drunkenly. Even to me, Leah suddenly seemed like an old maid, an albatross around our necks, a monkey on our backs. To my surprise, she gave me a sudden hug before they left. I didn't realize it was a different kind of goodbye.

I danced with Susan and Radha. I hung with them. I lost them and found them again. I wanted alone time with Susan but this was impossible, and she had a sharp emotional edginess to her that didn't allow for easy intimacy. At one point, and out of nowhere, she and I began an intense conversation about my North American Novel class. It started as an inquiry by Radha into what courses I was taking. Susan pounced on the novel class, my favourite, and there was a spark in her eye.

How many women novelists are assigned to the reading list? she asked.

The question took me aback. It had never occurred to me to count the women novelists on the reading list. This was not because gender didn't matter. The fewer women the better, I probably believed without consciously thinking about it. The novelists I revered were not women, they were distinctly, overtly men, and I did not jibe with a feminine sensibility. I liked my description of character, mood, tone, and moral outlook to be firmly rooted in landscape and action, salted with the premonition of imminent violence and the contemplation of emotional betrayal. But I had no interest in having an argument. We were at a house kegger, and I had fangs in my mouth, and Susan and Radha were wearing spangles and smoking cigarettes, and all I really wanted to do was suck on their breasts. But I understood, as I focused blearily on her darkly lined and unblinking eyes, that this was important for her. Susan wanted to play grown-up. She thought that college students stood around at parties and argued volatile differences of opinion, before they went off and fucked. She wanted the college experience. Well, I aimed to give it to her. So I rose to the challenges she offered, knowing she was a child before my withering intellect.

Who gives a fuck whether a novelist is a man or a woman? I asked.

She stiffened. Dimly, I sensed danger and realized I had just dislodged one of her crazy stones. She began poking my chest sharply as she spoke, becoming more worked up with each point. Even so, I thought: She must really want me. If this seems like an incongruous view, don't kid yourself; every man, in almost every situation, with almost every woman, imagines that she wants him and imagines what she would be willing to do.

Unless fifty percent of the novels you study are written by women, your class is nothing but bullshit, she said.

There were angry tears in her eyes. Fearing irreparable harm, I tried to make nice. Look, I'm just kidding you. There are a bunch of women on the list.

Like who? she countered.

I could only think of two names. Margaret Atwood and Eudora Welty.

Eudora Welty?

I was surprised that my offering hadn't mollified her more. No points for Margaret?

Eudora fucking Welty? she asked again. No Alice Walker, not even Toni Morrison? You probably don't have room, right, because there are three essential John UpCock novels on the curriculum?

I happened to like John UpCock. In fact, no one had taught me more about how to paint a nice coating of metaphor over the drywall of a story. But I didn't know how to say that.

Instead, I said: Wait a minute, you're telling me Toni Morrison isn't a dude?

I knew my situation had become hopeless. All I wanted to do was get her to the couch and start cuddling.

Susan looked to Radha for moral support.

This is bullshit, don't you agree? Only two women and all those men?

Radha was smoking a cigarette and eyeing us both. I don't know, she said. Who are you going to leave out?

I volunteered to get us more beer.

They were still with me at the party at two in the morning. Radha had curled up asleep on the end of the couch, her long black hair fanned out around her hidden face in a don't-fuck-with-me veil. Susan and I sat side by side. The tension between us was an electric fence. I kept willing my hand over but my arm didn't respond. I wanted to draw her to my side, even if it was only to fall asleep with her head on my shoulder, but I had to be content with her nearness. None of us were capable of driving home. It was going to be a long, uncomfortable night.

When Chris returned, he stood before us, grinning as though he'd discovered the source of the Nile after an epic quest. I'd never been so grateful for the easy forgiveness of male company. I registered his presence and grinned back, hopeful that he'd be impressed by my success at keeping two belly dancers close by. Radha remained asleep, curled a different way now, like a child in the back seat of a car. Susan remained upright but locked into a thousand-yard stare.

Nipples get cold? I asked him.

He was no longer bare-chested and bow-tied but wearing an old T-shirt I didn't recognize.

Nah, he said. I got raked pretty bad.

I didn't understand what he meant, so he turned to the side and lifted his shirt up from the back. I saw thick red gouges, like whip welts. It dawned on me.

Leah? I asked.

She does go in for some vengeful breakup sex.

Susan's head bobbed, as though she'd fallen asleep and woken up just as suddenly, and then she was sitting upright, her stare a little more focused, maybe ten yards out instead of a thousand.

I was awestruck by Chris, the way he handled whatever turns life gave him. Leah had left him, his industrial sex sessions were over, he was doomed to self-governed celibacy once again, and it did not even cause him a flinch. I would have mourned her, or mourned what was gone. His adroit indifference made him seem forever in control. He was one of the charmed ones, and I was lucky to be his closest friend.

Susan rubbed her eyes and crossed her legs, the triangle of blue bikini disappearing into the wedge of her naked thighs. She must have been cold with little but glitter to cover her. I felt brave enough, suddenly, to mark her as my possession. But at the very moment I meant to reach my arm over, she rose.

And then, to my disbelief, she was standing next to Chris.

They began to talk. They shared a laugh. They huddled closer together, Chris leaning over to hear what she was saying, Susan's hand reaching up to touch his shoulder and remaining there.

I started to rise, to insert myself into their conversation, to reclaim my stake. Then something in me, something small and despairing and angry, gave up, and I sank into the crumb-infested couch, three times heavier than my normal weight, and thought: This is where I belong, abandoned like a forgotten sock.

I watched them like I'd watch a movie. Beers appearing in their hands. Cigarettes. Chris didn't even smoke, but he was smoking now, holding the cigarette like he'd pinched a snake to keep it from fanging him. And then I blinked or passed out for a fraction of a second, and when I looked up again, I saw that they were leaving. No. I saw that she was leaving, and bringing Chris with her. His hand in her hand. He looked over his shoulder at me with a puzzled grin as she led him away.

I knew what was happening, but I did not understand how someone as cavalier and emotionally careless as Chris could win over the girl who'd argued with me about the number of women novelists in my first-year literature class. I did not understand the game, let alone the rules; but I knew once again I'd lost.

Ten minutes later, they were still not back. I went off in search of the bathroom. When I found it, I saw two women standing outside, banging on the plywood door with their fists, calling for the occupants to get their own room. I listened between fist bangs, and heard shower water drilling a tub, and the hollow thud of something knocking against linoleum over and over, and little yelps and little grunts.

Like a cuckold, I was too stunned to weep or flail, but went off to find a beer.

In the lonely days that followed, I fretted and obsessed about Susan. I wanted to call her and ask why. I knew that she loved me, not Chris. So what compulsion made her give herself over, in the same public fashion that Leah had? What compromises and allowances? What tweaky needs? The pain of the loss I felt was confused with the pain of desire, and the dark suspicion that the fault had been mine, that I'd made some fatal mistake. Maybe I shouldn't have made fun of Toni Morrison. How was I to know she'd win the Nobel Prize?

I didn't yet understand how determined Susan could be to get what she wanted, how strategic, how needy she was for the thing out of reach, the thing she shouldn't have. I didn't yet know about her fragile sense of self, her crazy impulses. And if I had understood all of those things, I doubt it would have made the slightest difference.

Then there was Chris. To my mind, he achieved something utterly magical that year. He'd bagged a hearty gust of chick wind and could avail himself of it like an expert sailor whenever he desired. He was, on top of that, physically in the best shape of anyone we knew, and in full command and control of his course work, and socially in sync with the world. By all tangible measures, he had reached that most elusive of psychological states known as *flow*. I only had to compare his situation with my own to observe the extremes that could be experienced by two different people in the same basic circumstances.

But, of course, Chris was actually experiencing his own inner torment, however unmerited that might have been. I learned the truth in mid-November when a series of severe snowstorms shut down the school and the city.

It was remarkable how much snow accumulated. You gave up shovelling your driveway because the stuff never ceased falling and the plows neutralized your hard work whenever they passed. Then the plows stopped coming because they had no place else to put the snow. The banks closed. The stores closed. Sidewalks got obliterated. Stranded cars disappeared beneath rounded humps.

We found ourselves with a few stolen days. We should have studied during that unexpected break, caught up on our papers and assignments. Naturally, we spent our time in Chris's basement, drinking beer, looking through *Playboy*s, and talking random shit. Such shit was the foundation of our friendship. In Chris's car, walking between classes, at the lake, standing bored at some house kegger, we talked and talked. We finished each other's sentences. We built on each other's ideas. We invoked twists on each other's ridiculous fantasies. Always joking. Always one-upping.

By Wednesday night, we got restless. The snow had stopped blowing hard despite our calls for it to keep going strong, and it seemed likely that, after one good plowing day, the world would start up again. Naturally, we headed for Oathill Lake around midnight with a football.

There was a full moon and the night was bright. The snow on the lake lay in drifts that mimicked waves on the beach. We ran like Charlie Chaplin across the ice, sliding, losing balance, shifting direction suddenly, and tumbling. We discovered that we could throw the ball wide of an easy catch and that the receiver could dive recklessly and slide along the ice for a few glorious feet and still conceivably manage a highlight-reel grab. We attempted it over and over until we were so snow covered, it was pointless to stay on our feet. Lying on our backs, we made obscene snow angels and then stared up at the moon-bright sky and watched the odd snowflake tumbling down in 3-D.

I feel like I'm meant to do something bigger, Chris said.

The words were so sudden and so discordant with the goofiness of our play that I was not sure, for a moment, he'd uttered them aloud. They might have been someone else's thoughts, blown to us like a snowman's hat.

Like what? I asked.

Silence. Then a pained laugh.

I guess that's the question.

I had never known him to question anything before. I watched the snow dazzle above and felt a strange and comforting power over my closest friend. I knew the bigger thing I was meant to do. I was going to be a writer. I understood now that Chris felt the lack of that. It made me appreciate all the more keenly his unwavering support, but I also felt a selfish and ignoble one-upmanship. I tried to cover that with humour, the familiar place friends go to for reassurances.

Give me a break. You're nailing everything that moves. You're coasting through school. You're going to be a kick-ass cop. What more do you want?

He didn't answer.

Maybe you should do the whole Navy SEAL–ranger-assassin thing, I suggested.

That got from him an easier laugh.

Yeah, well, maybe I will.

The silence came back. It was not ordinary silence but the silence of snow falling, the silence of solid ice beneath our backs, the silence of a city not moving, of an entire universe that had stopped to listen.

Actually, though, he said, I've been kind of thinking about doing something a little unusual.

Again, I did not have the words to answer him right away. I could have joked. Get a sex change? Try ballet? But I resisted, and maybe because I resisted, it gave him the freedom or the safety to utter what should never have been spoken.

You remember how we joked once how easy it would be to rob a bank? he said.

I did not remember at first because the context had been so different. Then it came back to me. It was one of our many running what-if conversations. What if zombies attacked— would you abandon anyone who might slow you down? What if there were no guardrails on the side of the bridge—would you be able to stop yourself from driving off the edge? What if you knew you could get away with it—would you actually rob a bank?

Yeah, I said, hesitantly, warily, not entirely lacking in curiosity.

Well, I've been thinking about that one a lot, Chris said.

I waited.

What do you mean, thinking about it?

About the process. About the mechanics of how to do it.

I laughed, but not too harshly. I was, I have to admit, sort of in awe. The process? The mechanics of it?

And I've come to the conclusion, Chris continued, turning his head to look at me across the shared blanket of snow, that it's completely doable. That, done right, no one would ever know.

I did not, could not, say a word.

I felt a kind of vertigo, as though the tectonic plates beneath us had suddenly forced our ice floor a hundred feet into the air, then dropped it a hundred feet back down. The vertigo was due to some innate realization, some unexpected illumination that Chris and Chris alone was fully capable of doing such a thing. Not merely robbing a bank—that was extraordinary enough— but doing it successfully and doing it without anyone knowing. Going on as before, as though nothing had ever happened, bearing secret knowledge.

Have you? I asked, a pit in my chest. I meant, Have you already done it? And I did not know whether that would have been a relief, or whether I would have felt betrayed and passed by if he'd said yes, the same way I'd felt when he got laid before me, and all those many times since.

No, he said. I'm not sure I could pull it off on my own. I'm thinking it takes two to commit the perfect crime.

That was what I wanted to know, and what I most feared. I wanted to be needed. I wanted to be essential. But I did not want to do the thing that was needed. I wanted only the knowing, not the being or doing.

If there ever was a time to stop the madness, it was then. A laugh. A disparaging comment. That was all it would have taken to quiet Chris about his feeling of lack, and his fantasy for filling it, to shove it all back within, and to force him to find other outlets or partners. Our friendship might have been altered forever, diminished by the absence of unconditional support, but I would have avoided the dangers that lay ahead. And yet, God help me, I said nothing.

More silence. Just snowflakes sparkling down in that *Star Wars* jump to hyperspace sort of way. I had no faith in hyperspace. To me, it had always seemed unlikely you could avoid being obliterated by a random meteorite.

Like a coward and a friend, I introduced that subject as a way of diverting our conversation.

Not surprisingly, Chris didn't share my doubts.

4

Every writer, Graham Greene might have said, like every
spy, and every homosexual, leads a secret, double life.

So began mine, as writer and bank robber both.

When I look back on the process of being convinced—or convinced enough to co-conspire, though burdened by the lack of any wholehearted commitment to the cause—I grasp it through the filter of Nietzsche's will to power. I'm not saying that Chris asserted his will over mine, dry-humped my values and viewpoints into submission like an alpha dog does to its smaller, less vicious companion, but I'm not saying he didn't either. I think that a battle of wills, if you can forgive the cliché, takes place in every relationship at almost every moment. I remember it from childhood, between friends, between myself and my dad, between me and the kid with the locker next to mine elbowing for space. I've seen it in the most intimate relationships I've had since, as well as with editors, agents, business clients, waiters, hair stylists, prostitutes, appliance salesmen, and neighbours. How little we understand what's going on between human beings when choices get made. His way or my way. Her way or the highway. Why do we lean one way, not the other? How do we learn to force others, imperceptibly, with the precision of acupuncturists channelling and shifting energy flows that no scientist can prove exist? I've seen children do this! I've had children do it to me! And yet this process of influencing, this jostle of personal power, this rough dance of desires and drives goes utterly unstudied. We don't even see it happening, though we feel the effect. No wonder, in the parlance of self-help, we're fucking morons when it comes to other people.

I didn't really believe Chris needed me to rob a bank. I didn't think for a second that any contribution I made would mean the difference between success or failure, that I could augment Chris's skill set. But I did have an inkling, the vaguest, most gossamer insight into what he was really looking for: he wanted nothing more and nothing less than my approval.

Chris must have sensed I was emotionally rattled—wrecked, really, thrown to the side of the road like a hit-and-run victim—by the very idea of robbing a bank, so he went easy on me at first. It was a psychological relief. We did a lot of jokey kid stuff. We played Dungeons and Dragons for the first time in a year. We ordered pizza and lobbed rancid farts at each other. We hung out at the mall, played video games in the arcade, and floated around the bookstore for hours. I talked to him about my ambition. He knew I wanted to be a writer, a goddamn great novelist, but it helped me to keep saying it aloud. I also told him about my deeper fear—that I was missing something, that I hadn't accumulated enough experience in life to write really great work, that I probably never would. I was an eighteen-year-old white male raised in a middle-class suburb in the armpit of North America. What kind of greatness could come from that?

You mean lopping off orc heads in a DnD session isn't going to cut it?

Chris got it. He always did.

Like all writers who lack life experience, I turned to writing classes to fill the void. I focused on one particular course in second semester that was restricted to seniors unless you put together a kick-ass portfolio. I wanted someone to recognize my talent and give me a shove in the right direction. I worked my ass off to produce something worthy, driven by my fear that ordinary life was a trap designed to funnel me toward mediocrity. For the next few weeks, I roused myself at five to write for a couple hours before getting on with the day. My strategy was not very productive. I was so ripped by lack of sleep that I occasionally threw up. I sat bleary-eyed before my typewriter, not typing more often than I typed. And the words that appeared during those intermittent bursts of gunfire often didn't sound right. But I was certain I had to squeeze the trigger on a regular, consistent basis, or die a failure.

In early December, the evening after I turned my portfolio in, Chris and I drove to the larger mall (called Mic Mac, after the neighbouring lake, and the Indians who presumably once paddled there) to do some early Christmas shopping. We aimed to find a counter where they sold Chanel No. 5 for the moms (since that was the only gift any mom had ever wanted or been given in the history of Christmases), and a store where some item not too expensive or embarrassing could be purchased for a dad. Chris drove. (He always drove; which put my role as the driver in his plan in an even more ludicrous light.) After we goofed around for a few hours and did our shopping, I felt migrained by the intense jangling, bright-lighted mall experience, and we slunk out into the slushy cold to go home. But instead of drag-racing through the parking lot for the exit, as we typically did, Chris drove slowly around the back side of the mall to a less parked-up region. He pulled into an empty slot away from the glow of lampposts and put the car in neutral, pulled up the emergency brake. Then did nothing more, just sat with hands in lap, staring toward the facade of the mall.

I started to laugh and say something, but stopped. Chris was not laughing, nor was he saying something. He was watching the bank.

It was still open on a Thursday night. The lights were on but you could tell that there were few people within. I had an itch on my forehead, but if I lifted my hand to scratch, I worried that my fingers would tremble. So I did nothing, and I tried to be silent even as I let out a ragged, timid breath.

They close off the mall entrance to the bank at eight-thirty, Chris said.

I tried to focus on what he was seeing.

For the next thirty minutes, he continued, there's usually only one teller at the counter, and the other three workers disappear into the back. If you parked here, he said, you'd be out of sight from the mall but less than five seconds from the curb. I go in alone, but when I come out, you're waiting for me, and we drive away. Not too fast, not too slow. The east exit is right over your shoulder. There's never any wait and there's no traffic light. We're on the highway within ninety seconds. The whole thing from beginning to end takes less than seven minutes.

Each word was a pulse in my forehead, a flick on the nerve along my cheek.

Chris seemed to break his own trance when he looked over to me finally, not with a mocking grin, or an air of all-seeing, all-knowing awareness, but an honest, straightforward question.

Robbing a bank has got to make you a better writer, don't you think?

I suppose, ladies and gentlemen of the jury, he got me right there.

I finally got fucked the next night, which seemed proof that some kind of cosmic realignment had taken place. How else to explain the progress in bank robbing, writing, and sex?

Chris had been seeing Susan on a regular basis since Halloween. This meant my time with him was rationed, and made our circumstances doubly painful, even tragic. Susan had been meant for me. Didn't Chris know that? I hated her for abandoning me, but I blamed him for allowing himself to be led, unbidden, into the bathroom and capitulating without a struggle when she stepped out of her clothes and showed him her back, bracing herself face-forward against the wall while he thrust into her over and over. I resented learning that this experience had been, according to Chris, the single most intensely erotic encounter of his life. To undercut his assertion,

I reminded him of Leah on the pier and a couple other stories he'd told me about. He contemplated the full set for a few moments and then agreed with me.

Yup, them too.

When Leah had swooned for Chris in a compromised setting, Susan dropped her like a hot potato, but Radha did not seem bothered by the bathroom incident and remained Susan's best friend. And so the four of us hung out. This set me on a spiral of self-pity masked by acerbic wit. Not that anyone seemed to notice my difficulties or care. The nights were often marked by a detour period in which Chris and Susan politely parted from us for a half hour or so, fucked, sucked, or whacked each other off, then returned. In the uncomfortable pause, I felt as worthless as a fluffer on a porn set.

The night after our shopping reconnaissance, we all went to a movie and saw *Less Than Zero*, which was great for the sex and the debauchery of college students but not so great for the descent into male prostitution. Shortly after it ended, Susan announced she had a tickle in her throat and wanted to go home. She was pretty sure she was getting a cold. She was wearing a red turtleneck sweater and her hair was in a tight bun, giving her a convincingly strained and weakened look. So Chris, the good soldier, offered to take her home even as Radha complained that going home would be the most boring thing in the world.

You guys should stay out, Susan said. You, of all people, she added, looking at me, should try to have a good time for a change.

I wondered what the fuck she meant.

After they were gone, I started to wake up to the fact that

Radha and I were now out on the town alone. Should we go somewhere for some nachos and maybe a Long Island iced tea?

How about a bottle of wine? Radha asked.

It turned out her older sister had an apartment in the city but was out of town on a business trip. We walked to the tower where she lived and into a large, shiny lobby. Radha nodded to the security man at the desk and led me to an elevator. We took it all the way to the top floor. The elevator actually opened into a living room, and a little white dog appeared before us and barked its stupid head off.

Ooh, aren't you the brave little poochikins, Radha said, and went off to give it some dinner.

I was astonished by the opulence and walked around. There didn't seem to be any curtains in the room. The windows ran floor to ceiling around the back of the couch, past the dining table. I could see the whole city, the harbour, the lights of the bridge, and even the insignificant twinkle of Dartmouth. Then I felt my toe nudge something and looked down. On the carpet behind the couch was a field of small turds. The dog must have shit back there fifteen or twenty times. Revolted, I backed my way out of that minefield carefully and waited for Radha to reappear.

She called my name from another room. It was the kind of call you think will never happen to you in real life.

I found her lying on top of the silk sheets, wearing the belly dancing costume from Halloween.

This, she announced, is what we should have done then.

Really? I asked.

I was too stunned to think of anything more romantic or witty to say.

Although I had read about sex and heard stories about sex and imagined sex so many times before, I did not know exactly how sex got accomplished in practice. But I'm happy to say, despite any expectations to the contrary, this time the good guy won and it all worked out very well indeed. We did what you would call foreplay, which involved licking, gripping, poking, and sucking each other for a time, and then we twisted, groped some more, rearranged, and pushed until actual penetration had been achieved. I stared into her enormous dark eyes with astonishment until they gently closed with what I could only assume was pleasure. I moved in and out of her slowly, as if testing the cushions on a new couch, and then I gained confidence when nothing terrible happened and began a more vigorous and rhythmic plowing. By the time stars were blinking in the dark cave of my skull and subterranean rivers of blood were rushing pell-mell through my veins, I took a moment to consider what I was supposed to do next. That's when I remembered asking Chris the very question: If you're not wearing a condom and you're not sure she's on the pill, what do you do?

I usually pull out and jerk off all over her tits, Chris answered. Then added, Especially if they're nice.

So that's what I did. Radha opened her eyes even wider and squealed in delight, and after I'd pulsed every last bit of myself onto her breasts, a lifelong supply of pent-up jism, she reached up and pulled me down, embracing me fully, smushing my chest into her chest, gallons of sperm squishing around between us, lubricating our skin.

That last part, I thought, was entirely uncalled for.

Just to further support the whole realignment-of-the-stars theory, the next morning, Chris went to work intending to quit, and then abruptly changed his mind for reasons that proved to have a significant influence on later events.

I worked every summer, as did most of our friends, but in addition to summer employment, Chris had worked the same part-time job all year every year since he was fourteen years old. A neighbour down the street, Mr. Baxter, was the manager of a Canadian Tire store. Canadian Tire was a kind of proto-Walmart, more giant warehouse than store, with enormously high ceilings and endless rows of goods, ranging from automotive supply at one end to carpeting at the other. In between, there were aisles dedicated to plumbing, electricity, athletics, clothing, lumber, windows, tools, televisions, and so on. The deep back corner, like a protected national park, was where the hunting and fishing supplies could be found. You knew because of the fringe of pleasant green Astroturf underfoot, which made you feel as if you'd entered a wilderness.

Starting at $3.15 an hour, Chris had worked his way up to almost $8.00 by the time he was nineteen, doing two evening shifts and one Saturday day shift every week for five years. While that kind of commitment to a menial task seemed utterly uncharacteristic for such a restless and devious rogue, Chris also liked his easy comforts. Putting on the uniform and hanging out with guys he knew well to sell products he was actually interested in selling wasn't such a bad gig, as gigs went. And he also liked the regular paycheque, however small, every two weeks.

But he had finally grown tired of it, and after several months spent contemplating the end, he'd resolved to quit. He had a tentative line on a job as a bouncer at a bar, and he figured that would be a far cooler way for a college student to earn spending cash. Certainly, it did a better job at combining his three favourite hobbies: money, alcohol, and women.

Because it didn't matter anymore, he showed up twenty minutes late for his 9:00 a.m. Saturday shift the morning after I got laid, only to discover the store in an uproar. The weekend cashiers, who were mostly teenage girls, had abandoned their posts and gathered together. The sales clerks huddled at the top of the aisles, as though afraid to venture too close but too curious to stay away. As Chris walked into the store and toward the staff room, he tried to catch wind of what was going on. The cashier girls watched him with big eyes. The sales guys shook their heads and grinned. He figured his tardiness must have been noticed by the CEO of the whole company or something, and he was about to be publicly flogged. But Ron, the manager of hardware, (who you knew was the manager because he had a combed moustache and wore the sky-blue polyester pants that matched the sky-blue shirt with the red pinstripes) gestured for him to come over.

Good day to show up late, hombre, he said.

Ron was not the kind of manager to lay into you for bending the rules. He was more of a player's coach, so to speak.

Why's that? Chris asked.

Because no one in management is going to notice today, that's why.

How do you figure? Chris asked.

Oh, I don't know, maybe because they're dealing with a little matter of being robbed at gunpoint about fifteen minutes ago.

Chris was elated and crushed at the same time. He'd missed an armed robbery!

No shit? he said. They catch the guy?

Shit no, Ron said.

They backed up as the store manager, Mr. Baxter, and the assistant manager, and some other suit-wearer, and three police officers suddenly emerged from the offices and strode toward the exit. Discreetly, Chris peeled his winter jacket off and dropped it to the floor, toeing it under the light-fixture shelf.

At lunch break, Ron and Chris grabbed some burgers and a couple of beers at the nearby bar, and he got the full scoop. The armed robbery had taken place not in the store but along the route to the bank deposit machine across the street. One of the management trainees had set out with the deposit bag first thing in the morning. Just as he was crossing the road, a motorcycle pulled up to the light. This was strange since it was winter. There were two men on board, both wearing helmets with full visors. The one on the back aimed an evil-looking thunder cannon and reached out for the bag. Shitting his polyester pants, the management trainee handed the bag over, and the motorcycle roared away.

Jesus Christ, Chris said in amazement, that wasn't too hard, was it?

Nope, Ron agreed. Like the candy and the little fucking baby.

They continued to eat their burgers and sip their beers thoughtfully. And then Chris said, How much money do you figure was taken?

Ron leaned in. I heard Baxter tell the cops the deposit was just shy of $115,000.

Holy living crap, Chris said.

He was so impressed, he forgot to quit.

That night, Chris and I had planned to get serious about studying for exams, so we packed all our books and notes and hit the library. But then we got hungry and distracted and gave up and went for beers. He was excited to tell me about the armed robbery at Canadian Tire and the ungodly amount of money involved. I was excited to tell him about getting laid. I got to my story first. He listened but seemed distracted, and I felt as though I were boring him. For Chris, getting laid was right up there with learning how to ride a bike, something that had happened so long ago, and involved so many rides since, that the initial exhilaration and stress—the huge fucking deal of it—was largely forgotten. So I embellished the details and the number of times we did it and the variety of the positions we'd tried—not grasping yet that it was the little miracles, the smallest pushes and reactions, the particular touches and smells that were really worth noting. After I'd stretched the truth as far as possible, I felt like I was approaching the level of a Chris story, and still he seemed to be not really paying attention.

What? he asked, when I said he was pissing me off.

I told him I thought he'd be a little more impressed on my behalf.

He got himself together and agreed it had been a hell of an accomplishment. He had an easy way with earning redemption. It was nearly impossible to stay mad at him for long.

There you go, he said. It looks like planning to steal a shit-load of money has done wonders for your confidence.

I let that sink in and wondered, Was that what had happened?

As well as your complexion, Chris added.

Despite my enhanced confidence, I didn't get into the creative writing class. I got my notice mid-December. Chris was even angrier than me. Motherfuckers, he said when I told him. We were in my basement for a change, on a lazy Friday, the girls having skipped a high school field trip to hang with us. Radha and I lay on the couch together; Chris and Susan lay on the floor. The letter was in Chris's hands. I felt burned too, but Chris took it personally, and his reaction, while it would have been appreciated had we been alone, seemed over the top and embarrassing in the presence of others.

Seriously, he said, what are they looking for? Stephen fucking King?

I doubt it, I said. I was self-conscious about Susan and her Toni Morrison thing. I always tried to sound smarter around her, knowing she read real books. Chris was a reader too, but he read indiscriminately. If a book was entertaining, well written, and kept him flipping pages, he enjoyed it. That meant he had no taste. Currently, he was on a Stephen King kick. To him, *The Shining* sat next to the *Iliad* and *Garfield at Large* in the pantheon of literary achievement.

Well, what story did you give them? he asked. That crazy one about the beach?

I willed him to hush. Didn't he remember what that story was about?

I didn't think it was ready, I said, hoping to divert any interest in its contents from Susan and Radha.

Ready my nutsack, Chris said. That was a kick-ass story.

It was no use trying to make him understand. But I knew that a creative writing class for seniors was likely to be looking for a certain kind of work, something literary.

Give me that catalogue, Chris said.

He meant the description of all available courses, a huge beast I'd thumbed through obsessively before registering last summer and that Chris had barely glanced at.

I heaved it to him and tried to work my hand down Radha's pants, subtly, so no one else but my throbbing cock noticed. Susan snaked her head around Chris's elbow and read too. Radha started to make little invisible grindy movements against me, so I figured she was getting my message.

Chris said, Is this the fucking course?

That required me to dislodge from Radha and look.

Yeah, I said. That's the one.

It made me feel bitter just acknowledging it.

Chris read the professor's bio. That guy's ancient. Is he the be-all and end-all?

He's kind of famous, I said. Mordecai Richler called him the Balzac of the Maritimes.

Chris flipped more pages while I tried to resume my grindy, grabby position with Radha.

A few seconds later, Chris interrupted again.

What about this guy? Did you apply to this one too?

I hung off the couch to read.

Crafting the Powerful Narrative. The truth was, I hadn't noticed the course, but an embarrassed part of me didn't want to admit it. It was in the creative writing department, offered by someone named Professor Delmore Rivers. He was an assistant professor, I noticed, nothing special.

I've seen him, Chris said. He's a young dude, and he seems pretty fucking all right. He came into my English class to invite people to submit for the school literary journal. This is the guy you want.

The course did have a portfolio requirement, so that meant it was at least exclusive. But it had the same deadline as the other course, already passed, so what difference did that make?

Too late, I said.

How's that? Chris asked.

Susan showed him the date.

Oh, fuck that shit. Where's the phone?

He went upstairs into the kitchen. He was gone for ten minutes. When he came back down, he had a grin on his face, like he'd just fucked the maid.

It took me three calls, he said, but I finally talked to this old bat in the department. She said the class isn't full and if you get your stuff in by 9:00 a.m. Monday, the professor will consider it. That's when the packages are getting handed to him.

It was two o'clock Friday afternoon.

Cool, I said, and felt hopeful for a change. I'll deliver it personally.

But use that crazy beach story, Chris said. I'm telling you. Nothing else you've written so far even comes close.

What's the beach story about? Susan asked. She met me with her academic stare, the clear-eyed, emotionally neutral, but intellectually curious expression she seemed to reserve for me.

The beach where you and I almost made out, I wanted to say, but shrugged instead.

Does it involve sex? Radha asked.

Dirty, nasty sex, Chris said, and started tickling Susan. Radha jumped on to pull him off. I jumped on Radha to complete the pile and managed to tickle Susan a little in the process.

Chris had read almost everything I'd ever written, so in that sense, he was pretty much the only person with the credentials to make any judgment about my work. But the crazy beach story wasn't ready. When the contortions on the carpet calmed down, I told him the story needed cleaning up. It needed tightening. It needed a beginning and an ending. It would take me days. My face was flushed, and I probably sounded more desperate than usual.

Well, Chris said, you've got about two and a half. Come on, girls, we're out of here. Get your boots and coats. Let's hit the road.

He slapped Susan on the bottom. He pulled Radha to her feet.

What are you doing? they asked.

Chris, who met all urgent deadlines with blithe indifference, was like a man possessed.

We're giving him space. You heard him, he needs a few days to get his story ready, so that's what he's getting. Let's go. Come on. We can watch a video at my place.

And just like that, they were gone.

It was, perhaps, my first bitter taste of the loneliness of the writer's life.

I wasted a night even getting started. I was distracted. I was horny. I was exhausted. I masturbated twice. I felt sick about the story. It wasn't good enough. It was a mess. Chris was wrong. It wasn't the greatest thing ever, or even the greatest I'd ever written; it was bullshit.

Chris called me from his lunch break at Canadian Tire the next day to see how it was coming. I wanted to lie and say, Great, but he'd gotten me into this mess and I felt petulant.

Fucking brutal, I said.

What do you mean?

I can't get it right.

Bullshit.

It's never going to work.

Silence. The airlessness of disappointment.

I think you'll figure it out. You just got to torture yourself for a while.

He hung up.

That night, still no words. It was Saturday night. I hadn't spent Saturday night at home in years. My dad asked if I was sick. I told him I had a story to work on. He didn't seem to hear. My mom asked me if Radha and I had already broken up. No, I said. I didn't even know she knew we were going out. Was it that obvious? Had there been fewer cum stains on my sheets?

Around nine o'clock, I got called to the phone again, and picked up the one in my room.

How's it going now? Chris asked.

No better, I said.

Radha wants to say hi.

A pause.

Hi, she said.

Hi, I answered.

I miss you, she said.

I miss you too, I said. And I did. I was miserable.

If you get your story done on time, I'll do something to you you'll never, ever forget.

I wondered if I'd heard her right.

What would that be? I managed to ask.

You'll have to imagine, she said, and giggled.

The phone got dropped. Was she drunk? Was she making fun of me? Voices echoed into the mouthpiece, questions, instructions, laughter. Finally, it was picked up again. Chris spoke.

There, that motivate you enough?

As if a call and a promise like that would suddenly boost my concentration. I asked them what they were up to. Then we said goodbye and I jerked off again.

This brings me to an important point. I knew at some level writers never jerked off. Not the successful ones. Instead, they channelled their sperm into bullets of supreme hardness that machine-gunned the page and left nothing but wondrous words. Failed writers, like yours truly, dribbled all their creative genius out in wasted days, pointless frustrations, self-pity, and weariness.

And then on Sunday morning, as the hopelessness peaked, something happened. I read the story again, angrily, ready to tear it to pieces, and this time, I saw a crack of light, an opening, and I pulled and clawed my way in, and when I stood there, on the other side of something, I had a sentence to start it all off.

A dead frog on its back, stuck in the oily muck, the white belly so much larger than the limbs, paunched slightly to one side.

Is this it? I thought. That's the way some sentences are supposed to feel. You react to them like jolts. Not just strings of words used to describe a person, place, or thing; instead, they are mood-setters and tone-makers. They contain the magic of poetry within the push of prose. And for the writer, they are pure freedom, even as they compel you to march forward. I knew I'd be forever grateful to that frog. He died for my sins that I might live.

My story was about Leah at the pier. And, to my amazement, it turned out to be from her point of view. I don't mean to say that I was Leah, and Chris fucked me. In one version, the version Chris had read, yes, I had described that sex scene in detail from a third-person omniscient perspective. But while the tension in that version was palpable, as they say, and the description evocative, the story itself had no reason for being. Who, except a perverted voyeur, actually cared? But when I wrote about what happened from Leah's point of view, I suffused every moment with some emotion inside her. The innocence of calling out to us on a perfect summer day. The unspoken tensions between her and Susan. The beauty of the lake, touched deftly and sweetly by a certain foreboding inherent in all water and what it contains, not in any malevolent sense but in terms of the immensity of life, of all lives, and the endless lifelessness beyond, the timeless emptiness of the universe. Then the pier, and the way pain and need and temptation got embodied and became irresistible, and you succumbed willingly, the instigator of your own destruction and shame.

But the moment of brilliance, the insight given to me in the delirious hours of my dream state, was to understand for the first time the power of absence. I ruthlessly severed some of my best paragraphs, including the ones, ironically, that had delivered me into the story in the first place, and I cut any mention or even hint of the sex scene that had anchored the original draft. I scrubbed it from the story and left the reader only with the knowledge that two people had departed the pier, and two people were left behind. And in that reading, the vagueness took on many possibilities. Tilt the story one way, and you understood that a murder was coming. Or sex. Or suicide. Or maybe nothing at all, the roiling emotions just so much darkness, like silt on the bottom of the lake.

It was, if I say so myself, very Hills Like White Elephants.

By the time Chris called to check up on me on Sunday evening, I was surging with energy and almost too wired to talk. I need to keep going, I said.

Go go go, he answered.

So I worked all night, and around three in the morning, I had perfection, and such a blissful sense of power and accomplishment that, when I sank back on my bed, exhausted, I didn't even feel like tossing one off. That's when you know you've really done something worthy.

Then I overslept the next morning.

I woke at 8:10. Under normal circumstances, it might have been okay. When you're eighteen, what does a little tardiness mean? But I had my 9:00 deadline, and if I didn't get my story in by then, I didn't have a chance of getting into the class. And I needed to get into that class or else I knew my writing life was over.

I rang Chris, risking a pre-noon phone call, but his mother, who was a night nurse, answered blearily and said, He's not home. Meaning, probably, he had never come home. What a trooper. I'm slaving away on a story. He's out on the town.

My own parents were already out, and there was not a car around. I emerged from the house with my boots unlaced and looked around for a neighbour with a car warming up, any ride I could beg, borrow, or steal. Then I thought of the bus.

We never took the bus. The damn thing never, ever stuck to any kind of schedule. Sometimes you could walk the whole route without a bus sneaking up behind you. But what choice did I have? If God wanted me to get into the writing program, God would supply a bus. And lo, verily, He did.

I ran for half a block to cut it off at the stop, and barely got on, bodychecking the chrome door when I threw my way inside. The driver was not amused and waited for me to count out the right change in my shaking hands before resuming his route. I sat, grateful for the rest, and checked my watch. I had thirty-five minutes. It was conceivable that I might make it. But when the bus reached the harbour, instead of turning right and heading for the bridge, it turned left and headed for the depot. This bus did not go to Halifax—it was terminating!

I broke out and ran for the ferry. Two ferries crossed the

harbour every half hour. It took twenty minutes for the ferry to make a single passage. Twenty-five minutes was all I had left. When I reached the ferry terminal, bus transfer in hand, I saw that the barrier had closed, and the ferry was revving up for its surge away from the dock. I felt a giant *No* screaming out of my chest and threw myself forward. I ran through the turnstiles, down the concrete incline, and leaped.

The ferry, by the time I was in the air, had separated itself from the dock by a foot and a half. If I slipped, I would be churned into pink foam in the water below, like a hapless bad guy in a James Bond film.

Instead, I landed on the slick deck, slipped under the barrier, and walked shakily past disapproving clucks and shocked stares from fellow commuters who did not know what it meant to be on a mission of genuine importance.

When I arrived at the English department office, eighteen minutes late, sweat was streaming down my face. They pointed down the hall when I asked for the creative writing reception. I chugged farther down, checking door signs, before finding an opaque glass door with *Creative Writing* written on it, like a dental office.

The door was closed. A tragic sign, I believed. I rapped, heard nothing, rapped again, and a voice called out, It's open.

So I opened.

I didn't even look up as I strode across the carpet. I was already in full explanation mode, apologizing for my lateness, inquiring whether there was still time, trying to talk or fling my way through the next set of barriers.

Hey, you!

The words, as I remember them, sounded accusatory, but it was a pleasant, sweet, and altogether familiar voice calling to me. I focused and saw Leah sitting behind the desk.

Her hair had been newly permed and her lipstick was brown, but I should have recognized her nevertheless. Still, I couldn't grasp that it was her for another ten seconds because I had no reason to expect her there. My brain did not compute. She guessed this, because she offered an explanation.

One of the receptionists is on maternity leave, and I'm temping for a few months. Whatcha got?

I held out the manila envelope that contained my form and story.

This, I said. I needed to gulp and pause and catch my breath again.

Oh, are you applying? she asked. Great, because I'm supposed to sort them this morning.

Professor Rivers isn't here yet? I asked. I was hopeful.

Oh, no, she said. He's on vacation. Back after break.

How's he going to know whether we deserve to get in or not? He needs to read our applications, right?

Leah was trying to straighten out my envelope—I'd gripped it so tight I'd left a sweaty, crinkly handprint on it. She gave up, pulled another envelope from her desk drawer, and exchanged it for mine.

I think everyone who wants to is getting in, she said. They don't have that many applicants or something.

I must have looked sick, because she asked me if I needed a drink of water.

No, I said, just some sleep.

Okay, she said. But it's really great to see you. How's Chris?

He's good, I said. I knew she wanted detail. I knew she wanted to know that he was miserable, or great, or dead, or married. But I could not embellish.

Maybe we can have lunch sometime, she offered. I'm here at least until March.

I told her I'd like that, too dazed to even consider the possibilities, and said my goodbyes and walked out the door.

It took me to the end of the hallway to remember that she had once been forbidden to wear underwear around Chris. She hardly seemed like the same girl. Then, as that pleasant and disturbing image played in my head, I stopped dead in my tracks, ice cold all over, and rushed back to the office.

She was startled to see me again so quickly but offered the same kind of smile—half administrative, half friendly.

What's up? she asked.

I stuttered, Could you please not read or even look at my story?

She winked. Wouldn't dream of it.

And although I wanted her to make the oath in blood, I knew that was the best I could do. As I walked off, it seemed to me that the ferocious bravery I'd felt writing such a piece the night before was nothing but false bravado when confronted by the possibility that someone with an actual connection to the story might encounter him or herself in it.

That's the fear I have now writing this book.

My first class with Rivers was on a Tuesday morning, the twelfth day of the year. His class was to meet only once per week for three hours each time. We would meet infrequently because we were meant to be doing the serious business of writing between sessions. We would meet for an extended duration because we were meant to engage in the intense and serious work of cutting each other to pieces during those sessions. But when I arrived at the classroom, there was a notice on the door. *Professor Rivers's class is postponed until January 26. In preparation, please gather and read (as much as possible) the following.* And a half-dozen books were listed.

No one seemed to know why class was cancelled for two weeks. One woman announced she was heading to the department to demand an explanation. The rest of us dutifully jotted down our list of required readings and slunk off in guilty appreciation of the unexpected freedom.

I was glad to find the list appropriately heavy and dark. It included Dostoevsky's *Notes from Underground,* Nietzsche's *Beyond Good and Evil,* Faulkner's *The Sound and the Fury,* Hemingway's *The Sun Also Rises,* and Conrad's *An Outcast of the Islands.* Not a Margaret Atwood or Eudora Welty among them. Fuck you, Toni.

Two weeks later, there was no notice on the door but neither was Professor Rivers there to greet us. Nine of us sat in the classroom that morning, six men and three women. At ten past the hour, Rivers still hadn't arrived, and a restless irritation began to build among my classmates. They had expectations about the obligations of professors, which I didn't share, and believed that paid-for services should be provided in full and as advertised. To me, every class was a mysterious collision of personality, performance, and the piecemeal revelation of arcane knowledge. You waited like an acolyte for whatever the master brought you, and hoped he wasn't a fraud.

Rivers arrived just before the revolt could grow. He pushed the door open with a shoulder, and we saw that his hands clasped the bars of two short aluminum crutches. There was a knapsack over his shoulder, which made him look young, even though he wore a blazer with elbow patches and a sweater vest and had a full beard. He stood on one leg stiffly. The other, as evidenced by the way the hem of his pants had been pinned up, was missing.

It was this second leg, the one that was not there, that we tried to inspect closely and also utterly ignore. The tension, the confusion in the room, was an electrical storm. I felt icy sweat on the back of my neck. I had not been told, I had not been warned, even by Leah, that Rivers was an amputee. I had heard no rumours. It made me wonder, suddenly, whether this was a recent occurrence, which seemed possible given the awkward way Rivers moved and the makeshift job on his pants. Had he missed class while recovering from some horrible surgery? We could only wait silently for an answer. Rivers in turn offered us a grim and unwelcoming expression, an accusation of blue eyes beneath dark eyebrows. I thought how much he resembled the young Ernest Hemingway, angry and wild, handsome and brutally serious. He regarded us all for a moment, and finally spoke. Come with me. Then he left the room.

We were puzzled and confused. We were also stuck to our chairs. We had our books out and our coats off. We had not expected an amputee professor. We had not been prepared to rise and follow. And yet, necessarily, we trailed after him.

116

Rivers crutch-swung his way down the long hall, like a perpetual motion device that had achieved enough anger to make forward progress. Someone asked him about our destination and whether we would need our coats. Rivers merely swung his torso forward contemptuously.

Down steps into a basement, ever so awkwardly, we doubled back along a lower hallway until we came to an old wooden door. Thrusting it open with a crutch, Rivers motioned us through. Three long tables with chairs were organized in a triangle formation. There were wires and cables along the floor, and the walls were covered with spongy foam, as though the wood panel had been pulled away to expose the insulation.

Have a seat at one of the tables, Rivers said, and he hobbled over to a sound deck and began flicking switches.

His arrangements completed, he looked back at us and hit a last button.

I wanted you to hear it clearly. This is the Vorspiel of Wagner's *Ring Cycle*.

The sound built slowly, and at first I didn't understand that it was music at all. I need to explain, however, how hard this piece hit me, how suddenly and quietly it came over me, like a dream that obliterated all my other questions, making them seem meek and pointless compared to a larger moral quandary.

A baritone hum began, emerging not so much from an instrument as from some gorge or crevasse. Then a new note arrived, pitched at an oblique angle to the first flat tonal groan. After a breath and a pause, you realized an awakened giant had just taken an enormous step, and then another, and that he was now looking around. You could suddenly see the mountains that surrounded him, multiple sharp peaks, along with clouds and the specks of distant birds. All of that visual information picked up speed as light sharded through and dark storms began to brew over far-off bodies of water. A hundred violins in strident chorus circled each other in dizzying spirals that kept climbing higher, building urgency with a slow but terrible determination, massing pure energy. And then you realized it was not sky they were climbing but a depthless ocean. A single flute rose slowly, like a swimmer, shimmering in the fractured light of water. Then there were more swimmers, moving faster, so that you could not tell whether they were desperate or elated. Together, they neared, while never reaching, some urgent point, like a treasure that flickered or a breath of life-giving air, surfacing finally with a single operatic gasp that became an argument of song.

Over the music, Rivers read a passage from a paperback in his right fist.

The will to truth which will still tempt us to many a venture . . .

He sat with the gone leg stuck out over the edge of one of the larger speakers; the noise must have caused vibrations on his pants.

What questions has this will to truth not laid before us!

He looked up at us and I didn't know whether he was now reading from the passage or talking to us from his own fevered brain.

What strange, wicked, questionable questions!

Then back to the text.

Who is it really that puts questions to us here? *What* in us really wants "truth"?

He gave a long, unbroken stare.

118

We sail right *over* morality, we crush, we destroy perhaps the remains of our own morality by daring to make our voyage there.

He read on.

Independence is for the very few; it is a privilege of the strong. And whoever attempts it even with the best right but without inner constraint proves that he is probably not only strong, but also daring to the point of recklessness. He enters into a labyrinth, he multiplies a thousandfold the dangers which life brings with it in any case, not the least of which is that no one can see how and where he loses his way, becomes lonely, and is torn piecemeal by some minotaur of conscience.

And then, looking directly at me.

Our highest insights must—and should—sound like follies and sometimes like crimes when they are heard without permission by those who are not predisposed and predestined for them.

He dropped the book, a mere release from his fingers, but never had such a passive gesture struck so ominous.

I could read from this all day. But that would only reinforce the things I have already said, and if you are not interested in entering this labyrinth or sailing past morality, then you will not understand me. I am here to teach you about writing. But writing cannot be taught. Writing is not about morality or goodness. It is about truth. The only thing I can teach you how to do is to be frightened of what you have an inkling you want to become—this thing called a writer—and to understand that you will not get there without recklessness and courage and a willingness to leave everything behind, including your morality and many comforts and any hope for the approval of others, because your highest insights will not be understood and they will sound like follies and sometimes like crimes to the people you give a shit about. The catalogue says this is a writing course. This is a course about power. Creative thought—in whatever form you articulate it—is an act of will. It is an output of an argument you must want to win. You can pretend that power doesn't matter because it doesn't make you feel good. But if you intend to generate something that is worth reading, to manufacture from your stunted and inconsequential library of experiences some account or tale that someone else in the world will get truth from when they devote to it their precious reading time, then you had better understand what writing takes. Otherwise, you are better off not beginning the voyage at all. Because it cuts even the great ones down.

We could not help, of course, but look at his leg, look for it anyway, that piece cut from him, in some battle in whatever labyrinth.

He dared us to stare at it. Then he said:

Writing is a life-threatening activity, and if you are not reckless enough or deluded enough to go forward, I suggest you give up now. We'll develop a schedule for submissions next week. You're free to go.

It goes without saying that I stumbled from that cave in a daze, blinded by the daylight of the world above.

In the weeks and months that followed, I became an unquestioning disciple, unafflicted by doubt or any divergence of views. In my world, Rivers was the God of Writing come down from Olympus to walk among us. He was the Oracle and the Answer.

Others disagreed.

Some students, some faculty, a cadre of the small-minded who feared what sailing over morality might involve, quietly and subtly ridiculed his intensity and machismo, his bullying past the sensibilities of others. They mocked his very notion that writing was as much a physical act as it was an intellectual one and that the stakes mattered and went beyond the words on the page.

This criticism extended to his injury. Although its severity was undeniable, blame was ascribed to his own recklessness and love of glamour. The accident had taken place on a ski hill in Europe, it turned out, but for the critics, the way Rivers carried himself, the grim purpose he'd adopted when he returned, made it seem as though he'd lost the leg on a battlefield, not a black diamond run.

But perhaps the root cause of resentment was his rigour. Rivers brooked no bullshit in the writing he reviewed. A number of my classmates banded together to complain to the powers that be about the intensity of the assignments and Rivers's harsh grading of their work.

I did not believe that Rivers liked my writing either, since he red-marked it so mercilessly. The welts were painful but I accepted them as an acolyte accepts his due count of lashes. They were meant to purify and kindle a fiercer commitment.

Halfway through the semester, Rivers invited two of us to his home. The fact that I had been included with Giles Osborne, the obvious star and talent in the class, was enough to make me swoon.

When we arrived, implements awaited. There was a tree that needed pruning. It had overgrown his veranda and was knocking the shit out of his shingles, and he needed us to climb the roof in the semi-twilight and hack and saw some branches down. Giles and I did it willingly, gleeful to be taking such lawsuit-reckless chances for the professor of our dreams.

Afterwards, Rivers invited us in for curry and beer.

His girlfriend, Megan, served the food. She was an attractive but subdued woman of Rivers's age who gave the impression she came from privilege and was slumming it with her bohemian boyfriend. The living room had low furniture and plenty of pillows, like a hookah den, and we sat on the floor, feeling self-conscious about Rivers's awkward positioning and his calls to Megan for whatever implements, condiments, or replenishments were needed.

We talked about various living writers and their latest books and the status of their careers. We talked about the circle jerk of book reviewing, and the bullshit of academia, and even some of the students in our class and their merit and potential. I vibrated with the inappropriate and adult nature of the discussion, its many dangerous edges.

When the food was done, Giles, in a typically brilliant stroke, pulled a bottle of Crown Royal whisky from his knapsack and stood it on the table. Rivers grinned and asked Megan for glasses and ice. I had never tried whisky straight before and struggled to man it down. The alcohol seemed to amplify Rivers's thoughts while honing our attention on his words.

He talked about the discipline of writing and reading. He had theories about how many pages a day were necessary to sustain a long and meaningful work, and how many words must go into the brain (through reading) to fertilize the number of words that came out in writing, a four hundred to one ratio. He talked about the dangers of academic instruction and the importance of life experience—thoughts that echoed and reinforced my own belief that a writer could become successful in an institutional sense and still have nothing worth saying. He talked about the importance of mental and physical health. We were young still, but we would need to exercise and learn to meditate to produce quality work over the long haul. Rivers himself ran marathons twice a year and practised yoga every day.

There was a silence, as we acknowledged the elephant in the room.

You heard I lost the leg skiing, I suppose, Rivers said.

These were sobering, accusatory words, and we gripped our glasses tighter, careful about jingling the ice.

It's amazing how people will twist the facts to cut you down.

No shit, Giles said.

I nodded but had nothing to say.

It's like *The Old Man and the Sea,* Giles said. Those fucking sharks. They were Hemingway's critics, you know.

This was meant for me. And I could only widen my eyes. The sharks were critics? It seemed bad enough they were sharks.

Hemingway's fuck-you book, Rivers said.

Goodbye, Hollywood, Giles said. Go to hell, Nobel Prize. Up yours, *Life* magazine.

Rivers leaned back.

What does it take to become a great writer? I've thought about that a lot this year. How much of yourself are you willing to give?

Megan stood and took plates into the kitchen; there was nothing too abrupt about her movements but some vibe of disapproval anyway. Rivers watched her and then shrugged as if to say, She doesn't get it.

Tolstoy fought in a war, Rivers said. Stendhal. Solzhenitsyn got thrown into the gulag for writing a letter criticizing his commanding officer. They wouldn't give him any paper, so he composed novels in his head. Cervantes fought on a galley and got his hand torn apart by a bullet. He went back to war a year later and fought one-handed. Then his ship sank and he was taken prisoner for five years, and when he got home, they threw him into jail for debt. Instead of killing himself, he wrote about a foolish reader who confuses adventure tales with reality and sets out to live them. In the process, he invented the goddamn novel.

Giles kept our glasses topped. We sipped, we pondered.

Hemingway went to war as an ambulance driver. He got his leg half blown off carrying a wounded soldier on his back. He fell in love with his nurse, and she rejected him—at around the age you are now. Those early experiences were so complex he kept living them out and writing them down for the rest of his life. He was an asshole and a drunk and a braggart, but he reinvented the English language by forcing us to use only the words that really matter. Do you think he could have summoned that kind of courage if he hadn't understood what suffering and brutality was like?

Conrad was a smuggler and a gunrunner when he was your age. He gambled too much and wasted his fortune. He fell in love with someone who didn't love him back, so he shot himself in the chest. The bullet went all the way through, and when he told the story later, he claimed he'd been wounded in a duel. And because he was broke and sick of himself and sick of his own lies, he joined the merchant marine and travelled to some of the worst places in the world, and the only way he could understand what he saw was to write it all down.

Faulkner was a drunk, too, but do you think he could have cracked thought into pieces if he wasn't playing Russian roulette with alcohol? Dostoevsky's epilepsy, the madness that infected his best writing, started the day he was lined up before a firing squad and shot with blank rounds. Balzac wanted to write the whole history of human futility and committed suicide through coffee, overwork, and lack of sleep. Joyce worked on the same book for seventeen years and went blind trying to get his words right. Burroughs was a junk addict and a homosexual who didn't have the courage to buck convention until he shot his wife through the head playing a doped-up game of William Tell. Mailer stabbed one of his six wives with a penknife.

He rolled the bottle on the floor between us until it clunked against the table leg.

They're right, he said. Writing risks nothing. But something that's so obsessively engaged in, something that squeezes out its power through brutal concentration and merciless scrutiny and the desperate pursuit of unachievable expectations, takes a complicated toll.

It was after eleven when he asked for help to rise and go to the bathroom. The evening had been mesmerizing, except for the frequent interruption of the telephone. Every so often, it burst with a sharp jangle and Rivers would break off mid-sentence until the answering machine in the bedroom came on. Bizarrely, the answering message was an Islamic call to prayer, and it went on in full warble for endless seconds, pausing then sounding again, before a hushed voice finally offered the dignified caller a chance to leave a message for Sinbad, sailor of the seven seas.

Megan had not returned from the kitchen. I'd assumed she'd slipped off home, but when I brought the last of the dishes in, I saw her sitting at the breakfast table, nursing a glass of wine, her face drawn and tired. I felt as if I'd intruded on some private intimacy and asked in a quiet voice whether she was all right. She answered only that she'd had a difficult day at the office and wished she could put Rivers to bed.

He's not well, she added.

I imagine it will take some time to get back to normal.

He hasn't been the same since.

My mind went to Nietzsche. It was easy to dismiss her concerns as the complaints of the small-minded, to write her off. Rivers had seen and experienced the unspeakable. Now he was sailing over the morality of ordinary men.

But then she said, Delmore thinks a lot of you. He told me he thinks you're going to be a great writer.

A trembling came over me.

Is that right? I asked.

She didn't say anything more, just gripped the stem of her wineglass and became submerged in tiredness once again.

Outside, Giles and I paused to say goodbye to each other.

Jesus, that was insane! Giles grinned. That guy's fucking nuts!

I was shocked at his betrayal. He'd hung on to every word Rivers said. He was the class star who knew that the sharks were critics. And now he was being dismissive, as though the great man was a homeless ranter at a bus stop. I understood, in that instant, Giles did not truly want to be a writer; he wanted to impress. Still, I didn't have it in me to call him out on the spot.

Most writers are nuts, I offered lamely.

Not like this fucking guy, Giles said. We'll be lucky if we get out of his class alive!

I laughed. Like Peter before the cock crowed. Then Giles rode off on his bike and I hoofed it home.

I took the long way around the lake, lifted but disoriented by the thoughts in my head. When I got home, it was after midnight and my parents were sitting in the living room in chairs we never used. I could tell by the aged expressions on their faces that something was wrong. A death, I figured. A diagnosis.

Where have you been? my father asked.

To realize that I was the object of concern unnerved me. For once, I'd been doing something healthy and positive, not the casually demented and evil stuff of a normal fuck-around night. I felt unjustly accused and got self-righteous in my tone.

I told you I was at Professor Rivers's house for dinner.

It's so late, my mother said.

I opened my mouth but no words came out. What did time matter? I was almost nineteen years old, going to college, and had just experienced one of the most meaningful evenings of my life.

I'm out this late all the time, I finally said.

But when you are, we know who you're with.

They meant Chris. They meant that being with Chris was better than being with Rivers. This was so ridiculous, I laughed out loud. Did they have any idea what kind of influence Chris was on me?

We called his house over and over, my mother said, and no one answered. How were we to know what was going on?

I blanched. So it was my parents who'd been calling that whole time? I thought of the messages they must have left, the prim, impatient requests, and felt sickened, too embarrassed to live.

Jesus Christ, I groaned.

In the next instant, my father stepped into me and swung, almost knocking my head off with the palm of his hand. My face blazed with heat and the tears flew to my eyes but I didn't cry. We stood chest to chest, the anger and adrenalin churning me to bits. I was wild with rage and power, and I realized for the first time in my life that I was bigger than him. I think he realized it too.

You've been drinking, he said.

Whisky on my breath.

So? I didn't bother to defend what didn't need defending.

What kind of man is . . . What kind of relationship . . .

What? I demanded.

He started up again.

Are you . . .

And he stopped once more, unwilling or unable to go on.

Am I what? I felt too shocked, embarrassed, and persecuted to say anything more articulate.

My father left the room.

A moment later, with all the horror and shame I'd ever felt, I grasped his unasked question. He wanted to know if I was gay. My mother and father thought I'd been ass-fucking all night.

I looked to her for some acknowledgement of the injustice. She'd flown toward us when my father struck me, begging us to stop. But I saw no understanding in her eyes. Like all mothers, she only wanted love and an absence of conflict in her home.

I went to my room.

Are you? My father's question was a virus that wormed its way through everything Rivers had ever said. His teaching had become contaminated. My elation over his attention had turned toxic.

The next day, I called Chris, so angry my voice shook.

Chris knew how excited I'd been to visit the great writing teacher, and he asked me how the night had gone. I tried to explain what had happened at the end, the embarrassment my parents had caused, the injustice. Unable to articulate the monstrosity of it all, the outrage, I finally blurted it out.

I think my dad thinks I'm a fag.

I couldn't have admitted that to anyone else. Even opening the door would have been life-threatening.

But Chris only laughed.

He's just figuring that out? I've known it for years.

As usual, it was the perfect thing to say.

My father is invisible to me now. I've blanked him. I no longer remember the presence of him except as a totem of reproach. I remind myself that he was tall and thin, that he enjoyed a drink or two in the evening, that he went to church every week, usually by himself, that he didn't like golf but liked tennis and running, that he read history books like they were novels and couldn't stand it when a war movie got something wrong, and that he dismissed the mysteries and self-help my mother read as nonsense and probably thought the literature I liked was contemptible too. I remember how dutiful he was about work, and how much his sense of the rightness of obligation seemed enhanced by the dullness of a task, and how that futile and dispirited pointlessness suffused what we thought was normal and gave rise to the urge for rebellion. I remember that I loved him, and that I disappointed him, and that to love him was to disappoint him.

And yet, when I think of fathers, I think of Rivers. At some point in life, if we're lucky, we try to make a clean break and become who we want to become. Around that time, we choose who we want our father to be.

One father wanted me to be reckless, to garner experiences no matter the cost, to be a great writer. The other wanted me to be safe.

I'm not sure Rivers was a good choice, and I'm not sure I followed through sufficiently to find out. And I'm not sure my father wouldn't have been a better father if I'd let him.

These are the kind of puzzles you spend a lifetime trying to solve.

Susan was another. Why did I think of her as the one for so long?

Is it because I often caught her looking at me when the four of us, or the three of us, were together?

Is it because she once walked between Chris and I and held our hands, and when it caused us all to laugh with embarrassment and surprise, she let go of mine a breath or two after she let go of his?

Is it because she dared me to kiss her one night when we were both too drunk and Chris had passed out?

Or because she gave me a letter the next day, but pulled it back and ripped it to bits before I could open it, though I could smell the perfume on my hands ever after?

Or because she pretended none of these things happened?

Of all the people I've ever known, she was the most unknowable.

I suppose that's why I've been looking for her ever since.

Over the next month and a half, as the term neared an end, I often felt angry and belligerent, and just as often sick and defeated. It was a nauseating, disorienting, exhausting time in my life.

Chris's persistent talk of banks was a kind of water torture to my brain, a drip of dread. The only relief came when we were with the girls, because he never talked about bank robbing around anyone else. Even so, my confusion over Susan, the many wrong signals and imagined opportunities, was another irritation. Poor Radha got less from me than she deserved. We were rarely alone, preferring group comfort to our own awkward relationship. This is not to say that our time was joyless. As a foursome, we usually watched videos and ate takeout, laughed hard, and even had many serious and interesting talks. At some point, on most nights, we split up for a time and hit separate rooms, finding beds if there were no parents home, or pushing back couches and hiding behind them, or even entering closets or bathrooms for briefer encounters. Then we'd gather again with sly comments about carpet burns, hickeys, or pulled muscles. For some reason, some mysterious soreness issue I happily ascribed to my enormous member, Radha and I jerked or even sucked each other off more than we actually fucked, but this was okay by me. I usually thought of Susan as we did it anyway.

No doubt, these moods, that kaleidoscope of longing, regret, panic, and elation, were good for my writing. I felt emotions more keenly and painfully than ever before. I drank too much in order to hide and massage my deeper worries and insecurities. As a result, I wrote tense, nervy scenes and sometimes whole stories that wound in on themselves so tightly, they barely breathed. Rivers told me he'd reappraised my potential, upgrading me from a plot-driven craftsman like Sidney Sheldon or Irving Wallace, to a modern Hemingway like Robert Stone or Thomas McGuane, writers I promptly devoured.

Then one evening, the carousel of date nights came to an end. Chris showed up at my house as dinner was starting. I would have invited him in for spaghetti but my parents were not the type to welcome strays. So I asked him what was up, bolognese sauce on my chin, and he told me Radha was through with me. I took the surprise blow hard to the stomach but didn't flinch. Instead, I managed to shrug and ask, Did she say why?

Chris shrugged in turn. Bad enough I'm stuck delivering the message. Didn't bother to get all the why stuff too.

Fuck why, I agreed.

But back at the dinner table, I spilled my milk.

With the end of the run of such an intense and rewarding social life, you'd think I could have sublimated all my energy and ripped off straight As and a novel or two, but it was all I could do to manage my course load. I drank even more frequently instead, and occasionally my belligerence got me into trouble, the odd scuffle and push, the occasional pounding on the sidewalk outside some sordid establishment. I fancied my activities as extra credit in the writing school of real life.

The encounter with my father, what Chris and I thereafter referred to in Robert Ludlum fashion as the ass-fucking accusation, inspired my desire to get a place of my own.

Ultimately, this effort sprang the trap I was trying desperately to avoid.

Chris seemed to understand the vulnerable position I'd put myself in, because he offered a complicated and self-serving plan to secure my freedom. I would need money to move out on my own, and money, in ordinary circumstances, required a paying job. Therefore, I should volunteer to my parents that I was going to double down on work that summer. I would accede to my father's wish that I serve as a replacement teller at the bank, and I would spend my evenings and weekends pulling rickshaw with Chris.

Why would I do that? I asked, never as rapidly devious as Chris.

Rickshaw is a great cover for money making, Chris explained. You can make enough in rides and tips to flash bills whenever you want, and we can hang out and drink all summer. But if you work at the bank too, you'll make your dad happy, and you can scout security and help plan a heist. It's a win-win.

It didn't feel like a win. It felt like death. But I could come up with no rebuttal worth uttering. My misgivings were not moral, they were steeped in the fear of getting caught and the dread of betraying my father. I doubt Chris would have understood either concern.

For this reason among others, I was occasionally petulant with Chris. But he seemed to take my moodiness in stride, never making much of it, allowing me to dissociate even further from any sense of responsibility, like a child. Robbing a bank involved more reconnaissance and study, more dedication and even professionalism than I thought Chris had in him. But like a secret hobby, he let the pursuit absorb much of his time. I understood that robbing a bank wasn't about the money to him. It was a theory he had to prove. And this gave me hope, however dwindling, that he would not get serious with the deed. Sometimes he asked me questions about my father's bank and my own experience as a summer teller, never so intrusively that I was put off by them, but frequently enough that I knew he wanted my secret knowledge. I supplied him—again grudgingly, petulantly—with as little information as I could, as though the conversation was merely boring. I began to feel sick just seeing a bank. Whenever I walked by one, I put my head down and strode a little faster to make it go away. Inevitably, at such moments, the sun was breaking through the clouds and the shards of light jabbed a migraine into my fevered brain.

Having said that, I must concede we barely talked about the

bank-robbing idea at all. Percentage-wise, we spent more time talking about the level of fitness I would need to acquire to work rickshaw.

Chris insisted that, in terms of body cut, I had more natural talent than him for muscle development, but I knew I lacked other more important ingredients, such as will, discipline, and desire. Still, he scared me good with stories of how difficult it was to pull a rickshaw up the steep Halifax streets, and got me into the gym and out onto the road on a pretty consistent training regimen. Two days a week, we did chest, triceps, and abs; two days, shoulders, biceps, and legs. Three days a week, I went running, but this I did by myself, on the sidewalks around both lakes, the Sony Walkman headphones on, Wagner or Pink Floyd playing. The closest thing to a great novelist is a composer, Rivers said. I heard novels that way, before I wrote them. I understood that mood and language and metaphor got introduced as themes with their own specific notes and refrains, and that they came together over the course of a piece in new and surprising ways.

I was less comfortable and meditative at the weight pit. The rubbery, mouldy smell of the place was the odour of intimidation. I felt like an interloper in a world of giants, men who pumped and groaned, heaved and clanked, stared like mesmerists at the bars above their eyes and lifted them by flaring their nostrils before letting them come crashing down like great continental plates smashing together. Most were athletes putting in their time, hockey players, football players, discus throwers, shot putters, but the truly serious were just bodybuilders, monk-like in their devotion, living to rep, repping to live.

By the time I began to feel somewhat confident about my abilities, Chris must have grown tired of my mood swings. After I bragged about a series of squats I'd just done, he called me out.

Don't kid yourself, he said. You ain't shit.

I guess that hurt, so I dared him back, and before I knew it, I bet him I could do fifty reps on a curl bar with twenty pounds.

Chris snorted. You do a hundred reps with an empty curl bar and I'll give you twenty bucks.

That was doubly insulting. A curl bar was the feather in your hands before the weights went on. I could curl it forever and not even feel it.

But Chris said, You just try, big talker. Give it your best shot.

The bar was light as air. I began my reps, counting quickly, running past ten before I knew it, feeling practically sorry for Chris and how foolishly he'd be parted from his twenty. At fifty reps, I was no longer smiling because I was bored. This was taking too long. At seventy, I started to worry. It wasn't the weight of the bar but the fact that my biceps were now engorged with blood. Soon it became difficult to lift the bar and I saw Chris's thin smile growing.

Fuck you, I said.

And Chris just nodded. Yeah, we'll see, tough guy.

At ninety, I knew it was impossible not to make it, and yet my biceps and forearms were screaming in agony. In fact, I was no longer sure where bar ended and flesh began. Through prayer and the fear of unbearable humiliation, I managed to contort and fling my body sufficiently to complete the last few reps.

136

See? I said.

You would have bet me five hundred reps if I'd suggested it, he said.

And though he was right, I still took the twenty.

That night, I knew my body was wrong. A mental limit had been surpassed. I felt broken inside and had a premonition that bad things were about to happen. I joined my parents for television, something I rarely did, because I did not want to die alone, but I spoke only in monosyllables and hissed breath. I had the strangest fear that I was turning to stone.

I went to bed early and woke in darkness unable to move my arms. They were frozen, bent at the elbows. Half awake, I tried to sit up but couldn't. The pain in my arms was too extreme. I went back to sleep and began to think, even before the restless dreams took me, of Rivers's missing leg. I wondered, half-deliriously, if I would still be able to write with no arms. I remembered the story of an armless boy who learned to play the flute with his toes. Perhaps I could type that way, I considered, or peck the keys with some stick taped to my forehead, an industrious woodpecker hunting for a good phrase.

By morning, I understood that the nightmare was real. I could not, no matter how I forced myself, move my arms up or down. The tendons were high-tension cables. In the bathroom, I could hold my toothbrush but not reach my mouth, so I bent and sucked paste from the tube, then swirled it with my tongue. Wiping my ass was like flailing with a mannequin's arm. In the shower, I could not reach my hair to shampoo it. Desperate, tearful, worried, I finally squirted shampoo on the wall and rubbed my head into the tiles.

It was a week before I could fully bend my arms again. During that eternity, I could not type or jerk off, and I realized that working out was a distraction from more important matters. I stopped going to the weight room. I stopped running. How hard could rickshaw be? I decided writers didn't need to be Olympic athletes, they just needed to be Olympian drinkers, and I adopted a sullen, wounded pose as my new drinking stance.

There was a good reason Chris did not consider two jobs to be any great shakes. While going to school, he was still working at Canadian Tire Mondays and Saturdays, and he had also taken on Tuesday and Thursday night shifts as a bouncer at the Billy Club, a bar whose customers were primarily police or police related. You might not have thought that a bar frequented by law enforcement types would require the services of a bouncer. A coat-check girl, maybe. A bartender for sure. But police and the people who loved them were heavy drinkers and indiscriminate brawlers and troublemakers. It was a measure of Chris's success in the weight room and on the speed and heavy bags that he had the size and vibe to serve as a general deterrent and occasional enforcer to unruly cops.

He invited me in, one slow Tuesday night, to hang out. It was strange to see him at the door in his button-down shirt and black pants, with his thin moustache and his surprisingly bulging muscles, looking adult and serious, but he gave me a grin and told me to hit the bar, and promised he'd pop by when he could.

I drank Jameson neat, because that seemed right for a writer undercover, and also ordered a Labatt Blue chaser, hoping at least one of them would be on the house. I took in the bar like a connoisseur of bitter dives. It was a low-key place, with lots of dark wood rails and round tables, and space for the dance floor and a disco ball overhead. Chris kept a drink behind the bar, which the bartender lifted up for him whenever he came by to talk. The DJ started up around nine and some dance music came on and a few of the women went out to the floor to groove together. I watched. One caught my attention. She wore a sexy but quietly sophisticated black dress and tall black boots, and when she danced, she did not exert herself overly but made the most of small, exquisite movements. Everything about her was mature and classy, except for a studded dog collar around her neck. This simple token, this elegant mark of outrageous perversion, fixed me with desire.

Chris came by on his break, and we spent the next half hour on stools as the place began to fill up. The men were thick-necked and bristle-cut, except for the occasional long-haired hippie type that Chris would mention, offhandedly, was in drug enforcement or an undercover agent in a biker gang. The women were mostly wives and girlfriends, Chris said. They were older, not quite old enough to be our parents but out of our league, and I felt like an imposter playing at adulthood. Nevertheless, I was on fire for the one in the dog collar and I kept an eye on her. She sat with a man and another couple, but every so often, I swear I caught her looking my way.

Finally, I couldn't stand it anymore.

Do you see her? Oh my God. What's her story?

Chris figured out who I was talking about, and turned back to the bar before answering.

She's a schoolteacher.

I couldn't believe it. What school?

Some elementary.

I pictured innocent children, and a leather boot–wearing teacher chained to the desk.

Dude, she's been looking at me.

But Chris just laughed and shook his head.

What's so funny? It's about time I banged a teacher. I've been imagining it for years.

She's a friend of mine.

A friend?

He lowered his voice. I've kind of been fucking her since I started here.

What do you mean? Her? Why didn't you tell me?

I was as shocked by the news as I was by the ever-so-casual betrayal of Susan.

I didn't want to make a big deal about it. She's married.

She's married?

Yeah, to a decent guy, too. He's here now and then. Works a lot of extended shifts though. She's lonely, I guess.

And she fucks you?

I think she thinks I'm older than I am. The other night, she finally figured out I'm only in college, and it kind of threw her.

What do you mean?

She told me she wasn't sure she could do this anymore. But when I woke up in the morning, she was blowing me.

Jesus. I paused to gather my thoughts. With the dog collar on?

He just grinned.

Handcuffs?

Not as of yet.

Is she kinky?

He burst out laughing. What do you think?

I did not know what to think.

I was still bewildered, and even more hammered, by the time Chris came back for his second break around eleven. I was reading a paperback, something by Bukowski, and the alcohol and the dance music and thoughts of dog collars were the rhyme and metre of my surreal Bukowski buzz.

I think we need to really do this, Chris said, when he sat back down. He was drinking openly now. There was no more need, apparently, to nurse and hide his cocktail.

Do what? I asked.

The bank thing, he said.

I was taken by surprise. I'd forgotten about banks, for a blessed hour or two, and was thinking mostly about dog collars. Now I felt sandbagged.

Are you serious? I asked.

Of course I'm serious. You think I've been just playing with myself the last six months? It's go time.

Go time. I didn't like the sound of that. But I kept whatever sang-froid I had in me on the surface and frosty.

We're in a bar surrounded by cops and you're talking about that.

Oh, fuck that, he said. They're off-duty.

We both laughed, me nervously and drunkenly, riding the sharp edge of anxiety, him generously, enjoying the irony.

What about a gun? I asked. Have you thought about whether you're going to carry one?

It was the thing I most wanted to know, and the thing I could not envision.

Of course I'm going to carry a gun, Chris said, as if there had never been any debate.

Why do you need a gun? No one's even packing at a bank, you said.

Well sometimes they are, but mostly I need it for other reasons.

Like?

To generate urgency, confusion, and a serious impression.

The practical way he spoke. Even his violence was carefully considered, and would be employed like a tool.

But where are you going to get a gun? I asked. I was looking for any way out.

Dad's got a few. He won't miss them for a couple hours, I figure.

I hadn't thought of that. A swallow of Jameson later, I asked the other question on my mind.

Will it be loaded?

Quietly, like Clint Eastwood, Chris gave me a squint.

Now what kind of fucking moron would carry an unloaded gun?

Doesn't that increase the chance you'll get shot?

They're still going to shoot you. You just won't be able to shoot back.

And he gave a dark, evil FV laugh. Somewhere, in some memory, I heard: This one tends to blow the head clean off the shoulders.

Chris went back to his post. I entered a zone of drunkenness saved for special occasions, a place where I felt bewildered by my inability to navigate life successfully, but certain in my superiority over others. I spent the next hour or so offering the bartender helpful characterizations of his customers, based on the drinks they'd ordered. I was heaps of fun, I assure you.

Finally, it was time to leave. Chris steered me outside into the cold air. I felt troubled by some worry I couldn't remember. Then, as we approached Chris's car, his mother's Volkswagen Rabbit, we saw two parka'd hombres leaning against it, smoking from a hash pipe.

Time to go, boys, Chris said, as if they'd been assigned guard duty over his car until he returned.

Get off the fucking car, you fucking fucks, I contributed.

This fucking car, one of them said, and he looked behind him as though surprised to see a car supporting his weight. Then he stepped away and launched a tremendous kick, knocking the side mirror from its base so that it dangled loosely, like a broken hand.

I readied myself for a rumble.

Chris sprinted suddenly and caught the first one behind the ear with a wild and unexpected punch; then, while that guy was bent over, holding his head, Chris punched the other guy four or five times in the gut, knocking him assward to the cold pavement. Without pausing to admire the quick takedown, Chris then turned back to the first hombre, grabbed him by the parka collar, and rammed his head through the driver's side window.

A cough of glass as the poor bastard bounced back and fell

to the ground. He writhed about, holding a red crown to the top of his skull.

That's using your head, I muttered. I scampered around the car and opened the passenger door. Chris delicately picked the larger pieces of glass from his seat and swept away the shards with his forearm, then climbed in and started the car. We drove away.

The cold air streamed through the broken window. Chris was grim and quiet. I had sobered enough to be filled with regret, even as I remained in awe of what I had seen.

Sorry, I mumbled.

About what? he asked.

The whole instigating a melee thing.

He laughed. You've got a knack for that.

More silence while I pondered what he meant and how he meant it.

I'm just mad at myself, Chris explained. You know how much a car window costs? That whole head-through-the-window thing just wasn't necessary.

I hesitated, relieved he was angry about that and not about me. Then the right words came.

Yeah, but I'm glad I saw it.

We were crossing the harbour and the lights sparkled in the blackness all around.

Good scene for your book, Chris agreed, as if me writing a book about what we were doing had always been in the plans.

It'll be a classic, I said. *Tom Sawyer* meets *Dirty Harry*.

Chris nodded. You might want to say there were nine or ten guys, though. Spice it up a little.

That'll work, I said.

And it did seem as though the chapters were writing themselves.

I have boxes of notes. I have letters, recorded conversations, court transcripts, photographs, photocopies, and maps with Xs and arrows representing actual robbery locations and escape routes. Those shards of pottery, those yellowed bones and corroded coins, are the artifacts of my archaeological dig, the midden of what we did and the evidence of why. But I am also reminded of the inadequacy of material explanations, the possibility that even elaborate and convincing theories can be completely wrong. Looking through my yellowed copy of *Beyond Good and Evil*, I hear Rivers read, Suppose we want truth: *why not rather* untruth? and uncertainty? even ignorance? Flipping through Dostoevsky, I hear another voice, a bit more shrill, coming from vodka-moistened lips and a sweaty brow, saying: Tell me, who was it who first declared, proclaiming it to the whole world, that a man does evil only because he does not know his real interests . . .

And I think to myself, this drunk beside me on the bar stool, the stinking old man no one else can see, this Dostoevsky of my mind, is on to something. There's a temptation when analyzing a wrong path in life to assess and ascribe motives. Especially if we know the person in question, and know him to be lacking in little and with much to lose, we want to grasp what secret reasons, circumstances, or forces led to the upsetting outcomes, to understand *why they would throw it all away*. Through gossip and speculation, we develop mental flow charts that show directional cause and effect, lining up influences and motivations. We say, They must have wanted X. Or, They must have thought it would lead to Y. But what if we're on the wrong track altogether? What if we lack the ability to understand the reasoning involved because the moral algorithm is too complicated or radical to grasp?

In *Notes from Underground*, Dostoevsky lays out an argument in favour of irrationality when it comes to making moral choices. He says, And what if it so happens that a man's advantage, *sometimes*, not only may, but even must, consist in his desiring in certain cases what is harmful to himself . . .

I knew, indisputably, what was good for me: to do well at school, to have a healthy physical body, to have sound relationships with my parents, to proceed with as few mistakes as possible toward a desirable future state. And yet—the feverish, writerly part of me wondered—what if reason is mistaken about what is good? What if going through with Chris's insane idea was the single action I could take that would lift me up from a mediocre writer with mediocre experiences to a Dostoevsky standing against the firing-squad wall as the blank rounds go off, or a Hemingway with a bullet-torn leg, dragging a wounded soldier to safety?

Robbing a bank has got to make you a better writer, Chris said.

Writing is a life-threatening activity, Rivers added.

What if writing a novel isn't like robbing a bank, Dostoevsky asked; what if writing a novel *is* robbing a bank?

But in spite of my occasional moments of feverish clarity, those times when I actually saw virtue in my own self-destruction, I never shared Chris's certainty in the ease of doing wrong. I knew that if we did go through with a bank robbery, I would get caught. And if I got caught, my meagre life would be over. And so I prayed—I actually prayed—for a way out.

Did God listen?

During one particularly fit-filled night, I woke in the utter darkness and lay there, my heart pounding and my tongue swollen and dry. I wondered if I'd heard a noise, a skulking intruder, a murderer, a ghost. I listened, and then realized it was not a noise that had woken me but an idea. If I didn't work at the bank, I couldn't be Chris's inside man. I would be of no use to him. He would have to do the robberies on his own.

When I reawoke, several hours later, I felt rested for the first time in months. I tried to understand why, and then I remembered the elegant answer to my problems, the escape plan that seemed divinely inspired. I carried the answer around with me all day. I tested its worth from every perspective and found it sound. No bank work meant no bank robberies. Which meant no getting caught robbing banks, and no ruining my father's career or destroying my own life. So that night, at dinner, I steeled my spine and told my father, under no uncertain terms, that I would go bank-less this summer. I wouldn't be working behind the counter or at a desk. No khaki pants. No overly tight necktie. No thumbing money or adding numbers. No form filling. No signature taking. No coffee making. No lunch breaking. I was going to haul rickshaws instead, and that would make for a summer worthy of the name.

The kitchen went silent. Not a fork was lifted, not a plate shifted. I did not swallow. My mother did not lift her chin. My father's face did not change in any perceptible way, but I saw reproach somehow deepen and grow starker, as though the sun itself had altered and the quality of light in the room had shifted, and his disappointment was the heaviness in all of our limbs.

Okay, he said.

It was the epitome of hollow victories. He did not add: Throw away the job. Throw away your future. You think the world will welcome you as a writer? You're delusional. You're probably homosexual. You are no son of mine.

But he did not have to. In his eyes, I might as well have announced I was off to Broadway to sing in musicals.

Did he have any idea what I was saving him from? I didn't take your stupid summer job because I hated it (which I did anyway). Instead, I threw away my future because it would have destroyed yours.

If only he could have understood: I did it for him. But, of course, we men typically cannot explain or reveal our complicated love until it is too late.

Chris was almost as disappointed.

When I told him I was going to pull rickshaw and that I was not going to work at the bank, I acted as though such complete commitment to our wanton summer lifestyle was like joining him in volunteering for the French Foreign Legion. I feigned ignorance of his down vibe. I knew that he wanted me to rickshaw *and* work behind a counter, that he wanted me in a tank top *and* wearing a necktie, because he wanted my freedom *and* he wanted insights, carefully gleaned, into the operations and security of a branch. He wanted a free man and an inside man, and I had defied him as much as my father in choosing one over the other.

It was my one way out. He didn't really need me to drive, he needed my access. Now that I was less useful to him, I hoped he would realize that, combined with my other deficiencies, I was not worth bringing along, and certainly not worth a cut. As a result, I hoped he would either abandon his plan altogether or leave me out of it.

This was my way of trying to save Chris too.

But I acknowledged none of these complicated calculations and showed raw exuberance instead.

Dude, a whole summer pulling rickshaw, getting suntanned, hauling women up steep streets while they whip our backs with purse straps. This is going to fucking rock, I said.

I felt so relieved, I began to have solid bowel movements again.

I should have known Chris would not be thwarted so easily. A week later, just before finals, he picked me up on a Sunday morning so that we could hit the library and study. Instead of heading for the bridge and across the harbour to Halifax, however, he drove deeper into Dartmouth, and left it up to me to puzzle where we were going.

To a strip bar? I asked.

Too early, he said.

To your gay lover's apartment? I asked.

Ha ha, he said.

Even as he passed through familiar intersections and down well-known roads, the destination and the purpose of our sojourn was completely mysterious to me. I still didn't get it when we pulled up to the curb outside the parking lot of the Canadian Tire. Instead, we sat in the car, sipping Tim Hortons coffees and watching the empty, closed store, as if Chris expected someone or something to exit at any time.

So? I asked.

This would be way easier than a bank, Chris said. Especially for the first time.

What would?

I was confused, and then it finally dawned on me, and the cold hand of fear crept down my back and cupped my balls.

But you work there.

Exactly.

They'll know who you are.

Nah. We do it like the last one; they'll think it's the same guys come back for more.

They never caught them?

That's what I'm saying.

We sat and watched. A door opened. Two people walked out—a young management type and a regular guy in jeans. The management type was carrying a bank satchel.

The only difference from last time, Chris said, is they've doubled their security.

He put the car into gear again.

May I remind you, he continued, the score that last time was $100,000. That's $33,000 to you just for driving my car.

It wasn't the right argument for me. It never was. But what does a coward do?

He shakes his head in awe and says, Holy fucking shit, that's a lot of money. He's still shaking his head later as though thinking, Money, money, money.

I accepted the new reality like you accept a diagnosis of cancer. You know that everything has changed. You rationally acknowledge that a new lifestyle with new limitations will be imposed on you as the treatment commences. You recognize the possibility of death, and it's always on your mind, but you also don't believe it, even though you wake in a cold sweat sometimes, or lose your train of thought and stare off in the distance when you catch a simple moment of beauty, a chipmunk in a park or the sun peering between two buildings, and think how strange it will be to leave this world.

Chris, on the other hand, became more steady and serious, even as he seemed to glide with ease from one moment to the next. If he was feeling any nervousness or doubt, he never showed it, not even a tremor, and that's all it would have taken, I believe, for me to abandon him in terror. As it was, his calm, professional certainty was hypnotic. I told myself, because he stated it with so much conviction, that we would never be caught, and if it was impossible for us to be caught, what was the harm in going through with it? No one would know. No one would be hurt. We would be richer and we would have accomplished something worthy of a novel, maybe even a movie, and the rest of our lives would be enhanced by that secret thing.

We did nearly a dozen dry runs, so many that I became bored of the practice and the planning. At some level, the preparation felt pointless. Even to me, the doing seemed simple. It was only the decision to do that had so many jagged edges.

On the appointed morning, however, I woke up before the alarm, dry-mouthed and clear-eyed, in awe of the moment that had finally arrived. As I moved about the house, every routine gesture was heavy with consequence. Of course, I saw lightness in Chris as his car pulled to the curb outside with as much impatience as if we were late for a movie.

It was 7:15 a.m. I got in without a word, and even sitting there, I still couldn't believe we were actually going to go through with it. The fact that we were up so early was the most compelling evidence of the seriousness of what was about to happen, like the executioner appearing at your cell door before dawn. Chris did a U-ey at the end of my cul-de-sac, where the swamp and woods began, then headed back through the neighbourhood and down the endless hill of Celtic Drive. Every house we passed had a familiar face. They'd seen us do a lot of crazy shit over the years, but I am inclined to believe they could not even begin to guess what we were up to on that quiet Saturday morning.

Lake Banook and Lake Micmac at the bottom of the hill were mist-shrouded and ghostly; if you listened, you might hear the paddles of war canoes slipping by. We shot through the rotary and onto the highway, no more than a half dozen other cars in sight. It seemed odd to me, at some level, that I was not behind the wheel, especially on this errand. But we both knew I was a lousy driver, prone to daydreaming, lacking good judgment, unable to make quick decisions, uncertain of the power of the engine.

We got a bit of time, Chris said. You want a coffee?

The question was typical of his thoughtful awareness of other people's needs, the limits of which could also be rather abrupt. I said yes because yes was all I could manage.

We went to the Tim Hortons by our old junior high school. The squat, brown brick building with the tin roof looked a little like a coffee cup to me and felt reassuring in that moment. We'd spent many freezing cold lunch breaks in there, during middle school, pooling our resources to split a fritter or a Dutchie. It seemed possible that by doing something as innocent now we could ward off the evil to come.

We did the drive-through rather than get out of the car. I couldn't stomach a doughnut. We broke our lids and took sips. When the requisite minimal amount had been drained away, we set out again, passing strip malls on our right and our left, and finally pulled into the parking lot in front of a gym Chris occasionally worked out at, called Nubody's.

Nubody's was not officially open until 8:00, and usually opened later than that in practice. This was one more element in Chris's master plan. Since the bank drop took place at 8:00, more or less exactly, and Nubody's never really opened its doors until 8:15 or 8:20, we had a built-in excuse for me to be sitting in a running car waiting for Chris to get back. We'd even brought gym bags along for cover. In mine, I had my gym shorts and an extra pair of underwear. In Chris's bag, he had a ski hat, gloves, a pair of ski goggles, a motorcycle helmet, and his father's stainless steel .357 Magnum with the custom rubber grip. The one that had a tendency to blow the head right off the shoulders.

My mouth was as dry as cloth, my palms wet, my guts twisting in a painful knot. Chris, on the other hand, did not seem nervous, just highly focused, as though mentally running through some last technical details.

Okay, he announced, I'll be back in a few.

And he was gone, his gym bag in one hand, his motorcycle helmet in the other.

He left the keys in the ignition and the engine on. I watched in the side mirror until he had hopped over the guardrail and trotted across the main road to the parking lot on the other side of the street. Then I got out of the car and stepped into the cold air. I could have slid across the seat to the driver's side but didn't want to spill our coffees or knock the gearshift. The second after I slammed my door, however, I realized that I had locked the keys inside with the engine running.

There are some moments of panic that last an eternity. I aged during that micro-forever. The emotions that attacked me were complex and exquisitely specific, like a torturer's gleaming tools. Not just the horror of being caught. Not just my life being over. Not even the pain of my parents finding out. But also the stupidity and the shame of my clumsy, idiotic failure, exposed for all to see. My knees gave way in a nauseated faint. I lurched forward to attack the door and then saw, in the next instant, that the lock on Chris's side was still in a popped-up position. I didn't believe in the mercy of my reprieve until I had stumbled around the other side of the car like a drunk and pulled up the handle. I sat in the driver's seat and leaned my head into the steering wheel, gripping it with shaking hands, and moaned. Then I realized that I'd sat on something, and leaned to the side to lift one buttock and retrieve the crumpled remains of Chris's silver-mirrored aviator sunglasses.

Across the street, Chris walked through the misshapen parking lot, passed Rocky's Billiards and the strip club, and ducked into the alley. The buildings had no identity from the back, all brick and aluminum siding. The pavement of the alley was cracked. The steel guardrails were flaking red paint, dented, warped, and caved in from years of trucks trying to manage that tight space. Emerging on the other end of the alley, Chris walked by the actual bank drop slot and crossed the next street to the pair of half telephone booths that stood on the edge of the sidewalk before the empty vastness of the mall parking lot. He hung the gym bag strap on his wrist and picked up the receiver to mimic making a call.

Though this was late May, and the sun painfully bright, it was also bitter cold. The early light bounced off the metal awnings of the building, the chrome framing of the telephone booth, even the long strip of white sidewalk. Chris had a clean line of sight to the store and the bank drop. That would allow him to watch the employees leave the store with the deposit bag and get into the pickup truck to make the brief drive to the bank.

A cop car drove through the traffic light and approached.

Most people, seeing a cop at such a moment, would have lost their nerve. Not Chris. Even as it neared, he kept it together. Yes, his heart thumped wildly and he wondered, ever so briefly, if they were on to him; but he assumed that its appearance was purely coincidental. Sure enough, it rolled on by.

I wish I could make even a small claim to Chris's grace under pressure. Sitting in the parking lot on the other side of the block, I saw the cop car appear in my own rear-view mirror a minute or so later. The vision hit me like a physical blow. I lurched forward, twisted around to look, and then slammed myself back into the seat in a single massive spasm as though defibrillator paddles had been applied to my chest. A moan escaped my throat. Then I saw it was going to the Tim Hortons. Fifteen minutes before, the lot had been empty; now it was full of cops. I counted four units up there, like a posse of sheriffs on a ridge, waiting to nab us as soon as we made our move.

My breath was so rapid, my vision started to sparkle. I realized that the cops were most likely gathering at the doughnut shop for the same reason cops have always gathered at doughnut shops. At eight in the morning, this was probably a shift-change ritual. I laughed then, a cynical, insane, desperate guffaw, and realized that for all Chris's planning, he had failed to take into account the fact that more cops would be in the vicinity on a Saturday morning than if we were trying to break into the precinct itself. I knew he would have to abort. I waited anxiously for him to appear, walking casually, plans cancelled. I could hear the blood squishing through the narrow capillaries of my head.

But by then, Chris had forgotten the cop car and was fixated on one concern: *Where the fuck was the money?* It was later than usual, and he wondered whether he hadn't blown the timing. Despite the cold, he was beginning to get hot and uncomfortable. No wonder. He wore his dad's down hunting vest under his own black jacket in the belief that the extra bulk would give him a heftier appearance. He also had a ski mask on, but it was rolled up over his forehead like a winter hat, and he was ready to put the motorcycle helmet on when the moment came. He'd chosen the helmet because that was what the suspect in the original robbery had worn. But his own helmet lacked a visor, so he had goggles too. He figured driving off in a car instead of on a motorcycle would help confuse the escape.

Just then the doors of the Canadian Tire finally swung open and two figures walked out. At the same moment, a car driving along the street veered suddenly to the curb and a young woman jumped from it and ran to the empty telephone booth next to Chris. This, even more than the appearance of the cops, seemed like a bizarre and unforeseeable event. Who uses a pay phone at eight o'clock in the morning? Since he already held the receiver to his ear, he began to talk into it as though in the middle of an actual conversation. He laughed and grunted a few times and kept his face turned away. Trapped, he could only watch the two Canadian Tire employees (one lugging a green deposit bag) hop into the pickup truck. Before it exited the parking lot, the girl's own telephone call ended just as abruptly as it began and she slammed the receiver down and ran back to her car at the curb. She drove off and passed the pickup truck going the other way.

Chris's mind cleared. The gods may have been having fun with him but he knew they were still on his side. He put the receiver down, then put on his goggles and popped the helmet over top. It was a tight fit. The world had yellowed. He was a predator able to see in the darkness. The pickup truck pulled into the parking lot across the street and Chris stepped away from the phone booth and walked toward it, feeling top-heavy, like a space alien. Until then, he'd been in complete control of his body, but as he neared the truck, his entire system flooded with a power surge. The muscles of his lower belly bunched together, his heart knocked against the wall of his chest, his legs felt as though they were moving faster than his torso. Everything peripheral—cars, cops, girls making sudden phone calls, even me waiting in the getaway car—was forgotten.

Except suddenly things were moving too fast. The truck was already in front of the drop-off slot, parked at a lazy angle to the corner of the bank. Chris had to reach the guy carrying the deposit bag before the money got dumped, irretrievably, into the deposit slot. At the same time, he realized his own heavy breathing was fogging up the goggles, making it impossible to see. He pulled them down so that they dangled around his neck, choking him with the chinstrap. He broke into a run and reached into the gym bag for the .357 Magnum with the custom rubber grip. The young man carrying the deposit bag turned around, startled by the motion behind him. Chris saw the muscles on the employee's face lose their strength and his expression slide away. Without breaking stride, Chris reached out and pulled the deposit bag from the young man's hand. He'd never before thought of what bank-robberish thing to say, however, and could only stammer, Don't look.

He bolted for the safety of the alley but shoulder-checked when he heard the truck gunning toward him, lurching over the curb, and heading for the wall at ramming speed. They're trying to kill me, he thought, but the driver was wild-eyed with panic, struggling to control the truck like a spooked horse, pull it back around, and flee. They were more afraid of him than he was of them.

I can't fully explain why I did what I did while this was happening. Waiting in the car, my mind began to play tricks on me. I'd turned the engine off, despite Chris's strict orders, because the exhaust was streaming out of the tailpipe and into the cold morning air like a distress signal. Twenty minutes had gone by since Chris left, and I knew something was wrong. Unable to stand it any longer, I got out of the car, climbed over the guardrail, and trotted across the street.

As Chris exited the alley, he was running so fast that his feet seemed to barely touch the ground. To me, he had become a demon out of hell. Silver helmet, black ski mask with that O around his mouth, yellow ski goggles giving him an extra set of bulbous insect eyes around his chin, jacket so bulky that he could have been a child in a snowsuit. In his right hand he held what could only be described as a hand cannon.

I expected some wave or shout telling me what to do, but Chris headed straight for me as if I was not even there. Then I glimpsed the money bag and understood that this job, this act, this big-balled robbery, had actually taken place. So I turned back toward the car and ran.

I felt as though my legs were stuck in quicksand. I had about thirty feet on him and my arms were windmilling, but he quickly ate the distance between us. As I reached the car, automatically going for the passenger side, I remembered that my job was actually to drive, so I leaped over the hood in classic *Starsky & Hutch* fashion but lost it somewhere mid-air. First I bounced on the hood, then I rolled, and finally I landed shoulder first on the pavement.

Chris appeared above me seconds later, that oval mouth amplified in appearance, ugly and murderously angry. *Keys!* it said, and I shoved my hand in my pocket and turned them over, as if to a carjacker. Then I felt a hand under my arm and got lifted to my feet like a child. *Get in!* And when I started for the driver's side: *Over there!* And I reversed course and ran for the other door.

He was turning the engine over before I even sat down. The gym bag, the gun, the goggles, the helmet, the deposit bag, all lay at my feet. Put that shit away, he said, in a calmer voice, and the car moved forward.

I put that shit away. The goggles and ski mask I shoved into a side pocket of the gym bag. The deposit bag needed some squishing and shoving before the gym bag could close up around it. The helmet I clenched below my knees. The hand cannon I slid underneath the seat. Even as I did that, I wondered about my fingerprints. I never wanted to touch a gun again.

Chris pulled us onto the main street, then headed back toward the Tim Hortons, the last place in the world I would have gone. I mentioned the cops. He told me to calm down, as if he'd always known they'd be there and it was a critical part of his plan. The sun had disappeared behind the inky morning clouds, darkening the world. Beyond the road and the strip malls that lined it, there were low forested hills all around, and I saw the peaks of house roofs and the simple cross of a church. Telephone poles, sagging wires, transistor boxes sitting next to traffic lights. The red turned green and Chris rolled forward again. More cars now. No cops following. No sirens. We're just going to drive like there's nothing to worry about, Chris said, as if in teaching mode. He waited at the stop sign, looked both ways for oncoming traffic, and rolled through, picking up the pace ever so slightly on the straightaway. We passed our old junior high school with the paved courtyard, the fence, and brown grass, and Chris hauled off his jacket and flung it into the back seat. Next, he tried to take off his father's poofy down hunting vest but the zipper was stuck. He gave it a ferocious yank and the material ripped open. Tiny white feathers exploded into the air and Chris spat them away from his face.

I wanted to apologize for fucking up. I wanted to close my eyes and never open them again. I wanted to cry. But with the appearance of the feathers, Chris started laughing and the laughter became surprisingly contagious. We were in a snow globe that had been shaken so vigorously, the world was dazzled with the sheer fucking wonder.

There is a familiar ritual in bank robbery. It is required that the perpetrators find a sheltered space and count the money as soon as possible. Most bank robbers, however, must not have part-time jobs or school. Chris's shift at Canadian Tire was starting in an hour, and my end-of-year party for Rivers's class was scheduled for that afternoon. So, Chris decided we would keep the deposit bag locked until we could get together, either late Saturday night or sometime Sunday, and celebrate like men.

He dropped me at home, then drove the two and a half blocks to his own house to put his helmet in the garage, return the .357 to his father's gun safe, hide the deposit bag behind the washing machine in the basement, dispose of the remains of his father's down vest in a garbage bag, shower, change into his uniform, put his workout clothes into the same bag, and drive back to work. I crawled into my bed to assume the fetal position and stare wild-eyed at the wall.

When Chris arrived at the Canadian Tire the usual fifteen minutes late for his shift, it was clear from the demeanour of the morning employees that something bad had happened. A robbery, one cashier confirmed. The morning deposit. As subtly as possible, Chris asked Ron, his floor manager, how much those bastards had gotten away with this time. Ron was only too happy to answer.

Baxter is saying over a hundred grand again.

That's a lot of dough, Chris said, a little snow-globed all over again.

Then Ron remembered it was Chris's last day on the job.

You picked a fuck of a day to quit, he said. If I didn't know better, I'd say you were the one who robbed the place this morning.

Ha ha, Chris said.

It was such a good joke, Ron repeated it ten or eleven times to other staff. Then, since the upper management types were so distracted with the police and the lawyers, Ron made an executive decision and decided to throw Chris a goodbye party at lunch.

Baxter would have done it himself, he reasoned, if he wasn't so distracted. You've been here six years or something, right?

Thereabouts, Chris answered.

His mind was on the deposit bag. But a goodbye party was better than working, so Chris allowed himself to be taken with four other willing male colleagues to the Brass Rail, the nearby titty bar, where the burgers were passable and the watery beer came in pitchers. The laughter and the conversation seemed particularly jacked up, an energy possessing all of them, and far more beer was consumed than usual. Chris was gifted two lap dances in appreciation of his years of service, and acted enthusiastic even though it was the middle of the day, and he was facing middle-of-the-day type strippers. When it was time to return, they stumbled back to the store to finish the shift. Within the half hour, Chris was confronted by a housewife complaining about the carpet cleaner she'd rented. Though drunk, he thought he was behaving in a professional manner as he listened. Then she smelled the beer on his breath and demanded to see his manager. Chris obliged by calling Ron over, glad to get away from the crazy lady. As he walked to a safer and quieter section of the store, he heard the woman screech in shock, and shout, You're drunk too! Then he saw her leaving the store in a huff.

One could only laugh.

Chris escaped to the warehouse for shelter from more irate customers. When he stepped into the cavernous space with towering racks for stored goods, he found another manager sleeping on some rolls of carpet. He looked around, hands on hips, and took it all in one last time. Then he grabbed his coat and left, three hours before the end of his shift.

He couldn't wait anymore. He needed to count that money.

I awoke as if reborn. I had never slept so soundly in all my life. I'd slept through the morning, slept through lunch, slept through the early afternoon. The light had changed in my room in the meantime. I opened my eyes without realizing I was finally awake. I saw shadows on the wall, and books on my shelf, and the motion of a bird hopping along my awning. I stretched out, and became aware of my body. I remembered the robbery as if it had happened a hundred years before. I was alive and I was free. I had been given new life, and I was experiencing an acutely new level of consciousness as well. No longer obsessed or fretful, a Buddhist sense of eternal now had possessed me.

I realized, in the most detached way, that it was time for Rivers's party. My house was empty, as any Buddhist's house should be, and I got dressed and ate. I absconded with an opened bottle of my dad's Irish whiskey and caught the bus to Rivers's place.

The party was in full swing, and included students from classes of previous years as well. Rivers's girlfriend, Megan, was there, looking flustered and sexy, bustling from kitchen to backyard with various necessities. Rivers himself sat in an Adirondack chair beneath a blanket, like FDR, and held court. I walked up and put the bottle on the broad wooden armrest, and he eyed it, and eyed me, and shook my hand in a way he wouldn't have when he was teaching the class. Have a glass with me later, he said, and I agreed that I would.

I saw Giles and nodded at him. He grinned and plowed his face into a burger. Then I saw Leah.

It was difficult not to see her. She wore a bright pink sundress, despite the chill, and I had never seen longer legs or a more beautiful neck, and never felt a stronger urge to grab a woman from behind and cup her breasts. Still, even these thoughts passed through me with Buddhist detachment. I was aware of my desires and her beauty more than I was weakened by them. I gazed upon her with a kind of reverent appreciation until she saw me and smiled with her peculiar enthusiasm.

What are you doing here? I asked.

I'm part of the team, she said. Delmore said that he couldn't have gotten through the semester without me.

It was good to be next to her, to be friends with her, and we had a relaxed conversation as we stood on the grass, drinking beer. Then Rivers called Leah over and she left me, and soon I saw her heading into the kitchen to help Megan.

In the full darkness, later that night, the bonfire roared, and the remaining people were huddled in chairs and on log stumps, watching the flames. I found myself next to Rivers, and he offered me a drink of the whiskey I'd brought. It was almost empty when I received my slug.

Loosened, Rivers began to talk. We all listened, but he was talking to me.

I finished edits on the novel. The publisher loves it, she thinks it's going to be one of the biggest books of the year, but she has no idea how to classify it. They're calling it a cross between *The World According to Garp* and *The Eiger Sanction*. I'm calling it *Transassination*. It's about a rogue CIA agent who gets a sex change to go undercover. It's outlandish and it's dangerous, and it's like nothing the world has ever seen.

There was nothing we could do but lift our glasses in cheers.

Gentlemen, he said, as the ice clinked, we're here to make axes for the frozen sea inside us.

Years later, I read the words in a quote from Kafka, yet they still seemed somehow cribbed from Rivers.

We congratulated him. We basked in his accomplishment. We cheered the bold choice he had made in writing a novel on the edge of such polar extremes. And yet, inwardly, even as I spouted off like the others, I was surprised, horrified, and strangely excited by the bizarre and unlikely combination. Sex changes and espionage? Garp meets Clint Eastwood? I'd never heard of such a thing before. Was this the future of the novel? I wasn't sure. I had my doubts.

Rivers seemed to sense my confusion, perhaps even my reticence, the skeptical cracks in my faith.

I didn't write an absurdist thriller because I think the world needs better airport novels, he said. I wrote it because the originality of my story will command attention, drive my sales numbers up, and allow me to do what I really want, which is to keep writing, and to keep shaking people up. You think that's a crime?

Of course not, I said. What did I, after all, know about crime?

He thrust the whiskey bottle at me again. I took it robotically and poured the dregs for both of us.

You and me, friend, Rivers said, are never going to be afforded anyone's attention the easy way. We have to hit people over the head with story, goddamn it. We have to make it impossible for the reader not to read us because the story we're telling is too goddamn gripping to put down. We've got to arm ourselves to the teeth, kick the doors in, take hostages, and still somehow get away with all the loot. You understand?

I do, I said. I do.

You can't bore readers with writing that builds to some important philosophical point. You can't drag them through three hundred pages of Kmart realism just so they come to know your everyman character. You can't expect them to give a shit about your nifty little postmodern jerk-off moves that have been old hat since Donkey fucking Coyote. You have to put a gun to their forehead and demand their cash. You have to grab them by the throat and choke the fucking shit out of their ears. Otherwise, they've got too many other distractions. They can watch *Hart to Hart* or read Sidney Sheldon. Or, if they want to feel literary, they can pick up the latest novel by whoever is currently getting their cock stroked by the *New York Times* or dig into whatever great master they pretended to read in college.

But that's okay, Rivers assured me, because being good at story is going to be critical for surviving in this business from now on. There will be no Bellows, Updikes, or O'Haras going forward. The nineties will be market driven. So that's what I'm doing with the novels I'm writing now; I'm making it impossible for publishers not to publish me and reviewers not to review me and readers not to read me, and that's what you need to learn how to do if you want to make it. Otherwise, it's too fucking hard. You won't be able to keep going. The rewards are too few and way too far between. You'll feel like a loser because everyone around you is making a living and you're not. You won't have the confidence to look people in the eye, or the time for a girlfriend, or the resources to support a family. You'll take up some shit job like night watchman, janitor, or dispatch agent to get by and because it gives you time. You'll end up living all alone, in some basement apartment, eating crackers and typing, masturbating once in a while for release, and thinking about shooting yourself in the head.

Do you get it? Do you get what I'm telling you?

I did not realize how drunk I was until I felt Megan at my side, nudging Rivers awake. You have to get up and go inside, she said, or you'll freeze to death. And Rivers said, I'm pretty sure I should have frozen to death on that fucking mountain, and closed his eyes again.

Can you help me? Megan asked.

I rose and tried to lift Rivers's arm. He pushed away from me.

Drape his arm over your shoulder, Megan said, and lift him that way.

Ow! Rivers said, and muttered something about us being cocksuckers.

I'll help, Leah said. Out of nowhere she emerged and gently edged me aside. She was wearing a leather-sleeved hockey jacket now, with the name Dave stitched onto the shoulder. It felt unmanly to step back but Rivers submitted more easily to her. Flanked by Megan and Leah, he hopped his way inside.

I was alone in the backyard.

I kicked a log in the fire and watched sparks rise. I wondered how such a day could have occurred, what strange humour God was in to conjure it into existence, whether life itself wasn't a hallucination of sorts, a tortured dream.

I had a long walk home, and set out.

It was cold away from the fire. My jacket was too thin for such weather. My legs and teeth were numb. The streets were shadowy with tall trees and strangely unfamiliar. I needed to piss, and decided that the picket fence of the house in front of me was as good a place as any. A dog started barking. A car pulled up behind me and stopped, headlights trained on me as I gushed urine. I could not look back. Just my luck for the house owner to arrive home as I relieved myself. But when I was done, and zipped, I heard a familiar voice.

I think I've owed you a rowboat ride for about a year now, right?

Leah. In a car.

It was a giant Chevy Impala sedan, rusty, misshapen with dents.

I pulled myself together and walked around to the passenger side and opened the door. It creaked like the cellar in a horror movie.

About time, I said, and felt swallowed by the front seat.

It amazed me that she would reference that afternoon at the lake, given what had occurred. It amazed me that she was the last to leave Rivers's house. All us writers gone, and Leah left over.

Rivers okay? I asked.

She shrugged and looked pained. He's not so hot these days.

I guess he's got a lot to deal with.

Meaning the leg, I thought. Meaning writing, maybe.

Megan is so sweet, she said.

I said nothing.

So, Leah said, you live near Chris, right? I'll head over there and you can direct me.

I was too drunk not to try something.

I don't want to go home.

What do you mean?

I'm sick of my parents. I had a big fight with my dad yesterday.

I was blurring fights in my mind, remembering the encounter from the last time I'd visited Rivers's house. I was making it up as I went along.

What did you fight about? Leah asked.

169

My future. Stuff.

Right, she said.

You ever have those fights with your mom? I asked.

She laughed. Nope.

I saw something there to leverage, a crack in a secret door.

Can I crash at your house?

What?

Seriously. I don't think I can go home tonight.

Don't be silly.

Well, just let me out near the harbour then. I'll grab a coffee somewhere and wander around for a few hours.

Of course, Leah was unable to allow me to do that.

She lived in a neighbourhood called Jellybean Square. It was a housing project made to look like a community, a maze of tightly packed duplexes, each unit with a front door of a different colour. The effect had been intended, no doubt, to be colourful and vibrant, to project a cheery, hopeful, even prosperous aura. But it looked cheap, as though every resident had stolen their door from some other house. And the moniker as much as the various social assistance programs seemed to give birth to the diverse racial mix of the inhabitants, black, white, red, yellow, brown, like so many leftover jelly beans stuck to the bottom of one of those candy dispensers.

She parked at the curb, and shushed me as we walked in. I was drunk, stealthy, and conniving. She bid me hold at the foyer and peered inside. I heard her huff in frustration over whatever she saw.

My mother's asleep on the sofa, she told me. You can use my room and I'll sleep in hers.

It was a wonder to me that such an arrangement could be made, and though I was exhausted now, I was also kindled by the thought of sleeping in Leah's bed, even alone, surrounded by Leah's smells, by her flakes of skin, by the stains of her fluids.

A small room, stacked high with stuffed animals and paperback books. A narrow bed.

The bathroom is down the hall, she told me.

I tugged her inward.

What are you up to?

I pawed her shoulder and touched her hair.

Aren't you the romantic, she said.

I said something charming.

Not a good idea, she answered.

With stubborn insistence, I convinced her to lie on the bed with me and talk.

We talked about Rivers and about Chris and about how many stuffed animals she had. While we talked, I rubbed her back and then, when the resistance proved minimal, I drew the outline of her breast with my fingers, and then, when it seemed her defences had been exhausted, I reached lower and fumbled my way along her thighs and beneath her skirt.

Please don't, she said.

It was a plaintive, surprisingly earnest but mild rebuke, as rebukes went, though unexpected. Why rebuke me? I thought. Others who should have been rebuked had not been; and it seemed unjust to rebuke poor me at this moment, with so little to offer or offend. I hesitated, fluttering like a butterfly before her, weighing the merits and the detriments of continuing, then plunged my hand in again.

I met wetness, a grotto swampy with desire. This too was a surprise and a concern. Why rebuke when the instinct was so strong, when her undercurrents were roaring with as much desire as I felt? Her voice changed, and went mousy. Then she twisted and restrained my shoulders with both of her hands rather forcefully, pushing me back an inch or so. It was all I needed to stop, her message clear enough even for me, even then.

She unwound and gave me a chaste peck on the cheek.

Wait, she said, and left.

I lay on the bed barely large enough for my frame and my God-like erection and took in the loneliness of this rundown room. Her life here, and me an invader. I felt the bed begin to spin and a buzzing start up in my ears. I felt dryness in my throat, and knew myself to be the worst kind of son of a bitch. I felt the heaviness of guilt pressing me down, and closed my eyes for whatever sleep was left.

I was awakened by her touch, and her pressing, grinding insistence, growls in her throat, and bites on my neck. She wore a T-shirt and I felt her naked hips and her knees astride my thighs, and I discovered that my pants were around my ankles. But something was wrong. I had gone sallow with sin. I was lousy with remorse.

We tried this and that to no effect.

Have you heard the expression *too drunk to fuck*? she asked.

I laughed bitterly at my shame. It was my oldest companion, my only true friend. And now that its presence in my life had been revealed publicly at last, I felt a tremendous relief. The rock-bottom kind. She cuddled my neck. It was probably for the better, we agreed. That way our friendship would remain less complicated. We needed each other. We were both abused, in a way, by the vagaries of a cruel world, and it helped to have a pal.

But then, after a mere hour or so of entwined sleep, the problem resolved itself, and we fucked so hard, she pressed a stuffed animal into her mouth to muffle the sounds.

5

Another writer who came along for the ride in Southeast Asia, naturally enough, was Graham Greene. If Conrad had fathered a child with the depressed wife of a British civil servant during a tepid monsoon in Bombay or Rangoon, Greene might have resulted. He was the patron saint of the post-colonial backpacker. By this I mean Greene revelled in a cheap, exotic kind of sordid, and his heroes were always *farang* and functioned perpetually as double agents, romantically cynical, traitors to their countries, their traditional values, and even their own hearts, the kind of betrayal and cynicism that tastes exquisite when there's a smell of clove cigarette in the humid air and you are drunk in the afternoon and intermittently engaged in conversation with some wayward, morally lost fellow traveller, of whom there are many. What Henry Miller was to the pubic louse, Graham Greene was to the poste restante; both wrote poems about the bliss of disappointment in foreign places.

But while I steeped myself in Greene's books, and occasionally got roused from a late-afternoon heat- or debauchery-induced stupor by some intense and unexpected insight into

the awful depths the human soul can crawl into, I never understood why the fuck he converted to Catholicism.

Yes, I know he did it for marriage, initially, to some reluctant
Victorian priss he decided was the one and later abandoned for
all the others, though, tellingly, he preferred to carry the stain
of adultery into all his serial transgressions. Clearly, this meant
he did not live much like a Catholic, if ever a Catholic did, except
to make a fetish of the guilt of sin, which all Catholics do. But I
couldn't understand his conversion at an intellectual level. Why
would an intelligent, literary, worldly man make such a choice?
You can believe in God, vaguely or even mystically, but why that
God, with such specific requirements and limitations? At that
point in my life, it seemed the stupidest of religions, except for
all the others. My father had been a devout Catholic, though
he'd never forced it on us, and while I retained a requisite fear of
God, I did not really know him or feel him in my life, moments
in foxholes notwithstanding.

It seemed to me that if you were Catholic, the thing you
would dote on most was the man himself, nailed to the cross,
experiencing the pain and sorrow of the failings of others. But
that wasn't a pain I could relate to, perhaps because I've never
suffered for anyone's sake my entire life. And so it seemed a
stretch, to put it mildly, to feel any desire or gratitude for someone willing to do that for me, some self-satisfied, superior type
who wanted to take on my sins and failings, which, after all, are
mine and mine alone, thank you very much.

No, the pain I could relate to was different, and later—I
think I was bombed then and alone, stoned or drunk or frazzled
with overindulgence—I glimpsed a sudden understanding into

the nature of Greene's Catholic fascination. He didn't truck with Jesus. It was Judas he got.

I knew this because, of all the bastards in the Bible, Judas perplexed me the most. Job was another I thought about, but Job's plight seemed self-indulgently juvenile, a mewling and unlikely series of woe-is-me what-nexts, conveniently blamed on God fucking around with Satan, all of it perversely fascinating in a Mary Karr–memoir kind of way but lacking plausibility. Cain, too, put a little hook into my consciousness, because Cain also seemed unfairly afflicted, and he'd even done something about it, something Job hadn't had the stones for, which was to lash out in defiance at God, who was clearly, at that point, a son of a bitch. The fact that Cain was forever damned for standing up for himself seemed poetic in an epic sense, rather than psychologically astute, a bit like Gilgamesh or Ulysses thwarted repeatedly by immature gods bent on petulant revenge.

Judas, on the other hand, his story, his predicament, really worried me—at some level even frightened me. Here was a guy they said loved Jesus a lot, like a brother, and he'd sold him out for thirty pieces of silver, then hanged himself out of remorse. Yet, since there was next to no explanation for the betrayal, I could not help but puzzle the reasons. (And for this plot twist alone, let's recognize that story as the Bible's big literary moment.)

Even as a kid, I related to Judas (and felt guilty about it) because his actions seemed so personally plausible. Who among us hasn't wished ill on a more successful friend, even fantasized about their cruel end? Who hasn't secretly felt like a traitor even in the midst of friendship? It isn't revenge or hatred that motivates such emotion, it's the bitterness born of love. So, like an emotionally neglected school chum, Judas turned on Jesus and lived (briefly) with the consequences. Distraught at what he'd done, Judas then went out to a field, found a withered tree, threw a rope over a branch, and hanged himself dead, thirty coins of silver glinting on the ground below his feet. Even worse, this act, above and beyond the betrayal of the Son of God, was the seal on his ticket to hell.

If weight could be defined in Biblical terms, surely its closest parallel is damnation. I get that part. They don't call hellfire *eternal* by accident.

What I don't get is the Biblical reaction. Where's the pity? Where's the compassion and understanding? Is forgiveness of that kind of betrayal beyond even Jesus? Wasn't Jesus nailed to the cross for Judas's sin, as much as every other man's? (Perhaps it's easier to forgive the transgression of a stranger than someone you really know.)

Furthermore, if we take the whole redemption of mankind through the betrayal of Jesus metaphor seriously, wasn't Judas necessary to kick-start two thousand years of religion? Every cardinal and pope, every parish priest should be on their knees thanking him. He's the guy who made your careers possible! He's the guy who let you slaughter infidels, sexually abuse minors, or siphon the donation basket and get the holy free pass.

But although divinity students explore the mysteries of the Holy Trinity and transubstantiation and the virgin birth, they pretty much skip the mystery of Judas's terrible guilt—the cause and effect of it, the lingering weight.

I believe the deficiency is due to a lack of literary understanding. We don't follow Judas from the point of view of plot, so we don't see the necessity of him. Maybe that's why a writer gets him more. Writers, by nature, are tearfully grateful for their plausible villains or faulty heroes because they make story possible. There's a little Judas in every great character Greene created.

Still, I recognize the spiritual danger here. A character in a story that we identify with provides a glimpse of understanding into our own psychological mysteries, however infinite and multi-faceted.

To say I identified with Judas is only a small step away from being Judas.

Chris, of course, was Christ.

I didn't get home until late Sunday morning, and was so bedraggled and hungover that my parents didn't even question what I'd done. I counted this a moral victory since they'd known I'd been at Rivers's party the night before, and the obvious suspicion they would have, I presumed, was that I had been ass-fucking until dawn. I'd gotten fucked all right, but the difference was all the world.

I was not, however, feeling any ease. My respite from the anxiety over the Canadian Tire robbery had ended, and I read the newspaper and listened to the radio with the kind of fear and dread that comes when you know capture is imminent and life is about to end. The cops would be bashing in our front door at any moment, and I was too paralyzed to do anything about it.

When the doorbell rang, I died a small death. When I saw that it was Chris, I rose to live again.

Strangely, it wasn't the robbery that flashed to my mind when I opened the door, but the fact that Leah and I had fucked. I felt oddly guilty about that, although Chris and her were over, as though I'd stabbed him in the back. Maybe it was because I had other, future stabbings in mind.

The afternoon was over, and dusk had arrived, but Chris was wearing dark Wayfarer sunglasses, grinning like Tom Cruise.

Sorry, he said.

He did not look sorry.

For what? I asked, assuming the worst.

For counting the money without you.

That was the last thing I was worried about, but I reacted indignantly all the same.

Asshole, I said.

Shoot me, he offered.

And you got new shades, I said, finally figuring it out, remembering the ones I'd crushed.

A hundred and fifty smackeroos, he said. Don't worry. I paid for them out of your cut.

It was an incredible, almost incalculable amount of money to us then.

Holy shit, I said.

Wanna go get wasted? he asked.

I didn't even mention to my parents that I was going out, just grabbed my jacket and left.

Fairy tales are filled with idiots who make lucky fortunes. They trade a cow for three beans and end up with a giant's treasure, they get trapped in a gingerbread house and live happily ever after, despite whatever fate they actually deserve.

We got drunk that night, foolishly, gloriously drunk. We hit on chicks. Twice I remember Chris warning me to shut my fucking mouth, in a good-natured and generous kind of way, and I'm not sure if it was because I blurted out something about robberies (a possibility) or merely expounded on the length and durability of my erection. I did, however, recognize a trend in myself, though I ignored the reasons or the consequences: I was becoming a bad drunk.

Chris, almost apologetically, told me he'd intended to wait until we were together to count the money, but then he figured that would be another twenty-four hours minimum, and he made an executive decision instead. After his parents went out for a dinner with friends, he pulled the deposit bag from behind the washing machine, cut it open along the zipper, poured out the innards and started sorting and counting.

His first reaction had been disappointment. After sorting the piles of bills and credit card receipts and checking the deposit slip, he realized the bulk of the money, seventy thousand dollars or so, was not cash. This filled him with anger. He was not remorseful about the job itself but about the lack of payoff. He'd wanted something glorious, something remarkable and noteworthy to begin his new and better life, and this small-time payout just didn't cut it.

But once he counted the bills for himself and sat on the number for a while, he began to feel better. Slowly, the reality of the bounty sank in. There was $21,892.18 on the table before him. It was, all in all, not bad for an hour's work.

Knowing I was busy, he scooped the money back into the deposit bag, except for a handful of C-notes, and rushed to the mall. He celebrated by himself, with a pure and magical kind of self-satisfaction, splurging on an extra-large Orange Julius and two pairs of Wayfarers. He delivered the second pair to Susan that night, after she finished her waitressing shift, explaining that he'd bought her a present with a little unexpected bonus money for his years of service at the store. In return, Susan blew him in the front seat of his car below her parent's bedroom window.

Maybe she's a little more materialistic than I realized, he said. He sounded mildly disappointed.

I told him never to question a blow job, and we decided those were words to live by.

Chris bought our drinks, and a few drinks for others at my insistence, all night long. I didn't even think about the money owed to me. Instead, I kept remembering Leah. I felt the heaviness of guilt and tried to heave it off.

Ah, shit man, I gotta tell you something, I said.

What? he asked.

I sensed a danger and didn't want to continue.

What? he asked again, less patiently.

It was with a certain perverse satisfaction that I told him.

I fucked Leah last night. I'm sorry, man. I feel bad as shit about it.

He looked surprised. He arched an eyebrow. He eyed me for what seemed like a long time, absorbing the hit, weighing the transgression.

No biggie, he said.

But I kept pushing it over the course of the next hour or so. I think I wanted forgiveness and I think I wanted to heap weight on Chris in turn. I wanted him to feel the remorse and the uncertainty that I knew so well.

Many drinks later, Chris told me to stop. Look, man, the reason I'm giving you a total free pass with Leah is because I guess I have my own confession to make.

My world, which had been spinning, screeched to a halt.

I accidentally fucked Radha.

Accidentally?

Like he slipped and his cock ended up in her vagina.

Unintentionally, he said.

I pressed for details. He told me it happened the weekend I was writing my beach story. The weekend, in fact, when Radha telephoned to say she would do unspeakable things to me once I finished.

I guess, Chris explained, she got worked up by that. You know.

I did not know. No unspeakable things had been done to me in the end. I'd asked her what she'd had in mind, considering the promise to be on the order of a blood oath, but she got expertly elusive when the payoff moment came and all I got was the usual.

Now I understood: she'd expended her warped energy on Chris.

Fuck it, I said. Well, I guess we're even.

We did not feel even.

You got the better end of that deal, he said.

And this, too, was painful truth.

When he dropped me off at my house, hours later, he reached under the car seat. I tensed. For some drunk and numb reason, I expected a handgun to appear. I was, of course, the weak link in our operation. It would only make sense for Chris to off me now, tie up my loose ends. Part of me even wished for it. Put me out of my misery and yours, Chris. Neither of us needed the weight. In every heist movie it is the same. You coddle the weak one at your peril. Your downfall is friendship.

But then I saw he had an envelope in his hand, not a gun.

Thought it best to give this to you at the end of the night, he said.

Probably a good idea, I mumbled.

I started to look inside but realized the futility and just looked at Chris instead.

Six thousand for being the man behind the wheel, he said. Then added, Sort of.

We both laughed about the sort of way I'd helped, the sort of way I'd been a man. But even more than the Radha business, I never quite forgave him for his little shot about my incompetence. It wasn't just a wisecrack but a betrayal of our jointly held illusion. It indicated he actually knew my failings acutely and always had and always would, even when he pretended to be oblivious.

No doubt, Judas would have understood my resentment.

My father grilled me the next night about rickshaw, and whether I was serious about it, and whether I was still intending to not work at the bank.

My successive nights of debauchery must have been too much for him to stand, but he couldn't have raised the topic at a worse time. I was flush with money and freedom. What need did I have of a bank? Besides, I still feared any ideas Chris might come up with if I did time as an inside man.

He asked me for specifics. He wanted to know how much the rickshaw cost to rent each week, how many rides were required to earn that sum, how many rides there were in a day, what the average per day was, and how many days a week were lost to rain on average. I made up numbers out of vague, plausible bits recalled from conversations with Chris. There was nothing convincing about my argument, even to me. I could not insert into the calculations the other factors that would have balanced the ledger: the suntan, the frequent flirtation, the random sexual encounters, the beer, the laughs, and so on.

I don't see how your numbers add up, my father said. How are you going to afford school in the fall?

I told him I'd get by. Meaning I had six thousand dollars currently stuffed into a pair of hockey skates below the stairs.

Your mother and I aren't your personal bank.

I told him I had no expectations of receiving any supplementary funds. I could take care of myself.

It went on and on. I did not move in my position, and he did not move in his. My mother was sick of us talking about it. She told us to let it go for the night, to talk about it more tomorrow, and I knew, in a way, that this was an acknowledgement of my victory, because banks and rickshaw rental services were not vague concepts; they did, in fact, require commitments, and my plan was to not work for the bank, and to commit on Sunday to

Dan the Rickshaw Guy, who owned the storage shed and rented the gear. My father must have also understood that by withstanding his barrage, I had achieved a win, because he could not resist a last dire warning.

I hope you'll make good choices.

He added that he didn't care if I became a truck driver so long as I drove to the utmost of my abilities. The problem was, he didn't want me to be a truck driver and I didn't want to be one either; I wanted experiences, the kind that sailed right over morality, that garnered higher insights that would be considered crimes, and so on.

I suppose he was asking me to be mature.

I understand maturity better now. I see it less as wisdom than an acceptance of weight. Children can treat life heavy, too, but the passage toward adulthood involves an accumulation of increasingly weighty concerns, a reluctant acceptance of burdens and responsibilities, until you're so heavy and tired, no one can deny your sombre maturity. There are people, rare beings, who seem to bear weight with lightness, who live life lightly while understanding its weight. I'm thinking of a few yoga teachers I've known, the Dalai Lama, a giddy philosopher or two, a few dementia-stricken seniors. But for most of us, maturity equals weight, and immaturity equals lightness. Think about your own moments of immaturity—at games or sporting events, during drunken nights or reckless fucks, while hanging out with childhood friends. For a time, you feel light and outside your weary self.

My argument with my father came down to that. He was afraid for me, and afraid of the world. He wanted me to be happy and to achieve my dreams, but he wanted me to be safe first. And if being safe meant forgoing happiness and dreams, so be it. Those would have to wait for some other life, a life of lightness.

I wanted a summer of lightness before it was too late.

I got an unexpected call, a few days later, from Leah. I had thought little about her since our tangle on the weekend, so much had happened in the interim. I had not called her because I did not think of her as the kind of girl who needed post-intimacy consideration. The sound of her voice, however, brought with it a rush of guilt and awkwardness. I did not want to seem withdrawn, since we had been friends, and had vowed to continue to be friends. I did not want to seem ungrateful or sullen, since we had done things together that had been wondrous in the moment and were still pleasing to remember. But I did not want to seem too happy or eager, either, because I feared being drawn into a relationship with her. This was not the time, and I had no space in my heart.

Relax, she said. I'm calling on Delmore's behalf.

Huh?

It turned out she was doing some secretarial work for Rivers, on the side, and he'd asked her to arrange a lunch date with me. Would today work?

Today? I asked.

Yeah. I told him there wasn't much chance you'd actually be doing anything with yourself yet, so I've got you down for 12:30 at the Shipyard.

Oh, like in two hours?

Yeah, like in two hours. I could have called earlier, but I didn't want to wake you up. Don't you love me?

Huh?

That's a joke.

Oh.

What are we going to call the baby?

What?

Another joke. You're hilarious. Don't be late for lunch.

I didn't even have the clarity of mind to ask her what it was about.

I wore my white jeans, suede boat shoes, and a relatively wrinkle-free lime-green golf shirt. My mom dropped me off at the ferry terminal, and I crossed over to Halifax with time to kill, so I hit a second-hand bookstore. A dusty hardback copy of Herman Wouk's *Youngblood Hawke* caught my eye, and by the time I'd read the jacket copy, I knew it was a fortuitous find. Youngblood Hawke was a writer of crude, rugged, and unpredictable personality, overladen with talent for language and story, who rode the New York publishing world as though it were a bucking bronco, taking from it everything any writer could ever want—fame, critical acclaim, wealth, sex—until he fucked it all up and died of excess. I felt as though I had discovered my autobiography, in a prophetic tome. Seven bucks was a lot to shell out for a used book, but I did it anyway, and strode off to the Shipyard to meet Rivers, well armed.

Rivers occupied the crow's nest table, a beer and a Reuben

sandwich with fries before him, his crutches to the side. I greeted him and laid the book on the table. He did not hold his hand out but looked at me with stern disapproval. Had Leah told him about our encounter?

I couldn't wait any longer, Rivers said. Why don't you order something from the bar.

It was only 12:35. Had Leah told me 12:00? Or had she sabotaged my meeting? I didn't know what to think. At the bar, I ordered fries with gravy, a local delicacy, and a Coke. For some reason, I didn't feel right ordering a beer in front of Rivers.

When I returned to the table, Rivers was flipping through my new book.

Have you ever known a famous man before he became famous? he asked, reading the first line.

Have you read it? I asked.

I read the *Reader's Digest* version, he answered.

I tried to hide my surprise. Would any real writer read a *Reader's Digest* book? It seemed a kind of sacrilege.

Who's got time to read Wouk? he asked me. Minor writer, bloated as hell. You can get the vital stuff in condensed version and save your time for Dostoevsky, Stendhal, Conrad. Same with William Styron. Everyone raves about *Sophie's Choice* like it's the great novel we've all been waiting for. And I agree, it is a powerful story with terrific characterization, but it's flatulently told. Saul Bellow, same bullshit. Have you read *Humboldt's Gift?* Fantastic novella, seven hundred pages long. Don't get me started on *Augie March*. If you're going to write a great novel, it has to be great all the way through. It can't be lined with layers of fat just to heft it onto the impressive shelf.

No, I agreed. That wasn't the way to true greatness.

What does your father do? he asked.

I adjusted to the change in direction.

He works at a bank.

Doing what?

Some kind of district manager stuff. I shrugged.

I knew what my father did but I did not want to sound conceited or elitist. I shouldn't have worried with Rivers. Elite, superior, successful—those were okay by him.

So is that what you do in the summer then—work at a bank?

I could have choked on a fry. Had Rivers and my father become co-conspirators?

Not this year, I said, and when Rivers nodded approvingly, I felt brave enough to elaborate. I'm pulling rickshaw.

Rickshaw? You mean, around Halifax? Up those hills?

Yes.

Rivers snorted. Do you wear a toga?

Ha ha, I said.

You can make money doing that?

Like waitering. Good days, bad days.

How much?

Jesus, was he my father? Enough, I said.

Well, I suppose you might get a good story or two out of it.

I nodded. That's what I was thinking.

Work has to do one of two things. Either it has to pay the bills and give you enough cushion to write, or it has to give you good experiences that give you stuff to write about.

I waited. He had switched to guru mode, and I was comfortable with my role.

Take teaching. I'm tenure track, have a decent salary, and the course load is light enough to give me time to write, meaning on balance it's a good job. But it provides me nothing in terms of material.

Nothing? I was surprised. I figured all those people you meet, the social situations.

Rivers dismissed my suggestions. Nothing about it is real. And worse, try grading all that writing and see how much juice you have left for your own. The job takes more than it gives. Marginally supportive at best.

But teaching, don't you hone your understanding of craft and technique?

For a few years, after that nothing. You can't imagine the drain. Now, take journalism. Sounds good in theory. You get paid to write, research, investigate, and interview, all valuable skills, but it's the wrong kind of writing, and the research, investigation, and interview work gets ground up and processed like innards to make cheap hot dogs and nutritionless articles. Plus the pay is terrible.

There's always crime, I said.

Rivers nodded. Police work can be fantastic from the story perspective. The money, not so good. Unless you're willing to work a lot of overtime, which cuts into your writing time. And it's dangerous.

Didn't Nietzsche say we need to live life dangerously?

And Flaubert said live like a bourgeois to be violent and original in your work.

This, from Rivers, was surprising.

Maybe I should rob banks, I offered.

I think you should be a medical doctor, Rivers said, ignoring my attempt at humour.

It took me a moment to understand him.

I have a friend who's in family practice. Makes eighty Gs a year working part-time. Gets to know the intimate secrets of a lot of people. The downside is the seven to ten years you put into the education. But if you've got the stamina, you're still young when your sentence is over. You walk out a free man with a lot of loot.

I nodded thoughtfully, as if he'd struck a chord. I had no more interest in medicine than I had in banking.

But I didn't ask you here to talk about that. I have a proposition. *Transassination* comes out in the fall, and I'm going on sabbatical. I'm going to write my next novel with that break. I'm a third of the way through, and it's really amazing. Something that will blow Bellow and Styron off their bar stools. I'd like to try you out as my apprentice this summer.

Apprentice?

Three days a week. Minimum wage. You'll file, make copies, pay bills, do my laundry, and learn more about writing than you could in a graduate program at Iowa.

Oh, I said. I had no better answer. I was surprised by the idea that washing Rivers's socks and paying his electric bills would somehow make me a better writer.

Well, think about it, Rivers said, sensing my hesitation.

We finished lunch. I offered to pay. He didn't dissuade me. I felt self-consciously like a big man, peeling off a twenty. I tried to thank him again for the offer when we shook hands at the door, but his dark brow had furrowed and he was irritated by the crutches and he swung his way out onto the sidewalk like a deranged vet.

Part of my hesitation, part of the reason I didn't call him immediately that evening and beg to be reconsidered (for a position I hadn't actually turned down), was because of my father. I'd established the plan for rickshaw work with such conviction that any deviation would immediately undercut my entire argument and make me seem flighty and whimsical. In other words, I feared my father's disapproval more than I feared missing an opportunity to work with someone who could, potentially, be the next Bellow, perhaps even the next Dostoevsky.

But my summer of lightness did not start off well.

A snow squall struck that Sunday morning, laying four inches of white on the streets. It was a rare, though not unheard of, happening, and it struck most people with humour, even as it devastated the rickshaw industry. Ha ha.

I sat around for another week, and felt the weight of unmet expectations. Each glance from my father confirmed his disappointment. I should have been employed at the bank. Rickshaw was a colossal waste. In desperation, I called Rivers a week after Leah had called me, hoping to get on board as his writing apprentice. I connected only with his answering machine and that Islamic call to prayer and the voice asking me to leave a message for Sinbad the sailor.

My hell eased by that Friday, when the snow had melted away. The sun showed up on Saturday morning, and by Sunday, I was outfitted with my rickshaw kit.

I got my first paid ride late Thursday afternoon, nineteen and a half hours into my new career.

A pair of seniors wanted to go from the harbour front to the Old Spaghetti Factory. I didn't know where the Old Spaghetti Factory was, so halfway through the ride, I needed to stop and ask for directions, and ended up going twice as far as necessary. When we arrived at our destination, the old couple asked me how much, and since I had forgotten to set a price beforehand, I resorted to a trick Chris recommended, suggesting they pay me what they liked. I should have guessed that seniors heading to the reduced price dinner wouldn't be filled with largesse.

There was not much camaraderie at the shed, either. Chris had sung its praises as a man cave of ease and debauchery, but to me, at least at first, it lacked all mirth. It was situated below an old abandoned hotel and served, officially, as our storage space for rickshaws and gym bags, plus dispatch office. The immediate enclosure gave way to a cavernous space in back filled with treasure and mystery. The midden was extraordinary. There were countless boxes and old bottles and several chandeliers and dozens of broken chairs, bed frames, and dining tables. Broken rickshaws and collapsed couches served as our furniture. Old paintings in wooden frames offered targets for randomly thrown objects.

Everyone was in a foul mood that week. There were nine of us on Dan's crew in total, though only myself and two others worked those first few days. Chris didn't bother to show up at all. He tried to convince me that it was worthless to venture out before the weather warmed, especially given our secret pile of loot, but I didn't have the stones to lie around the house another week. So I endured the sullen hostility of my new colleagues who knew each other, and knew Chris, but didn't give a fuck about me.

Saturday afternoon, Chris finally arrived, the last of the boys to show for work, winning some kind of prize for being the laziest bastard in the process. It was hotter than hell all of a sudden, as if we'd gone from full winter to full summer overnight. No one else wore suntan lotion—in fact, Chris used baby oil to build a faster tan—so I didn't either. As a result, I was sunburned and dehydrated by five o'clock. That's when I got my first real fare.

Two young women. I learned later that Chris steered them to me. Naturally, as they boarded, I assumed the ride would conclude in some kind of three-way. The girls played it up. Giddy and flirtatious, they ordered a trip to the top of Citadel Hill, the fortress that overlooks the city.

I launched into the journey hopefully, but soon realized what a fool I'd been. The vertical climb was brutal. My heart pounded beyond all safe limits and hot drool began to run freely from my mouth. I pulled off on a side street and bent over as if to tie a shoelace, then couldn't lift my head again, and sank to one knee. My customers stepped out and approached me with concern. It turned out one was in nursing school. She took my pulse and forced me to sit on the curb despite weak protests, mercifully suggesting that I'd be all right as long as I took it easy for a while. I didn't care if I died at that moment, I only wanted to be alone. Her friend pushed a twenty into my hand. I was too shaky to even grip the paper. After they'd gone, I walked weakly across the street to a takeout pizza joint and bought a Gatorade. Then I went back to my rickshaw, still parked where I'd dropped the handles, and sat in it, comforted by the plush seat that hugged me like a blanket.

The first one always gets you, Chris said later.

You got to pop your cherry the hard way, a co-worker named Tim seconded. My first ride I puked on the sidewalk right next to the Shipyard.

They were right. The pain eased up after that, and the work became more fun, though I didn't make much money. I got a fare or two a night, earning twenty or thirty dollars tops. But I always remembered to pry a roll of twenties and tens out of my pocket and drop it onto the coffee table or kitchen counter at home as proof of my day's success. The money, of course, came from the stash below the stairs, and its steady accumulation above ground, like mushrooms popping up from a submerged fungal mass, was my way of laundering dirty funds. Instead of working our asses off, most nights we drank beer in the shed for the first four or five hours. Someone rigged up a broken rickshaw so that it was tipped back and we filled it with ice every night to keep our beer cold. Pleasantly wasted, we'd head out around eleven or twelve and park in front of a hopping bar or late-night donair and pizza joint, waiting for female fares. We refused to haul men, unless they were part of a couple.

I never once got laid working rickshaw that summer, but for Chris, it was a near weekly event. At times, I wondered if my sole purpose as Chris's partner in crime was to provide cover for him in case Susan showed up. She worked at a nearby restaurant, so this happened frequently, three or four nights a week. I got good at lying to her. I told her he'd just snagged a long fare and to call him the next morning, or that he'd twisted his ankle and was at the hospital, or that the Billy Club had called and asked him to fill in for a shift. I didn't really care if she believed me or if the alibis held up. Maybe that disdain was the secret to being convincing. No matter how outlandish my story, she merely put her hands on her hips, looked around as if to see if he were actually hiding behind some pile of boxes, and nodded. All right, see you later.

I was usually drunk, and that made me indifferent to the emotional needs of others. Besides, part of me gained a smidgen of satisfaction whenever Susan's needs were thwarted. If only she'd chosen me.

The episodes of Chris's cheating never failed to be entertaining to the rest of us. He was good about letting us in on the stories. He did not treat women poorly, as many successful philanderers do. In fact, Chris always seemed genuinely moved by some special quality of beauty or uniqueness in each one.

He never slept too late at an apartment or house when he had made a conquest. He always tried to be home before Susan called in the morning, so as to take her out for breakfast or coffee. As a matter of principle, he also tried to have sex with Susan as soon as possible afterwards. It was a kind of cleansing ritual, a way of proving that she was the one who mattered. I'm not sure Susan would have understood, but I'm not sure she wouldn't have understood either.

I can't fully account for his success. He was not that much better looking than the rest of us. He was not as witty as me or as charming. But he seemed to have something that women wanted. None of the encounters became serious or steady. He was, in his way, totally committed to Susan. I would say that it was merely impossible for him to stop, but that would imply he had any desire to stop. He didn't. He saw no contradictions. He was utterly light.

My only accomplishments that summer were physical. I got into better shape. I became hard and developed stamina. I began to take myself seriously as a physical force. I got pleasantly buzzed on beer each evening, and hammered down highballs each night. At least once a week, I said something so belligerent and offensive to some passing shmuck that a fight ensued. Only two or three times did Chris have to come to my rescue.

Most nights, the Halifax police would show up with paddy wagons and scoop up the most offensive drunks and brawlers. Three times I was among those transported to the drunk tank. The first time, I had just been kicked out of a bar by an overly officious bouncer, so I proceeded to tear the flowers out of the flower bed in front of the club and fling them across the street. On a second occasion, I decided to recite a poem (actually the Bob Dylan song Forever Young, spoken rather than sung) to a group of women who'd refused to take us up on free rides, and when they began to mock me, I stood on the back of a park bench, impressively balanced despite my inebriation, and shimmied my shorts and underwear off while I howled the final words of the chorus. Who knew that was a public offence? The third time, I was simply too drunk and indifferent to scatter when the police busted a joint frequently cited for underage drinking. Since I did not have ID on me, they took me in. Each time, Chris showed up with the appropriate funds to get my release. Not bail exactly, but some kind of fee. Like a parking ticket for being hammered. The details I left to him, and of course, there was no question of ever paying it back. We had a slush fund for that sort of thing.

While I earned plenty of material for stories that summer, I did no writing. This, as much as any lingering guilt I felt about the robbery and betraying my father, and the frustration I experienced over my lack of sexual success, was the reason I engaged in such a slow, glamorous, self-destructive suicide. I had been reading Dylan Thomas and Charles Bukowski and other poets of the damned. Maybe that fed the downward spiral, the romantic belief that I needed to grind myself into the gutter.

I should note, however, that although my behaviour was random, unpredictable, and seemed beyond my self-control, I never acted out too badly when Chris was not in hailing distance.

I did not spend much time at home. If it rained, we went to the movies or spent all day at a diner, or I went to the library and slept on one of the big couches. Sometimes, stumbling blearily back out into the world, I wondered who I was. At some point in August, I realized I was down to my last eight hundred bucks. I had no idea how the funds had been depleted so quickly, and I felt both relieved and stupid to have spent so much money on alcohol and food. I had not bought a bike or a stereo or saved for school or brought home flowers or paid for some sick kid's cancer treatment. I also felt wonderfully, blissfully free knowing the money was almost gone. I could never admit to Chris that I'd been so profligate, but that was okay. He didn't need to know. And then one night, he admitted to me that his own stash was almost blown. This, more than anything, astonished me and put the world back into balance. You blew eighteen thousand bucks in three months! Well, sixteen thousand, he rebutted, looking both sheepish and proud. On what? I demanded, as if I were vigilant as an accountant in my own money habits. You know, Chris said—and the astonishment on his face was genuine—I honestly have no fucking idea.

The money had simply disappeared, as though its magic properties had an expiration date. Since it happened to both of us, we knew it wasn't our fault, and this absolution made me feel lighter.

Then Chris announced we would need to do another job to replenish the coffers.

How could I have been so blind to that inevitability?

We took weeks planning it, and we laid out and discussed many possible armed robberies. There were, when you really dug into it, quite a range of options, from the traditional bank job to the lucrative but less conventional deposit-bag snatch, to still more innovative options. I could not help but contribute creatively to the brainstorming sessions.

What about a Brinks truck? Chris asked.

What about a grocery store? Or a jewellery store—

What about an expensive restaurant? Chris interrupted.

Or a movie theatre? I tried.

That's actually pretty fucking brilliant, Chris said.

Neither of us had ever heard of a movie theatre being robbed before. But when we considered the number of seats, the outrageous price for tickets, and the crowds, we quickly saw the potential.

Any idea that steered Chris away from a bank job seemed good to me.

Chris, however, had a cowboy-like desire to notch a bank on his belt. So my suffering began anew.

The only salvation—and I knew it was a temporary one— was that Chris could not decide on which bank. Some he dismissed because they were stand-alone structures and he would have drawn too much attention approaching or leaving. Some he scratched because they were located too deep within a mall— and running down the hallway would be time-consuming and chancy. Others he didn't like because they were too far away from our neighbourhood and we didn't know the driving routes well enough to mitigate any uncertainties.

Fuck it, he said, let's just do the CIBC at Penhorn Mall.

This struck me as inconceivable.

But that's the bank we opened our first accounts in!

So?

We still have accounts there. They know our names, our addresses, everything!

I don't think they're going to run down a list of account holders to see who could have done the job.

Jesus fucking Christ, it's about a five-minute walk from where we live!

Yeah, and who knows the back roads and the woods and the lakes and every other nook and cranny around here better than us?

He was right about that, no one in the entire history of mankind knew the contours and features of the neighbourhood like we did. Even so, his logic seemed indescribably flawed to me.

To accommodate his lightness, I doubled down on my drinking.

The worst element was the psychological delay. I was never sure which forces of preparation, circumstance, and what-the-fuckism needed to be aligned in order to make a decision to go for it. Chris held that secret formula in his own head. My only job was to suffer and be ready.

Running out of cash, and more desperate now to have this rickshaw summer pay off financially, I took to working afternoons. There was little payoff, but one day, standing next to my chariot, I saw Rivers exiting a café.

He seemed more at ease with his crutches, and he had a knapsack slung neatly over his shoulder and wore a beret like a Frenchman. He kissed the cheek of a woman he'd been sitting with and headed down the sidewalk.

I hesitated and then called out to him. He stopped, saw me, and smiled. I walked over.

You look good, he said. How are things?

I suppose he meant I looked in shape and well tanned. I knew that inside I was poisoning myself. I was corrupt, cirrhotic, ulcerous, cancer ridden. I was a mess, and I had not written in months.

I confessed that last bit to him.

He nodded. Happens sometimes. People think discipline is just determination and a schedule. That's like saying writing is just a pen and a piece of paper. Discipline is a desire stronger than any other desire to produce something. Maybe you don't have your story yet. When you do, the discipline will come.

I blinked in relief. Was this an example of the wisdom I had passed on by neglecting to seize his apprenticeship offer? If so, I wanted more.

I think I've got a story but I'm not sure I can write it, I said.

Technical challenges?

Personal challenges. It's about people I know.

Ah, potentially destructive to others in its truthfulness? The insufficiently disguised *Bildungsroman* autobiography?

Probably.

I knew my story was the source of my cancer. It was eating me from the inside out, a vicious baby angry to be born.

Write what you can now, he said, even in diary form, and come back to it in ten years. If it's powerful enough, it will infuse everything else you work on.

Ten years? I said.

Seems like a long time, doesn't it, he said.

Seems like forever.

It's not. You'll get there. Or it'll get you.

We stood before each other. He seemed to decide something.

I'm going abroad for my sabbatical, he said.

Abroad?

I can't sit in the middle of this vast America and build the bomb that's going to blow it up. I need some exile, silence, and cunning.

Europe? I asked. Thinking Hemingway, Fitzgerald, Henry Miller. You name it.

Too expensive. You been to France or Italy lately?

Not lately.

Me neither. I'm thinking Southeast Asia. It's the Paris of the twenties. Cheap, affordable. You get a beach hut and a desk for a couple dollars a week. You throw in beer, food, and a massage every other day for a few dollars more. You want a coconut or a mango or a swim, you go out your front door, walk five feet, and get one. If it goes well, I may stay two years, maybe more. I can write at least two novels with that kind of time, perhaps a good chunk of a third.

Wow, I said, feeling abandoned and wondering about the implications for his teaching career. They'll miss you at school.

He grimaced. I have an offer to make. You come over, you can hang out with me. Get a hut nearby or something. We'll be neighbours. You can work on your stuff, I'll work on mine. If I need a mango or a beer, maybe you'll bring it over. If I need someone to motorcycle into town and post something, maybe you'll do that too. No obligations, mostly just company. I'm a little worried about being cut off from good conversation. I'd like a small hand-picked community.

This time he did not seem so expectant of an immediate response.

Think about it, he said. I know you've got school to consider, and your parents. Sell it as a semester abroad. That used to be the done thing.

It was the kindest invitation I'd ever received. He needed me, or something about me, and he liked me, too.

I said I would think it through, and tossed it in with the mix of concerns already keeping me up every night.

The next week, my parents went away for their summer vacation in Maine. They'd rented a house down there, and while I was formally invited, my presence was not expected or even particularly desired. I'm sure they were as happy to be free of me as I was of them. I felt the weight lessening on my shoulders as their car pulled away. They even left me a couple hundred dollars to cover groceries and expenses.

That night, Chris decided we should go somewhere too.

We were sitting in broken rickshaws drinking beer, readying ourselves for another pointless night out on the Halifax streets, he to get laid, me to get tossed in some paddy wagon.

Go where? I asked, assuming he meant a bar.

Montreal, Toronto, Boston. Let's just do it.

How? I asked. He may as well have suggested Mars.

How much money you got left?

Maybe two hundred plus the two my parents left me. I'd tightened up as it dwindled. I was no longer so large-hearted buying rounds. I had hardened around my own solitary drink.

I've got seventeen hundred. Let's go spend it.

I struggled to offer a rebuttal. Once again, he'd flabbergasted me.

What if we run out when we're away from home? I finally asked.

Like that's a problem, he said.

I think he was joking.

Let's get rid of what we got. Clean our plates. Have a good time. Get some motivation for the next job.

I felt the cancerous mass within start to gyrate. Feeding on me.

Twelve hours later, hungover and wearing sunglasses to hold out the brutal blink, we arrived at the Halifax International Airport with gym bags containing the minimal change of underwear, socks, and T-shirts. It had been Chris's job to buy the tickets, but he'd forgotten to do so. We looked at the departing flights and tried to make a choice.

London leaving in forty minutes, Chris said. Blimey.

That's London, Ontario.

Whoa. That would be a mistake. What about Sydney?

That's Sydney, Cape Breton, I said. How about Toronto?

Fuck that, Chris said. I hate the fucking Leafs. How can you beat Montreal? Let's go there.

But when we arrived at the counter, the attendant was puzzled by our request for two tickets to Montreal.

Yeah, Chris said, I'd like to buy them. For the 11:30 flight. How much?

She punched numbers in her console, bit her lip, punched more numbers.

I'm afraid that flight is totally full, sir.

We did indeed dig the *sir* stuff.

Okay, what else you got?

To Montreal? Three-thirty, also full. Seven-thirty tonight. I could get you on that.

No thanks, Chris said. I don't think we can wait nine hours in an airport. Unless you're getting off soon.

I shook my head. Chris working the airline attendant.

She smiled, joked about a husband, and seemed to get into the spirit of things.

Is it only Montreal you're interested in?

What else do you suggest?

I've always loved New York, myself.

New York would be ace.

She punched, frowned, punched some more.

I can get you on the last two seats on the 1:15 to LaGuardia.

Is that near New York? I asked. It sounded suspiciously like Quebec.

I need your decision now. I can't hold these for long.

Sold, Chris said. If we can return Sunday. He looked to me. Got to go to Susan's place for dinner Sunday night. First time meeting the father.

And he shelled out $642.00 for the two of us.

The attendant wished us an excellent vacation. I can't imagine what she thought of us.

We had a few hours to kill, so naturally we hit a bar. We sat at a table and split a pitcher, our gym bags tucked under our feet. We were mighty pleased with ourselves, and then a strange look came over Chris's face. He'd gone utterly expressionless. Holy shit, he muttered. Don't turn around.

What? I asked.

A grin came over his face. You're not going to believe this. There's three Dartmouth city cops in plain clothes sitting at the bar.

I whirled around, practically knocking the pitcher off the table. Chris kicked me, so I whirled back.

A little more casual, please.

I gripped both sides of the table. Do you think they're following us?

It seemed possible, in that moment, that they were waiting to see if we'd leave the country before arresting us. I could no longer breathe.

Nah, Chris said. Crossed my mind for a millisecond. But that would be a little above and beyond the call of duty, I think.

I tried to calm down.

How do you know they're Dartmouth police? I asked.

Let's see. Because I've seen two of them at the Billy Club at least seventeen times. And the third guy is Drury. You know, the cop who lives up on the Horseshoe.

I almost—but caught myself just in time—said, You mean the one who showed up when we chainsawed the tree house?

Drury, I said. And felt the weight bearing down.

Evidently, they spotted Chris, because he suddenly nodded, smiled, and lifted his beer glass in cheers. Then he went back to drinking.

They're packing up, Chris said. See? Nothing to worry about.

Then the three men stood before us. One of them, whom Chris called Officer Green, asked Chris what he was up to. It was a friendly question, a make-conversation question, but there was malice to it, as far as I was concerned, cop-like suspicion.

Pulling rickshaw, Chris said, making a little coin before school in the fall.

You still applying to the academy? Green asked.

Yes, sir.

Dartmouth City or RCMP? the second cop asked.

Chris didn't answer, just grinned.

What do you think? Green asked his colleague.

A low snicker of laughter all around.

Well, if you don't make RCMP, we'll probably take you, the second one said.

They took you, didn't they? Green said.

Then Drury spoke up. Where are you boys headed?

Drury didn't do small talk. Drury did cop talk. Suddenly, I was sitting in the back of his car, holding a towel to my chin, answering every little thing he asked. Did he remember me?

But Chris didn't blink. Just waiting for a friend flying in. Where are you fellows off to?

New York, the second cop said.

I almost passed out.

LaGuardia? I asked suddenly.

They all gave me a funny look.

We're going to catch the Yankees-Jays series this weekend, Green said.

Have a blast, Chris said.

And they were gone, though I swear Drury gave me the extra-long stink eye.

Shit, shit, shit, I said. There goes New York. They got to be flying the same flight. They just fucking got to be.

Calm down, Chris said. We'll work it out.

Jesus, Chris. You told them we were waiting for a friend. If we show up on the plane too, they're going to get suspicious.

He sat for a moment, rocking on his seat, then said, I got an idea.

We raced to the terminal before the boarding call started. Chris explained to the attendant that I had a disability and needed boarding assistance. I began to sway and twitch like I was mentally retarded. This was something we could all do, when needed, since making fun of retarded people was second nature. But I had never needed to sustain the act under such scrutiny and pressure and for so long a time, and the hilarity of it soon changed to shame and desperation. Our seats were the last two on the airplane, by the bathroom. Chris figured that if we boarded first and deboarded last, the Dartmouth cops would never see us, unless they used the bathroom. Knowing they'd had a few beers beforehand made this all but certain. So we pretended to sleep the whole flight with our jean jackets over our faces. Somehow, lulled by the jet engines and the alcohol in my system, I actually managed to get a few winks.

We had no idea where LaGuardia was, or how it fit in relation to Manhattan. But there were more cabs lined up outside the terminal than I'd ever seen in my entire life. We got in one. The driver was a princely looking Pakistani guy not much older than us with photo booth pictures of his six or seven kids stuck on his dash. Man, you must fuck a lot, Chris said, immediately grooving with the whole New York thing, and the driver laughed and asked, What else when you have no money?

He asked us where we wanted to go. We mentioned Times Square, mostly because it was the one place other than Central

Park either of us had heard of, and we figured sleeping in the park was probably out. The taxi hit the highway hard and got immediately swallowed up by traffic, everyone gunning, surging, stopping, and honking in a clusterfuck of pointless rage.

The driver asked us what hotel and we said we didn't know.

We're in your hands, Chris said.

I got you, the driver said. A very good place.

It was shabby and unremarkable from the outside, but there was a doorman in a red uniform out front and that looked promising. The driver jumped out and spoke to the doorman for a moment. I saw something pass between them, and then he was back to Chris's door, letting him out.

Thank you, my man, Chris said, palming him a fifty.

The doorman took our shitty little bags.

The lobby carpet was worn to the floorboards; the front desk had a Mason jar of plastic flowers.

This is a shithole, I said to Chris.

Who gives a fuck? Chris said. We didn't come here to sleep.

We got our room, two single beds and a coin-operated television, dropped off our stuff, and hit the street again.

What didn't we do? Central Park was a jungle of forest, lake, and boulders with suspicious-looking men in jean shorts offering come-hither glances. We walked all the way down the West Side to the very end of Manhattan, stopping at a half dozen bars along the way. We crossed on the ferry to the Statue of Liberty and climbed into her piss-smelling head. We slept on the ferry back, and only woke up when a heavy-set cop kicked our legs and told us no loitering. We wandered into Lower Manhattan, passed graveyards and old churches, and found Wall Street, which, it turned out, was an actual fucking street, and went on to the World Trade Center towers. We paid for the double elevator ride, and went up first one tower, then the next for two distinctly identical views of Manhattan and the world beyond. Face against the glass, I felt as though I were on the mast of the largest schooner in history, plowing the vast ocean at tremendous speed.

We stared at sex stores and street vendors and sidewalk peddlers. We gawked at high-booted, short-skirted women and enormously Afroed black men. We found ourselves in the general vicinity of the Empire State Building and went up that too. We agreed that the view from this vantage point was somehow more special than the World Trade Center, but conceded the possibility that it was the night sky and all those amazing lights that made the difference. New York looked clean and magical from above. On the street, it was jungle warfare, all leeches and gnats.

But to me, there was something enthralling about it. Gazing down, I realized this is where I wanted to live and die, churned into bits by the discordant, complicated, electron-like hum. I vowed someday I would return, then I actually screamed it into the darkness as I shook the protective cage. I shouted that New York had not seen the last of me. Chris nodded. Yeah, I can see how a guy like you kind of belongs here.

Back near the hotel, Times Square had become a radiance of neon and hookers. We found ourselves in a strip bar where all the women wore cowboy hats. One stood before us with her tray, naked, but for her Texan. Then I noticed something gold and glinting near her vagina, like Frodo's ring.

212

What the fuck is that? I asked.

She told me it was an earring.

An earring for what?

For my clit.

Does it hurt?

She laughed. Not anymore.

Can I touch it?

Sure.

So I reached forward and gave it a little bump with my finger. It was the closest I'd come to a pussy all summer. A wonder my hand didn't explode.

I thanked her and tipped her, and she touched the brim of her hat in acknowledgement and walked off. Moved by some sensory need, I tapped my teeth for signs of life, and they seemed wooden, making me aware of just how exceptionally drunk I'd become. I looked for Chris and realized he was gone. Had he even come to New York? At some point, an old bearded man had sat next to me, looking a bit like Walter Huston in *The Treasure of the Sierra Madre*. I asked him how he was doing. He said he was doing well enough. I could tell he was homeless, or close to it. There was a way he gripped his drink. I bought us both another round the next time cowgirl came by, and asked him if he ever got tired of looking at strippers.

Not yet, he said.

You seen any Dartmouth City cops around town tonight? I asked after another round.

He laughed and muttered something about no cops showing their faces here.

Good, I said. Those Dartmouth ones are motherfuckers.

He pulled something bushy and black out of his jacket pocket. It looked like a rabbit's foot, except nine inches longer.

What you got there? I asked, watching him stroke it.

Squirrel's tail, he said.

I was impressed. It sure as hell was a squirrel's tail. Big, bushy, and black. I wondered, Did squirrels' tails fall off like lizards' tails? Did they shed? Then, blearily, I noticed a red nubby stump at the end of the fur, and a sober understanding came over me.

You ate that, didn't you.

Walter Huston gave a secretive chuckle. Spent the whole day lying on a park bench with a noose and a peanut, pretending to sleep.

A noose and a peanut, huh.

Then I yanked him tight but good.

What'd he taste like? I asked, though I already knew the answer

Chicken, he confirmed.

He asked if I wanted to smoke up with him. I was surprised and touched. We were on the street soon, sparking up.

I couldn't tell if there was actually any hash in the hash, but pretty soon there were three others with us, all women. Then Chris joined. I'd forgotten about him. My cowgirl waitress was with him, in her clothes and out of her hat.

I asked her how work had gone, how long she'd worked there, where she lived, what her name was. She had a squeaky voice and a bit of acne on her nose, and probably was around my age. She was my sweet and grimy princess.

Chris pulled her away and proceeded to talk to her, arm over her head, holding up the alley wall, her giggling, shrugging, nodding, staring up into his eyes with a certain bemused invitation.

You motherfucker, I thought. You move in on anything I even look at.

But it turned out, he'd made a deal for me. And that's how I got laid in New York City.

We had twenty-nine dollars between us when we got back to LaGuardia, and spent it on an I Love NY T-shirt for Susan, a bottle of Tylenol for me, and a pack of Juicy Fruit for Chris, the gum closest to a nutrient-supplying fruit or vegetable. We did not see Dartmouth City cops on the return flight, and I'm not sure they would have recognized us regardless.

That Friday afternoon, Chris strode down the mall corridor and into the bank of our childhood with a large duffle bag. He was wearing a motorcycle helmet, a leather bomber jacket, a pair of acid-washed jeans, and a bright white pair of running shoes. The motorcycle helmet belonged to someone from the shed, left behind because of a sudden downpour and forgotten. Chris snagged it because of the tinted visor. It was not unusual to see someone in a motorcycle helmet walking through the mall. Guys who parked their bikes outside to make a quick purchase did that all the time. The bank was so busy on this Friday that the lineup for the tellers extended twenty feet into the mall, and this made Chris smile as he walked past them. He loved it when an element of planning turned out even better than expected.

He had never felt so calm. He had never felt so strong and sure.

The manager's office was next to the entrance, across the lobby from the tellers. Chris walked in and saw the manager smile, despite his confusion. Chris reached into the duffle bag and pulled out the hand cannon, the rubber-gripped .357 Magnum, kept it low at his side and spoke calmly.

You know why I'm here. Open all the tills.

The manager paused only a moment to hang his head and close his eyes, then rose from his desk and walked into the lobby. In a voice loud enough to be heard by all of them, he told the tellers to open their tills and step back. Chris leaped niftily over the counter. He waved them all farther back with the water cannon and walked past each teller in turn, scooping out the large bills and shoving them into the duffle bag hanging over his shoulder.

It took about sixteen seconds.

Chris walked by the bank manager.

Thank you, he said.

In the corridor, he broke into a run.

I sat in the brand-new black Fiero Chris had leased for the occasion, and waited. I was parked along the side of the woods, on the other side of Somerset, but less than a mile from our own neighbourhood. I was parked downhill, emergency brake on, because it seemed that gravity would give us an advantage that way.

The eternity of waiting diminished my sense of time. I was content to sit in a black Fiero forever.

When the thing, the creature, crashed out of the woods twenty or thirty feet down the hill from the car, I did not know what it was. It flailed and struggled through the thick brush like a sasquatch. The head was enormous and bulbous, and it dragged one leg behind it, a dark stain on the hip. I saw the thing reach up and remove its own head, and there was Chris looking wildly about, wet haired and pink cheeked. He saw me and grinned. All this took less than four seconds. I responded to that grin by popping the car into gear, releasing the emergency brake, and surging forward, stopping curbside next to him. He opened the door, threw the duffle bag in, and hissed, Go.

So go I did.

Our plan had been to hit the highway and disappear into traffic, but there were sirens speeding toward the mall, cutting off our exit. You never quite forget your first siren. The quickest way home was to turn around and head back over Somerset Hill, but I did not want to draw attention to such an odd three-point turn. So I hurtled the car left instead, into the neighbourhood above our old elementary school.

Chris asked me what I was doing. I didn't answer, just set my teeth and shifted into third gear. For once, he did not over-rule me. I suppose there wasn't time.

Sirens below us, too. A major road looped the two largest lakes, Banook and Micmac, and I could tell that police cars were coming up toward the mall from that direction as well. So I turned right on the last street above the school and gunned it. We both knew it was a dead end.

What you got in mind there, pal? Chris asked.

I wasn't sure if I had anything in mind, if there was any mind to it. I did know that we were being pincered from two directions, and probably from a third, and that there was no conventional access road out. Maybe, in retrospect, I'd intended only to park and duck down, pretend it was an empty car, or abandon the car altogether and run. I'm not sure when I remembered, or how I mentally measured the space require-ments, but at some point, some fraction of a second during that drive, I thought of the path up from the highway that we sometimes took as middle school students, when we had, for whatever reason, wanted to avoid the overpass. The path was gravel and steep but it ran directly down onto the highway next to the pillars of the overpass. I could not recall a ditch or any other impediment. I remembered only a smooth transi-tion to blacktop.

This was the path I had walked up the day Dusty broke my arm in a fight.

I did not slow down until the Fiero was on top of the incline. I remember Chris reaching over with his seat belt and punching it into the clasp, then leaning back and bracing him-self with both feet planted on the floor. I tipped the car nose over and felt the tremendous angle threaten to somersault us, but I geared down at the same time, and the tires bit into the gravel. We slid all the way down, fishtailing, swooping, and grinding. I kept us from toppling by twisting the steering wheel this way and that like I was playing an arcade game. We were almost sideways when we reached bottom. We were also facing the right direction. I pulled onto the road and accelerated. It happened so fast, I'm not sure any witnesses would have even believed their eyes.

My expert driving manoeuvre made Chris feel extra satisfied by the entire undertaking, and he suggested we celebrate big time. Instead of counting the loot in a basement or at the shed, we decided to get a suite at the nicest hotel in Halifax, the Sheraton. I was good with this. It seemed right. Something about participating in an active way had changed the game for me a little. I was still ragged and heavy but there was a part of me that had enjoyed myself.

First we had to stop by Chris's house for a new pair of jeans and to return his father's gun. The acid-washed jeans were ripped along the side, and Chris's leg, from hip to mid-thigh, was scraped bad and oozing blood. I was relieved it was only a scrape, having assumed, from the blood stain and the awkward way he stumbled out of the forest, that he had been shot. But no, that wasn't it.

Chris had a bit of wonder in his voice.

I was running faster than I've ever run before, and when I got to the high grass that sinks down the hill before the forest, I just kept going and jumped like I was jumping off a cliff.

I was a little alarmed at the idea that he could be so filled with bliss as to try and fly.

I expected to land on dirt, Chris continued, but there's all kinds of shit down that hill. I think I hit a shopping cart, a concrete block, and a truck tire before I stopped rolling. Not sure how I scraped the thigh. I was so adrenalin-pumped, I didn't even know it happened. I was a little off line and couldn't find the path, so I kind of threw myself into the blueberry bushes and cut straight over. And then—he paused—you'll love this part.

I knew I wouldn't.

When I finally crossed the path, I immediately came across these two kids walking up from the lake.

I felt myself go cold.

What are the odds of that? Chris asked. They must have been swimming, and then they were heading home through the woods. They were barefoot and still dripping. And we just kind of stared at each other for about five seconds, before I crashed through the woods to the street and found you.

Fuck, I said. It was this kind of thing, an impossible-to-predict occurrence, that I knew would be our downfall.

Don't worry, Chris said. I had my helmet on. They didn't see squat.

Never tell a heavy not to worry. Naturally, he'll do nothing but.

Chris paid for the hotel room with cash he pulled out of the duffle bag. This seemed inadvisable to me, but the clerk at the desk acted as though it were done all the time.

The room was a hell of a lot nicer than the dump in New York. Two king-size beds. A desk and a couch and a giant TV. A view out over the city. Some kind of steam shower in addition to a humongous bath. Two toilets, one without a lid, which Chris explained to me was a special washing kind for French people.

I felt an incredible pent-up urge to take a dump, and

announced that the bathroom would soon be uninhabitable. I left the door half open and my grunts and other sound effects actually echoed within. I heard Chris laughing in disgust, and then he tossed something in, like a package of a half dozen bars of soap or some plastique.

At least do something useful while you're in there, he said.

A block of twenties sealed in grey plastic. I leaned over, stretched out, and picked it up. The heft on my bare thighs was remarkable. I had nothing to cut it open with so I gnawed through, like a hyena tearing into the sinews of some carcass. When I finally ripped the plastic, the bills spilled out like cards from a new deck, slippery and distinct. It was the freshest money I had ever handled. I sat for the next half hour and counted, laying the stacks on the floor at my feet.

Eight thousand even, I said when I emerged, my pants still around my ankles.

I'm assuming you washed your hands before counting, Chris said.

Holy shit, I said, seeing more piles of money all around him on the bed.

I just got to ten thousand, he told me. Maybe another thousand still to go in small bills.

I noticed a green Heineken bottle between his knees.

Where'd you get the beer?

Mini-bar, he said. Nothing but imported shit.

I leaned over and pulled out a green bottle.

Grab me a pack of those six-dollar smoked almonds too. I'm feeling flush.

We were drunk without having had much to drink. We'd stacked the bills and divided them accordingly, six thousand for me, the rest for him, and about nine hundred loose bills left for the night. We ordered room service and had surf and turf, though neither of us were big lobster fans. It was, however, the most expensive entree on the menu. We watched TV while we ate. Some pre-Olympic track meet was on, and the announcers were very excited about the one hundred.

I wonder if I started training for real if I could make the Olympics, Chris said.

I snorted.

No, man. I bet I ran as fast as any of these guys today, running across that parking lot.

I could tell he was serious.

Maybe if sirens are going off while you're running, you might not finish dead last.

He threw a lobster tail at me.

We were both bored soon, exhausted, and yet utterly amped.

Problem is, Chris said, I just don't feel like going out.

I seconded that.

He picked up the phone and took the receiver off the cradle.

Let's see if Susan wants to come over and party.

Oh, great, I said.

He called the restaurant where Susan worked. No personal calls were allowed, but he convinced whoever answered that it was a family emergency. A minute later, Susan came on and he told her to calm down, that everything was fine.

I closed my eyes and tried to calm myself down. I listened to Chris telling Susan some bullshit story about how we'd come into money. Some rich family from Saudi Arabia with about thirty people had ordered rickshaw rides for the evening non-stop and then tipped a thousand bucks. Yes, a thousand bucks. And now we were splurging on room service at the Sheraton.

All right, he said. Great. See you around eleven.

He hung up.

She believed that shit? I said.

A woman will believe pretty much anything, he said.

Well, I guess I got until eleven before I find myself a taxi home, huh.

I had been hoping to rage all night, but I was tired enough to go home.

Nah, brother, she's going to bring a friend from work. You might just get lucky or something.

We both fell asleep. When I heard the pounding on the door and the voices outside, my first thought was that the cops had arrived. But then I could tell it was not cops, and I stumbled over and opened the door wearing only my jeans.

Room service, Susan said.

She was wearing her work skirt and the golf shirt that went with it, and plastic flip-flops.

This is Rebecca, she added. We cocktail together.

Rebecca was taller and bigger-haired but dressed the same way.

I can't stay long, Rebecca said.

Chris called them in. I stepped aside, still sleepy but aroused. Rebecca was not my type but how could I complain?

Susan walked by me, surveyed the room, and then slid onto the bed next to Chris, also shirtless, sockless, and tussle-haired.

So what have you two really been up to? she asked.

Just like I told you, baby, Chris said. Arabs and rickshaws. I'm a Ben-Hur motherfucker.

The girls were hungry so we ordered nachos and chicken wings, just before the kitchen closed. We also asked for two bottles of champagne.

Saudi guy insisted we get champagne, Chris said.

I think I need a Saudi guy, Susan said.

Sheik Abdullah at your service, Chris said.

He offers very special magic carpet ride, I added.

By the time the food arrived, we were all sitting on beds, Rebecca on the edge of mine, which I took as a sign that she could barely control her lust for me.

We had a weird energy going on, as a group. Susan was more sarcastic and critical than normal, but also flirty and awkward. At one point, she picked up a chicken wing and drew on Chris's chest with the barbecue sauce. He told her to fuck off, so she hopped off the bed and drew on my chest too. I did not protest as much, though the odd-shaped appendage was a creepy, if not stomach-turning, pen. Rebecca put her feet up and mentioned her sore legs, so soon I was massaging her calves. Then she flipped over and I was massaging her shoulders and lower back, and I had a full and upright erection poking through my jeans, clearly visible to Susan and Chris, but they made nothing of it, just watched us as we all continued to converse.

Wait, Susan said.

Wait what? Chris said.

Isn't this the hotel with the indoor-outdoor pool? she asked.

Chris picked out one of the brochures from the fancy leather folder and said, Yeah, the one and only.

I want to try it, Susan said. She told Rebecca how cool it was. You can swim indoors, but if you want to go outside, you swim under a barrier, and you're on the roof so the view is amazing.

One problem, I pointed out. I don't think any of us have any swimsuits.

Ain't anyone swimming right now anyway, Chris said. Pool's got to be closed.

So let's go! Susan said.

I don't think so, Chris said.

Why not? Susan hit him on the chest.

I fell today and scraped the shit out of my thigh.

Where? Susan asked.

On the concrete sidewalk.

I mean where on your thigh. Not too high, I hope. She started to undo his button fly.

Chris stopped her. Last I knew you weren't a nurse.

Oh, you want your mother or something?

Jesus, why don't you go swimming?

He was joking, I think, but it sounded a bit harsh.

I'm up for investigating the situation, I said.

For once, I was more sober than Chris. That explains my cunning.

So Susan, Rebecca, and I headed out for the pool. We left Chris with the remote control, flipping channels.

The hotel was utterly silent, except for our hushes and giggles. The elevator opened up, and although the room was dark, we could smell pool and see the filtered green light of the water, glowing. We stood on the deck and Susan pointed out how the edge of the pool was blocked by a window, but if you swam below the window, you were outside.

So who's going to swim? she asked.

I don't think so, Rebecca said. No suit.

What's the difference between bra and panties and a bikini? Susan asked.

Rebecca shrugged.

Suit yourself, Susan said, and she pulled off her shirt, winnowed out of her skirt, and stepped into the water like Aphrodite returning to the surf.

I eyed Rebecca and encouraged her to do the same.

I can't, she said.

Someone better come in, Susan said, treading water.

I pulled off my shirt and dropped my jeans. I wanted to cannonball but refrained, and merely jumped feet first.

It's nice and warm, I said.

Susan turned around, and with two dolphin kicks, she was under. I saw her faint undulating form swimming away, toward the glass wall, and shimmering under it, as though she had passed into a dream.

I'm going back down, Rebecca said.

Whatever, I thought, and followed Susan under the water.

When I emerged on the other side, I could not find Susan at first. The water was flat and undisturbed. I felt some alarm, as though I had indeed been chasing a dream. Then I saw that she was out of the water and perched on the roof ledge, knees hugged into her chest. She was looking out at the harbour.

I swam close to her and hooked my chin on the edge of the pool, then floated with my arms and legs free, as nonchalantly as I could manage.

Nice view? I asked.

There was a full moon that night, or nearly full. It cascaded upon the harbour and us. Susan was wearing a black bra and red panties, and the moonlight on her skin made her the most beautiful sight I'd ever witnessed.

You still hate me? she asked.

I blew at the water like a horse. The noise seemed inappropriate, like making a rude sound in church.

I did not know what she was talking about—what hatred, from when, or how it had transpired. I only knew the answer.

No, I said.

I would have climbed out of the pool but my ginch was sloshy with water.

It's beautiful out there, I said.

I'd like to leave, she said.

I did not know how to answer. I loved Halifax. But I would have left in a second for her.

Where to? I asked.

She shrugged. Somewhere else. Maybe Vancouver. Maybe Japan.

Once you finish school?

I suppose.

What about Chris? I asked.

How could I not? I realized she was crying.

The city gave up strangely distant noises from below, and there was a smell in the air that could have been rain.

What's wrong? I asked in a softer voice. I should have climbed up beside her. But she had folded up into a tightness of bent neck and arms and legs.

Nothing, she said. And she wiped tears and smiled quickly at me and looked back out on the harbour.

So I said nothing back.

Rebecca must have taken my room key, because it wasn't in my jeans pocket. We knocked on the door of the room and it was strangely silent inside. It became uncomfortable, because I knew what must be going on. I wondered if I should steer Susan to the ice machine or onto the street for coffee or some other ridiculous place, just to give Chris time to escape from his latest predicament unscathed.

Then the door opened, and Rebecca stood there, her big hair even more messy than before, but a sleepy expression on her face.

Sorry, she said, and added, Chris is totally conked.

We went in. It seemed true, to my relief. Chris was twisted on the bed, his head tipped awkwardly back on a pillow, his jaw hanging open, his hand dangling off the bed. I had hoped that this once he would be caught. He got away with everything. And Susan, like his parents, like his teachers, like his police friends, suspected nothing.

Can I stay here? Rebecca asked. I'm too tired to go home.

Susan walked by without answering.

Of course, I said. It's a king-size bed. Plenty of room. I meant it. Innocently even.

We took turns using the bathroom. I was last. My underwear was soaked. I saw Susan's soaked underwear hanging over the bathtub faucet. I took off my jeans and wrapped a towel around my waist, left my shirt on. There were two hotel toothbrushes, both opened from their plastic seals. I did not want to use one that Chris had used, so I took a chance and used the one that seemed most recently wet. I brushed and urinated and looked at my face in the brightly lit mirror, and did not recognize or like what I saw. Then I turned out the bathroom light and went back into the room to go to bed.

The lights in the room were off too, and it was pitch-black. I stumbled, swore, heard rustling, found a bed, climbed onto it, then under the sheets. There was plenty of room. The towel was rough against my skin and I tugged it off.

I stuck to my side of the bed. Rebecca was on the side closest to the middle of the room, as near to her protector, Susan, as possible.

I think I fell asleep. But I'm not sure if it was for ten seconds or an hour. I felt beneath the sheet a touch on my leg. Just a toe or a heel. The touch stayed. I could sense the warmth of a body. I became as erect as I had ever been. But I didn't dare move or even breathe.

I opened my eyes and stared into the darkness. The blackness was gone. The room was flooded with the pale light of the full moon outside. It must have manoeuvred its way into our portal, on the ship we sailed across the sea.

I could make out Rebecca's head on the pillow next to mine, and the line of her shoulder. I felt her hand reach back, blindly, and touch my stomach. My entire body jerked with the shock.

Then nothing. So I waited, barely breathing, my heart thundering in my chest.

Finally, unable to stand it any longer, I slid closer and spooned Rebecca from behind.

I was not wrong to do so. I felt her back press into my front. Her hand pulled my hand onto her breast beneath her shirt. I felt her large nipple. She bent her head away from me and exposed the nape of her neck. I knew I was meant to bite there. So I did, as quietly as I could, and Rebecca responded as quietly as she could. We did not even rustle the sheets.

But when I opened my eyes, I saw that Susan, lying on her side on the bed opposite, was watching. With the moon, her face was as clear to me as if the light was on. The only thing that made it difficult to see her was the way she had huddled into the sheet. She was tucked into it, from the chin down, and her large eyes were unblinking.

I stopped nibbling on Rebecca's neck and stared back. Susan did not move. She was so still that I wondered if she slept that way, eyes open, like some kind of vampire. I would have stopped if I could. When doing illicit things, you always stopped and backed away when you were caught. But Rebecca had not stopped. I closed my eyes without meaning to and felt the sweat on her back and below her arms and the tightness of her neck.

It became ridiculous, and I pulled Rebecca onto her back and entered her from above. Though we remained silent, we did what we did as though we were alone.

I woke up to a shitstorm, and while it was impossible to pretend I was asleep, it was also impossible to extract myself from the twisted covers. Susan stood in front of the bed with a breakfast plate in her hand. She was wearing panties but no bra, and her tits, finally revealed to me, were even more beautiful and perky than I had ever imagined. Chris sat up in bed, a breakfast plate in his lap. I saw a trolley with more breakfast dishes and shiny covered plates in between the beds. I did not see Rebecca. I wasn't quite sure how I could have slept through the arrival of such an enormous breakfast, or the departure of Rebecca, but I certainly could not have slept through Susan's screaming.

I want you to tell me the fucking truth, she said. She was kicking something with her foot, and I heard the rustle of newspaper. Don't give me this Saudi prince shit! Acid-washed-jeans-wearing motherfucker!

You think I robbed a fucking bank? Chris said, his voice calm but beginning to rise in volume, a growing wrath I'd rarely seen. Think about what you're saying. You don't want what I give you, why don't you stop fucking taking it!

Then fucking take it back!

And she threw the breakfast plate at his head. He flung himself out of the way, none too gracefully, the plate on his lap flipping off the bed, his torso caught up in the sheets as he fell off, and he thumped to the floor with one leg still entangled. But at least he'd avoided the heavy porcelain, so sturdy that it did not even smash when it thudded into the wall. The contents slid down the wallpaper in a slow spreading smear.

I expected to be next, once her wild eyes locked on mine, but she turned her back instead, and pulled her skirt on over her head, something I'd never seen done before and never imagined possible. Next her bra and shirt and then she scrambled around on all fours to look for her flip-flops.

And why don't you guys just fuck each other and let me know how it is!

And with that, and a horrific door slam, she was gone.

I waited for some sign that it was safe to speak, and when no sign came, I slowly sat up in bed. I looked around. I was naked and the sheets had bundled together at my groin. I could see Chris now, still lying on the floor with one leg tangled up in the bedclothes. He looked back at me, then picked up a piece of bacon from his chest and took a bite.

Holy fuck, she can get dramatic, he said.

I swung my legs off the bed and tried to get my bearings. Chris tugged himself loose of the sheet and crawled around to the foot of the bed. I heard more rustling of paper and he stood up, naked, a newspaper clenched in his fists. He scanned each page in turn, throwing them aside when he'd finished.

You want a coffee? he asked as he continued to flip pages. There's a pot there, unless the fucking she-demon knocked it over.

I found the pot on the trolley, and a mug that was under the TV stand. I poured a cup. My hand was shaking.

Here it is, Chris finally announced. He read silently for a moment, then he crumpled the paper up and chucked it away.

Jesus Christ, I am not fucking lanky.

I retrieved the newspaper ball, smoothed it out, and began to read, my heart thumping madly.

I read about the robbery of the Penhorn Mall branch of the Canadian Imperial Bank of Commerce. I read about a lone male still at large, armed and considered dangerous. I read that no one was injured. I read that officers had arrived at the scene within minutes, and then spent the rest of the afternoon and evening with a tracking dog. I read the word *lanky*. Police described the man they were seeking as white, about six feet two inches in height, lanky in build, clean-shaven, with short blond hair, between twenty and forty years of age, wearing acid-washed jeans, a brown leather jacket, and a black and silver motorcycle helmet with a black visor. Police were not releasing details on the amount of money taken but said none of the money had yet been recovered.

Susan thought it was you because you wear acid-washed jeans? I asked.

Yeah, he said from the bathroom. What kind of bullshit is that?

The injustice of it.

Were you chased? I asked.

I heard a flush. No, that's fucking bullshit too.

He emerged, face washed, scrambled egg picked from his chest. He put on his shirt.

I lowered the newspaper to my lap and lay back down, paralyzed.

Come on. Get up, he said. I'm sick of this shit. I can't get the smell of scrambled egg out of my nostrils. And I can't even flush the toilet from the dump I just took. I practically had to beat the thing back with my shoe just to get out of there alive.

So I rose, as bidden, to get dressed.

Lanky, Chris said. Fucking chiselled god is more like it.

At the front desk, we turned in the keys. Asked if there were any additional incidentals beyond the room service to charge to the room, Chris said, Yeah, the mini-bar. The desk clerk said, What items did you have from the mini-bar? And Chris said, All of them. So we added those in too, and did not cop to the Led Zeppelin–like condition of the dishes and walls, not to mention the unholy terror Chris had left in the toilet. It seemed, all things considered, that we were being unusually honest and more than fair.

In the Fiero, I asked him once again about Susan.

You think she'll tell anyone?

Tell what?

What we did.

No. I'll convince her she's crazy when I talk to her later, and I'll act all pissed off for a day or two and then everything will be all right again.

If you say so.

And then, my next area of concern.

What was Susan so mad at me for? I asked.

What do you mean? He was impatient with my question, still irritated and grumpy.

You know, the shit she said about us fucking each other. What was up with that?

I could not stop thinking about Susan watching me when I was having sex with Rebecca. Had I misunderstood her stare?

Oh, that. He laughed, still grim, but more amused suddenly. That was just a bad strategic move on my part.

I asked what he meant.

Thank you for using the 3M Self CheckOut

Title: Killer/ Jonathan Kellerman.
ID: 31812039883849
Due: 03-05-14

Title: Robert B. Parker's Bull River / Robert
Knott.
ID: 31812049680169
Due: 03-05-14

Title: Flagged victor : a novel / Keith Hollihan
ID: 31812049340491
Due: 03-05-14

Total items: 3
2/12/2014 1:14 PM
Checked out: 3
Overdue: 0
Hold requests: 0
Ready for pickup: 0

Automated Phone Renewal (412)622-1895

It's personal, he said.

Fuck that, I replied. What is it?

You really need to know?

I really need to know.

Jeez. Okay. Well. Susan and I have had the occasional conversation about her interest in girls.

I hesitated, then asked for more detail.

She did a little experimenting in her youth.

Her youth?

When she was fourteen or fifteen or something.

What kind of experimenting?

With a couple other girls.

Experimenting what?

They were playing the doctor thing.

The doctor thing.

And it went a little further than anyone expected.

Further like how?

Like pussy licking far.

I blinked stars from my eyes.

So naturally, Chris continued, when she told me about that particular series of youthful incidents, I've brought up the idea a few hundred times since.

The idea?

The obvious logical extension.

Of her having sex with a woman?

Yeah, but like with me.

A threesome.

Three's a good number. Four. I like all kinds of numbers.

Holy shit, I said.

Yeah, he agreed, I could pretty much die fulfilled after that.

A long pause while we contemplated our own individual agony. Then I forced a point of clarification.

But you were talking about you, Susan, and other girls, right? You weren't talking about anything to do with me.

He grimaced. Fuck. Just when I was getting the smell of scrambled eggs out of my nose, you make me feel all sick again.

Well, what the fuck did she mean when she said we should go fuck ourselves?

Don't worry about it.

I'm going to worry about it until you tell me why.

Jesus, fine. He winced. This morning, I suggested Rebecca as a candidate. She's always saying how cute Rebecca is, and how nice her breasts are, that kind of shit.

Oh, I said, and remembered the stare. Had that been its reason? A chance to imagine the threesome?

Is that why Rebecca left? I asked.

No. I didn't suggest it while she was there. I was a total gentleman about it. I suggested it when she'd left.

But when I was there?

You were asleep.

And what did Susan say?

She blew me. So I have to assume the idea was not unappealing.

When I was there?

Like I said. You were asleep. Is there an echo in here?

But—

Chris interrupted. I actually could use some quiet time for a bit, he said. I'm a little wiped out.

So I stopped talking and let Chris drive. I was hungover, exhausted, sick to my stomach about the newspaper, and somewhere, in a place of far less prominence than it deserved, satisfied about the sex I'd had with Rebecca last night.

Fucking lanky, Chris said, as if to himself. I got to get to the gym.

6

And now begins the sad and weepy part of my tale.

Chris was right. Susan was back on board within days, as though nothing had ever happened. I had no idea what she suspected, whether her concerns were mollified or merely repressed, or whether part of her liked the ambiguity. Either way, Chris could care less. For her birthday a week later, he gave her a card with five C-notes inside.

I told her I'd saved it up all summer, he said. She kissed me like I'd just donated my kidney to her dog. I guess she enjoys the fruits of my labour just fine.

For me, on the other hand, matters took a bad turn.

The day my parents returned from their vacation in Maine, I realized that I'd forgotten to register for classes in the fall.

It was a bad moment. I had not thought of school all summer, but I'd always taken it for granted that I'd be attending in September. The deadline passed on the Friday Chris and I robbed the bank. I called the registrar's office as soon as I'd realized my mistake, but they offered me no reprieve. I made an appointment to see the registrar that week, and when I arrived, early for once, and dressed as properly as I knew how, carrying the goddamn course calendar and a copy of *Humboldt's Gift*, the registrar was unmoved by my pleas. He was a balding, infinitely patient man, Yoda-like in his bemusement, and he offered that perhaps I had not been as ready to return to school as I believed myself to be.

But then, he admitted, I'm a Freudian.

In any event, a single semester wouldn't kill me. Perhaps I would be more focused when I returned.

As for the killing part, he didn't know my father.

There are some events that do you in. They take away your nerve, your stomach for adventure. They exile you from your future. Looking back on it now, if only I'd had more courage, everything might have turned out differently.

I told my parents of my error. I did not have it in me to concoct a story. Not enough fight remained. My father knew that it was rickshaw, and my debauched and wayward summer, that had been my demise. We all knew it would never be allowed to happen again.

I should have thought about Rivers and his offer to join him in Thailand. If only I had kept my head when I forgot to register for school, forcefully denied that rickshaw or laziness or poor character was at fault, and made a convincing argument for apprenticing with Rivers instead, I might have saved the day. But I lacked the stuffing. Like any heavy, I accepted my punishment before I had even been tried and convicted.

This meant I would go back to work at the bank.

The last few weeks of summer, I did not even have the heart to work rickshaw. I visited the shed once in a blue moon and I paid my rental fees promptly, but there was no life for me there anymore. I was like a football player on injured reserve. Hanging around, I was just bringing the other guys down, taking their mind off more important matters such as drinking beer and getting laid. Even when the busker festival came to town, and a colourful circus of flame-eaters, jugglers, contortionists, banjo players, and scam artists filled our streets, I could not be bothered to watch. I was a beaten man.

I called Rivers and told him I couldn't pull off the trip—because rickshaw work had not paid out like I'd expected. He was understanding. Don't put too much pressure on yourself, he said. Enjoy school. If you let things weigh you down too much, you won't make it to forty.

Rivers himself sounded light, cheerful, and full of bravado. He told me that his book had been given starred reviews in both *Publishers Weekly* and *Kirkus,* a rare event, and that the publishers were on fire for it and getting ready to make him a writing star.

Meanwhile, he said, I'll be on the other side of the world writing my next book. The one that's really going to blow them away.

I wished him well, and said I hoped I'd make it over sometime. He wished me well, and said goodbye. A week later, a brown envelope showed up in the mailbox, addressed to me. I opened it up, and a thin copy of Conrad's *Lord Jim* spilled out. Inside, Rivers had scrawled a note: *Essential reading for every writer setting out on a journey.*

I put the book on a shelf in my room, and there it sat, accusing me from its perch.

Of course, Chris had forgotten to register for school too. But for a person of lightness, this was not the end of the world—it was actually kind of hilarious.

My second day at the bank, the week I should have been back at school, Chris walked in. I was working behind the counter as a clerk and my first thought was: He's here to rob the place. I watched him warily, wondering whether he might, at some opportune moment, lift a hand cannon into the air and fire to get our attention.

Instead, he politely let others in line go ahead of him until my counter opened up, then he stepped forward and laid a pile of cash in front of me.

What's this? I asked.

I'd like to open an account, he said with a grin.

I hated him for that.

My manager needed to assist me. I was forced to count each bill in turn, and when I had added them all up and announced the sum, Chris told me I was wrong.

No, man, there's got to be sixty more dollars in there. I'm sure of it.

And my hatred for Chris grew.

I felt my manager's disapproval at my curt and impatient manner. But when I had slapped each bill and finally came to the end again, we all saw that Chris was right. I had been exactly $60.00 short of the sum of $3,280.00.

The manager kept an eye on my incompetence ever after.

Chris was waiting outside the bank when I finished that afternoon, sitting on a new motorcycle. He tossed me a helmet.

Come on, man, let's go get a beer.

I put the helmet on and hopped on the back. There's nothing so unmanly as hugging another man from behind on the back of a motorcycle. You might as well give him a reach-around.

The bar faced the harbour, with outdoor seating, and if you didn't mind the seagull squawks and the seagull shit and the putrid seaweed smell, it was pleasant.

Chris told me he was sorry to give me a shock at the bank. It was just a little joke.

You're really funny, I said, then added, I'm stunned you're putting stolen bank money back into a bank.

Who's going to know where it came from? he asked.

He had a point, but I did not feel like acknowledging that.

Besides, he continued, I put most of it back into the CIBC at the mall.

These words, and the audacity they indicated, could have turned me to stone.

You're shitting me, I said.

I put about eight thousand back in the CIBC, in my old account. He grinned.

When did you do this?

About three days after the job. People in line were talking about the robbery.

My jaw dropped.

It was like John Dillinger had been there. You'd think I'd rappelled from the ceiling in a ninja outfit and strafed machine-gun bullets around the room.

Our wings came, and our nachos. I had no stomach for them.

I did figure out the whole lanky business, though, Chris said.

The lanky business?

You know, the part where they described me in the newspaper as lanky.

How did you figure it out?

I asked Dad about eyewitness testimony, whether it's reliable, and he said it's a well-known if little-divulged fact that eyewitnesses are worse than useless. They never give a reliable report of a crime. The only reason it's not common knowledge is that the police don't want defence lawyers to know.

Why?

Because then every goddamn lawyer would have eyewitness testimony stricken.

The waitress was hovering, smiling a shy smile, like she wanted Chris's autograph.

Chris asked her what was up. She asked whether he owned the motorcycle, and wondered whether he'd mind moving it farther from the door for fire code reasons.

Oh, sure, he said enthusiastically, and didn't move. We watched her ass as she walked away.

How did you go about asking your dad a question like that?

I told him I was studying for my police academy application.

I was struck, for the thousandth time, by the difference between us. My lies so heavy, his offered up with ease.

In other words, Chris said, there's no way we can get caught.

We watched a pair of seagulls fighting over a french fry, squawking and flapping. Chris kicked a plastic beer cup toward them.

I heard the tellers were kind of shaken up, though, he said. A few of them were given a week off and therapy to get over the trauma.

To emphasize the word *trauma,* he made air quotes with his fingers.

That sucks, I said.

Yeah, and it's bullshit, too, Chris said. I was the most polite and considerate bank robber they'll ever encounter.

I did not know what to say.

You're bringing me down here, Chris said.

I apologized, and said I had a cold.

Yeah, I'm cold too, he said. Been thinking about going to Australia.

Australia? I was stunned again.

My grandfather is there. And a couple cousins. I barely know any of them.

Why did your grandfather move to Australia?

A shrug. Hated my grandmother, I guess.

Maybe he was a convict, I said.

That's not funny, Chris said. Anyway, since school is fucked this year and rickshaw is almost done, I'm thinking: Why not?

Why not? Rivers wants me to go to Thailand to hang out with him while he writes.

Why don't you?

How could I explain to Chris the meaning of weight?

Not enough cash, I said.

Yeah, I need more too, he said.

And in the pit of my stomach, the beast gave a kick.

It's almost three large for a ticket to Australia, and we burned through the last pile so fast. I've been thinking it's time for a bigger job, something that will tide us over for an extended period.

What kind of job? I asked.

Something significant. A Brinks truck should do the trick.

I closed my eyes and wished the whole world would disintegrate.

Would they have more cash than a bank? I asked, trying to steady myself.

Usually, he said. At the CIBC, I just went after the tellers. Kind of loose cash. But the Brinks guys are delivering for the safe. I'm guessing a drop-off might be ten times what we got last time.

Two hundred thousand?

Maybe you could reconnaissance the facts and get a round estimate.

Don't those Brinks guys carry guns? I asked.

Indeed, they do, Chris said. But they're rent-a-cops. No different than mall security.

But guns, I insisted.

Yeah, he said. You'd have to neutralize them pretty quick.

What do you mean neutralize? You mean take away their guns?

I don't know. I'm still working on it.

The waitress returned. She did not mention the motorcycle parking job. Instead, she offered to replenish our beers. I said that I needed to split. Chris said that he was taking Susan out for dinner. He needed to break the Australia idea to her over an expensive night out.

How soon do you think you'll go? I asked.

Soon as we can get the money, he said.

I took the ferry home, then the bus after that. It dropped me off on the main road, and I descended on foot into our neighbourhood as the Indian summer sun was setting. By the time I reached home, I had a plan.

I visited a travel agency on my lunch break the next day and bought Chris a ticket to Australia. It cost me over five thousand dollars. It would have been less, but I chose a departure date that was only a week away. I figured not even Chris could get his shit together in that amount of time to pull off a Brinks job.

When we went out, that Friday night, I waited until we had had a few beers, then I slid the envelope across the table to him.

He looked inside. He looked up. He looked back inside.

I told him it was a gift. I was just going to piss away the money anyway. Why not put it to some good purpose, like him seeing his grandfather one last time?

Chris was more touched than I ever would have imagined, and he asked me, before the end of the night, to watch over Susan while he was gone.

I know you two don't always get along, but I'd feel better knowing you were checking in on her.

I promised that I would.

It's difficult to describe the emptiness of the world with Chris gone. My bearings were off. There was a little uncertainty in my step. I felt as though I'd woken from a long illness and was only starting to make my way around again, putting my life back into place, readjusting my understanding of what was normal. Even the weather seemed to struggle to know what to do with itself.

As soon as the rickshaw season ended, the rains started, grey, listless, chilling days of endless drizzle. I wore sweaters and fought a cold. It was difficult to make it through a mere eight-hour workday and have any energy left over. Once, we'd casually and thoughtlessly packed a week's worth of life into every single day and drop-kicked every night.

The bank was a suitable place to spend such muted time, sedate, orderly, rule-bound, requiring the maximum amount of the minimum of my attention. I felt like Kafka as if he'd never written and stuck to clerking instead. At lunchtime, I left the bank and sat in my car—the black Fiero Chris had left for my use even as he kept up the lease payments—and read. But I did not read the difficult works. I read for escape. Books like *Lord Jim* were rebukes I couldn't handle.

Above everything else, I missed a good laugh. I had not suspected until then how essential our shared sense of humour had been to our friendship, how intensely freeing and light this immaturity was, and how little there was to enjoy when he was gone. I thought of him in the past tense, and while I missed him terribly, I was also relieved he was out of my life.

I did, however, get the occasional postcard. A beach shot with two bikini-clad women from Sydney, both wearing baseball caps that said Sheila. A *Close Encounters of the Third Kind*–shaped mountain from a place called Alice Springs. A koala bear, slant-eyed and pleasure-stricken, holding a beer can in two sloth-like paws, as though it were masturbating with a slow languor. I did not know where to send a note to Chris, so I did not write him back. I'd planned, at one point, to write an ongoing letter and to send it to him once I did get an address. I didn't bother to start because I had nothing to write about, and because our friendship had become dangerous to my health and well-being. If I could, I would have been the one to choose exile. I wanted to be forgotten.

Chris wrote in surprisingly precise, small print. On one of those postcards, maybe the koala bear, he asked how Susan was doing. He had not heard from her and missed her. Then he mentioned that the local girls were very accommodating to the needs of a foreign tourist. He said that Australia was just like Canada, except the beer was better, there was sand instead of snow, and everyone banged everyone all the time. Then, in even smaller print, he asked me again to check in on Susan, and to see if she needed anything.

I called her on a Tuesday evening, and we agreed to meet for drinks on Friday afternoon, when her classes were over. The sky had broken open and spilled a bit more Indian summer on us all. It did me good to drive into the city, in the black Fiero, wearing Chris's sunglasses, the ones he'd bought with the proceeds of our first robbery and forgotten on the dash when I dropped him off at the airport.

Susan wore jeans and a tight T-shirt and pink sneakers, and she looked to me like a vision of freshman purity. I'd forgotten her caramel skin, and the way her hair looked when it was pulled back from her face. She greeted me with the exuberance of a child, jumping up and down in place a little, rising up to hug me hard, holding onto my neck, breathing into my chest, releasing, beaming up at me.

You bastard, she said. Am I not allowed to see you or something when Chris is gone?

We sat down at the table. I was confused and muttered something about the phone system working two ways, but I suspected she was right. Some barrier I'd set up, a kind of tension or force field, had prevented contact between us.

We had snacks and a pitcher of Long Island iced tea (it seemed like a dangerous drink to start an afternoon off with) and talked about the end of her summer and the beginning of her school year. She was angry with me and Chris. She called us idiots for not registering in her first year. It would have been so much fun to be together. At least Chris had a reason—he had planned this trip to see his grandfather for years—but what was my excuse for not being at school? She had so much energy it was pleasurable to be with her in the moment, but it also had an unsettling effect on my sense of reality. She was rewriting history as we talked, as though, in her mind, Chris had indeed saved his pennies from years of part-time jobs to take this trip, as if the Sheraton had never happened, as if she'd never stood in her panties, braless, and thrown a plate of scrambled eggs at Chris's head, as if I'd never fucked her friend in the bed beside her. She had the air of a person who'd entered recovery and chosen to believe in a different world.

When the pitcher was finished and the waitress was going off shift, I asked Susan if I could drive her home. She glared at me across the table and said, You're not getting rid of me that easily. So we left the bar and went out to dinner instead. The nicest steak restaurant we knew. It felt good to spend money again.

I asked her how she was enjoying university. She told me it

was the best thing that had ever happened to her, and that she felt free for the first time in her life. I asked her what English courses she was taking, and made a comment that it was too bad Rivers was on sabbatical, and that I wished I'd gone with him. She stopped chewing and looked at me.

Leah did.

Leah did what? I asked.

Leah went with him. That's the rumour, anyway. Can you believe her?

I tried to think that through. Leah went with Rivers to Thailand? Did that mean she was apprenticing for him, or was she something more?

Wow, I said.

No kidding, she said.

For some reason, this news sobered me up and pricked a dormant determination to write. I had the feeling that I had been lulled into sheep-like compliance while revolutionaries were being lined up against walls before firing squads.

So, Susan said, are you going to tell me the truth?

I wondered which truth, of the many dozen possible versions, she was referring to, and carefully asked her to be more specific.

About what Chris is up to.

I realized she must be talking about the bank robberies and collected my meagre mental and spiritual resources to tell a lie.

Susan interrupted my confession before I began.

Does he really have a grandfather in Australia?

It took me a moment to recover. A grandfather. I forced a laugh. As far as I know, I said. And then, just because Judas would, I allowed for a shadow of doubt. But you know Chris.

She grimaced, and that sour face was her admission. She did know Chris.

So what's he really doing over there? she asked. And when I looked blank: Let's keep it simple so you don't have to lie. What's he *doing* on an average day? Is he working? Is he suntanning? Is he fucking everything that moves?

He told me he's written you about five letters. You probably know more than me, I complained.

Yes, but he doesn't *tell* me anything, she said. He tells me so much that I learn nothing.

It was an old technique of the compulsive liar. Cover up whatever you are doing or have done with a storm of plausible and entertaining details.

I bet he is fucking everything that moves, she repeated.

You cannot hear a woman use the word *fucking* thus, and feel unstirred.

Chris? I asked, as if we were talking about the pope.

Yes, Chris. Fucking everything that moves.

I doubt it.

What's to stop him?

You.

I'm ten thousand miles away.

I mean, he wouldn't want to cheat on you, even over there. He wouldn't want to jeopardize what you have.

Had I ever spoken a larger lie? Or was there some truth in there also? I could no longer tell the difference.

You wouldn't tell me even if you knew, she said. You're thick as thieves.

And we both knew that was true.

Is he ever coming back?

I shrugged, the most honest answer I'd given all night. I didn't know. I wasn't sure. I had a bad feeling either way.

She began to cry. She went weepy, as drunk girls often do. She drew attention to herself with her tears. I'm sure the other diners and the uncomfortable waiter and the glaring female bartender assumed that this was our high-priced, low-class breakup meal. Naturally, I was the perpetrator because I remained stony-faced and was eager to hush her up.

Do you want to go someplace else? I asked.

Yes, she answered in between sniffles.

We ended up at the Sheraton. We had more drinks at the bar. Both of us missed Chris badly, and it seemed that by sharing more time together, we were resurrecting his presence. The decision to get a room seemed, even to me, to be a chaste one. It was for sleep, not sex—the sleep of consolation and loneliness and a desire to escape from the false and strained and, yes, fucking drab lives we were both leading absent Chris's magic spell. So we lay together on the bed, in our clothes. I allowed myself the taking off of my socks. Her eyes closed tightly, as if she were trying to squeeze out the memory of a nightmare. She was very drunk. I kissed her forehead and her nose, and brushed her hair, and listened to her breathing.

If I knew Chris was never coming back, we could be together, she said.

I did not say anything. What lies could I offer? What comfort?

By the time I'd worked my mental gymnastics to a suitable conclusion, I realized she was asleep.

That fall, Rivers's book hit the shelves, and hit them hard. I could not help but see it whenever I went into a bookstore. Have you ever known someone famous before they were famous? So this is what it looks like, I thought.

I did not buy his book. I could not read it.

Was I proud? Was I bitter or envious? Was I numb?

I was all of these things, in complicated proportions, at various times and moods. But I wish that I'd wished my friend luck more wholeheartedly before his luck arrived. I wished that I felt lighter about his success and less anxious about my own floundering future.

I finally got a letter from him in mid-October. It was sent from Thailand. Inside was a yellowed piece of newsprint, torn from the *New York Times*. On a second sheet of paper, in marker, Rivers had scrawled his note to me: NYT review. Complete bullshit. Complete misunderstanding of my work. Interview all lies. Never said any of it.

Then: Leah says hi.

Why had he sent it to me? I wondered. The review was harsh, the interview harsher. It called Rivers an overhyped, blustery talent whose claims for greatness were only surpassed by his talent for profanity and his derision of other authors more noteworthy than himself. The tone was bemused and insular. I felt for him, a flush of shame in my face, an ache of anger in my belly.

I wrote him back. I used as much profanity as possible to press my solidarity with him. I talked about Nietzsche and high crimes and morality sailing, and I told him it would all be worth it when they wrote about him again, years from now, and called him truly great.

I feared that this review would knock him down, alter the trajectory of his career. My fears were realized. His book seemed to falter afterwards. The tone of the *New York Times* review crept into every later review. Soon, the copies in stores were no longer stacked in piles, and became reduced to a few, spine out, stuck on back shelves.

I did not hear back from Rivers right away, and when another letter came, at the end of November, it was written by Leah.

She went on at length about her arrival in Thailand, the confusion of Bangkok, the change in climate and diet, the monsoon that had gotten them stuck for weeks halfway to the islands. They'd settled on Koh Atsui, which was sufficiently infrastructured to provide the necessities, but not too overrun by tourists.

I have to say, she wrote, I love it here. I love the gentle culture, and the gentle pace, and the gentle warmth, and the surprising moments of everyday beauty.

And then, without warning, she told me what had happened to Rivers.

He met a friend, she wrote, an Australian named Mike, who was a brilliant poet, and they made a habit every week of visiting a bar on the other side of the island. You know how important conversations are to Delmore. They always rode on Mike's motorcycle, Delmore on the back. Neither wore a helmet. It was not always possible to see the road, especially in the dark and unlit central part of the island, and they must have struck a fallen tree. Mike was killed. Delmore survived.

She told me the grim details. He was recovering in the hospital in the main town on Koh Atsui. She'd begged him to allow her to transfer him home or at least to Bangkok, but he insisted there was no point. The injuries to his chest healed better than expected, but his left arm, crushed and dragged along the road, became infected and had been amputated a week ago.

He's very depressed, she wrote. It's understandable. I feel like I've aged twenty years in the last month. I'm living like a nurse. I look after him every day. He hates being an invalid confined to bed, and he hates needing me, and he hates himself most of all. I'm afraid of what he will do. Your letters would be very meaningful to him. Please keep writing them. I wish you were here to spell me. I've told him that I'm telling you what happened so you don't need to pretend not to know.

I could see Rivers lying on his back in the open hospital ward. I could smell the mix of smells around him, burnt sand, rotting garbage, coconut milk in rice, antiseptic gauze. The palm leaves outside the veranda were so crisp and dry they looked inauthentic. The ward itself was cool and pleasant. The concrete floors were splashed every few hours with a bucket of water, and this simple, casual, almost indifferent act seemed like a votive offering when the coolness rose up. White sheets hung like a maze of walls throughout the large room, dividing it into sections, filtering the sun, taking away its bite. The only unexpected sounds were the occasional bleat of a scooter, moments of chatter, sudden laughter, the clank of silverware on porcelain. I could see Rivers closing his eyes and sleeping, horrified whenever he opened them again and remembered what had happened.

His right leg, his left arm. I cried for him. It seemed, to me, as though he were dead. That even though he lived, he no longer actually counted. I tried to understand why and realized that it was because two such injuries made him worse than an invalid, they made him a spectacle. He had become a monument to tragic failure and bad luck, to clumsiness and poor decisions, a warning of the dangers of trying too hard and fucking up.

I wrote him a long, meandering, and heart-soaked letter, filled with pomposities. I used descriptions of setting to articulate my feelings, as Hemingway might. I described the autumn here, and the slow death of everything green, and the tang of decomposition in the air, and the smell of an old bookstore, and the mundane comfort of working a simple and undemanding job so that I could be violent in my writing. I lied and told him that I was rereading *Lord Jim* as a way of recovering from my own personal wounds, which I did not elaborate on. And I ended by telling him that I needed him to hang on and be strong, and that the world needed him too, because he had so much greatness yet to give.

Just before Christmas, he wrote me back, a postcard with an empty beach and two mysterious islands jutting like emerald mushrooms from the blue water of the bay. A half dozen words were all he offered in exchange for my ten-page ode to bullshit.

Writing, he wrote, is a life-threatening activity.

The tragedy—and I know I must explain why anyone should pity me—is that I was different by the time Chris came back. I had sobered. I had become serious of purpose. I woke every morning at four-thirty to write before work at the bank. And when writing time was over, I lay on the floor and did fifty push-ups and two hundred sit-ups. This did not mean I was settling in to a staid vocation. I knew I did not want to be employed in the bank forever. I'd had my fill and was ready to return to school. I had decided to finish my degree in two muscular years, apply to a famous American graduate school in creative writing, publish my first story in the *Atlantic* or the *New Yorker*, sell a novel, garner big reviews, write bigger novels, become famous, and die wretched. If I could have maintained my austere and monk-like devotion to routine, and my solitary relationship with drink, I might have become something noteworthy.

But the obligations of friendship could not be avoided.

He called me two days before Christmas, and my heart was immediately filled with dread. I had not heard from him for over a month, had gotten no more postcards or letters, and I had not tracked down Susan since the Sheraton, so his absence was total. In fact, it had come to seem as though he had never been in my life, that he was a heroic character I'd created, not a reliably unreliable friend. The phone call was collect, and because of this, I assumed he was calling from overseas and that made it easier to put enthusiasm into my voice. But then he told me he was at Halifax International Airport. He needed to repeat himself before I understood.

Then why are you calling collect? I asked, still unable to understand.

Because I don't have any money, he said.

Not even a dime?

His laugh was the sound of my doom.

I told him I would be right there.

I did, after all, have his Fiero.

When I arrived at the airport, he was standing outside. A foot of grimy snow edged the sidewalk and most people were hunched over to avoid the cold, wearing hats and mittens, scarves and boots. Chris wore a T-shirt, dark sunglasses, and sneakers. He was also holding an enormous surfboard.

I didn't greet him or pound his back, I just asked how I was supposed to get the board into the car. There was no way it would fit.

Don't worry, you fucking nancy, Chris said.

We drove the ten miles or so back to town with the passenger window open. I shivered, shook, and sniffled. Chris held the board flat to the side of the car, without complaint, and seemed unmoved by any pain.

School began again. We both returned to our studies. And we resumed, in a stilted, awkward way, the pattern of our past friendship. One evening, a week into the semester, Chris asked me if I wanted to walk to the mall. We had given up walking anywhere years before, and this invitation seemed so innocent that it was appealing. My heart opened up a little. He met me on the street as we'd done a thousand times before, and we walked through the cul-de-sac, into the woods, and across the parking lot. I tried not to think about the bank job we'd done five months before.

But Chris, apparently, wanted to think about it.

There's something about that job I've always meant to tell you, he said.

I did and did not want to hear more.

Remember the two kids who saw me that day? he asked.

In the woods?

Yeah, coming up the path, he said.

What about them? I asked. I feared the worst. Had one recognized his face?

They were us, Chris said.

I didn't understand.

I saw us on the path. The two of us, you and me, walking back from the lake. We were just younger. Twelve or thirteen. But it was us, no doubt about it.

I waited for him to break into a grin and admit he was joking.

Okay, I said.

Weird, huh?

You mean like we travelled through time or something?

Another shrug. Maybe. Anyway, when I saw us, as kids, I knew everything would be just fine. You know what I'm saying?

And I said that I did, as any good friend would.

We pumped quarters into the video games at the arcade, like we would have years before. We played Asteroids, and Tron, and Missile Command.

Susan said you looked in on her, Chris said, after we left the arcade. Thanks for doing that.

I nodded, knowing this was the conversation that preceded my execution.

I missed her like crazy when I was gone.

She missed you too.

I got pretty serious with someone though. She owned a dive shop. We lived together for two months.

Wow, I said, and thought about Susan. *If I knew Chris was never coming back.*

She had a cute little girl who started calling me daddy.

I laughed. No shit.

Yeah, it felt really good.

I didn't know what to say. I wondered if he was telling me that he was moving back to Australia. Maybe he wanted me to break the news to Susan.

I told her I was a doctor, just out of med school, and taking a break before doing my internship.

Why?

He shrugged. I don't know. I just did.

We left the mall and walked across the field toward the forest, the barrier to our neighbourhood.

I think I lied to her because I wanted it to be true, Chris said.

You want to be a doctor? I was surprised.

No. Not a doctor. I want to do something serious. I want to accomplish something.

I was reminded of a night when we lay on our backs on the frozen lake, staring up into the snowflaked sky. Before all this shit started up. The causal event.

Like what? I asked.

I've decided I'm going to get serious this semester, get some kick-ass grades, get my application in for police academy. I can keep studying for my degree while I'm at the academy. Dad says it's a lot of work, but a few guys manage it, and I know I can be one of those guys if I apply myself.

I was impressed, if unconvinced. That's a good plan, I offered.

We stopped in front of my house to say goodbye.

I just need some money to get me through the next twenty to twenty-four months, he said.

And because he was sincere and I was his friend, I nodded at this too.

He had in mind the Brinks job, and I could not dissuade him. At least we did not talk about my involvement, and it occurred to me, with incredible relief, that he wasn't asking for it. Perhaps a Brinks job didn't require my services? This made discussing the particulars of his strategy more academic. If I was merely a consultant, I had less at stake, less need to steer him away from particular ideas.

The critical question in Chris's mind was, How do you neutralize the guards? He said it so often, to himself, that I began to make fun of him.

Would you like to get a coffee, I'd say, or do you need to neutralize the guards?

Or, I'm going to take a giant shit now, unless you need me to neutralize the guards.

Or, I was jerking off the other night and suddenly I thought, How can I neutralize the guards?

Ha ha, motherfucker, Chris said. He was a good sport but he did not like to be mocked.

Then, one afternoon at his house, Chris asked me to come into his parents' bedroom and try something out.

I did not know what to think as he led me down the hall and

opened the door. The room was remarkably neat and orderly, with a sort of military precision to it, but there was a prissy quilt on the bed and overly stuffed pillows.

Chris went to the closet doors and opened them up. It was the first walk-in I'd ever seen.

Like the Batcave, I said. I stood on plush carpet, surrounded by rows of suits. Before us was a shiny walnut door with a combination lock.

What's that? I asked.

Gun safe, he answered.

Chris did the combination and pulled open the heavy door. The interior was slightly smaller than a fridge, except loaded with weapons.

Three rifles with dark metal stocks stood at attention in a nest of green velvet shag, as though someone had used them to club a pool table to death. There were flat shelves and drawers as well. Chris slid out one of the shelves and showed me the handguns resting inside.

Recognize this bad boy? he asked.

It was Chris's preferred weapon, the one guaranteed to blow the head right off the shoulders.

Mr. FV himself, I said.

Indeed, it is, Chris agreed.

Then he opened a drawer and took out a mini spray can.

Right Guard? I asked.

It's mace, you stupid fuck.

I'd never seen mace before. I expected it to look different.

Otherwise known as guard neutralizer, he added.

Oh shit, I thought. But said, Cool.

I want you to spray me with it, Chris said.

What? I asked him.

I want you to spray me, he repeated.

I could not fathom why he was asking me that.

Because if I'm going to neutralize two armed guards with it, I want to make sure it works.

Why don't you spray yourself? I said.

I can't pull the trigger. I tried. So I need you to do it. Blast away, big boy.

Jesus. What do I do?

Just point it at my face and press the trigger.

At your face?

Where else?

I held the can and hesitated. Really?

Chicks do this, he insisted. Don't be such a pussy.

The magic words. I took a step back and lifted the can and aimed at his face.

His eyes were absurdly wide open.

At least close your fucking eyes.

No, he grunted between clenched teeth. Do it!

So I did. It was not unlike my first frog kill from long ago. But unlike then, when my aim had been true, this time I was way off. The spray shot out from the can in an unexpected arc over Chris's shoulder like a stream of confetti. When it landed, it struck a navy pinstripe suit hanging from the rack.

In slow motion, I saw this, but in real time, I wrestled with the spray can like a fire hose. I tried to get it under control but the nozzle must have been stuck, and I sprayed all the suits from that first suit on, a steady flow cutting across each shoulder in turn.

I could hear Chris yelling, Fuck! Enough!

I could barely breathe let alone respond. My lungs had seized up. My nose and mouth were smeared shut with melted skin. My eyes were boiling in their sockets. The air was hellfire eating into my hair follicles.

I collapsed. I plunged my face into the cool waters of the carpet. I wanted to dive below the surface and escape the corrosion of the chemical fire. I did slow swimming kicks with my feet. I tore at carpet tufts to diminish the agony.

Chris, it turned out, was doing the same thing.

When we could finally see and breathe again, we sat up in wonder.

Holy shit, Chris said.

I'm sorry, I blubbered.

Fuck that, he said. I asked you to do it. If you'd hit me, you might have killed me.

Chris was not the kind to dwell on mistakes. He pronounced the mace perfect.

Perfect? I asked.

No guard is going to have the wherewithal to shoot me if he gets a dose of this.

Oh, I said. Great.

Now how are we going to clean these fucking suits? he asked.

All along I'd assumed this was a solo gig, and I was merely a sounding board, or a chronicler of heroic, legendary deeds. But, of course, I was not to get off so easily. Chris wanted me to drive. Like I'd driven the other jobs. He'd assumed all along that I'd wanted to drive. So he hadn't even bothered to mention that part.

Rather than acknowledge my shame—rather than spare myself the possibility that I'd be sent to prison for the next twenty-five years, and that my parents would die while I was still inside, and that my education would end, and that my writing career would never start, and that I would be man-raped on a casual but frequent basis—I acted as though I too had been intending to go all along.

We did it on a Tuesday morning. Unlike the previous two jobs, Chris did not bring me along for any dry runs. For this, I was grateful, if a little surprised by the laxness. I was familiar enough with the location, but I did not know it from the point of view of someone casing the joint, as they say. I have found, in my limited though pertinent experience, that you never truly know a place until you have planned to commit a crime there. Absent that concentration, you do not see the physical details, the flow of pedestrian traffic, the angle of sight around corners, even the most decorative features.

We arrived a half hour early. Chris knew the precise time that we needed to be on hand. I did not. We were running on his clock. In reaction to my fear, I had become abnormally quiet and calm, and did not show any outward signs of panic. My hands did not shake. My skin did not sweat. But my reactions were imperceptibly delayed. Each moment of delay was a private eternity.

He directed me to park behind the mall, out of sight of the doors. This was my waiting zone. He acknowledged that this particular parking lot was the worst one yet. It seemed exposed in every direction to lines of sight from a multitude of other cars and store windows. What's more, there were no easy exits. We would need to drive a hundred yards or more in any of three possible routes to reach a road, each of them easily cut off by a single car—no matter if it was a cop car coming up on us fast or a granny in a Nova fucking up on a parking job. Once out of the lot and onto the street, the roads lacked quick branches and off-ramps. Even a single red light could render us stuck as the police converged. Our best hope was acting in contrast to the confusion. If the turmoil within the mall drew enough attention, the parking lot would be less scrutinized. If we were calm enough in leaving, we might go unmarked. If you can keep your head when others around you are getting theirs blown off, you'll be a man, my son.

When you see me come around the corner, it's go time, Chris said.

I nodded.

You got everything you need? I asked.

Got the gun and my helmet, Chris said. What more can a fellow ask for?

And the mace, I said.

Chris checked his watch, noted some important increment in the passage of time, and popped the door open. He looked at me before he got out.

I decided I didn't need the mace, he said.

What are you talking about? I almost grabbed his arm.

His voice, ever calm, hypnotized me again.

I found out from my dad that Brinks guards are actually paid bonuses to shoot robbers. If you couldn't squirt me in the eyes when I was standing still, how am I going to hit them in the middle of a heist? Way too risky.

So what are you going to do? I asked.

But he had shut the door. And that's when I understood how wrong everything was about to go.

I watched him walk toward the back of the mall, its grey aluminum siding capped with the red trim of a flat awning, a bit like an elongated Pizza Hut. He put on the motorcycle helmet and reached into his jacket pocket, probably to check on the gun.

He did not need the mace.

I should have driven away. Left him behind. But when you are half paralyzed by fear and laden with assorted weights—the weight of friendship most of all, the weight of obligation conjoined to that, the weight of shame not to be overlooked as a contributing force—the easiest alternative is to do nothing.

I raise a glass to nothing. I acknowledge my sympathy with this monster, Mr. Silent Death. I blow a kiss in the direction of its sweet centrifugal darkness. Someday, I know, I will join it, my private weight emulsifying into the density of this densest of black holes. Where all our weight goes. To be redistributed to the next poor sucker in the cosmic karmic lottery.

Knowing that matter can be neither created nor destroyed.

But weight can do whatever the fuck it wants.

I checked my periphery. The strip of parking spots behind the mall was still empty, except for me in Chris's black Fiero. I saw an abandoned bicycle, pretzelled and rusted, next to an industrial trash bin overflowing with cardboard. A path led up the grass berm behind the trash bin, and then along the ridge of it, the kind of path a kid would take. I thought of the kids

Chris met on the path in the woods after the last job. They were us, Chris insisted, and I did not doubt that they had been, and I wished I could see them now, standing on the ridge, looking down at me, wondering what the fuck I was doing.

When Chris entered the mall, he walked in with the tinted visor down. This was winter. Shouldn't that have caused alarm? Nah, a few crazy bastards rode motorcycles whenever the roads were clear. And besides, Chris did not worry about plausibility. He understood that gestures only seem out of sorts when you are uncomfortable making them. If a novelist flinches, you know he's faking it. If a bank robber hesitates, his gun looks smaller.

The entrance was an elaborate arch, Hindu-like in its gaudy splendour, a temple devoted to cheap convenience.

A long, wide hallway. The ceiling low, the steel roof beams exposed, generous skylights up above, blotched with snow so that the light within was dim. Everywhere tile. The floors were tile. The pillars were tile. The walls were tile. The ocean of tile was marked by several islands of wood-framed boxes overfilled with wild, waxy-leafed, exotic jungle plants. Surrounding the boxes were benches propped on stubby wooden pillars. Chris sat, oblique to the bank machine, and pretended to look through his wallet.

Seven minutes and counting. He was checking his wallet as if searching for a receipt. Mostly old people in the mall that morning. White-haired women. Old men wearing ball caps and leaning on canes. But some high school kids too. What were they doing here? Skipping school. On recess. He noticed only the girls. Feathered hair and blush. Short T-shirts. Grime-hemmed winter jackets tied around their waists. Mouths working, chewing gum or talking. Jeans dragging ratty along the floor beneath a sneaker. He did not look directly at the bank, except to note that it was open. He felt the door open at the end of the mall, experiencing a slight change in air pressure, and knew it was the Brinks delivery. He heard the cart rattling across the tile floor. He stood and walked to the window of the store next to the cash machine and looked within, as though deciding whether he needed to shop there.

It was a card store. There were aisles of cards. There were plush teddy bears on top of each aisle. There was a pregnant woman in jean bib overalls standing in the aisle closest to him, looking for just the right happy birthday message. She glanced his way and there was something in the glance, enough of a sudden tightening of her lips, to make him dead certain he could do her. He'd had sex with two pregnant women already, both of them happily married. They couldn't seem to control themselves. They came and came and came.

He touched the handgun tucked into the waist of his pants, just to make sure it was there. It occurred to him that he would feel very foolish if it fired at that moment and blew his cock off. Perhaps the noise and subsequent screaming, followed by a second shot as he fired into his own temple, would be enough to make the pregnant woman go into labour. He angled the butt of the pistol a little to the left. Better to sever his femoral artery and bleed out in a minute or so, the pregnant woman hovering overtop of him, bathing him in tears of regret.

He knew they were coming and knew what that meant, and yet he did not register the awareness physically. His breathing stayed normal. His heart rate stayed normal. He was surprised, as ever, by this calmness. It did not seem quite right. But he didn't give a fuck.

He stepped over to the cash machine, as if making a withdrawal.

This was his one spontaneous moment, and it was a reminder never to do anything unscripted. Without thinking, without the brake of deliberately running through a scenario, he almost put his bank card into the cash machine slot. He stopped himself just in time. How nice it would have been to leave an electronic record of his presence. This near mistake rattled him slightly, pushed his heartbeat up a tick. He took another breath and tried to concentrate on making the bank machine transaction look real. But like a debut actor, he hesitated, almost forgetting his lines. How many buttons do you press? How long do you wait before cursing and pressing them again? Fuck it. He focused on the Brinks guards walking by, watching their reflection in the metal mirror. They did not look over at him. He put his wallet in his back pocket and pulled the handgun from the waist of his pants, holding it low against his thigh.

They didn't react when he turned around. They were intent only on reaching their destination, one pushing the cart, one striding after.

He shot the first one, the man following the cart, through the side of the thigh. The man's leg kicked out from under him as if he had been yanked by a rope lassoed around his ankles. Chris was so surprised by the swiftness of the fall that he hesitated a moment too long before turning to the second man.

The second man was on his way into a crouch when Chris shot him. But because of the sudden change in height, the man's thigh was twenty or thirty inches lower now, and Chris accidentally shot him through the chest instead. The bullet flung him back.

At some level, Chris could not believe what he had done.

At another level, Chris was very pleased with what he had done.

Quick Draw McGraw.

The motorcycle helmet muffled the noise. Nevertheless, he was amazed at the loudness of the cannon blasts. He felt as though birds from every waxy jungle plant must have flocked heavenward as a result. He vaguely saw that the birds were old people and teenage girls running away.

Like a vampire rising from a coffin, the chest-shot man sat up and fired. Chris only registered the movement after the glass behind him shattered. He was almost too stunned to understand how it had happened.

And then he realized, Motherfucker's wearing a vest.

He straightened his arm and stared down the barrel of the gun. He fired once and the man was tossed away. He fired again and the man slid along the floor. He fired again and the man wrenched terrifically, twisting his arm behind his back to scratch at the unreachable place where the bullet went in. He fired again and the chamber clicked empty. He turned to the leg-shot man and saw him fumbling to lift his weapon. Chris ran straight for him, leaped over the cart, and kicked out with his size-eleven sneaker, as though he were trying to launch a soccer ball over a fence.

I will always be grateful that I did not leave, no matter what awful things might have been happening inside.

I stayed, and in retrospect, I looked brave.

I saw Chris walking toward the car. His motorcycle helmet

dangled from one hand. He walked casually, without urgency. I gripped the steering wheel so tightly I could have ripped it from the driveshaft. I did not know whether to gun the car forward or remain still. I remained still. He barely glanced my way. There was no money in his hands, and I knew that meant something. He reached the car, opened the passenger door, flung his helmet to the floor, and sat down.

There was still no urgency. No command to flee. No reason to move.

What? I asked.

I didn't do it, he said. His voice was calm and filled with weight.

We parked at another mall, because parking at a mall was easy to do, and he told me what happened.

It was all coins, he said. No cash. A trolley full of coins.

He was angry. He was struggling with his emotions.

Not in twelve or fourteen times did I see them deliver anything but cash. It boggles the fucking mind.

It all boggled. It boggles still.

I had just pulled my gun out and I saw the stacks of coins, so I twisted around, stuffed the gun back in my pants, and walked right by them.

I pictured the graceful pirouette, the delicate avoidance of death.

We sat in silence. Minutes went by.

Fuck! Chris screamed. He lifted a fist to his mouth and then stopped, halfway to the destination, and lowered it again. He put his head back and closed his eyes.

What were you going to do without the mace? I asked.

It was the kind of question you do not ask.

He tilted his head toward me. I had a plan.

Would you really have shot them? I asked.

Not in the head or anything. In the leg.

In the leg?

I loaded the .357 with .38 target rounds. I didn't want to use big ammo because I knew they'd bleed out all over the place. So I went with smaller bullets. Way less kick, far less lethal.

I'm going to grab an Orange Julius, I said, and opened the door.

I need a nap, he answered, closing his eyes again.

I didn't come back to the car. I wandered the mall for a couple hours, then snuck out a different exit and caught a bus home.

And that was the end for me. I had reached my moral limit. We parted there. We went our separate ways. I went back to school. He went on with what he did. And what happened to him later happened because of his own agency. I was—at least at some judicial level—an innocent bystander. I saw and reacted with horror like everyone else. The kind of horror that's different in the aftermath of consequence. Before consequence, before the weight gets piled on, we're all drawn to lightness. We look up and marvel at the birds and the clouds. Afterwards, we cluck in disapproval and wonder how someone could ever do such a thing.

Tsk tsk, rip, drip.

7

Except, of course, I did not abandon him, not even at the mall parking lot after he told me he'd intended to shoot two guards. I did not wander the mall for hours, merely minutes. I stepped into a bookstore and bought a collection of Hemingway journalism pieces, stuff he wrote before he became a novelist. (I was very curious about what kind of life the great writer had lived before he was great.) There were two other books I would have bought, if money hadn't been so tight, and I exited the store in a funk of defeat. The lack of money was due to the failure of the robbery, I knew, but I also suspected that the failure of the robbery was somehow due to me. I bought two Orange Juliuses (Julii?) with the seven dollars remaining in my pocket, one for me and one for Chris. I sat at a table and sipped from mine, and the sweetness unfurled in the back of my throat like the taste of rotten fruit and with the sudden cough came vomit. I vomited between my legs, as people around me stared or tried not to stare, and when I could see straight again, I abandoned my cup of Orange Julius and walked away with the other cup. When I got back to the car, Chris had repositioned himself to the driver's seat and was looking impatient about my delay. Did they make you make that yourself? he asked, as I handed him the cup. He took a few slurps from the straw to lower the level and then put the cup between his thighs and we drove away. I noted, as we reached the rotary, that the sky was looking like snow.

When I was passing through Kuala Lumpur, during my travels in Southeast Asia, I found a guest house in the Chinese district where I could sit on the narrow balcony off my room and drink tea and look out on the street below. The balcony rails were painted robin's egg blue, with decorative touches of yellow, green, or pink. It was soothing on the eyes and the conscience. The room next to mine had a bamboo birdcage, like a hanging plant, on its balcony. I loved to watch the small yellow bird hop from perch to perch, twitching its head impulsively at any sound or sight.

Checking out a few mornings later, I saw a paperback on the shelf, leaning against the container of complimentary biscuits. Travellers were always leaving books behind as they travelled, and I never failed to check what some other wanderer had thought I might like to read. So I stepped over to the shelf to examine the title. When I turned it over, I saw that I was holding St. Augustine's *Confessions*.

Flinching a little, I put the book back, and finished paying my bill. After we were done, and the old Chinese woman had nodded her thanks, I swam upward through my anxiety to the light above, and asked her if I could have the book.

She looked confused. I picked up the book and gestured with it, pulling it toward me, pushing it back to the shelf. May I?

Take, take, she said, in an irritated frustration, shooing it off her shelf like it was a fly.

On the train south to Malacca, I started *Confessions* and found some of the things I was looking for inside.

I knew, because I had read about this memoir, that there would be a story within of a man who had done many wrong things in his youth and then turned to God. I did not want to turn to God. I was terrified of turning to God. But I read anyway because a little bird had chirped in the balcony next to mine.

I expected accusations. I expected to be called out.

I was not disappointed.

Like Augustine, I carried my thoughts back to the abominable things I did in those days. Like Augustine, I loved my own perdition and my own faults. Like Augustine, I swam in a sea of fornication. Like Augustine, I stole pears, not because of hunger, but for the sin that gave them flavour, and the thrill of having partners in that sin.

And then I read on about Augustine's closest friend.

He was my companion in error, Augustine wrote, and I was utterly lost without him.

I knew what it meant to have a companion in error.

A lump in my throat, I learned that Augustine's friend fell mortally ill with a fever. After all hope was lost, the friend was baptized. But instead of dying, the friend recovered and woke.

When Augustine, who had never left his friend's side (oh, how this comparison pained me), was finally able to exchange words with his friend, he teased him about the baptism. But the friend, who weeks before would have shared the cynicism, looked aghast and admonished Augustine never to treat the miracle of faith so lightly again. Otherwise, Augustine should leave, no friend worthy of the name.

Augustine took the rebuke, mystified by the intensity of his friend's reaction. His guilt compounded a hundred times over when the fever returned and the friend died a few days later.

I lived in a fever, he wrote, convulsed with tears and sighs that allowed me neither rest nor peace of mind. My soul was a burden, bruised and bleeding. It was tired of the man who carried it, but I found no place to set it down to rest. Everything that was not what my friend had been was dull and distasteful. But if I tried to stem my tears, a heavy load of misery weighed me down. The god I worshipped was my own delusion, and if I tried to find in it a place to rest my burden, there was nothing there to uphold it. It only fell and weighed me down once more, so that I was still my own unhappy prisoner, unable to live in such a state yet powerless to escape from it. Where could I go, yet leave myself behind? I left my native town. So from Thagaste I went to Carthage.

For years I searched for Carthage, and only occasionally did I understand what I was doing, where I was going. Finally I moved to Brooklyn, the Carthage of New York.

I wrote that after the Brinks job I left him, because in some ways I had. Unfortunately, such endings never happen as neatly as they should. Poetically clean breaks are the way storytellers dramatize the truth. In my case, the mind was willing but the heart was weak.

I had returned to school in January, but I was a shadow. I attended classes, studied for exams, wrote papers, and drank and partied like a champ, but I had nothing inside. I was no longer among the living.

Or, you could say that I was completely the opposite. That I was invigorated, angry, forceful, wilful, charming, deceitful, curious, and inclined toward extreme experiences.

A hollow shell or a shit disturber extraordinaire. Take your pick. Such is youth, the myriad state.

The Brinks job was our bad mood, our seasonal affective disorder. With that trolley of coins, like some cursed treasure in a fairy tale, the skies darkened and our luck turned.

Simultaneously, and by no means coincidentally, I became more active as Chris's partner in crime, at least in the planning of it, which was a great step forward toward total complicity. The failure of the Brinks job, and the slight but ever-so-nagging lack of faith I now had in Chris's thought processes, prompted me to step up, as it were, and start pulling my load.

I had one predominant motivation. I did not want him to do a Brinks job again. To me, the risk was incalculable and, therefore, should be avoided at any cost. Accordingly, I betrayed my father and offered up a bank instead. I convinced Chris the score would be sizable. I'd worked long enough in a bank to understand its operational weaknesses. The most cash-inundated times. Why rob a Brinks delivery, with those guns and sprayed bullets, when you could intimidate unarmed clerks? Bank employees were not paid to thwart a robbery, they were instructed to be obsequious and helpful. I hinted that my father was motivation for further revenge. I was sick of him. I was tired of his authoritarian rule. I wanted to storm, like Carlos the Jackal, into the boardroom of his corporate universe, take hostages, demand ransom, fly to Cuba.

This was my desperate play, the ace card I had been holding back.

The first month of the new year always seems longer than the other months, as though it is the most mature month, the most sober, the getting-down-to-business month. And yet, Chris did not get down to business. He failed to return to school, as he had vowed to do. He abandoned his workouts, listless about the effort required to heave and clank. He did not seem particularly into Susan, nor particularly driven to cheat on her. He came across as tired and emotionally depleted.

Still, when we were out for drinks on the last Thursday night of the month, he surprised me by announcing that tomorrow would be the day. The day of what? I asked. The day we rob the bank, he answered. He seemed almost belligerent in tone, as though looking to pick a fight. I had no choice but to agree.

The next day, we parked in the same area where we had parked for the aborted Brinks job. I waited once again. Amazingly, I did not feel any paralyzing nervousness. Whatever happened, getting caught or getting rich, would be done without bloodshed. I was grateful at least for that.

But when Chris returned from the bank, running at high speed, those long strides gracefully covering the distance, I saw no money in his grip.

Go, he shouted.

So go I did.

I spun out of the lot. I had forgotten about the adage to be calm and normal. Chris put a hand on the steering wheel to wake me up.

Slow down, he said.

Sirens converged as I eased into traffic. Cops from three directions at once. We sat behind a Volvo at a red light. The light turned green, a few cars jerked forward but then stopped as a police car burned through the intersection on its way to the mall.

Police car gone, the green light turned to red. We waited some more. We could not help but see police cars everywhere. Then, mercifully, green came again, and we moved forward in the flow of others.

Always late, Chris said. Cops are such stupid motherfuckers.

I found out soon the stupidest motherfucker was me. In an icy voice, Chris told me what had gone wrong. The bank kept all its money in a central safe, not in the tills. Chris had stormed over the counter, but the clerk only looked confused and said he had no money. So Chris moved on to the next clerk and told that motherfucker to empty his till, and that motherfucker in turn said he had no money. The money, the second motherfucker explained, was kept in the central till behind the cage.

We did not have a cage at my bank. I had assumed that every bank would be like mine. I felt the heat rushing to my face.

Was the cage difficult to get into? I asked. I scowled to make it seem as though I was pissed off.

I never tried, Chris said.

Why not? I asked, talking as though pissed off—my money too, that sort of thing.

Because it wasn't in the plan, Chris said.

And that was that.

The plan, however much it might alter according to the dictates of circumstance, was the Ten Commandments, the Constitution, and the NHL Rulebook rolled into one.

We were never able to stay mad at each other for long. We got drunk that night. There may have been a dozen beautiful women in the bar, but all we did was huddle over our drinks and argue philosophical problems.

Is it better to be lucky or good?

I'd say good. Luck is random. Nice to have but you can't rely on it.

If a hot chick was willing to do one incredible thing with you and one thing only, what would you do?

I'd say threesome. Still stuck on that idea. Got to get it out of my system.

Who'd win in a fight, Kirk or Sulu?

Much as I like Sulu, I'd have to go with Kirk. Unless we're talking Sulu with the virus.

Yeah, Sulu with the virus could beat pretty much anyone.

Except Spock.

No one could beat Spock.

Except maybe evil Spock with the goatee.

If a hot chick offered you a chance for a threesome and the other girl had a great body but the ugliest face you'd ever seen, would you do it?

Probably.

If you had to choose between getting caught and living as a fugitive for the rest of your life, what would you do?

I wouldn't get caught.

That's not what I asked.

Then the question is too theoretical to be relevant.

As opposed to Spock with the goatee fighting normal Spock?

That's at least conceivable.

Come on, man. Which would you do?

Life as a fugitive.

Never see your family and friends again.

No biggie.

Never see Susan.

Let's not get personal. What about you?

Me too.

Then you see it is a stupid question, isn't it?

I guess so. It seemed profound in the moment.

That's because you're on your seventh rum and coke.

Could be.

Actually, the whole fugitive lifestyle could be kind of fun.

Don't get started on the Butch-and-Sundance-still-alive thing.

Don't know if I'd be into riding a horse every day though. Bonnie and Clyde would be more my style. Except with a faster car.

They're dead too, you stupid motherfucker.

You'll believe pretty much anything you see on TV, won't you?

Hours later, when Chris finally dropped me at my home, I stumbled inside. I tried to sleep and couldn't. The bed did spins.

Occasionally, I rose from bed and stumbled into the bathroom to throw up, retching horribly. A few times I got up just to urinate or drink another glass of water. I dreamt of Bonnie and Clyde all night. Those rustling bushes. That hail of bullets. The shattered glass and blood-splattered love. The long last look. Then torn full of holes.

The next morning when I stood over the toilet to piss, I noticed speckles of blood in the bowl. I got down on my hands and knees to look more closely. Was it really blood?

That evening, without a word, my mother gave me a pamphlet on alcoholism. It reminded me of the stack of pamphlets she had handed me a week or so after my first wet dream, when I was fourteen. Those pamphlets were short paragraphs with simple graphics about birth control, the mechanisms of impregnation, masturbation, and sexually transmitted disease. So silently offered, they'd seemed to rebuke the wonder of whatever had happened to me in that dream a few nights before. Had I shouted out, Hallelujah! in my sleep? The lightness of newly discovered pleasure became the weight of guilt. Despite the secret shame, I brought them to school the next day to show my friends, with all the bravado I could muster. Now, years later, another pamphlet. How To Know When You Are Drinking Too Much. I saw it as an ode to obviousness. My first argument was the very premise: Define *too much*. For each circumstance, each different night, the quantity Too Much was just a spin of the roulette wheel. The numbers rarely coordinated exactly with the results. I also argued with the general idea that alcoholism is a disease and not a response to mood or moment. Clearly, the author had never been in the bank-robbing business, nor been a college student for that matter. There were simply too many instances I could think of when drinking yourself into oblivion was not only sensible, it was the right thing to do.

I put the pamphlet on the stack of bills on the counter in the kitchen. It remained there for several days, an unspoken, unresolved argument among us, and then it disappeared.

I did know, however, that I needed to get my own fucking place.

Two weeks later, we decided to go again. We were, by this point, so broke we felt like rock stars who had once been worth millions and now desperately needed a comeback album.

Once again, it was my idea. The movie theatre. The blockbuster payoff. The bank alternative.

Let's do it, Chris said.

My only hesitation was that it might be better to wait for big-time movies. In February, the movies weren't hits. They did not draw lineups. In the summer, the take would be much bigger.

Fuck summer, Chris said. If it works, we'll do it then too. Call it a sequel.

On go night, we went out for drinks. It seemed smart to have a few before we did the job. It was raining and cold. The world's shittiest weather combination. I was on my fourth or fifth rum and coke when Chris said I'd had enough.

Because of the rain, Chris had a yellow raincoat. Because of the cold, Chris had a hat with a ski mask. He carried a smaller pistol because there was little chance of armed adversaries at the theatre. A black Ruger loaded with .22 calibre bullets. You could almost call it a chick gun if the damn thing didn't look so James Bond.

I parked in the cul-de-sac, near the swamp where we'd built the coolest fort ever, all those years ago. The rain pelted the windshield and steam rose from the hood of the car. The swamp was a Scottish-moors kind of spooky.

When Chris walked into the lobby, the last movies had already started, and all movie-goers were inside. He saw, however, that there was only one cashier at the ticket counter, and that made him wonder whether he'd blown the timing. He could have turned away, saved the job for another night, but he was frustrated, so he walked up to the cashier, pulled the Ruger out of his gym bag, and angled it toward her. Sandra was her name, according to the tag.

You know why I'm here, he said.

Maybe Sandra knew, maybe she didn't. Her eyes went wide, like a deer in the headlights. Then she was gone. She bolted from the back of the booth before Chris could repeat the order.

Standing there all alone, he thought: Fuck. Now what do I do?

The problem was getting into the tills. He'd never operated one before. Never paid attention at the Canadian Tire. He saw two ushers in their usher jackets standing at the rope line that separated the ticket lobby from the theatre lobby. They were staring at him as if he were a madman. He lifted his gun and pointed it at them as he strode over.

Bobby and Arnold, according to their name tags. He grabbed Bobby, the least quivery of the two, and dragged him over to the cashier booth. Later, the police would call this physical contact a dangerous escalation.

Open it, he said.

Bobby leaned into the booth, hit No Sale, and the drawer popped open. Chris flung Bobby away.

Lacking time for finesse, he pulled out the entire tray and shoved it into his gym bag. Then he ran.

This job had not gone according to plan. It had taken longer than expected, and he'd only gotten one tray. He was pissed.

But the rain and cold felt good. He'd gotten overheated in the raincoat because of the adrenalin and frustration, as though he were saran-wrapped inside a garbage bag. Running in the cold was a relief. He loped across the parking lot like a cloaked avenger, hooked onto the path, into the woods, and was gone. Zowie. Who was that masked man?

The bag with the till was awkward on his shoulder. Sticking up, the plastic corner kept knocking against the side of his neck. The only difference between the path now and the path when we were kids was that some knucklehead had put a fence across it, making claim to the woods as an extension of his backyard. If we were still kids, we would have kicked the shit out of that fence and used the boards for the walls of a new fort.

Chris did not break stride but reached out with one hand for the top of the fence and swung his legs up and over. Then he scrambled down the path, slick with pine needles and exposed roots, to the cul-de-sac where I waited in the car.

I had gotten out of the car and was standing by the open driver's door, willing Chris to appear from the woods. I was not sure how much longer I could wait because of the police sirens that screamed into the dark, rainy night. I could see blue and red lights flying along the main road above our neighbourhood. This meant they were driving away from the mall and toward us. They could not possibly have gone to the mall first, assessed the situation, and then reacted. So they must have reacted as soon as they knew a job had taken place. And they must have known in advance that this cul-de-sac was one of the great exit points for anyone doing a job at the mall, especially at the cinema. They were on to us, and they were coming to get us.

Panic unmans the best of us. There's something addling about fear, something awful in the way it undermines our more rational intentions. I saw Chris emerging from the woods, yellow-slickered and sliding, and screamed for him to hurry up.

I got back in the car, slammed my door shut, and reached over to push open his door so that he could get in faster. He slipped and hit the side of the car with a clumsy bodycheck, then looked back over his shoulder at the police car rocketing along the highway as he tossed the bag in.

The till caught the frame of the door and money exploded into the sky like confetti.

You've got to be fucking kidding me! I screamed.

There was money on the car seat and on the dashboard and even stuck to the inside of the windshield. There was more money outside. Chris bent over and scooped piles of the stuff into the car, handful after handful, shovelling it in, while I scraped the stuff off the dash and windshield and tried to fling it to the floor.

Leave it! I said.

But he kept scooping and the cops kept coming. Finally, he hurled himself into the car.

Go, he said, in as calm a voice as I'd ever heard.

So go I did.

I'm not sure where my own calm came from. I wanted to hit the accelerator with both feet but I drove slowly even as Chris frantically stuffed cash back into his bag. We passed my house and turned the corner toward Oathill Lake. Another car came out of nowhere, some driveway or side street, and tucked in front of us. It rattled me, and I wondered if it was an unmarked police car. Then I saw an actual police car pull up behind us. Its lights were not flashing, but there was no other reason for it to have shown up.

Stay easy, Chris said.

If not for the car in front of us, I would have gunned it. Somehow, someway, I drove calmly forward. We approached the intersection where there was a three-way stop.

When the car in front of us reached the stop sign, it tapped lightly on the brakes but did not fully stop. As if nervous of the police behind us, or utterly unaware, it picked up speed and drove for the lake. I reached the line and stopped carefully, trying not to panic.

The cop lights flashed, and suddenly we were in a blue and red world. I squeezed my eyes tight and felt every cell in my body implode, a million little aneurysms at once. The cop car gunned forward, surged around us, and chased after the car that had rolled through the stop sign.

I did not know what to do.

Just drive, Chris whispered, as though the cops might hear us.

We rounded the bend and saw that the cop car had cut off the other car, angling it onto the curb. Two uniformed cops were standing outside their car with their weapons drawn and aimed at the driver within.

Give a wide berth, Chris said, and go around like nothing is happening on Sesame Street.

So I did.

Chris's house was a block away. We drove up the gradual hill, still hugging the contour of the lake, and around the corner. I could not help but gun it on the straightaway, and Chris didn't stop me. When we reached the house, I launched into his expansive driveway. All my delayed panic had flooded my system. I turned off the ignition, my hands shaking, and looked to Chris.

Jesus, you're bleeding, I said. His chin and neck were wet with blood, an ugly open slit was puckered with gore. Were you shot?

He touched the blood.

I think the till caught me in the face when I jumped the fence, he said. Got any tissues?

What bank robber carries tissues? I had none. Chris took a few bills and smeared the blood away from his chin and neck. It did no good whatsoever, so he lifted his shirt to his face and towelled himself, Shroud of Turin style. It only smeared the blood more.

I think we should get the fuck inside the house, I said.

Chris thought that was a good idea. We could still see the pulse of blue and red police lights strobing in the air. Chris tucked the gym bag with the money behind the hedge near the front door. A moment later, the door flung open and his dad stood in the entranceway.

I stared at Mr. R even as Chris, to hide his blood-smeared face, turned his back and looked out on the street.

What's going on? Mr. R said. He was gazing off toward the strobing lights.

They pulled over some melon head in a sports car rolling through a stop sign, Chris answered.

Is that all? Mr. R said.

I guess, Chris said. They drew down on him and slapped the cuffs on.

No kidding? Mr. R said. He looked impressed.

We stood there watching the street for the next thing that might happen.

Must have been flagged victor, I suggested.

Mr. R said nothing, then asked us if we were coming inside or taking a shower together on the porch. Chris laughed, told him we'd be right in, but didn't turn around.

I released my held breath and leaned against the wall to stay upright.

Flagged victor. Finally, us.

Chris wanted to see Susan and go out and celebrate. I wanted to crawl home and die. Before parting, we did manage to laugh about the cash flying everywhere, but I was shaking as well.

Just like when Butch and Sundance used too much dynamite to blow up the train safe, I said, You sure know how to blow things up, Butch!

But after ten minutes or so of tearful side-splitting laughter, Chris announced he needed to go get laid immediately.

Despite the rain, I walked down to the lake and stood on the pier. I could not help but remember that other night when

I had stumbled out of the woods after chainsawing Paul's tree fort and ended up in the back of Officer Drury's squad car, blubbering like a baby.

How far you've come. How far.

I realized that I had no sense of agency in my life. Everything that happened to me happened because of someone or something else. I was not the main character in my own life story, at best a trusty sidekick. This was no way to live. The epiphany left me feeling depleted, if not annihilated.

When I finally got home, my father was already in bed, my mother in the kitchen. She was puttering. Cleaning counters that looked clean. Reorganizing a cupboard full of Tupperware. She looked tired but managed a small smile when she saw me.

You're soaked, she said, and threw me a tea towel.

I took it and put my face into the rough, recently washed cloth. It smelled of home.

Your father's not well, she said, while my face was still buried.

I looked up. I had never before heard her say anything like that.

What do you mean? I asked.

He had some tests done today at the hospital. We'll know more soon.

What kind of tests? I asked.

She looked uncertain, as if she'd said too much.

Some blood in his stool. It could be anything.

A word that could only make one laugh. But I didn't laugh.

Could be anything like what? I asked. I felt like a little kid. This was why no one trusted me on anything. I panicked. I needed. I was heavy.

Could be hemorrhoids, she said. Could be an ulcer. There's

no point in speculating. It only leads you to worry. We'll know more next week.

I started to say something else.

It's okay, she said, and smiled. It will be fine.

I stopped. Okay, I said.

Oh, I forgot to tell you, she said. Chris just called. He asked you to call him. No matter how late.

He did?

That's what he said, so I guess you better call him.

Okay, I said. I made no move for the phone.

I think I'll get changed first, I said. I'm getting cold.

This was the only way I could think of to escape to the other phone. And with that, I bolted upstairs.

I dragged the phone by its extra-long extension cord and huddled on the floor beside my bed. I even listened for sound from the other receiver as I dialed the number.

When Chris answered, his voice was so cheery, so light in its lack of worry, that I wondered if I was going mad.

What's going on? I asked.

He hesitated. Long enough to make me wonder.

I hid the till and counted the cash. Now I'm heading over to Susan's. We're going to kick back for an hour or so. Then go out for drinks. Splash out a bit. Figured you ought to be there.

You guys haven't had a lot of fun lately, I offered magnanimously. Go spend some dough on each other.

Very kind of you, sir, very kind. Want to know how much?

I didn't want to know how much. Yeah, what'd we take?

Just over two grand.

Silence.

Shit, I said. I did not know what I meant by that.

Yeah, he said. I bet we could have tripled that if I'd gotten there five or ten minutes earlier. Should have had you in the lobby, spying on the whole deal and giving me a signal. Probably not a one-man job.

I supposed he meant it didn't take a man to drive the car. I agreed with him.

Live and learn, I said.

Live and learn, he repeated.

More silence.

One minor setback, he said.

My heart beating. What's that?

Can't find the gun.

What do you mean?

Must have fallen out somewhere.

How?

I could hear him shrug. I'm not even sure what I did with it. Can't remember if I stuffed it in the waist of my pants or in the bag. But it must have popped out at some point.

Man, that's not even funny.

Not funny at all.

You check everywhere?

Everywhere I could think. Behind the hedge, under the seat of the car. I even drove back to the cul-de-sac, looked around where we parked, walked up through the woods.

Heart thumping thumping thumping.

Did you see any police?

Not just then. Did find a couple twenties though. Just lying there in the wet.

Money everywhere.

You look all over the woods? I asked. Where you jumped the fence?

'Course I did. Darker than fuck though. Couldn't see much.

You didn't bring a flashlight? Like I was Mr. Common Sense.

Didn't exactly want to advertise my presence.

Oh, right.

Anyway, I'm heading out. Just wanted you to know the situation. If you change your mind, we'll probably go to the hotel like last time. Don't be shy, come on by.

And with that, he clicked off.

Just heading out. Just wanted you to know. Don't be shy, come on by. All that lightness dazzling in its insanity. I crawled into bed and lay in the dark, the weight of the cosmos pressing down.

Three-thirty in the morning, I still hadn't slept. But I knew where the gun was.

I got up as quietly as I could, crept downstairs, and drank a glass of water. I was amazed by my awakeness. I put on a jacket and boots, and snuck outside.

The world was silent, a post-drip haziness and calm. The aloneness of it comforted me.

I walked the block and a half to the swamp. All of the houses around were dim and asleep. No one would have noticed my ghost passing through the mist.

I'd expected orange cones. Yellow tape. Signs that police had crawled all over the place, were crawling still. Nothing.

I walked up the path into the woods.

When I was a child, I would explore the woods with all the time in the world. Back then, I'd been hooked into the universe. It had been my friend. The memory made me realize how divorced from that connection I'd become. Was that the origin of the wrongness in my life? I drove those thoughts from my brain and thought about nothing. I only saw. I saw wet leaves and exposed roots and pine needles in pools of water. I squished. I stepped. I hopped easily over the fence.

I saw the gun beneath a clump of leaves, handle sticking out, nozzle poking through. It gleamed in the no-light. I leaned over, picked it up, and tucked it into my pocket.

I thanked the woods and the rain and the universe and I walked home.

I slept in until ten-thirty and only awoke because my mother was pushing my shoulder. She had the phone in her hand. It's Chris, she said. Do you two need to move in together or something? You're like a married couple.

I did not like this joke. I took the phone and asked her to leave. She was used to being asked to leave when I woke up. She probably thought it was because I was grumpy. Hopefully, she didn't suspect my enormous and unbreakable morning wood.

What? I croaked.

I need to tell you something, he said.

What more? I thought.

Susan knows.

What?

She knows.

Okay.

I suppose I figured she'd know eventually, but the way he was telling me felt conspiratorial and strange.

You want to join us for brunch? She's eager to see you.

That got me up, but did nothing for my morning wood.

We met at a diner in a portable trailer that served East Coast food like fish cakes made with salt cod. Have them with over-easy eggs. Nothing like it to cure a hangover.

Susan and Chris sat beside each other in the cramped booth. I sat across. Susan looked stern, disapproving, her mouth slightly pouty. It vibed like an act. It was strange to see her across the table and to know that she knew, and knew other things besides. I wondered how much she knew about my involvement, or how accurately or generously Chris had characterized it, but I suspected from her attitude that he had appropriately played up my role. Perhaps it served him to buttress my reputation and sidestep his own primacy of initiative.

I can't believe you two, she said.

Chris only grinned.

I grinned back because I was such an inauthentic fuck.

All this time, she said.

Heh heh heh, we said.

You're dangerous together, she said.

We arched eyebrows and looked pleased.

You're meant to be together.

We tried to hold our grins despite this vaguely homosexual insinuation.

You'd do more for each other than you would for anyone else.

Easy now, Chris said.

Did you figure it out on your own? I asked. Or did he blurt it out in his sleep? Any way to change the subject.

Chris laughed, for no apparent reason.

Every time he came over to pick me up and he had wet hair, Susan said, he'd also have a pocket crammed full of cash.

Wet hair? I asked.

I always showered after a job, Chris said. Robbing banks makes me sweaty.

So you put two and two together? I asked.

Oh, and there was the time when he didn't have pockets in his shorts so he asked me to hold a couple thousand dollars for him, she said. That added up too.

Yeah, I guess it would, I said.

And then there was the time he told me he was going to the gym and I checked his bag to see if he ever washed his gym clothes and saw the biggest gun I'd ever seen in my life.

It wasn't that big, Chris said modestly.

And there was the trip you guys took to New York. And the trip to Australia. And the fact that I read about the movie theatre this morning and Chris asked me to go to that movie theatre about ten times in the last six months.

Our secret history got unfolded before us. Then our breakfast plates arrived.

We were on second cups of coffee when Chris brought the conversation to more practical matters.

About the whole movie-theatre thing, he said. His mouth was full of food, so he slowed down, chewed and swallowed. After I went home this morning for a change of clothes, there was a cop car in the driveway.

My fork in the air, halfway to my mouth.

Apparently, Mom was out in the backyard earlier in the morning, throwing away some compost, and she found the till I'd chucked in the woods, so she called the cops.

She fucking what?

Easy, big fellow, Chris said. You can't blame her. She knew there'd been an arrest on the street last night, and she knew the movie theatre had been robbed, and she found a till in our backyard. What else was she supposed to do?

Holy shit, I said. If my heart beat any harder, Susan and Chris would go dim before my eyes.

Don't worry. The cops figure whoever did the job probably ran through our yard on the way to the lake.

We leaned back as the waitress poured more coffee.

Actually, it makes total sense, Chris continued. Our house happens to be on a direct line between the mall and the lake as the crow flies.

Some crow, I said. I could not believe how calmly he was taking it. Nor Susan, either.

Chris went on.

So they found the till. It's not worth worrying about. My clothes were washed. My car was clean. The cash was at the hotel. Everything's A-okay.

Except for the gun, I said.

Yeah, he said. That part sucks.

What gun? Susan asked.

Nothing, Chris said.

Don't nothing me, she said.

No one spoke. We waited for Chris.

I dropped it, Chris admitted. Somewhere in the woods.

Oh, shit, Susan said.

I could have let him spin. I could have provided Susan with some doubt about his sanity. But I did not have it in me to be so devious.

I found it, I said.

Really? Chris asked, more hopeful than I would have expected.

I took a walk through the woods this morning and found it under some leaves.

Wow, that's awesome. He was relieved and started to laugh.

Jesus, Susan said. You guys are going to get caught, and then what am I going to do for a boyfriend?

Don't worry, Chris said. I'll never get caught.

I noticed that he didn't say *we*.

Susan and Chris began to see even more of each other, as though removing the enormous lie between them brought them closer together. I didn't mind. I think I'd finally resigned myself to their inevitability. I had also become more comfortable in my loneliness, and saw it as something that might propel me to other places, another life.

Our take from the movie theatre had not been that large, so I figured it would only be a matter of time before Chris approached me for another job. After two months went by, however, I wondered if his bank-robbing career might have ended. Perhaps the solidity of his relationship with Susan, the new honesty between them, had extinguished his strange urge to risk it all.

I used my own money to move out. I think my parents were just as relieved as me. My father was being treated for stomach ulcers, and this had reduced his activities outside of the house. He went to work only three days a week. Being around each other so much was more than either of us could take. I found a basement apartment in a nearby neighbourhood. It was not glamorous or exciting but it was my own place. Chris figured I'd get laid way more often now. I urged his words to hasten to God's ears.

Between rent, food, and gas for the piece of shit car I'd bought, I did not have the money to go out much, however, so my opportunities to meet women became woefully rare. I felt lonelier still. I thought about Rivers often, and wondered what might have been different if I'd gone to Thailand with him, what seemed like a lifetime ago.

And then Chris told me that the jobs had not stopped after all, they'd merely stopped for me.

We were in my basement apartment drinking beer and watching a hockey game on my black and white TV. The news floored me.

How many have you done?

Four, he said.

Four was a torrid pace. That meant a job every two to three weeks. I couldn't believe it.

I need to read the newspaper more often, I said.

Chris shook his head. Nothing big time. We're taking it slow. An IGA. A jewellery store. Smash and grab stuff. No banks. No Brinks. No glory.

Who's we? I asked.

He shrugged, as though uncomfortable.

Me and Susan.

And this, as much as anything he'd ever told me, blew my mind.

You're shitting me. I can't believe you got her into this.

I felt like an old grandmother suddenly, but I was upset. It seemed unfair to involve her.

It was her idea. I told her no fifty times. She begged me.

I couldn't believe that, either. It wasn't the Susan I knew. Or was it?

Why?

I don't know, he said. The thrill, I guess. The chance to be a bad girl?

So I was the only one who had misgivings? Everyone else in the world thought robbing a bank was the high of a lifetime?

How does she do? I asked. I suppose that was the next most relevant question when it came to destroying my dignity.

Actually, Chris said, she really sucks.

Don't get personal, I said.

Ha ha. No, I mean it. She's a wreck every time. One time, I was just about to go into a bank and I saw an off-duty cop go inside, so I blew off the job. She rolled the window down and hurled.

I laughed.

Another time, a cashier chased me out of a store until I finally turned around and pointed the gun at her, and when I got into the car, I saw that Susan had wet herself.

Wow.

She said she'd spilled her Slurpee, but you could tell it was piss by the smell.

At least I never pissed myself, I said.

Man, you had some amazing moments, Chris said. Remember when you drove down the embankment onto the highway? That could have been in a movie.

I grinned.

Also, Chris continued, I have to admit celebrating with Susan hasn't been as much fun.

Oh, come on, I said. There's no way that's true. You guys probably fuck like dogs afterwards.

Well, that's true. But partying with your girlfriend just isn't as much fun as partying with a friend.

Or with girls you don't know.

Exactly. Although, if she wanted to party with her, me, and another girl, that would be all right.

Still working on that threesome?

Just need the dominoes to tip the right way.

So how good have the scores been? I asked, ever the practical number cruncher.

Only a couple thou each time. It's hardly even worth it. Just lifestyle maintenance.

Are you kicking the habit?

I think so, he said, nodding. Can't do this forever, right? Neither can Susan. I feel sort of over it. I want to go to cop school. She wants to go to law school. We'll probably get married and have kids. Can't exactly hire a babysitter and then go out and rob a bank, can we?

You know how fucked up that sounds? Law school and cop school, babysitters and bank robberies. You couldn't write a better movie.

Maybe you should, he said.

That had always been part of the deal.

It'll work its way into something, I said. I'll just change the names to protect the guilty and add in a few shootouts and helicopter rides.

We clinked bottles.

Amen to that, brother. Never let the facts get in the way of the truth.

8

I need to explain how it came to be me who pushed for
one last job.

School ended at the beginning of May. It was a moderately successful semester for me. I did fine, but I had no life-transforming courses. There was no Rivers on the curriculum, only plodding and rote learning, a marking of time on a straightforward journey to a credential. At some point, I woke up to the death this represented.

I think it hit home when my father's illness returned. He entered the hospital and got lodged in a bed. When I visited, he seemed unusually happy to see me but also gaunt and tired. I tried to get a grasp on his condition, and so, when visiting hours were over, I walked my mother to the parking lot and badgered her for answers. What did they know about his illness? What were they doing to treat the ulcers? My mother said, He doesn't have ulcers, he has cirrhosis of the liver. It took me another minute to understand what she had told me. Had I misheard her before? Had I imagined ulcers?

Cirrhosis? I asked. She hugged me goodbye and got in her car.

Later that night, lying on the pullout couch in my basement apartment, I understood how artfully she'd lied to me, and what that implied about my entire life. Never any blatant falsehoods, but an atmosphere suffused in falseness. Was she saying my father was an alcoholic? He drank regularly after work, two and sometimes three drinks, but this seemed normal, a way of winding down. He did not thrash and roar. He merely grew quiet, sullen, removed, and went to bed early. Cirrhosis of the liver meant drinking yourself to death. The speckles of blood in the toilet. Had I done that or him? Was I my father's son? If my father was an alcoholic, a secret, desperate, quiet one, what did that say about the way he lived his life? There must have been pressure and stress and dissatisfaction at a level I hadn't understood. My father couldn't stand that I'd wasted a summer pulling rickshaw. But he was drinking himself to death going to work at a bank. He was killing himself and offering me the same gun.

At some point that summer, as I worked my bank job and Chris pulled rickshaw and trained for police academy, I decided that the last thing in the world I wanted to do was go back to school. It wasn't that I hated school, it was that I enjoyed it. If I didn't guard myself against that enjoyment, I might be satisfied with the path that school made possible. I would get the sensible job. I would find the sensible wife. I wouldn't write with the madness of Dostoevsky or the astonishing keenness of Hemingway. I needed to break wildly from this death march and do something bigger and life-altering. I needed to irrevocably wreck the life I was living and cut myself off from safe harbour.

I fixed on a life abroad. I'd find Rivers and get a hut near him, and write and write and write. I wrote him a letter, only the third since his injury, and in it I described my plans. I laid out for him all my biggest fears. I told him about the kinds of books I wanted to write and the greatness I wanted to aspire toward and the fearlessness with which I would attempt it all. What did obscurity and failure and poverty and disregard and frustration and unhappiness matter to me? Even if no one ever learned my name, there would be more glory and honour in that than in whatever success could be achieved by taking the straight and narrow.

I must have passed some threshold or test, done enough to be forgiven for past transgressions, or said the right magic words, because this time, I got a message back.

A postcard of a beach, and on the other side a few words: See you whenever.

I read it as a promise of greatness. I just needed the money to pull it off.

So I set about working my way back into Chris's confidence as his getaway driver of choice for one last job.

I did not expect this to be very difficult. I was surprised, therefore, when he did not respond as enthusiastically as I was hoping. The first time I asked him, we were out drinking, and maybe I was a little boisterous about it, throwing my arm over his shoulder. He laughed a little at my proclamations that we were fearless daredevils and peerless badasses, that Butch and Sundance were our genetic ancestors, that every woman in the room should volunteer for our harem, and that we ought to do one more job. He apologized to the waitress for my lack of manners and later, when we were outside after closing, he stood by watchfully as I tried to wrench a park bench from the ground and then pissed in a fountain filled with pennies and nickels. As he drove me home, I recited Leonard Cohen.

On another occasion, I tried a more sober approach. We met over coffee on a Sunday afternoon. It was a rainy day and he was taking the weekend off from pulling rickshaw, suffering from a tweaked knee. I asked him how things were going with the police academy application, and he expressed frustration with himself for not being more disciplined about studying. I commiserated, but I'd never heard Chris acknowledge a weakness before.

Then kick it into gear, I said, encouraging him to get serious. The summer's not even one-third over.

I will, he promised.

I asked him about Susan. He told me she was great. She was working out—something he'd always nagged her about—and she was making bundles of cash cocktail waitressing, and they had never been so close.

So you're not banging anyone else? I asked.

Well, I wouldn't go that far, he said.

There were a few. The dog-collar schoolteacher was a semi-regular event. He'd had a potentially great but ultimately dissatisfying one-nighter with an incredibly hot eighteen-year-old before sneaking out her window, carrying his clothes and his hard-on, as the mother banged on the locked bedroom door. A couple others not really worth mentioning.

Nothing serious, he said.

I wondered if Susan had any idea. He did not think of them as serious, so he did not carry the weight in an obvious way. Same went for the robberies. Who would suspect him?

I asked him again about one last job, and he became more evasive. He agreed with me that it would be a good idea to do a big one, and that we should get it set up. But he failed to follow through on that notion with any concrete plans and even snapped at me once. In this, he reminded me of my old passive-aggressive self.

Another month went by. I got darker and became more frustrated with my life. My father was back to work, doing better on his carrot juice and roughage diet. I felt as though I were being strangled by my work as a teller. I tried to explain my woes to Chris on an afternoon when we went swimming. We were at Oathill Lake, where we'd met Susan and Leah a million years before. We had a dozen beers with us and discovered it was not easy to swim out to the floating dock, laden in such a way. But the attempt reminded us of other crazy things we'd done, and seemed worth the effort. We drank in the sun, standing up to piss into the lake whenever needed, then lying back down.

I'm fucked, I said. Chris asked why. I wanted to tell him. But I couldn't. I shrugged instead. Too drunk to get back to shore, I explained.

I got an idea for another job, he said.

I listened. I needed it. I tried not to show how much.

There was a new store near the old Canadian Tire doing amazing business. It was called The Real Atlantic Superstore and it was eating Canadian Tire's lunch. Chris had screwed a girl who worked cashier there and she was amazed at how much money they kept in the tills. It seemed like a no-sweat way to make forty or fifty thousand without going through the hassle of actually robbing a bank or shooting any Brinks guards. I was good with all that.

It took us another month to get our act together. My will never wavered, though I sensed that Chris's did. He hemmed and hawed about a go date, and even when we set one, on a Tuesday evening the second week in August, he cancelled two days before, citing a bronchial infection.

Can't do the forty-yard dash if I'm wheezing like my grandfather, he said, and coughed for good measure.

A week after that, I called him and laid down the law. I didn't want to go back to school. I needed to go to Thailand, but I'd just registered for school because I had no other fucking choice, and the reason I had no choice was because he wouldn't commit to doing one fucking job, after all the times I'd done what he asked. It was time to do right by me.

His voice went cold in response.

This has got to be a mutual decision, don't you think?

Our decisions had never seemed very mutual before. But was that his fault or mine? I could not win for losing.

But Chris, who was also my friend, relented. We'll go tomorrow, he said.

He showed up at my place late. It was not too late to do the job, but it was late for my nerves. I asked him where he'd been. He told me he and Susan had been in bed together.

I think it was the best sex we ever had, he admitted.

It was not the kind of thing I wanted to hear.

We cracked a few beers to work up our courage and discuss

some last-minute details, but Chris was still marvelling about their sex session.

Actually, it wasn't the sex, he said, it was the after-sex. We lay in each other's arms for over an hour. Maybe cuddling and affection isn't full of shit after all.

Spoken like someone who gets enough sex, I said.

He laughed, but before we were done drinking, he mentioned again how amazing it had been to be entangled with her.

I almost couldn't force myself to leave, he said.

Then he stood up.

Let's get this shit over with so I can get back to Susan.

I gave a last glance around my shitty apartment with the shitty sofa bed and the shitty black and white TV and followed him out the door. I didn't even bother to lock up.

We took my car instead of his. Chris had a feeling the black Fiero might have been spotted on a previous job, and he didn't want to use it. I didn't want to use my car because it tightened my own complicity, but I could hardly say no. We drove the half mile or so to the Superstore and parked near the entrance. We had about fifteen minutes until closing and there was suddenly no reason to hurry. Chris didn't fidget. He just sat. I sat too. Although we'd done these jobs a million times before, there was a sense of ending. We'd never do it again.

I've got an idea, I said. We'll go to Australia and start all over. They've got great banks loaded with money. They've got more hot chicks than they know what to do with. Plus they speak English.

I was summoning Butch Cassidy. I meant that we were a duo, and we'd been through a lot together, robbed some banks and trains, loved the same woman, jumped from cliffs, travelled to New York, and that it was our last job.

I don't think I can do it, Chris said, which wasn't in the script.

Australia's not so bad, I said.

I mean I don't think I can do this job, Chris said.

A panic fluttered through my chest.

You've got to do it, I said.

I'm not sure I can.

It was unsettling to see Chris waver. He'd never wavered before.

It's easy, I said. You've done it a hundred times.

Doesn't feel right, he said.

Just because it doesn't feel right doesn't mean it won't go right.

He looked at me, a little more determination in his eyes.

You're probably right, he said.

I know I'm right, I said.

Same as always, he said.

Easy as pie, I said.

You'll be here, he said.

Always am, I said.

Then let's get her done, he said.

And he left the car.

I watched him walk across the parking lot and into the store.

Now, knowing what the years brought, I'd have given any-thing for a Butch and Sundance ending. Gut shot, a last look, a last joke, running out into the daylight together to face all those rifles.

Chris insisted they got away. I knew better. Which of us was right? The evidence is on my side. The moving picture stopped moving. The frame froze. Butch and Sundance, guns blazing, got nailed to the crucifix of consequence.

But I also know that, dead or not, Butch and Sundance got off easy.

The real crucifix is time itself, and the way life keeps moving on, and the way you can't undo anything you've done, no matter how heavy that time weighs on you.

Drip rip tock tick.

He came out running. I was late turning the corner of the parking lot, so I probably left him standing all alone on the curb for ten or twenty seconds. For this I will be eternally sorry.

When he was in the car, I gunned out of the parking lot, and then slowed to the speed limit on the street. I glanced over at him. He looked fine. I asked him how it went. He said it went fine. I drove. He started rooting through the money, then said we should just get rid of it. I asked him what the hell he was talking about. He told me something wasn't right. I insisted that everything was just fine, he'd said so himself. He told me we should drive to the harbour or the lake and dump the money. I told him he was out of his fucking mind. He calmed down by the time we got home.

It was a pleasant August evening, and we stood on the grass of the house where I had my apartment. We congratulated ourselves on a job well done. We didn't feel the urge to celebrate, or at least he didn't. He had better things to do than count money together and drink from a mini-bar, or maybe he just wanted time away from me. It hurt a little, but I had what I wanted, a bag full of freedom. I could quit my job, quit school, and head out for Asia. I could finally leave Chris and Susan behind.

We shook hands. He said that he would see me later. He got into his black Fiero. He was heading back to Susan's. I had my complicated feelings about this. As I watched him go, I was warmed by the late sun, the perfect calm. I felt free, finally, in a way I'd never known before. He drove slowly around the corner, up the hill, and out of sight. It was over. What was over? His life. It ended on the highway. And part of my life ended too.

9

They stopped him on the highway for speeding. They asked him what was in the bag and pressed the muzzle of a gun against his temple. They yanked him out of the car and hand-cuffed him, a dozen officers on him at once. They drove him in a squad car to the police station. The cuffs were tight on his wrists. The steel cut into his skin and bent his hands back in a bad way, so he leaned forward and rested the top of his head on the Plexiglas. He stared at his knees and couldn't believe what was happening.

They took him to the processing room and strip-searched him. They took away his belt and his shoelaces so he wouldn't hang himself. They led him down a short corridor lined with empty cells. They gave him the larger corner cell and left him alone for the next four and a half hours.

He figured the endless wait was one of their mind games. He figured there would be more mind games coming, and that he'd be so tired and out of sorts as they arrived that he'd only understand them to be mind games in retrospect. His dad had told him enough stories like that to fill a book.

He finally heard keys in the door. He did not recognize the officer standing in the entrance. Politely, the officer asked Chris to come this way. The tone of voice—helpful, friendly, even warm—inspired an unlikely hope. Was he going to be released? He knew this was not even remotely possible. He thought about it anyway.

He was led up the stairs to the second floor, through a large office with a maze of desks and file cabinets, and into a room that was walled with white perforated foam board, the kind that muffles sound. Officer Drury, our friendly neighbourhood cop, sat behind the table in the middle of the room.

Drury greeted Chris. Chris nodded. He knew Drury was a robbery and homicide detective now, no longer just a patrolman, but it still surprised him to see such a familiar face. Drury represented the neighbourhood and people they knew in common, including his parents. Those were connections that brought home the consequences of what was happening to him. But Drury's presence also gave him hope. He'd seen Drury four or five times over the past year, once at a backyard barbecue, and never did he get the sense that Drury had been on to him. Chris reminded himself that he'd been caught on only one job. They didn't have him on the others. And he'd had no bullets in his gun. He'd taken out the clip and would never need to admit the gun had been loaded. No bullets. A first and only offence. Even if they stomped on him with both feet, he wouldn't get a heavy sentence for one job, no more than three years, likely less. This was disastrous and tragic but less awful than it could have been. It was a deal with God he was willing to strike. That optimism gave him just enough strength to still the tremble in his hand.

As if reading Chris's mind, Drury turned in his chair, motioned behind him, and asked Chris to look. Over Drury's shoulder, Chris saw that the back wall was covered in sheets of paper, pinned there like a kid's science project display.

Go ahead, Drury said. Feel free to get up.

He did not want to look, but he walked over to the wall anyway. Mentally, he was sluggish, and taking extra time to process even the simplest things.

He saw his life pinned to the wall.

Every job he'd ever done was described in great detail. Maps, dates, amounts, times. Photographs. Eyewitness quotes. He saw pictures of himself pulling rickshaw. He saw pictures of himself sitting in the Fiero, drinking coffee. He read the dates and flight numbers when he had left the country, and the dates and flight numbers when he returned. He saw coloured dots marking his hangouts, and geometric lines tracing his frequent routes. There was a Polaroid of a shoe print on a muddy hill. There was a still from a security camera as he walked out of a bank. There were Polaroids of a mud-encrusted deposit bag pulled from the bottom of the lake, held aloft by a scuba diver in one shot, spread out on the dock for several others. There was a scribbled note of a partial licence-plate number and an arrow drawn from that note to a document stapled directly to the board. He flipped the pages and saw that it was a transcript of an interview of the cashier who'd chased him across the parking lot. The partial, he read, had been obtained under hypnosis.

He walked back to the table and sat down. He wanted to hang his head but didn't. He established a neutral expression to meet Drury's gaze. Inside, he was floored by the painstaking nature of the case they'd built against him. How long they'd known. The amount of evidence they'd compiled. The accuracy was chilling and also impressive. He wouldn't have guessed the local cops had it in them. And still they'd needed to catch him in the act. He wanted to lift the table and throw it across the room. He wanted to be in Susan's arms.

There was nothing, he realized suddenly, about Susan on that wall. Nothing about me. He wondered if Susan and I were in another room, facing our own interrogators. He didn't think so. It came to him that he was all alone, and he felt a strange comfort in our absence. The monster had missed us. We were safe to run out of the cave while he waved his torch and drew the attention of the beast. A moment passed. He shook his head, feeling less woozy, and stretched his jaw open. He hadn't known how tensely he'd been clenching it.

Drury started in on the questions slowly, asking mundane details. Every two or three questions seemed to circle back to the same unimportant matters. Which car did he drive the night he robbed the movie theatre? Had it been a Tuesday or a Wednesday when he did the jewellery store? The questions were trivial and irritating, and sometimes, to stop the irritation and shore up some temporary mental space, he'd answer one and force Drury to write something down. Not enough to incriminate himself. Nothing that could be used against him. Then, Drury would circle back again, to some other mundane fact, and insist he'd said something he knew he hadn't. It became increasingly difficult to think clearly. He drifted during one answer and forgot what he was about to say. Drury slammed the notepad down on the table, and Chris jerked up in surprise, heart racing, as though he'd fallen asleep. The slam sounded more like a slap, a pathetic impersonation of force, and the attempt at being tough pissed Chris off. He narrowed his eyes and glared at Drury and dared him with his glare to try that shit again. The questions resumed. Mundane details. Repeated details. Issues and clarifications that were not incriminating. Then Chris forgot to put a brake on his words when Drury asked him what kind of gun he'd used at the CIBC, and he told him it was the .357 Magnum. Drury noted that, jotting it down with the same care that he'd noted all of the bullshit so far, but now Chris's heart was thudding vigorously. He put his mind back on track. He willed himself to concentrate, to be completely present. Drury looked tired. Chris had more stamina, more mental strength. The nice officer delivered a cup of Tim Hortons coffee and a ham and cheese sandwich. Drury looked pissed off at the interruption. Chris took bites and chewed. The ham tasted peculiarly strong, and the bread was like wet newspaper, but the coffee actually settled his stomach, despite the lack of cream. Drury asked him about the motorcycle helmet, and why he'd used a ski mask sometimes, and he felt all the energy of the food leaving him. He stared numbly at the table and couldn't remember what he had been saying.

It became pointless after a while, knowing what they knew. He kept glancing up and seeing the pictures and the map and the dates and amounts. He found it difficult to focus on more than one or two cautionary thoughts at a time. And then somehow, Drury spooled another detail out of Chris about a run across a parking lot, and it meant (he realized all of a sudden) that he'd now admitted to the first CIBC job. He thought of that leap and how free it had felt at the time, flying through the air.

Four hours later, he'd signed a twenty-page confession. The way Drury carved the admissions onto paper amazed him. It was fine craftsmanship. Detail work. A chisel cut here, a light brush with sandpaper, a blow of air to clear away the obscuring dust. Even as the fight slipped away from him, Chris kept his remaining energy focused on one immovable dispute. No matter how many times Drury asked, no matter how righteous and angry Drury seemed to get in imminent victory, Chris insisted, with disdain and irritation in his voice, that he'd done every single job alone.

You think I needed anyone's help?

He stared at Drury as if our friendly neighbourhood cop was the biggest idiot in the world.

Drury blew air out of his cheeks, cracked his neck, and grimaced, and inside, Chris thought, Fuck you. Fuck you.

His lawyer was baffled that he'd revealed so much information voluntarily. At some level, still exhausted and in shock, Chris was baffled too. His father was furious for the same reason, but there was also a desperate regret in his anger. I thought you would have known better, his father said. Even if they'd caught you with a smoking gun in your hand, I thought you would have known better than to say a goddamn word.

The lawyer considered appealing the twenty-page statement on the grounds that Chris hadn't been offered a phone call. It seemed a trivial technicality to Chris, but any hope was worth chasing down.

There's all kinds of stuff in this case that stinks, the lawyer said. I don't completely understand it. There's something they're not telling us.

Privately, after his father left, the lawyer told him what to expect. In his favour, he was from a good family. His father was a cop, for God's sake. He was a responsible young man and had been a productive student. He was not a drug addict and had never been convicted of anything before, not even a misdemeanour. He did not fit any profile, and the justice system was built on profiles. On the other hand, the court might be tempted to go hard and make an example of him, to show justice being done. The media was all over the case. They loved every aspect of it. Chris had been big local news for two days running and would continue to be of interest during the course of a trial. A lot of attention would be on him and his family. The legal fees would be expensive, approximately $100,000 for starters, just to go to trial with a not-guilty plea, but that might be worth it considering that Chris was facing eighty-nine counts of armed robbery and a possible minimum of twenty-five years in prison.

Given that his life was at stake, Chris told the lawyer he wanted to go to trial. But at the bail hearing, he was denied. The announcement that he couldn't go home, even for the weeks or months leading up to the trial, sucked all the life out of his body. They shackled him up, legs and wrists chained together, as though he were a rabid animal, and walked him out. No chance to even speak with his parents. He waited in the court cell while arrangements were being made, and sensed that something else had gone wrong. An hour went by. Another. He couldn't believe he wasn't going home. He'd counted on the reprieve of bail to catch his breath. Even if it was just for days, he wanted to stand on grass again, sleep in his own bed, talk to Susan.

The court officer finally appeared at his cell and said that it was time to go back to remand. Because there was so much media waiting outside, he suggested that Chris pull his jacket up over his head to hide his face. Chris okayed the idea and regretted it almost immediately, the shame it represented, the cowardice. He shuffled out of the courthouse with his shoulders slouched and his head covered, seeing nothing but feet around him, jostled by the elbows, the shouted questions, until they loaded him in the caged van.

This is the way we saw him on TV.

It was impossible to see him in person. So Susan and I saw each other instead.

I finished my summer job at the bank. I started school. I gave no thought to Thailand and Rivers. How could I abandon Chris now? It seemed possible, too, that I would be forbidden to leave the country. I lived in terror of being visited by the police. I went about my life as if nothing had changed, but I was numb with fear and haunted by the plight of my friend. I began an affair with Susan. It was initiated during one of our support sessions, those long evenings or nights we spent together talking and not talking, hugging when she needed to be held. Soon enough, the hugging became an expression of a different kind of need. I don't know who needed what more. Guilt-ridden, I've wondered a thousand times where the balance was tipped and by whom. I'd like to say I wasn't responsible, but there were things

I indisputably did and much evidence against any proclamations of innocence.

We got addicted to that rhythm of solace and sex. It was a kind of mutual masturbation. Like masturbation, it helped relieve the stress, and passed the time, and also felt unhealthy and wrong. She visited my apartment three or four nights a week after work or school and we would fuck hard, cry hard, and hold each other. Once or twice, we talked about escaping together, fleeing to some faraway place like Europe or India, beginning a new life. It felt as though Chris were already dead and we were making plans with each other to console ourselves for his loss.

As Chris's closest friends, we actually received some sympathy for what we were going through, for a time. People treated us initially as though we were victims—not victims of what Chris had done, but victims of circumstance and of the police and of the confusion and shock that had fixated us all. Even my parents. They worried about how I was handling it. Perhaps they were too traumatized to put the pieces of the puzzle together. My father asked if Chris had been addicted to drugs, or whether he'd needed money to support some kind of gambling habit. In other words, why? Like others, and certainly like a banker, he couldn't believe there was no money left over from all the jobs. How had Chris spent it? He was less angry at Chris than I would have expected, and this comforted me a little, made me wonder what compassion could overcome. My mother expressed astonishment that I didn't know what Chris had been up to. After all, we spent so much time together. Then she quickly cut off whatever doubts might have been penetrating by observing that Chris had clearly been a master of disguise, as though he were a caped villain. How could his parents not have known? In this question she implied something else. How could they have raised him so terribly? These conversations were rare. I didn't visit home often, but when I did, my parents seemed to treat me more respectfully than before, as if they'd been kick-started into thinking of me as an adult by the adult nature of Chris's predicament. In the newspapers, he was referred to as a twenty-one-year-old man. I always wondered who they were talking about when they used that description. Not my friend Chris. Not me. We were just kids. We were still cutting down tree forts and shooting frogs.

I saw Chris's parents only a few times, and they were guarded around me but needy. Chris's mother spoke about Chris's innocence, as though he was the victim of a police conspiracy. She talked just as fervently about how important his closest friends were now, an implication in this about some kind of reckoning, a scrutiny over loyalty. Meeting her litmus test required subscribing to her beliefs without question. Her innocent child had been framed. Chris's father only asked me to help Chris bear his time inside. Write him when I could. Visit him when I was allowed. I think he knew better than any of the parents what might have happened. He was the least likely to be naive.

Susan and I geared up for the trial, telling each other that the light at the end of the tunnel was getting closer, that something good might even happen. But we both dreaded it, particularly any scrutiny about our own roles, the questions about how much we'd known. We knew that Chris was going to fight the charges, fight the arrest, fight the twenty-page statement. His lawyer was publicly questioning the police tactics in the investigation and the Crown prosecutor's ethics in sharing evidence. There was the matter of a gun that had been recorded into evidence but couldn't be produced. There was noise about an inquiry into how and why the police had determined to stop Chris's car on the highway. It all seemed very overwrought, and yet we could not help but hope.

My anxiety was like a paralysis slowly taking over my body and mind. I could not eat or move my bowels. I could not concentrate or finish a complex sentence. I could barely sleep. When I did sleep, I had terrible nightmares. I saw a courtroom filled with the curious and the bereaved. I saw Chris sitting in the witness stand and heard lawyers picking apart the flaws in his logic, the mistakes in his reasoning. What had been a debatable philosophical idea, and a somewhat thrilling adventure to conceive of before the consequences landed hard, now struck everyone, even me, as an unimaginable transgression.

Then, without warning, two days before the trial was slated to begin, we learned that Chris had decided to plead guilty, forgoing the need for witnesses or the presentation and arguing of evidence beyond what the prosecution had already brought forth. There would be no inquiry, either. Chris's lawyer came to an agreement with the prosecutor for Chris to serve twelve years in prison for fifty-two counts of armed robbery, assigned concurrently. It was, according to the newspapers, a surprisingly good deal, and one that had the whiff of expediency about it.

Five days after sentencing, Chris was shipped to Dorchester Penitentiary, a decrepit and fortress-like maximum security prison in New Brunswick, three hours away. To us, it was as though he had been taken across the River Styx and into Hades.

We couldn't understand why he pleaded guilty. It puzzled us like a mystery. Susan thought it was her fault. Chris's father had told her that Chris was worried about Susan having to testify.

His mother blames me, Susan said. She thinks I led him into it. She thinks I'm this evil witch who wanted all kinds of stuff Chris couldn't afford to buy.

She burst into tears again. I held her, and yet, if I was to confess one more secret, I was getting tired of holding her while she cried.

Another bout of sex broke the monotony of strained emotion. We even laughed a little—I kept brushing back her hair and it kept falling over her eyes, which seemed funny at the time. Then we got sad again because we felt terrible for laughing. It seemed we should be in mourning forever.

But there was also something horribly freeing about Chris pleading guilty and beginning his sentence. It reminded me of Kafka's *The Metamorphosis*. There is the grim, sick confinement of the man who has become an insect, and you're horrified for him and horrified of him, and you hope for a miracle that will cure his condition or end the nightmare. But the miracle never comes and the condition becomes harder to stand. You want him not to die but when he does die, when he's gone, you are relieved, and you walk out into the sunshine for the first time in months, stirred by the breeze, with a lighter heart. Maybe you hate yourself for this. And maybe you hate yourself because you don't.

Was this what lightness demanded?

We decided to go out for a change. We were sick of hiding in my apartment, as though we were contagious, and went to a bar in Halifax to be among people, and perhaps less among ourselves. It was a Tuesday night and the bar was not one we'd spent much time in back in the day. The baseball game was on. It was the World Series between the Oakland A's and the San Francisco Giants. I paid more attention to the game than Susan. The Oakland A's were a juggernaut that year, and it was awe-inspiring to watch a lineup that included Rickey Henderson, Jose Canseco, and Mark McGwire, as though Achilles, Hercules, and Theseus had decided to play ball. Around the third inning, a guy I knew from the rickshaw shed, named Steve, appeared in front of our table. He was wearing jeans and a white T-shirt. He had a leather bracelet around his wrist and a silver hoop through one ear. I didn't like him, particularly, but I said hello. He told me to go fuck myself, and he greeted Susan by calling her a cunt.

Susan's face went pale. She looked as though she'd been punched in the stomach.

I asked what the fuck was his problem.

I saw you two holding hands, he said. He had a look of disgust on his face, and at some level, I was amazed, after all that had been said and done in the shed, all the lying and the cheating and the misogyny and the sexual escapades, that any member in good standing could be disgusted by anything done by another.

I also couldn't remember holding hands. That was how unconsciously we must have done it.

We're friends, I said.

I bet you fucking are, he said, and he put his foot on my chair and pushed it away from the table. I felt as though I had been shifted by a giant.

Please don't, Susan said.

Shut your fucking mouth, you skank, Steve said.

I stood up.

It was impossible to stop his fury. He came at me with both barrels, two fists flying, and I took punches to the head and the mouth and the nose and the neck while only trading weak and flailing shots in return. I remembered hearing Susan screaming. I crumpled to the floor and he began to stomp on my back and kick me in the ribs with the sharp toe of his shoe. Each punch, each kick was an explosion of gratitude. I deserved every blow.

The bartender and a couple of his companions stopped him. Steve demanded that I be thrown out onto the street. We know you did it, you rat bastard! he yelled. Why the fuck aren't you in prison too, huh? Why did Chris take the whole fall?

Nobody called the police. Nobody moved to help me except Susan. She was weeping and shaking as she grabbed my jacket and keys. We helped each other out.

You deserve each other! Steve yelled after us. You're both fucking cunts!

Susan wanted to take me to the hospital. I didn't want to go. It was difficult to breathe, but if my ribs were broken, there was nothing that could be done. I could move my arms and turn my neck and I had not lost any teeth. I just needed sleep.

She lay with me on the sofa bed. It sagged badly with one occupant. It was almost impossible for two. You needed to cling to the edge so as not to slip into a huddled middle, poked at by springs. I almost wished that she would leave, except I was as low and lonely as I'd ever been in my life. I missed my friend badly. I remembered the time, all those years ago, when Dusty had kicked me in the face and broken my arm. Only Chris had called for justice. Now Chris was gone, and the beatings were back.

Do you think it will ever get better? she asked.

And because I hated myself and hated her too, I said, I hope not.

She seemed ready for my cruelty. She seemed to need it in that moment.

The next week, while San Francisco was still paralyzed by an earthquake and the world could only watch, she tried to kill herself with pills. It was a half-hearted attempt, one of those so-called cries for help. After she recovered, her parents sent her across the continent to Vancouver, where she moved in with an aunt. I heard that she began classes at the university that winter. I never saw her again.

10

I was lonely, and I was not well liked. I had a lab partner who didn't know me, and we went to the local art house cinema. Milan Kundera got me laid. And when I said that the lightness of that moment was a blessed relief, a visit by a nymph who, for one night, held a bowl over my forehead to catch the dripping venom, that does not adequately capture the pain I was in. Without sounding any more melodramatic than I already do, how can I describe how close I was to killing myself as well? I don't mean that I was going to jump off a bridge or swallow a bottle of pills, but I wanted my life to be destroyed. I looked for other people and other means to do it for me. I drank as hard as you can drink. (Like father, like son.) I got myself beat up whenever possible. (Each punch, each kick, an explosion of gratitude.) I did it because my friend was in prison and I was not. The light one was heavy, the heavy one walked lightly away.

How do you live with your own lightness when someone is willing to carry so much weight?

When the semester ended, I bought a backpack, gave up my apartment, and told my parents I was going to travel in Southeast Asia. My father, who had never understood me, understood me less than ever now. But he gripped my hand and then hugged me and told me that he knew I'd find my way. I was less certain of this than ever, and skeptical of his born-again lightness, but I will forever cherish the weight of that embrace. I wish I'd known how much an ending it was.

I flew to Hong Kong. I arrived at night, dazzled by the lights of that very foreign city, and made my way through its dense glamour and money into its dingiest squalor. I rented a bed in a room with five other men, all migrant workers, in an apartment complex. My window overlooked a wide garbage chute that must have been created when the neighbouring buildings got conjoined. In the evenings, a rat the size of a cat would appear on the sill of the open window and stare at the food being cooked on the hot stove. One of the men, a Bangladeshi who spoke English, always said hello to the rat and called him Charlie. I could tell this was done for my benefit.

I bought a typewriter in Hong Kong from an old Chinese man who spoke English with a British accent. The shop was at the top of the stairs in a building that was bursting with other stores, on a busy side street near the stock exchange. The old man asked me what kind of work I was doing, and I told him I was a writer. It was the first time I'd ever told anyone that my work was writing. He asked me where I was living in Hong Kong, and I told him I was not living here and not staying for long. I was travelling. I wanted the typewriter to fit in my backpack.

You travel with this? he asked in astonishment. It's too heavy!

I told him I could handle the weight, but that I would need extra ribbons.

At airport security, they became upset by the unusual device I was lugging. Everyone was on edge because of Salman Rushdie and assorted terrorist threats. They pulled out my typewriter and exposed it accusingly, demanding to know what it was. It was very odd to see a typewriter emerge from a backpack and I could understand their confusion. Dissociated from the harmless act of typing, linked to the dangerous act of bringing strange items onto planes, it seemed sinister, even threatening.

It's a typewriter, I said, not a bomb.

And that seemed to bring us all to our senses and made everyone laugh.

But later, as I typed, and each key punch exploded off the page, I was no longer sure it wasn't a bomb after all.

I flew to Thailand. In Bangkok, I stayed on Khao San Road in a guest house where I had my own room. The walls between the rooms were thin plywood and I could hear everything around me, the coughing, the farting, the fucking, the flicking of lighters. The restaurant on the ground floor was a collection of tables in a garage open to the street. Like every restaurant, it showed movies every night. *Apocalypse Now. Easy Rider.* If you didn't like what was playing, you could stroll down the street and catch a different movie somewhere else. The air was layered with smells and the sounds of Western music and bleating horns. The streets were filled with vagabonds, and I got some solace walking anonymously among them. Everyone had come from somewhere else. Everyone was going somewhere different. No one knew what I'd done, who I'd hurt, or how much I dreaded every new morning.

One night, I forced myself to sit through *Butch Cassidy and the Sundance Kid.* I bought a train ticket the next day to head south for the islands and look for Rivers. I figured if anyone could understand what had happened and how I could somehow manage to use that in my writing, it was either him or Joseph Conrad.

A suspicious robbery and homicide detective might ask, Where did he, this uncharged friend of a bank robber, who'd needed one last job, get the money to travel the world?

In Halifax, after Susan tried to kill herself, I received a letter from Chris. It was the first prison letter he'd sent me. My hands shook when I opened it.

It was a long letter, written in stages and in different places—remand, county, maximum. The type of paper changed every two or three pages, too. He apologized for not sending it sooner. Stamps were hard to come by. Sometimes the letter was detail oriented, as though he were trying to sort through the confusion of what he was experiencing by relaying as many facts as possible. Sometimes he confessed how frightened he was, and how he was learning what to say and not to say, and whom he could be friends with and whom he should stay away from. Sometimes it was funny. He had a way of making light of the most awful fears. He told me about some of the inmates he was getting to know, and what he'd learned about what they were in for. He told me that he received a big pile of forwarded mail when he arrived and that among the envelopes was his orientation package for police academy and a late notice and dire warning for a hefty unpaid credit card bill. Both institutions, he said, would be a tad surprised by where their correspondence had ended up. He did not mention any lack of letters from me.

Intermittently, he talked about how much he missed Susan, and asked me to look after her. He must not have known what she had done to herself, or that she and I had gotten together. He wished that he could understand why she wouldn't write or respond to his letters. He imagined it must have been just too hard on her. She probably had no idea how hard that was on him.

I know she's going to need to move on without me, he wrote, because she sure as shit isn't going to wait twelve years. Nor would I ask her to. So I wish nothing but the best for her, and I'm sorry for what I put her through. You too.

He'd heard from some of the boys that I was being blamed for his predicament, and he was doing his best to send word that it wasn't true. He'd caused his own problems. Still, he was touched by how many people had written him letters of friendship and support, even if they often included details about how they were going to torture and kill me.

Then he told me that he wanted and expected me to be a great writer by the time he got out. If he was going to do his time, survive this fucking hellhole, and emerge with a life worth living, I had to live up to my part of the bargain too.

He signed off: Start writing, motherfucker.

I read and reread the letter often over the following week. I worked my way through it so many times that it began to dry and yellow. Then I noticed an odour to some of the pages and realized those were the ones that were most yellow. The odour was distinctive, acrid, and familiar. I realized suddenly that it was urine.

I put down the paper. I felt as though I'd been exposed suddenly to the degradation and squalor of the prison. How and why had piss gotten on his letter? Had an inmate desecrated it? Had a guard? I no longer wanted to read it, or touch it.

In the middle of the night, waking out of unsettled sleep, I finally understood. I found a lighter and held the letter up to the flame and read the other message he had written.

I stood by the side of the lake three nights later, in early November, the water so cold it frightened me. I wore long underwear and track pants and a ski mask and gloves, and I carried a long knife and had a flashlight taped to my arm. I turned on the flashlight, stuck my arm in the water, held my breath, and pushed forward.

I swam all the way to the floating dock.

When I got there, I wasn't sure I could take the cold any longer. I lay on the wood and tried to catch my breath and stop my heart from racing. I thought, I'm going to have a heart attack out here, lying on this fucking dock. Summoning whatever will I had left, I rolled to my side, shone the light underneath the dock and stuck my face in the water to try and see. I couldn't find what I was looking for. I took the knife and I slid back in and went under and held my breath and squeezed my eyes tight as I sawed at the rope that kept the floating dock tethered to the concrete block far below. My hand and my arm and my chest and my cock went numb. I feared that I would drop the knife. Finally, the rope frayed and separated and I felt the umbilical cord of our life detach. I pushed the floating dock to shore, kicking and churning the water behind it.

No other kids would ever use the dock again, I thought, as I flipped it over. Fuck them, I said out loud, my teeth chattering uncontrollably. I was doing them a favour.

The amount he'd saved from each of the jobs was wrapped in plastic and stuck in one of the four barrels that kept the dock afloat.

The money allowed me to escape. The money bought me freedom. The money saved whatever was worth saving of my goddamn miserable life.

I took a ferry to the island where I knew Rivers and Leah had been. I sat on the iron deck with my backpack propped beside me, gifted with a bit of shade from a paint-flaked gunnel.

There were others like me on the deck, all backpackers, young, unshaven or unkempt, dressed like hippies with colourful troubadour clothes, multiple piercings, and sandalled feet. I had already exchanged my old clothes for this kind of outfit, but I didn't go all the way with the colour and the flamboyance, which made me stand out and look more serious. We gained a cheap kind of camaraderie as a group, stuck together in the same circumstances, on the way to the same island. A woman started talking about a temple she had visited in India, and how hot it had been there. A man mentioned a volcano he had climbed in Indonesia, and the difficulties of gaining access to the area because of local unrest. More stories got traded. I noticed that this happened whenever a group of backpackers were forced to spend time together for some reason. I thought of them as road tales. They reminded me of the way Chris, in his prison letter to me, had described inmates trading details about their lives. You knew the stories weren't the complete truth, that they were shaped and constructed for various reasons, to garner credibility, for instance, to justify a choice. This kind of casual and unverifiable lying suited me just fine.

When the ferry docked and the assault of touts met us on the shore, we disbanded (an urgency about us, a hastening in our step) and set off in separate directions. It was as if we never wanted to see each other again.

Those were my kind of people.

I did not find Rivers on the first island or the second. But I did read *The Unbearable Lightness of Being*. Beyond the discussion of weight and light, and the ramifications of existential choices, the passages I read most closely, with the most recognition, were the ones about interrogation.

The hero, a surgeon named Tomas, is the epitome of lightness, but under interrogation, he finds his inner weight, refusing to collaborate, to name names, to recant his personal views, even though this means sacrificing his career in medicine.

I felt that Kundera had a special understanding into what happens when you are being questioned. Even so, it seemed a fictional stretch to me that Tomas could be so stalwart and fearless in refusing to sign a trumped-up confession, despite having so much to lose.

But because it is a novel, this is what happens, and Tomas still gets laid.

I kept looking. More islands, more beaches. I came to a beach that was so difficult to access, it made me hopeful. You needed to hitchhike to the far side of the island and hire a fisherman in a pontoon boat to take you around the coast to a sheltered cove, bordered with unclimbable rocks and a dense coconut palm forest. It was the kind of place you might go if you wanted to avoid being found.

The pontoon boat brought me to within twenty feet of the beach and then lodged on something shallow. The fisherman, his flat and ancient feet straddling the gunwale for balance, leaned on a long bamboo pole to steady the boat and allow me to get out. The water came up to my waist, and I lifted my backpack above my head and waded to shore, like a marine carrying his rifle.

I put my backpack down when I reached the open-air restaurant with a palm frond–covered bar. It was lunchtime, or thereabouts, and a few travellers were seated at tables in their bathing suits and sarongs, eating salads, drinking lassis or water, playing backgammon or reading. They did not look up. One of them looked a bit like Leah, in her bikini, from long ago.

I sat at an open table. I was very tired and not feeling well, perhaps a little dehydrated. A boy around thirteen in bare feet and bare chest asked if I wanted anything. I told him I wanted a bottle of water and a hut. He came back with the bottle of water.

I must have fallen asleep. When I opened my eyes, the restaurant was empty, and it was later in the afternoon. I sat up. I saw a Thai woman behind the bar. She was older, perhaps forty, and she was putting away glasses. When she saw me, she walked over.

Her name was Sunny. She was the owner. I asked her for a hut, and she led me along a meandering path past coconut trees and clumps of tall grass to a place I could rent for three dollars a night. It felt good to slip my backpack off again. It had never seemed so heavy. I felt as if I'd been holding myself together, and now I was coming apart.

Before Sunny left, I asked her my question.

Have you seen a man with one arm and one leg? He was with a beautiful young woman.

She looked at me as though I was joking or crazy.

I kicked off my sandals and lay on the bed. A breeze came

in through the window above. I could hear the rustling of palm leaves outside, and I swear I saw a monkey peek in to check on me.

I slept so heavily I did not know who I was. When I woke, it was night. I was so thirsty I walked to the restaurant, my feet uncertain on the sand. It seemed as though everyone else was asleep now, and I wondered if I'd slept through the entire evening.

Rivers was the only one still at the restaurant. He sat at a table by himself, before a bottle of Mekhong whiskey. He was reading a book. There were two glasses. I did not recognize him at first because he had both arms and legs.

Hi, I said.

You don't look so good, he offered.

This coming from him.

I've been better.

He poured me a drink. I would have preferred water, but I clinked glasses with him.

Where's Leah? I asked.

It was an abrupt question, and it sounded accusatory.

She got restless, he said. She's not tired enough to be here yet. She has a beautiful soul.

I know, I said. I had a feeling that Leah had been the strongest of us all, the most capable of living. I missed her.

Where did she go?

He waved his hand toward the ocean. Malaysia. Singapore. Indonesia. She wanted to see the world. I'm happy here, he added. So I stayed.

It seems like a great place to write.

It probably is. But not for me. I'm not writing anymore.

What do you mean? I asked.

You've seen what writing did to me. It demanded too much.

I did not know what to say. I wanted to protest: But you told me that writing was a life-threatening activity!

He read my thoughts.

I heard you lived through your own firing squad, he said.

I looked down at the book and saw that he was reading my copy of *Lord Jim*.

I thought it would make me a better writer, I said.

He smiled, gently, mockingly, sadly. Wherever did you get that idea?

I felt the stillness of the air and the stillness of the stars and the stillness of the sea. The entire universe was still. The only weight within it was me.

When I looked up, he was gone, and the things I wanted to say to him went unsaid. Like Jim, I might have unburdened myself, unleashed the torment of my soul, if only he had been there to listen.

I wanted him to be my Marlow.

Eventually, I understood. He was telling me I needed to be my own Marlow.

I spent a week in my hut recovering. I don't know what illness had come over me, but whenever I thought about Chris and Susan and Rivers, I felt ill again. When I woke up at the beginning of the second week, I was healthy enough to walk to the restaurant. Sunny and a few of the regulars who were sitting around a collection of tables applauded my appearance.

By the end of the second week, I was swimming every day. I swam short distances at first, and I rested frequently. Then I got stronger until I could swim all the way across the cove and back without stopping. I joined the daily beach volleyball game.

One night, after everyone had gone to sleep, I remembered that I wanted to be a writer and why. I remembered Chris telling me it was time. I thought about Rivers and Marlow and firing squads and floating docks. There was a full moon rising above the cove. I walked into the water and swam toward it. I swam as hard as I could as far as I could and rolled over on my back, breathing shallow breaths, and stared up at that moon until I calmed down. I'd almost swum too far to return.

I unpacked my typewriter and set it up in my hut. I tried to write about Chris but I couldn't. There was a hole in my story, a darkness I couldn't jump into or explore.

So I wrote about something else instead, a tale of a couple who backpack through Asia robbing other backpackers to keep travelling, and I threw into it everything I understood at that point in my life about morality and consequence and the lightness of being and the relief of a reckless fuck.

I worked feverishly. I went out for meals or to swim across the cove, but I did not like to leave my room. If Chris was confined to his prison cell, then I would be confined to this hut. I did push-ups and sit-ups and jumping jacks to keep myself going. I meditated afterwards, my breath slowing. I paced off the area of the room and realized it was the exact dimensions of Chris's cell as he'd described it to me.

One afternoon, Sunny appeared in my window. She was angry about my typing. The exploding keys.

Bang bang bang! she yelled.

I must have looked half crazy, desperate, and perhaps dangerous to her, because she did not make me leave the complex. Instead, she moved me farther away from the beach to an older area, deeper in the forest, that must have been abandoned. Six huts in a circle, shrouded by palm trees. A few of the huts were sagging or half-collapsed, one cleaved in two by a fallen palm tree. Only one of the huts was remotely livable. We cleaned it up together, scrubbing on our hands and knees, and we hammered mosquito netting across the windows, and she brought me a good mattress. Later, she sent over a girl to give me a free massage.

I was alone in the jungle writing. But I saw, after a day, that the other huts weren't entirely empty. They were occupied at different times by a troop of monkeys. I noticed that they had stolen things from the huts and restaurant where the other travellers were staying. I saw sunglasses. A bottle of suntan lotion. A bikini top. A clench of brightly coloured panties. There were even a few books, including my own copy of *The Unbearable Lightness of Being*. I had not realized it was missing. I retrieved it from the scattered pile of ill-gotten treasures, chastened to discover that such a precious belonging had been forced to magically find me again.

The book I was working on changed after that, the angle tilting in a new direction. One of my main characters, slowly, and against his will, under the influence of the full moon and the tropical heat, became a monkey. This meant he could do whatever the fuck he wanted whenever he wanted but that he was also graced with a deep and abiding understanding of the universe. Being a monkey meant being light and heavy all at once.

My book ended up being twelve hundred pages long. It was the *Moby-Dick* of travel novels. I put within it everything that could be said about travel, and those who did it, and what it allowed them to do, and what it turned them into. It made me famous and lots of money.

Ha ha.

I told myself there was more glory and honour in having written it, and remaining unknown, than there would have been if it had been made into a movie starring Leonardo DiCaprio.

11

I rush now through many years, knowing this story has a hole in the middle that must be filled.

I travelled for several of those years, writing in many huts and many hotel rooms as I made my way through Southeast Asia. When my stash ran out, I moved to Japan for more of those years, where money was easy and who I was didn't matter. Then, as emotional attachments formed, I fled to Eastern Europe and found myself in the same city that Kundera had grown up in. It didn't matter that he'd gotten the fuck out as soon as he was able—I was from someplace like that too.

Chris joked that he wore through his address book, erasing my old addresses and pencilling in new ones. His address remained unchanged.

In his letters, he told me about life inside, the insanity and comedy, the setbacks and low times. He never complained or despaired. Indeed, he was certain that he would have a more meaningful and fulfilling life once he got out because of the things he had learned about himself. I collected it all as research for the great prison novel I would write someday, the *Moby-Dick* of crime and punishment. In return, I wrote him embellished stories about the women I had been with and the crazy things I had seen and done.

Through it all, one quiet miracle: we remained friends.

Compared to Chris's seriousness of purpose—his goal to create a better future for himself, his dedication to self-improvement, and personal responsibility—I was feckless. I had no commitments, except to myself. I made money easily, but it flowed away without notice. I could not maintain a long-term relationship. I went from party to party, job to job, country to country without leaving a mark.

Finally, the light one had become heavy, the heavy of us light.

The only thing I took remotely seriously was my writing, and this I toiled on diligently, but my curse, my gypsy curse, was that writing did not take me seriously in return. Or at least, the guardians to the kingdom of publication did not see fit to allow me entrance. I continued to send out the *Moby-Dick* of travel novels to agents and publishers, revising and cutting like an expert sashimi chef after each rejection. I wrote stories in between, sending them to magazines around the world, hoping for one bright spark to kindle an enormous fire. I started other novels too, about other mes, but nothing I worked on seemed to flow or even matter. I was haunted by the life I still couldn't write about.

I had foreseen withstanding obscurity, with all its honour and glory, for a few years, but a decade and longer was a little too much even for a guilt-ridden motherfucker like me.

Maybe Rivers had known what I was in for all along.

I got married and moved to Brooklyn, the Dartmouth of the five boroughs. I got divorced and stayed there.

Chris was let out of prison a few years early. I had never managed to visit him. He moved into a halfway house for six months, then into a shitty basement apartment near my old place.

How far I've come, he wrote, how far.

Yet, the difference between inside and out was all the world.

We started talking on the phone once he could afford a line. We talked about what he was doing, but mostly, at his urging, we talked about my writing. He kept telling me how great the stories I showed him were, and expressed as much frustration as I had ever felt about my ongoing failure.

You got to figure it's only a matter of time, man, he said.

It was just like the old days.

We talked about what a great novel his story would be. And he was willing and eager for me to tell that story, warts and all. That had always been part of the deal.

I told him all kinds of bullshit to explain why I couldn't make any significant progress. I told him that I still felt too close to the story. That too many people would be hurt by the truth that would be revealed.

You can't hold back, he said. It's got to be all or nothing. People can tell when you're lying.

I wondered if that was part of my problem.

Through one of my rejections, I got a series of gigs ghostwriting thrillers for authors who were either dead or had better things to do. This, initially, felt like a huge accomplishment and perhaps a break, and the money gave me time to do more of my own writing. I even worked on Chris's book, tackling it from various angles, trying to parse out the truth, to lay the evidence bare. I wrote a thousand pages of backstory to explain what we did and why. I talked about who and what and where. But my straightforward, nonfiction account failed to move even me. There was nothing you could hang a story on, or an author.

The glory of ghostwriting tasted more bitter than sweet after one of my authors made an appearance on Oprah without me. But the assignments did give me good excuses to talk to Chris. I called him whenever I couldn't work out a plot point in the notes. Chris always had the perfect plot-driven solution.

I didn't tell him anything about his book. Unlike every other thing I'd ever written, I couldn't talk to him about his own story.

In particular, there were certain plot points I couldn't discuss with him.

I asked him once, my heart beating like a drum, Do you ever regret what happened?

He paused for what seemed like a minute.

Nah, he finally answered. If I hadn't done all that stupid shit and brought the whole fucking world down on my head, where would I be now?

Ha ha.

Then he added, But there's one thing that still bothers me. I can't figure out how I got caught.

He was surprised that he, of all people, had not committed the perfect crime. To me, this represented a level of delusion so staggering, I did not know what to say.

Then I thought, How delusional am I?

Then I asked myself: How delusional do I need to be?

Through the ghostwriting gigs, I met an agent at a party who was actually interested in my fiction. At one point, I told him about the *Moby-Dick* of travel novels, and when I sensed his attention flagging, I interrupted myself to tell him about the book I was really working on, the story of my oldest friend who'd robbed banks over a two-year period.

He arched an eyebrow and looked impressed.

He was the son of a police officer, I said.

A thin smile. He nodded. That's good. Tell me more.

It was all neighbourhood stuff but done under the noses of everyone we knew. There were some very comic moments.

I described the movie theatre job, the money plastered wetly to the inside of the windshield.

I love it, he said. It's a comedy of errors. The Keystone Robbers. In fact, that's what we should call it.

Yes, I agreed, willing to agree with whatever he said.

And it's a true story, he noted.

It wasn't a question, but I answered it that way. Yes, I said. It's all true. Unbelievable but true.

I immediately regretted the use of the word *unbelievable*.

A memoir, he said.

I made a sound that was partway between agreement and How interesting. I did not yet know where his ducks were lining up.

Memoirs are selling very well these days, he said.

And it was my turn to smile and arch an eyebrow, as though he were finally coming around to my way of thinking.

I haven't seen a caper memoir in some time, he said, something with action in it, instead of simple malaise or emotional abuse, at least not one from the point of view of a nice middle-class boy like yourself. You usually see these written by ex-criminals, people from Boston.

Right, I said.

Where is it set? he asked.

In Halifax, I said.

He arched the eyebrow of confusion. The one that meant, Elaborate, or possibly, Did I hear you correctly?

Halifax, Nova Scotia, I clarified. In Canada. That's where I grew up. And then, as though apologizing for having had anything to do with the country whatsoever, I told him I hadn't been back in almost fifteen years.

I like the story, he said. I like that it's true. Do you think we could change the setting?

I simply was not able to compute what he was asking.

To a different city, he said. Maybe Seattle. Seattle's probably a lot like Halifax. I wouldn't want Maine. Too many editors vacation there now. They don't want to shit where they eat.

Absolutely, I said, willing to say anything.

Get me fifty pages, he said, and I'll sell it on spec.

When I got home from the party, I got straight to work.

Laptop keys don't explode with quite the ferocity of a typewriter, but there was a familiar vigour in my typing nevertheless.

When Kundera wrote about Tomas, it seemed to me that he was writing about himself. Be thankful you never experience the artful interrogation. No one is strong enough. Everyone's complicit. This was his own personal confession, written in the guise of fiction.

I began to write mine.

I got my fifty pages done in a month. It wasn't perfect, but it hummed with story. I'd taken every lesson I'd ever learned from thriller writing and applied it to Chris's life. The agent loved it. He said that he wanted to talk to Leonardo DiCaprio as soon as I had a full draft. In the meantime, he was going to start priming publishers and I was to get back to work.

A few months later, James Frey became the most hated man in American letters for admitting that his memoir had been made up. Larry King denounced him. Oprah publicly flogged him. His agents abandoned him. His publisher agreed to place millions of dollars in sales aside for refunds. A bunch of suckers had assumed that just because it was in print, it should have been true.

I was among those who would have picked up a stone to throw, but for different reasons. The son of a bitch had gotten caught before I'd even had a chance to commit the same crime.

I knew the phone call was coming. My agent, who'd laughed at my stories of Chris's escapades, who'd told me that I was going to kick the doors of publishing down, had a different tone in his voice now. He sounded like a school principal dealing with a disappointing child.

Is everything in your story fiction? he asked.

Of course not, I said.

Is everything in your story factual? he asked.

Of course not, I said.

Are there things you're not telling us? he asked.

What do you think? I said.

Before we hung up, he promised to consider the matter carefully, but I knew it was over. He would have made a good interrogator in Czechoslovakia.

Unlike Kundera, Frey signed his letter of retraction.

I didn't initially think of what I was writing as nonfiction or fiction, memoir or autobiography, he wrote.

I altered events and details all the way through the book, he said.

I made other alterations in my portrayal of myself, most of which portrayed me in ways that made me tougher and more daring and more aggressive than in reality I was, or I am, he admitted.

Hadn't he read *The Unbearable Lightness of Being*? It's the guy who doesn't sign the confession who ends up getting laid. The guy who signs just ends up getting fucked.

I put aside Chris's book. I didn't bother to approach dozens of new agents. I was an experienced unpublished writer by this point, and I knew the answer would be the same. The gypsy curse lived on. The weight of the universe could not be avoided. It pressed and pressed and pressed.

I got married again, and divorced a few years later. I still couldn't handle commitment. I kept writing, though, as seriously as ever.

You pin your hopes on one story after another, one agent after the next. You struggle through the tumult of disappointment and the busyness of everyday life to write something worthwhile. You need the words to be beautiful and the characters to make sense and the story to miraculously cohere, even as the entire exercise must satisfy the mood of each gatekeeper in turn, and the latest reading trend. You need endless determination and a great deal of luck to make progress, and more love than any fault-ridden and ill-formed person deserves. And when the magic doesn't happen, you call it failure. And if you have the strength and self-delusion, you try it all again.

This is how a few more years went by.

At one point, Chris asked me what I would need to do to pick up the pieces on his book again. This was the most impatience he ever showed me.

I told him I thought I needed time and space. In other words, money.

There are some books, I said, you need to rob a bank to write. Ha ha.

We came up with an idea for a money-making thriller we could both write, a murder mystery set in prison. I pitched it to my circle of publishing contacts as *The Name of the Rose* meets *Oz*. We made a reckless and heartwarming deal, Chris and I, to split the profits fifty-fifty, since his experiences and my skills would go into the writing of it in more or less equal proportions, and we also decided to go with a pseudonym as the name of the author. But when the pitch worked, and the deal was struck, for far more money than I'd anticipated, I lied to Chris and told him it was a tenth of the amount. Twenty-five thousand dollars was still a respectable deal for a first novel, and replaced the money he'd stashed under the floating dock. But I needed the big dollars to pay my bills, to support my ex-wives, to survive in New York, to write the damn thing.

I'm pretty sure Chris would have understood, if only I'd trusted him enough.

As Jesus said to Judas at the Last Supper: Do what you need to do quickly.

I had a modicum of success with the prison thriller. Not so much that you would notice, but enough for me to feel the freeing effect. It changes everything. And when they asked me what my next book would be, I told them about my friend who had robbed banks. They gave me an advance and said they wanted to see more.

With that validation and money, and the time it secured, and having doubled or tripled down on my guilt, I finally found the space to tell Chris's story truthfully, even loaded with falsehoods.

I Skyped Chris and began a rhythm of talking about his story, every few days. Patiently, with infinite generosity, he fed me details. Things that had happened, things that he'd felt. I could have written an amazing novel from his point of view. He was an indisputably great character, a combination of Nietzschean overman and Don Quixote, if only I'd had the ability or the grace or the luck to get it right.

But that wasn't the story I was able to tell.

I dug out my old copies of *The Unbearable Lightness of Being* and *Lord Jim* and *St. Augustine's Confessions* and lined them up on my desk. I found my old notes. The midden of what we did and the evidence of why. I put up pages of quotes, recorded like aphorisms, and tattooed my walls with the seriousness of my intentions. Suspending moral judgment is not the immorality of the novel; it is its morality, Kundera wrote, in one of his books on writing, and he ought to know. I've never heard of a crime which I could not imagine committing myself, wrote Goethe, allegedly. It is not the business of writers to accuse or prosecute, but to take the part even of guilty men once they have been condemned, said Chekhov, as any doctor would. I am forced to the appalling conclusion that I would never have become a writer but for Joan's death, said Burroughs, referring to the spouse he shot through the head while playing William Tell. I was trying to write a book that simply would not come, admitted Graham Greene, who then added, How twisted we humans are, and yet they say a God made us . . . And from Nietzsche, What if the "good" man represents not merely a retrogression but even a danger, a temptation, a narcotic drug enabling the present to live at the expense of the future? More comfortable, less hazardous, perhaps, but also baser, more petty—so that morality itself would be responsible for man, as a species, failing to reach the peak of magnificence of which he is capable? What if morality should turn out to be the danger of dangers?

It had been a long time since I'd travelled and Chris had been in prison. It had been a longer time since we'd committed Chris's crimes. What if morality was the danger we'd successfully avoided all along? What if the lives we'd led would have been less . . . less what? Less propelling, less challenging, less formidable, less noteworthy, less ours had we lived them any differently? Shouldn't you be willing to commit the same crimes, no matter how horrible or trivial, and to tell the same lies, over and over again, for all eternity? Isn't that the lightness with which you should live?

I looked back on Conrad's *Lord Jim* and was struck for the hundredth time how brief the incident that generates the book is compared to the book itself. The accident on the ship that sets off Jim's shame is but twenty pages long. The discussion of that shame, and the making amends for it, comprises the rest of the long story. Conrad got heaviness. He knew that we who are heavy are haunted by our failings for the rest of our lives. We make amends, as we can, perhaps by telling a Marlow, perhaps by becoming one.

My own Marlow now, I try to write it well enough to get it down. As Conrad wrote, There was not the thickness of a sheet of paper between the right and wrong of this affair.

And so, I need to make this final brief confession in a book and a life spent avoiding it. It was not Chris's fault that he was caught on his last robbery, it was mine. It was not his lightness but my weight that doomed us both. The heaviness settled on me not from the day we began to do the robberies but from the day we cut down that tree fort, from the moment I walked out of the forest by the lake with my cut chin. My relationship with Drury started then, when he picked me up in the squad car and asked me to tell him who else was in on it.

He asked me, so I told him. I would have told him anything to avoid the shame of him telling my father. And years later, after a string of robberies had occurred, and his suspicions of Chris became overwhelming, Drury approached me again.

I tried to resist. I tried to tell him that I wouldn't turn my friend in, that I would take the rap myself. And he let me believe that, and he gave me the time and space to become very afraid.

Once he teased that fear out of me, he had enough of a grip to yank out the rest. There was nothing I wouldn't tell him. Interrogation did its work. The story that spilled out on the walls of the police station was the first draft of this novel.

But heavier than my confession was the need for my complicity. Like Judas, I had been necessary. Drury needed to catch Chris in the act. So I helped make that happen too. Pushing Chris to do what he did not want to do, calling Drury when he was about to do it.

Do what you need to do quickly.

Afterwards, the horror of what I'd done was measured by the immensity of my cowardice, and I tried anything to prove that cowardice a lie.

Worse, I was even successful. I let Susan think that she'd abandoned Chris, when the abandonment started with me. I let Chris spend years in prison alone, and let him think he'd been caught because of his own mistakes, not mine. I left my parents and poisoned my childhood and became an exile from my hometown. I shed all that weight with the money Chris had saved and the freedom he'd sacrificed.

How bitter that made the money.

How heavy that freedom felt.

I write. I look back on the wreckage of my life. I read about the files unearthed that exposed Kundera's faltering, and know it doesn't matter whether he did it or not. We're all complicit.

Chris, bearing the weight of what we did, lives lightly. He has a good life. He's done well for himself and his family.

Given more time to think through my decisions, or less time to falter, I might have made different, perhaps better choices. But as Chris has joked about all the time he served inside as the result of his mistakes, Where would I be now?

And as I falter further, as I grow tired of the burden I've been carrying so long, I wonder if I should lie down and sleep, or whether this is the very moment when I should rouse myself and live.

Life when you are pinned to the eternal cross of consequence is very long. Life when you are light seems as though it might be terribly short. Which is the life worth living?

There is the chance, the certainty even, that I will make more mistakes, make millions of them, perhaps even a few monstrous ones, as terrible as the mistakes I made back then. I ask my interrogator, Are they all worth making?

You tell me! You tell me.